D1086920

THE
THINGS
YOU
DIDN'T
SEE

OTHER TITLES BY RUTH DUGDALL

The James Version

The Woman Before Me

The Sacrificial Man

Humber Boy B

Nowhere Girl

My Sister and Other Liars

THE THINGS YOU DIDN'T SEE

RUTH DUGDALL

This is a work of fiction. Names, characters, organizations, places, events, and incidents are either products of the author's imagination or are used fictitiously. Any resemblance to actual persons, living or dead, or actual events is purely coincidental.

Text copyright © 2018 by Ruth Dugdall
All rights reserved.

No part of this book may be reproduced, or stored in a retrieval system, or transmitted in any form or by any means, electronic, mechanical, photocopying, recording, or otherwise, without express written permission of the publisher.

Published by Thomas & Mercer, Seattle

www.apub.com

Amazon, the Amazon logo, and Thomas & Mercer are trademarks of Amazon.com, Inc., or its affiliates.

ISBN-13: 9781612187181
ISBN-10: 1612187188

Cover design by Ghost Design

Printed in the United States of America

To my great-uncle, George Hair.
I never met you, but you have been there with
every word I wrote.

PROLOGUE
HALLOWEEN, TWENTY YEARS EARLIER

Holly

In the blurred dusk someone moves, dipping in and out of the hedge. The girl searches the shadows, too nervous to call out, then in a swell of relief sees it's Jamie, her brother. He turns his torch on her – the beam makes her blink. 'Go back home, Holly! Quit following me.'

'I want to come ghost-hunting too,' she whispers, tugging the hem of his coat.

'You can't come, you're too little!'

'Let me or I'll tell Dad you're here.'

Dad's forbidden them to go outside the fence at night and especially not to the farm – he says because of the machines it's dangerous. But Holly knows the real reason: the farm is haunted. Everyone at school says so, lots of them have seen the ghosts, a woman in white and the falling man. Back on the airbase, her friends are collecting bags of candy and the only ghosts are pretend: that's why she followed Jamie. She's not little, she's almost nine.

'Fuck's she doin' here?' Coming behind them, too large to be quiet, is Carl. His family just arrived, bringing to the sleepy Suffolk airbase all of his American bulk and brag. Holly doesn't like him, doesn't like how Jamie gets louder when Carl's around.

'Squirt followed me,' Jamie grumbles. 'But she'll keep her mouth shut.'

They move through the wood, Jamie leads with his torch, then Carl, then Holly bringing up the rear. In the distance is the farmhouse. The setting sun hits the window panes so it looks like bloodshot eyes are watching their approach.

Holly's feet feel heavy. She's getting tired, but daren't say so. A lone car crosses the plain, headlights strafing the far field, making for the town. She suddenly wishes with all her heart that she were in that car, going to Ipswich to see a film – her favourite treat – eating sweet popcorn and snuggled into a blue velvet seat. Safe.

The sound of cracking twigs, behind them. Holly gives a yelp and moves so close to Carl, they bump arms and he says, 'Fuck's that?'

Jamie stops, searches with his torch, finds yellow eyes glittering low in the grass. 'Cat.' He kicks out and Holly hears a feline cry of pain, then rustling as it scrams. He continues, and they follow, trudging onwards.

The house appears, stone sides suddenly upon them.

'Fucking spooky, isn't it?' says Jamie, giving Carl a triumphant punch on the arm. 'That's Innocence Farm.'

The spreading glow of the setting sun has bathed the house red, as if the blood has seeped from the eye sockets and the whole face is bleeding. Holly clenches her hands, pushing the nails into the fleshy part of her palm to keep from screaming. They should go home now, she thinks. Time to turn back.

In front is the farm, but going back isn't possible either. Something is behind them, cracking twigs as it moves, casting shapes against the inky sky. Telling herself it's only the cat returning, she puts her hand over her mouth to stop the scream that's building inside. But the noise comes closer, the shape much larger than a cat.

'Holy crap,' Carl says, pushing Jamie and snorting in surprise, 'the freak actually showed.'

The shape approaches, shrinks, and turns into the outline of a teenage boy.

'All right?' he asks, bending into the light of Jamie's torch. It's Ash, who's in Jamie's year, who lives in the cottage along the lane. Jamie raises his hand and they press each other's palms in a high five. The sharp slap of it makes her flinch. She looks at her brother, confused, but it's too dark to see his expression. He bullies this boy, calls him weirdo and freak – why are they acting like friends?

Ash notices her. 'Why'd ya bring the little kid?'

'She followed us,' says Jamie, landing a sharp kick on her shin.

Ash lifts the latch and gently opens the barn door, just enough for them to snake through the gap. Inside, the smell is sharp and makes her eyes water. She can hear angry clucking.

'We've gotta be very still,' Ash says, leaving the barn door ajar, and pulling a bale of straw in front of it for them to crouch behind. 'This is the best place to watch from.' His voice is shaking like he's cold, but she thinks he's excited too. Jamie and Carl are popular – everyone at school and on the base wants to hang out with them – but now they want something only Ash can show them. 'The ghosts only come when it's really quiet. And not every night, so I can't promise you'll see summat.'

'We better!' Jamie says, smacking Ash on the arm with his fist.

It's uncomfortable on the uneven earth with the straw bale in front of her, and she wants to sneeze. Around them the chickens are getting brave, coming closer on red-clawed feet, beaks open as they cluck warning sounds.

'Come on, ghosts, it's your night. Come join the party,' Carl booms, not caring that the others try to hush him. He takes a bottle from inside his jacket, then stands and raises it towards the house before taking a swig as if to toast it. 'Halloween! When the dead walk the earth.'

Holly reaches for Jamie, moves close to him. 'Please can we go home?'

He turns on her, hisses, 'No one asked you to come.'

Carl turns his moonlike face at her, smug. 'Scared, are ya? Don't worry, we'll protect ya.' He pulls aside his Red Sox bomber jacket, which makes him look like a fat cherry, and she sees a BB gun wedged into the belt of his jeans. Black and stubby, a lot of the boys on the base have them.

Jamie grins. The light of the torch makes his teeth glow, as he pulls something out: he has his air rifle.

Holly gasps, her heart pounces. 'Jamie, you shouldn't!' He's only allowed to shoot cans in the backyard when Dad is watching.

'Shut the fuck up, Holly,' he says, the glittering barrel moving wildly as he does. He reaches across to take the bottle from Carl, and she smells caramel. Carl has stolen whisky.

The boys take turns swigging from the bottle – even Ash gets a go – as they crouch behind the straw bales, watching the farmhouse. They're tense, but as the minutes tick past, they fidget. Jamie starts messing with his gun, turning the safety catch off and on. Finally, they're all still. The empty bottle rolls over to the chickens, who stalk away from it, alarmed.

Holly wants her bed. She closes her eyes.

'Holy fuck, it's the woman in white!'

She wakes, realises immediately she's in the barn and shouldn't be. There's danger here. She needs to go home. This time, it's Jamie who presses against her, swaying, voice both slurred and afraid. 'Shut up,

Holly, don't fucking move,' he orders, though she was doing neither. She couldn't move or speak even if she wanted to.

In front of them is a pale shape, moving slowly towards the barn. Moving from side to side like a mechanical toy, face definitely human. Human, but with blank, dark eyes. A person, but absent, dressed in white.

'I want Dad,' she whines, her whole body shaking from stomach out. She's going to be sick.

In a reflex action, Jamie pushes Holly behind him.

Slowly, mechanically, the ghost looks their way. It walks towards them like a zombie and Carl swears, lifts his BB gun onto the straw bale, but it slips from his sweaty grasp. Jamie's shaking so much that it takes him three goes to release the safety catch. Ash pulls at the barrel – 'No, Jamie, stop!'

Jamie ignores him, lines up the barrel so it's pointing at the ghost, just as Ash lunges forward to stop him. Carl reacts too, and all three fight in the dark. The chickens fret and cluck, bustling around, as the ghostly shape moves closer.

Jamie fires the gun, she hears the crack, then the cry.

The ghost cries out, then moans as it falls to the ground. *It isn't real,* Holly tells herself. *I'll wake up soon.*

The ghost is on its side, clutching its chest, where white cotton is soaking red. The lights in the farmhouse flash on, bright white, and a gruff voice shouts, 'Who's out there? I'm callin' the police!'

Jamie grabs her by the wrist, Carl follows, and they run from the barn. Back through the scrubby farmland, through the woods, not stopping until they're safe within the fence of the airbase, hearts thumping, chests ready to burst.

They can hear the distant sound of an ambulance, coming closer.

It is only then that she realises Ash isn't with them. He stayed behind.

1

HALLOWEEN, NOW

Holly

'Oh, your poor face!' Holly said, wincing, a hand to her own cheek.

'*Ja*, stuff of nightmares, isn't it?' Leif grinned wickedly, turning to show how on one side he still had the unblemished face of a Swedish Viking, tough-jawed and roguishly handsome – the face that had persuaded her to agree to this date in the first place. But now the left side was scored white, raised like pulp, with red blood-like marks streaked through it. His eye had been taped down at the corner so the skin there looked burned.

It was only stage make-up, to team with the Freddy Krueger red-and-black-striped top and fake-knife fingers, but as he touched her with the plastic tips, she felt heat burning her cheeks.

'I'm actually a bit tired, Leif,' she said desperately, wondering how she could get out of this date that no longer seemed such a good idea. 'I'm working tomorrow anyway, so maybe it's best if I cry off. We could do this another time, yeah?'

'Did I say something wrong, Holly?' His handsome face fell, his seafarer eyes suddenly solemn, but there was a glint there too, like a naughty puppy who knew his cuteness could allay any punishment. 'It has surely taken me months to persuade you to give me a chance. And now I have made a mistake somehow?'

'No, of course not . . .' How to begin explaining? She simply couldn't. 'Just one drink then.'

Leif gave a playful 'Hurrah!' and took her hand, leading her along the communal balcony past the front doors of the flats, towards the concrete steps leading to street level.

The moon was a perfect disc of white, with more abstract light cast by glow sticks and torches. The streets were teeming with werewolves and witches, ghosts and vampires of all shapes and sizes, but it was Leif's disguise that Holly felt most sensitive towards. She had to stifle an urge to flinch every time she looked at him. Her own effort at a Halloween costume was pathetic. Thirty minutes ago, she'd been standing in front of her wardrobe, assessing her limited options. Eventually she'd picked out a plain black top and leggings, re-beaded her hair so it stuck up in tufts like ears, and marked her cheeks with kohl eyeliner to represent whiskers. As a final gesture, she'd pinned a thin velvet scarf to her bottom, hoping it would pass as a tail.

Tonight, Ipswich town centre was a playground for kids. Children who would normally be in bed were hyped up on freedom and sugar. Portman Road, adjacent to the flat complex where Holly and Leif lived, usually the haunt of lone men in slow cars picking up prostitutes, was alive with childish screams and nervous laughter, enough to jangle Holly's hypervigilant nerves. They came to a group of primary school-aged children who had just yelled '*Trick or treat!*' and left a house with small packets of sweets in their clenched hands. Now they were pointing at Leif's face and squealing in delighted fear.

'We don't have this tricking or treating in Sweden,' Leif told her, watching the children with indulgent good humour. 'It's *underbar*. Really wonderful!'

Holly, being half-American, had grown up with the yearly festival and thought it was, at best, an excuse for children to beg for candy. At worst, it was a festival that celebrated ghosts and demons.

Leif held her hand more tightly as they manoeuvred past the group. It had been a long time since she'd been touched, and though he was younger than her and not her usual type, he was easy company and – usually – very easy on the eye. The fact that he was Swedish meant that he couldn't 'read' her: he didn't have the cultural short-hand to glance at her and see the troubled past and her 'otherness' that was about neither of these things but something else, a unique trait, that marked her out as different. Holly had synaesthesia; it had started when she was eight years old. When it surfaced, as it always did, previously keen men turned cold, but Leif had yet to notice the signs and persisted.

'So who taught you to do make-up?' she asked, forcing herself not to notice how the red greasepaint made his skin look scorched, how the white foundation gave the impression that his eye had melted. 'Not the Clinique counter at Debenhams, I can see that.'

'*Nej.*' Leif waggled a plastic-bladed glove at the gaggle of pre-teen trick-or-treaters across the road. 'Trish, my colleague in the film department, specialises in costume and stage design. She used me as her workshop project today. The Film and Media students liked it very much.'

'I bet they did.'

Holly knew, from their conversations in the shared walkway out-side their flats, that Leif was from Malmö, but had started studying for his PhD at Orwell University a year ago, lecturing and taking occasional seminars while writing his thesis on the films of Ingrid Bergman. No doubt the undergrads saw him as the perfect package: clever and cute. Holly couldn't imagine studying films for a living, being locked in a fantasy world where anything can happen because it's made up. She preferred anything dramatic to remain firmly within her control.

Their destination was the Poacher and Partridge, popular with students and lecturers alike because the booze was cheap, so Leif's usual haunt. Flaccid orange balloons hung from the light fixings, and a greenish skeleton stood in the corner, pointing a bony finger in the direction of the loos. Cobwebs had been strung across the ceiling – although Holly couldn't be sure they were just decoration – while crudely carved pumpkins with candles flickering in their gashed eyes lined the bar. She challenged herself to stay in the pub and try to be sociable, although her senses were so alert that her skin felt flayed. She'd rather run away, had to fight the instinct not to. Running away never led to anything good.

'There they are! Come, Holly, meet the gang.'

Leif led her to the darkest corner, where two round bar tables holding several empty glasses had been wedged together. Three ghouls sat in a coven-like huddle around the flickering tea lights: a man with albino colouring in a white coat stained with blood; a second figure in a hairy werewolf mask who could feasibly be of either gender; and seated between them a sexy blonde, carefully made up with cat's-eye flicks and red lips, sucking on an e-cigarette.

With one arm around Holly's shoulders, Leif pointed to his friends, shouting to be heard over the loud music and laughter. 'The mad surgeon is Neil and the werewolf is Adam; they're both technical wizards in the media department. The *True Blood* geek is Trish. As well as turning me into Freddy, she's also my PhD supervisor.'

Holly looked again at the vaping blonde, who was clearly a multitasker. She wore a tight white shirt, open at the cleavage, revealing two bite marks on her neck, and her name badge said she was SOOKIE STACKHOUSE. Holly avoided horror or crime films, but guessed this must be a character from one of these.

'Hi, Holly,' Trish said, in a loud voice no doubt used to projecting across a lecture hall, flashing Holly a smile that did not reach her eyes. 'Come and change the conversation! I'm sick of talking to these film geeks about who's the most sympathetic killer, Dexter or Hannibal Lecter. And now that Leif is here, the conversation is bound to turn to Ingrid Bergman. I'll gaslight myself if it does.' She gave a huge theatrical yawn, then winked at Leif, who grinned. Holly had no idea what Trish was referring to, but it looked like she was enjoying this moment of shared intimacy with Leif.

'Tell us about real stories,' Trish said, pointing the e-cigarette at the empty stool nearest her, though her jaw still looked a bit set. 'Leif says you're a paramedic?'

'Not yet. I'm still in training.' Now she knew for certain she should have stayed at home rather than face this interrogation from Trish. 'And right now, I'm just a cat – a thirsty one. So, can I get anyone a drink?'

It took an age before Holly reached the bar, which was pressed into her ribs by the swell of customers behind her, all vying to be next in line. The bar was sticky with spilt beer, and she felt it ooze through her T-shirt to her skin.

The half-sloshed barman finally noticed her, his eyes already sliding lazily to the impatient crowd behind. 'What can I get you, Beyoncé?'

In order to be heard, she stood on tiptoe, and saw that across the bar area, in the games room, which had a full-sized snooker table and a dartboard, trouble was brewing. The source was a tall, lean man, wearing a black hoodie to obscure his face. She could see only his mouth. He was speaking loudly and fiercely to someone she couldn't see, and brandishing a snooker cue above his head.

The barman tapped his fingers on the bar. 'Come on, Puss, I haven't got all day.'

She saw Hoodie's face blanch with rage as he raised the cue higher. Her senses switched to alert and she knew that things were about to kick off. Her drinks order forgotten, she snaked through the three-deep throng behind her and made her way around the bar.

She stopped at the threshold, assessing the situation. Hoodie was poised threateningly over a smaller bloke cowering close to the ground, his hands raised in defence. Judging by his top hat and ginger wig he was obviously supposed to be Willy Wonka, but there was nothing funny about the scene. Hoodie brandished the cue like a sword with a fixed grip that Holly felt in the palms of her own hands. Then he brought it down, slamming it on Wonka's top hat so the cue splintered in two as the victim toppled sideways, his knees at an odd angle, his head hidden by the hat, both arms protectively covering it.

Holly's synaesthesia registered the blow as if she herself were the victim, gritting her teeth as she moved towards Hoodie. Her own hands ached from the force of wielding the imaginary cue – she was able to feel this sensation too. These heightened responses, both a curse and a gift, meant she had no choice but to intervene: it was why she was training to fix people. She hoped being a paramedic might cure her synaesthesia, might mean she could lead a normal life. It hadn't happened yet.

'That's enough, you leave him alone!' She threaded herself in-between Hoodie and his victim, trying to ignore her splitting headache.

Willy Wonka crouched behind her, his hand tugging the edge of her jacket, and said in a wheedling voice, 'I'll get it for you, mate, I promise. No need for this, is there?'

Hoodie was repositioning half of the cue to strike again. Holly's palms felt again the strength of his grip as he raised it, her brain assessing both assailant's and victim's reactions. After this blow, Wonka wouldn't be able to speak.

'Move, Catwoman. I'm not done with this idiot yet.'

'I'm not letting you hurt him.' Holly planted herself more firmly in Hoodie's way, unable to stop herself from intervening, now she knew the consequences of running away.

The pub had fallen silent. Everyone was watching the stand-off, and Holly could see Hoodie was weighing up just how much damage he wanted to do, and how publicly. Finally, he lowered the shattered cue, pointing its tip at Wonka. 'I'll give you one day. You pay me what you owe, mate. Or else.'

Wonka nodded, frantic, backing away on all fours. Then he scarpered. Holly's headache eased as Hoodie's grip on the snooker cue loosened, and she relaxed. It was over, the pain had cleared, and she could return to the bar to order her drinks.

This time around, the barman leapt to serve her, and she returned with a tray of drinks to Leif and his coven in their candlelit corner. They stared at her wide-eyed, as if they had just watched her perform the best trick of all that Halloween.

'Very impressive,' said Trish, aka Sookie Stackhouse, grudgingly. 'I can see that black cats really are lucky. Our Swedish boy will never have a dull moment with you around.' And then she winked again at Leif, who gave a satisfied grin.

Hours later, woken by the sun's watery fingers of light, Holly assumed she was in her own flat until she realised that, although the layout of the bedroom was identical, the bed was smaller than her own. The sheets felt suspiciously budget, not the Egyptian cotton she had treated herself to last year, to celebrate the start of her new career. The flat was the same but different, and then she realised why: *Oh fuck, I've fucked Krueger.* That'd teach her for drinking three pints of snakebite on an empty stomach. Still though, her body felt peaceful; there was a sweet stillness in her core that she experienced after good sex. A rare pleasure, given her poor track record with relationships.

Beside her, Leif stirred but remained sound asleep, and she rolled on her side to study him. His Scandinavian-blond hair was matted but his face still looked fresh, even after a night on the booze, although she could see red smears on the white pillow where the other side of his face had rested. Typical man – he hadn't removed his make-up properly.

Looking down, she realised she had matching red marks all over her breasts. Yuk. She touched her hair, and found her 'ears' were still in place; one advantage of inheriting her father's coarse black hair was it tended to hold its shape, so it was passable. The same couldn't be said for her skin, which was now covered in dried sweat and stage make-up.

She checked her watch: 6.50. Still plenty of time to go home, shower, and make herself presentable before she checked in for duty. Since finishing basic training, she was now shadowing and supporting the response team, gathering experience for when she'd be one of them. As she plucked her scattered clothes from the floor, she saw, hung up, a navy uniform. She hadn't noticed it the night before. Leif half-opened his eyes and yawned sleepily.

'I didn't know you were a police officer,' she said, sounding more annoyed than she had a right to.

'I'm not,' he said groggily. 'Just a special.'

'Don't you need to be British?'

'I just had to wait until I'd been resident for long enough.'

A volunteer with the police – strange he hadn't mentioned it. Not that it mattered; she had no plans to see him again. She had her clothes, including the velvet tail, in her grasp when her mobile phone began to vibrate. Holly stepped into the lounge to take the call, so as not to disturb Leif.

'Holly, it's Jon.'

Holly immediately stood straighter, as if her supervisor were in the room with her. 'Yes, Jon?'

'Control have just taken a 999; it's an attempted suicide. You haven't dealt with one yet, I don't think?'

She shook her head, then realised he couldn't see her. 'No.'

'Okay, well, this should be good experience. Our patient used a gun, so it'll be messy. If you've got a pen, I'll give you the address.'

Holly looked around, picked up a bitten biro from the desk and held it over the back of her hand. 'Okay.'

'It's Innocence Farm, in Kenley. The police are there, securing the scene, so we should already be inside when you arrive.'

Holly's hand didn't move. She didn't need to write down details of the address. Her body was already protesting, her hands had become slick with sweat and her head felt woozy. Once the call was ended she bent at the waist, hands on her knees, waiting until the nausea subsided. It wasn't a hangover, not from last night at least. It was the past, catching up with her like she knew it would.

Then she straightened, breathed deep, and set about her work.

DAY 1

SATURDAY 1 NOVEMBER

2

Cassandra

I'm confused when I wake.

There's a sound, whimpering, like a trapped animal is crying for help. I must still be dreaming: I'm groggy, unsure of where I am. Then I remember, with a sinking feeling, that I'm back at Innocence Farm. The noise must be Jet, who sleeps in the barn but comes inside during the day. Janet will have let him out when she arrived. It must be time to get up.

It's a struggle, but I pull back the duvet, then freeze: I'm naked, though I fell asleep wearing bra and knickers, I'm certain. The back of my hair is slick with sweat – in fact, my whole body feels sticky, and I wonder if I was sick again, though I can't remember. Maybe I was hot and tugged my underwear off in my sleep, though when I look there's no sign of it on the floor. Yesterday's blouse and skirt are folded neatly on the chair. I hurry to pull them on.

My limbs feel damp. Despite being sick after I'd taken it, some of the trazodone must have made it to my bloodstream and hit me hard, taking me to that deep unconsciousness where the body struggles to move, and instead wraps itself tightly around bedding, getting overheated.

Downstairs, Jet's barking has become frenzied and I think I hear crying. Human crying.

Dressed, though feeling vulnerable without my underwear, I make to leave the bedroom but stumble. One hand on the wall, I catch my breath and realise a headache is gnawing on the edges of my brain.

A sharp bark makes me jump out of my skin. Jet jumps up, scratches my stomach through my thin blouse, pushing me with his long spaniel snout so I fall back against the wall, my arm catching on the sharp corner of the door frame.

'Stop, Jet!'

But he won't. He runs away from me, to the backstairs that lead to the kitchen, not normally used by us, though Janet is forever up and down them with piles of ironing and cleaning products. Jet's paws slide as he scrambles partway down the wooden steps, then he rushes back up to me, barking.

'Okay, I get it – hang on.' I follow him to the top of the stairs. 'Why are you so manic?'

Looking down, I understand.

There you are.

There you are, lying in a delicate heap at the bottom. Dad is crouched over you, shuddering with sobs. The scene tells its own story: you fell, he found you.

'Mum!' I take the stairs two at a time, stumbling to reach you.

Your red silk nightdress has ridden high on your slender pale thighs. Your head is facing the wall but your knees are in the other direction, as if you're a toy twisted by a cruel child. Your dark hair streams across the wooden floor like a broken wing.

'Mum?'

I shake your shoulder and your head rolls, faces me. Blood drips from your scalp, down your lovely face, pooling in your hollow cheek, matted in that glorious black hair of yours.

Then I see something that chills me to the core: a short distance away, long and silent and deadly, is the rifle from the gun cupboard. I can smell cordite and iron – gunshot and blood. A smell from the barn. It doesn't belong in our home.

'Oh my God, Dad, what's happened?'

His bloodshot eyes find me, he struggles to speak, then says, 'She did this to herself. Do you understand?'

'No, she wouldn't,' I say desperately.

There's a wound on your slender neck, a black hole from which blood is leaking, onto me, making me recoil. Blood seeps into the floorboards, spreads its stain on your red nightdress. Your eyes are wide open and bloodshot, the pupils large and even darker than usual. I stare in horror as they fill with my reflection, my own face.

'Mum!' I shake you again, and from your nose a spray of crimson lands on me. 'Oh God, Mum, who did this to you?'

Jet cowers at my raised voice, snarling and baring his teeth, something I've never known him do before. Both of us are panicked and afraid.

Help, I must get help.

The phone lives in your study, so I run upstairs.

The study door is half-open. Unusual.

Inside, it looks as though a bomb has exploded: filing cabinet drawers are extended on runners like loose teeth, papers and clip-files lie scattered on the floor. With a shiver, I see that the gun cupboard hangs open, which should never happen, though Dad organised a shoot yesterday so maybe he wasn't careful locking up. It wouldn't be the first time he's been forgetful and none of us were thinking straight last night. A space reveals itself, where the rifle should be.

I've started to shake. Why is the study such a mess? Papers are scattered, letters about the Port Authority's plan to buy our land and make Innocence Lane its lorry depot.

They've been hounding you for months, but you resolved it yesterday. You made your decision.

I spy the phone, grab it, dial.

'999 emergency. Which service, please?'

The relief at having the call answered is like nothing I've experienced before.

'Ambulance.' I'm gasping like I've run a marathon. The longest two seconds of my life, then a different voice comes on the line.

'This is the Ambulance Service. How may we help you?'

'My mother's been shot. I don't know what to—'

'Can you tell me where you are?'

'Innocence Farm. On Innocence Lane, Kenley.' It's so early, the sky hasn't woken up yet; it's still a watery indigo. The birds are impatient, heckling the sun to rise.

'Okay, yes, someone has already called this in. We have police and paramedics on the way. What's the condition of your mum now?'

'She's breathing, I think, but not conscious. There's a gun, a rifle, beside her.'

'The earlier caller said she shot herself. Can you see the wound?'

'There's blood on her neck – it's hard to see. But I don't think she . . .'

'Okay, love, I'm going to talk you through what to do, until the ambulance arrives. You need to put some pressure on that wound.'

'I'm not with her, I'm upstairs.'

'Can you return to your mother?'

I put the phone on speaker and stumble back down to the bottom of the stairs. The sight of you – white flesh, red silk, black blood – is a shock all over again. I feel dizzy, fear I might fall.

'Okay, are you with her?' asks the operator. 'Can you put your ear to her mouth and tell me if she's breathing?'

Dad seems to rally. He follows the instructions as best he can while I hold the phone. He practically smothers you as he checks for signs of life, pushing hard on your ribs, his mouth searching for yours as he repeats your name, shoving Jet so roughly, he cowers from his master.

I watch and pray for the ambulance to hurry. Instructions keep coming from the operator. She's good at her job: she has all our names and keeps up a steady flow of instructions.·

'The ambulance is just ninety seconds away now, and you're doing great. I need you to breathe into Maya's mouth on my count. Are you ready, Hector?'

Dad is trying his best, but he's crying too hard, doesn't have the breath to save you. He looks up at me but I'm afraid, too afraid, to touch you. It's the blood, black in the half-light of the hallway. And you're so exposed, pale skin in red silk, dark hair matted with blood.

'Hector? I need you to continue counting so I can hear what you're doing. Shall we count together?'

He's sobbing now, and you, sweet mother, are deathly still.

'It's too late,' he says. 'Maya's left me.'

'No, Dad, she's still here!'

Something kicks in, a feeling I thought I'd lost returns and I push Dad away, pull your mouth to mine. It's soft and cold and I push my life into you. I ram both my palms hard on your chest, feel your fragile bones give way under the cool skin, all the time trying not to look in your terrifying eyes.

The operator counts: 'One, two, three . . .'

Oh please, oh please. Between gulped breaths, I silently beg you. Or God. I won't stop, can't stop, until you breathe again. Dad slips to the floor, weeps noisily, calling your name. Jet won't leave him be, wet snout and yelps. And still the voice comes from the phone, delivering calm instructions.

'Okay, Cass, the ambulance is very close. Keep going until the paramedics take over. Now push: one, two, three . . .'

3

Holly

Outside and all around, the season had changed, seemingly overnight. Just a few days before, Holly had tasted the air as cinnamon sticks, autumn smoke and spice. A rich clothing of red and orange leaves seemed to make every tree along the street glow copper. But the advent of November had brought with it cool silver skies and the taste of tin. The trees looked withered, as if their autumn dress had been stolen, leaving them naked and vulnerable to winter, and the sky was heavy with rain.

Holly's paramedic uniform was a short-sleeved tunic and cotton trousers. She shivered as she got into the car, a Fiat 500, her mint-coloured bubble against the world and the unwelcome sensations it gave her. Her work bag, in the same forest-green shade as her tunic and trousers, was on the passenger seat along with her Superdry jacket. She'd likely need that later.

Despite the passage of time, she didn't need to look at a map. Her internal navigation knew this journey as though she'd travelled it every day of the twenty years she'd kept away. After leaving the A14, the minor road to the outlying villages was a tunnel of trees, oak and sycamore, their leaves burnt and brittle, hanging from black skeletal branches. On and on she drove, down the familiar twisting lanes, then a sudden turn and a change in light, like coming up for air. A cheery farm shop on the left – it hadn't been here back then – advertising bread and local milk. Then a sign announced Kenley.

Kenley village was still just one row of houses, terraces built for farm labourers way back when. The local pub was in need of a lick of paint, as was the red-brick school, its navy-painted door and eaves peeling with neglect. When her family had lived here, the American soldiers at the base would volunteer to do tasks like this: good deeds in the community to ease the disquiet of the locals, putting up with a military base in their midst. But in the eighties the Cold War thawed, the base was run by a skeleton of staff through the nineties and closed completely after the invasion of Iraq; it became a ghost town. Today the playground lay empty. Half-term, Holly remembered, school was out for the week, although there were no children on the street either. Too early. And the headmaster wouldn't let them play on school premises during holidays, so they'd be left to roam the fields and woods nearby.

There was just one new addition, just one sign of change in the twenty years she'd been gone – a six-foot banner, hung across the front of the school building, emblazoned in black capitals with the message: HANDS OFF OUR COUNTRYSIDE!

Once she was through the village, the landscape turned barren. Here, the road was flanked by flat fields of turned earth with dirty pigs snuffling around domed metal huts. She turned down Innocence Lane. She'd always known she'd have to return one day, but still she didn't feel ready.

The hedgerows were untended and bleached by the sun with singed grasses and wires of ivy. Beyond, fields sprawled, stubbly with cut corn. When they were younger, she and Jamie had played here until they were spotted and shouted away by the farm workers. Before. Rooks jumped on the ashy white soil and cawed to each other in warning, rabbits darted around the muddy mounds. This stretch of Suffolk was remote – not an area a tourist would simply happen upon, so the perfect spot for a controversial American airbase, now derelict. In the distance, the perimeter fence still stood intact, but grass grew through the cracks on the sidewalk and the roads led to abandoned homes. The Yanks had gone home. Now this was a site of controversy and debate, given the lack of houses locally, but no one wanted to live out here: no shops, no employment. It was a problem. Something had to be done with the place.

A few hundred yards further down the lane came a wooden sign that hadn't been there before. It had a fat pink sow painted alongside a plump red hen and cheery script with the name INNOCENCE FARM. Staked into the mud beside it was a long banner, the twin of the one outside the schoolhouse: HANDS OFF OUR COUNTRYSIDE!

An uneven track, better suited to a tractor than her Fiat, eventually opened onto a gravelled drive that must once have been grand. In the middle was a stone fountain, the pump long since broken, judging by the mossy stone beneath. A squad car and an ambulance were already parked on the gravel, the police had secured the scene and Jon and another member of the team would be inside, expecting her.

There was the black skeletal barn that had both drawn and repelled her so much when she was a child. She looked away, unable to stand the memory. Instead, she looked up at the farmhouse, solid and square with its proud red-brick facade, dark glassy eyes for windows. A building that had seen generations of people come and go, and knew it would outlast them all. Holly pulled her Fiat in beside the ambulance, switched the engine off and left the safety of her small car.

Inside the farmhouse, Holly's senses picked up the faint metallic tang of gunshot, and it spun her back two decades. She followed the scent, past the grand entrance with its wide staircase to the back of the house, where, in a dimly lit hallway, two of her colleagues were working to save a woman's life.

A few yards away was a pale, stocky man with slate-grey hair – Hector Hawke, the farmer who had shouted her off his land so many times. Now, he lay slumped on the floor, one hand cupped to his chest, in a posture of defeat. Holly felt an ache along her left arm, a painful tingling in her fingers that mirrored his pain, as a black spaniel ran in crazy circles around him.

Seated on the third step, a confused expression on her face, was a woman in her thirties, who Holly hadn't seen in twenty years. Cassandra Hawke had attended the Victorian primary school, just like Holly, but the four-year age gap was too wide for them to have been friends. Besides, their worlds were radically different. Cassandra was the posh girl who lived in the haunted house, beautiful and aloof. She had been a figure of fascination to Holly, but as unapproachable as the Queen of England. Her cheeks were puffy from crying, and Holly felt her own cheeks dampen and swell. Despite this, the woman was as beautiful as ever, a sheath of golden hair falling to her shoulders. Except that the tips were matted with blood, as were her hands.

'Holly,' called Jon, suddenly noticing her, 'come over here and make yourself useful, please.'

4

Cassandra

It takes a moment, then I differentiate the uniforms around me: the bottle-green uniform of the paramedics, a man and a woman; the navy blue of a police officer who wears white overshoes to check upstairs and then pulls on blue gloves to remove the rifle.

The paramedic introduces himself as Jon, then asks what your name is.

Dad whispers, 'Maya. My Maya.'

They move quickly towards me at the foot of the stairs, and Jon smoothly positions himself just where I'm kneeling, taking over. 'Cassandra, is it? You can stop now: we have her.' I lean back, suddenly in the way.

You lie, limp and pale, your hair shrouding you like a black veil dipped in blood. Bruises are appearing on your neck, red as garnets. Your nightdress has ridden up, so you're exposed, but no one seems to notice.

'Hello, Maya, my name's Jon and this is Hilary. Can you hear me, love?'

The paramedics work together in a tightly choreographed dance. They snap on purple plastic gloves, then she unzips a blue kitbag, folds it out to reveal syringes, tubes, medical objects.

Jon puts on a pair of clear safety glasses before checking your mouth and nose.

I wince as a metal object is slid into your mouth.

'Okay, I can see the cords. Airway compromised, blood occluding,' he says to Hilary, withdrawing the metal tool. 'Unknown damage to neck and lower jaw, possible fracture at base of skull. I'm going to have to intubate to protect the airway. Get me a size eight.'

Hilary moves swiftly to the bag and brings forth a pump-driven machine. 'Here's the suction.'

Jon slips a tube into your mouth, looking all the time at the position. With a balloon-like object at the other end of the tube, he pushes air into you, counting to ten, stopping to check his watch, counting again. Hilary connects you to an octopus-like machine with many tentacles. At the end of each is something different: a peg to place on your finger, a cuff for your arm, several sticky dots for your chest. I'm watching a horror film, disconnected from me but still terrifying. I want to turn it off, but can't.

Another paramedic arrives. She's pretty, with caramel skin and the darkest eyes I've ever seen, I assume she's mixed-race. Something about her feels familiar. She looks at me, wide-eyed as if she's seen a ghost, then kneels beside Jon and looks away.

'Okay, good, airways clear and she's breathing,' says Jon. 'Circulation, Holly?'

She checks the machine, though I can tell she's still aware of me. 'Pulse is weak, low BP. Saturation is only seventy-five per cent.' Speaks the foreign language of medicine in which they're fluent.

'Take over the bagging, Holly. I'm going to cannulate for fluids.'

A needle is inserted in the crook of your arm and I shudder on your behalf.

Jon unravels the clear tube from the needle then shows her a bag of fluid. 'I'm going to put up a 500-millilitre bag of sodium chloride, 0.9 per cent, expiry 2020.'

Hilary lifts her head from checking the machine, glances at the label. 'Yes, confirmed.'

The work continues, but I see how the third paramedic leans forward, pulling gently at your nightdress so it covers you again. Giving you back your dignity. I am more grateful for this than for any of the life-saving tricks that have saved you.

Jon checks his watch. 'Okay, we're six minutes in and she's stable enough to travel. Let's scoop and run. Make sure the hospital knows we're coming and they're ready for us in Resus. Holly, you can meet us back at base.'

My thoughts slide into the fog.

I sit on the stairs, my body heavy and aching. There's a lull, a calm in the activity as the fluid enters you and Jon looks up, to where I'm perched. I feel him notice me and look down, see my stained blouse and realise it's obvious I'm not wearing a bra. I cross my arms over my chest, lower my head and feel the damp tips of my hair on my throat. When did it get so bloody?

'You've done well. I heard you had to resuscitate her. Relax now. We can take over from here.'

'I'm going with her to hospital,' says Dad aggressively, as if a right is being denied.

A stretcher is brought in, and it takes forever to move you. I notice the third paramedic is talking to you, almost lovingly, the whole time.

I wish someone would talk to me like that. I'm feeling absent. I have to slide my hands between my thighs to stop my body shaking.

Dad says you shot yourself, but that makes no sense to me. I want you to talk to me, tell me what really happened, but you can't speak, have barely moved. All I can do is watch helplessly as they open the stretcher into two halves and slide each side under you, scooping you up. Then the two who came first begin to carry you out.

The third paramedic comes forward. 'Cassandra?' She hesitates, then tells me, 'We're getting ready to take your mum to hospital, and your dad will be travelling in the ambulance with her. She's in good hands, and the hospital are waiting to take care of her. Is there anything we can do for you?'

I shake my head. All I want is for someone to tell me what happened, since I can't believe you shot yourself, and she can't tell me that.

Down the hallway, near the backstairs, Jon continues his loud monologue: 'Okay, Maya, we're just taking you out of the house now to the ambulance.'

His voice comes closer as he and Hilary carry the stretcher through the hallway, past the door to the front room, and I see the breathing tube and line into your arm being held over your bloodless face by the third paramedic. Strands of dark hair spill over the side of the stretcher, long and fragile like silk, and I want to reach and gather it up, in case it gets caught and hurts you. As if she can read my thoughts, the paramedic reaches forward and lifts your hair back in place.

Dad follows, like a condemned man. 'How could she have done it?' he mutters to no one in particular. No one looks my way, I've become invisible. Minutes later, they're out on the gravelled courtyard and the ambulance starts to scream its warning. A blue light is sent swirling around the room as it pulls away. The house is finally silent.

The third paramedic returns. She guides me away from the stairs, where I think I'd wait forever if I could. Her hand tries to steady me, but she must feel how much I'm shaking.

'Come on, Cassandra. We'll go in the front room. Take a breath.'

Now you've gone, everything looks just the same, the clock is still ticking to the right rhythm. How is that possible? She helps me into the armchair, and lifts the bedding from the sofa so she can perch on the end. *Dad slept here last night, after your argument.*

I can see her mouth moving, I can hear the words, but they seem to have nothing to do with me. Then something breaks through. 'Cassandra?'

'I'm sorry,' I say. 'What did you say?'

'I was saying I could drive you to hospital, if you like? You probably shouldn't drive yourself.'

I remember I should call Daniel. 'Please . . . I need the phone.' It's somewhere at the bottom of the stairs, from when I was on the call to the emergency operator. The paramedic goes to fetch it, returning swiftly and watching as I dial. He picks up immediately.

'It's me.'

'Cass? What's happening?'

'It's Mum. She's just been taken to hospital in an ambulance. She's been shot.' Three short sentences, not enough to convey the confusion and mass of questions in my head.

'Is she alive?'

Poor Daniel – he's always loved you, and you him. He's the son you never had, the man who cured your cancer.

'Just,' I say. Then I can't say any more.

'Keep strong, love. It'll be okay. I'll meet you at the hospital.'

He doesn't ask who shot you, or for any details, and I'm grateful.

As I disconnect, I realise there's something happening in the hallway. Someone has arrived to disturb the silence. A voice is calling my name. For a moment, I don't recognise Ash when he finds me. He's shockingly pale, his scruffy sandy hair dangles in his eyes. Never the cleverest of men, now he looks utterly dumbstruck. His thin fingers agitate the frayed edging of his battered wax jacket.

'Cass! How's Maya?'

An angry thought follows: *What the fuck's it got to do with you? You're only the housekeeper's son.*

The paramedic follows behind him, looking concerned. 'I'm sorry, but I don't think she's able to talk at the moment, she's just had a terrible shock. Why don't you come back later, when things are more settled?'

'I have a right to be here!' He turns aggressively, then stops when he sees her face, his eyes widening with recognition. 'What are *you* doin' here?'

'I'm a trainee paramedic. I'm here as part of the emergency response.'

Ash looks around him, confused. 'Where's Hector?'

'Mr Hawke has gone to the hospital, with his wife.'

'Is Maya gonna be okay?' He's usually the last to catch on, yet he's grasped the situation far quicker than me.

'We don't know yet,' she says. 'I hope so.'

Ash moves from one foot to the other, still watching the paramedic. 'It *is* you, isn't it? The sister.'

'Holly Redwood. Jamie's sister.' She glances at me, her skin flushes. 'I used to live round here, on the airbase.'

Ash remembered her, and now she's said her name it sounds familiar to me too. I examine her face again – her caramel skin dusted with dark freckles over her nose, her very dark eyes. She's studying me with an intensity that makes me uneasy. I feel like I've been unwrapped and everyone is seeing the very fibres of my being. I want to go back to sleep, and wake to find this is all a bad dream. I want Ash gone.

'Holly, can you show Mr Cley out so you can drive me to the hospital. He doesn't belong here right now.'

Ash looks at me, disbelieving, his mouth hanging open. 'Cass, what do you mean? I'd do anythin' for you and your family, you know that. It should be *me* drivin' you!'

I can see Holly assessing the situation, wondering what to do.

'He just works for us, you probably remember that.' I refuse to catch his eye. 'Dad employs him to manage the pigs and the poultry, and he lives in the cottage we own, down the lane. That's all.'

'That's all?' he repeats, gormlessly shaking his head so his dirty-blond hair falls in his eyes. 'Cass . . .'

'Go away, Ash,' I say, my fingers straying to the scar on my collar-bone. 'You're not welcome.'

He blinks, fighting back tears of surprise. Holly takes advantage of his momentary shock to guide him outside. His head is droopy, his chin almost to his chest. He doesn't want to go, but he has no choice.

Finally, I'm alone as I've never been, not here at the farm. I came here yesterday because I needed your help, Mum – I was slipping again. I was so wrapped up in myself, I didn't see this coming. I hear footsteps, Holly returning, and before I can stop myself I say, 'I don't believe my mum shot herself.'

Holly stands close to me. Her gaze is intelligent and sympathetic. 'It must be very hard to come to terms with.'

'No, that's not it. What I mean is that I *know* Mum wouldn't do that.'

She frowns. There are furrows between her dark eyes. 'Maybe that's just what you want to think?'

'No.' I'm determined that she should believe me. 'Suicide is for cowards, and she's not one of those. My mum is tough – she's run this place since she was in her early twenties, she's seen through two recessions. She isn't a quitter.'

Holly breathes in, looks around the room, then back at me. 'You think someone else did this?'

'I'm certain.'

I wait, expecting her to dismiss me, but she doesn't.

'I'll have to write a report on this, but it doesn't include a space for feelings: it's a medical form. But I'll tell my supervisor what you've said, and ensure it gets passed back to the police. It's their job to investigate anything suspicious. We should go to the hospital now.'

Pacified, I let her lead me out.

5

Holly

Holly pulled her Fiat into her parking space and looked up at her flat with longing. It was small and hardly a triumph of design, built out of breeze blocks that fitted together simply, rather than with style, the rooms all small and square. But what it offered her was priceless: a place with no noise, no stimulation of any kind and, especially after the day she'd had, a chance to think of nothing at all. She removed the keys from the ignition, and gathered up her coat and work bag. Opening the car door, she was hit by cold air, a biting wind that promised frost.

As she walked across the car park, she saw that Leif's light was on, and that he was watching her from his kitchen window. The last time she'd seen him was this morning, he'd been naked and she'd had to tread over two used condoms to make her exit. So much had happened since then, she could hardly believe it was just twelve hours ago. What an idiot she was: relationships were bad news, she didn't need the complication, and fucking a man who was a neighbour was bloody stupid.

She planned on slipping quietly into her flat, but when she arrived on the walkway to the flats he was there, waiting for her. She saw he was wearing the navy police uniform she had seen hanging in his bedroom that morning.

'*Hej du*, Holly, have you enjoyed a good day? Fancy a *fika* with me?'

She tried to think of a response that would set the right tone, given she'd fucked him twice already today. 'I'll have to say no, I'm afraid,' she said. 'I need a quiet night rather than sex.'

Leif feigned offence, one hand to his chest. '*Fika* is coffee and cake! You English, with your dirty minds.'

She smiled at the misunderstanding, but still had no intention of taking this any further.

'I'm too tired, Leif. It's been a tough day.'

She took her key from her bag, keen to disappear inside her flat and close the door on Leif and any possibility of them being more than neighbours.

'Me too!' he said, as she was turning away. 'I was called in as guard duty after some woman tried to blow her head off.'

Holly's key was still in her hand, frozen in space. 'Where was this?'

'At this creepy farm out in the sticks. I had to stand for hours, bored and cold. That's why I need coffee and cake.'

Holly slid her key back in her bag. 'On second thoughts, cake would be perfect.'

Holly found herself on Leif's sofa, listening to his lyrical Beowulf accent describe being called in for duty, which as far as she could work out consisted of standing outside the front door of the farmhouse and taking people's names as they came and went.

'So the police think there was foul play?' she asked. After she'd driven Cass to the hospital, she'd been to see Jon and done as she promised, telling him of Cass's suspicion that her mother had not shot herself. He'd put a call through to CID, and a chain of action had been triggered. One that, it seemed, had included Leif.

But he seemed blasé. 'An attempted suicide isn't a crime, but because of the gun they have to check there's nothing suspicious. The forensics team came and went very quickly.'

Holly's only knowledge of such things was limited to the rare times she'd watched a police drama on TV. 'So they didn't find anything to say it wasn't attempted suicide?' She seemed to care so much more than Leif. His eyes were heavy, and he looked almost bored with the conversation.

'I don't think so, but it takes time, Holly – all the tests they do.' He yawned, stretching his arms over his head. 'My only other visitor was a nosy neighbour, and a reporter who kept trying to take photos whenever I turned my back. But I promised you cake. Actually, let me feed you properly. Come!'

The sudden change in focus stunned her, and she found herself with more questions than Leif was willing or able to answer. She leaned on the doorway of the kitchen, wondering how Cass was doing right now, and if Maya had woken yet. Leif grated potatoes and whipped eggs, and all the time her thoughts kept returning to Innocence Farm.

'How many are on the investigating team?'

'Hmm? It's a routine investigation, so not many. Our SIO said it was a waste of resources because . . .' He paused, looked down at his cooking. 'Sorry, I shouldn't be telling you.'

'It's okay,' she said, trying not to appear too eager. 'You can trust me.'

He sighed. 'He said farmers have the highest suicide rate of any profession. It's a hard life, and there are guns on hand. One thing leads to another, yes?'

Holly recalled Cassandra saying, *She thinks suicide is for cowards.*

'But enough of this. *Raggmunk,*' he said, handing her a plate. 'Potato pancakes to you. Best served with cranberry sauce.' He opened a jar and spooned a dollop onto the pancake.

'Yum,' said Holly, taking a bite. Its savoury wholesomeness was very welcome, almost transporting her from her circular thoughts, and she ate quickly. 'God, this is delicious.'

'Missed lunch, *Sötnos*?'

Holly felt her lips twitch at the corners. 'Who are you calling snot nose?'

'It's a term of endearment. Literally, sweet nose. Which, by the way, you have.' He was still busy, making cups of sugary tea. 'The only drink that goes with *raggmunk*. Come on, bring your plate.'

She followed him back to the lounge, where she cleared her plate while Leif knelt on the floor by the TV, soon brandishing a black-and-white DVD, *Murder on the Orient Express.*

Holly laughed. 'Don't you have anything more modern?'

'This is a timeless classic, *Sötnos*. Give it a try.'

Stomach sated, Holly sipped her tea. 'Okay. But I can only stay another hour.'

She was shocked at the spookiness of the opening scene, the newspaper features that flashed in front of the screen telling the story of a kidnapped child who was eventually slain. The house from which the child was taken was large and forbidding, and her mind clicked back to Innocence Farm, though not as she'd seen it today. As it had appeared to her twenty years ago, when she was a terrified eight-year-old.

'This is really creepy. I thought Agatha Christie was supposed to be twee?' she said, and Leif turned to her with mock horror on his face.

'Don't tell me you've never seen this?'

'I've never seen any Agatha Christie.'

'But for sure you must recognise this man?' Leif pointed with his knife. 'Albert Finney, from the Bourne films.'

Holly didn't tell him that she hadn't seen any of the Bourne films, which would open up a line of enquiry she didn't want to answer. She didn't watch films because she'd literally experience every touch, every smell, and be bombarded with emotions she couldn't predict. It was as if, that Halloween long ago, her synaesthesia had been born in the place of her conscience. While she was running away from something – or someone – in pain, her senses were rewiring, to ensure she'd never do it again. It made life unbearably close and loud, especially before she knew what was actually wrong. Over the years, she'd learned tricks to manage it, and training to be a paramedic was her latest and best effort to lead a normal life. *If I confront the very thing I did twenty years ago, if I deal directly with pain and suffering, then my senses will quieten.* That, at least, was the hope.

She didn't own a TV and avoided books, especially crime novels. She didn't even watch the news if she could help it. But this film, perhaps because it was set in the 1930s, or because of the formulaic investigation by Hercule Poirot within the gilded confines of the luxurious train, pulled her in and amused her. His was a type of detecting, now hopelessly outdated, that relied on a sort of cod psychology that surely wouldn't stand up in court. The ending shocked her.

'So Poirot is going to let them get away with it?' she said, feeling disappointed in the detective she'd grown strangely fond of during the course of the film. 'Twelve people, all guilty, walking free.'

'Well, Samuel Ratchett did deserve to be murdered,' observed Leif. 'He organised the kidnapping, and there were all those repercussions for everyone on that train. He was a nasty piece of work.'

'Surely that's not the point?'

'You're overthinking it, Holly. It's just a great twist.' His Nordic blue eyes were sparkling with energy. 'Twelve people in this conspiracy, all surely guilty, each one stabbing the victim. But none knows which of the others dealt that fatal blow.'

'Preposterous,' said Holly. 'And a police officer's nightmare, I would think.'

Leif leaned back, his arms behind his head. '*Ja*, it's a tough job. Even from what I see, I wouldn't want to do it for a living.'

'But you do *see* things.' Holly coaxed him back to the subject, unable to leave it alone. 'Like the shooting at Innocence Farm today.'

Leif looked confused. 'Did I say the address?'

She shifted awkwardly. 'Actually, I was there – one of the paramedics attending the scene. I'm still in training, so I didn't do much.'

'But why didn't you say so?' He sounded hurt. 'Why the secrecy?'

She had no good answer. 'I'm sorry.'

'Anyway,' he said, wiping his hands clean on the legs of his jeans, and reaching for her with carnal hunger, 'it's unlikely a crime was committed. There's nothing suspicious about what happened. So my small part in it – and yours – is finished.'

6

Cassandra

Waiting. Watching through the café window at every doctor who passes, lifting my head every time a nurse in squeaky shoes walks along the corridor.

Waiting to know if you'll survive.

Then, suddenly, Clive is crouched beside me, holding my wrist and peering carefully into my eyes. Dr Clive Marsh, esteemed psychiatrist and – I like to think – my friend.

'Cassandra? Daniel called me, and I drove straight here. Oh, love, I'm so sorry about what's happened to your mum.'

He hugs me, and I breathe in the barky scent of pipe tobacco, my chin against the tweed of his jacket. I can't let go, can't cry. I'm still too stunned. I didn't ask Daniel to contact him; it makes me nervous that he did.

That was two years ago – a bad time, I tell myself. He's not here to lock you away. He's your friend.

'They're saying Mum shot herself,' I tell him, as if hearing the words out loud will make me understand. Dad's still outside, standing in the cold air. He's chain-smoked since we arrived, and I feel like he's avoiding me.

'I'm so sorry, love. Why do you think she did it?' Clive releases me and lowers his rather bulky frame gingerly onto the plastic chair. His battered jacket smells of cold air and smoke, familiar and comforting. His kind, crinkled face, his unkempt beard, his round glasses behind which twinkle gentle brown eyes. He's here to help me. I don't need to be scared any more. And I need to talk to someone.

'I don't believe she did. Yes, she was angry about everything that's been happening with the farm, and I know she'd had a big argument with Dad about it, but she wasn't depressed.'

Clive is turned to me, twisted in his chair despite his girth, so he can hold my hands. His assessing gaze scrutinises my face. 'Suicides aren't always the result of long-standing depression – it can be much more impulsive than that. You know this, Cassandra.'

He pauses. I feel the fingers of my right hand moving to the wrist of my left, where the old scars are. Yes, I know this, better than most.

'Mum thinks suicide is a sign of weakness. Even back when she was first diagnosed with cancer, she never spoke about giving up. She's a fighter: she tried everything to save herself. That's how she met Daniel, how he came into my world.'

Clive knows the story of how Daniel cured you – most people in Suffolk do, since Daniel talks about it on his radio show most Fridays. I was away at university when you were first diagnosed, so I didn't see your daily struggle, but you'd tell me when I called about this amazing man who was healing you using ancient ways. When I came home, fatigued and stressed with finals looming, you made an appointment for me. You introduced me to Daniel, and he became mine instead of yours.

'Mum's a fighter. She always has been.'

Clive looks unconvinced. 'Hmm. It's not always possible to predict things like this. A suicide attempt knocks any family sideways, but your mum is alive, and you've said she's a fighter.'

I remember something then. It comes to me in a hot flush of panic. 'Clive, I've forgotten Victoria! She'll be waiting at school to be collected for half-term. I don't know if Daniel will have remembered to call her. If not, she'll just be stood there, waiting for me.'

'I'm sure he'll have sorted it out – he sounded very calm when we spoke. He was organising everything so he could come here as soon as possible. But I can check if you like?'

He slides his Nokia from his pocket and begins to search for the number in his contacts. I place my hand over his to stop him. I want him to understand, because panic is rising in me.

'What will happen to Victoria's cake?'

He frowns, the phone in his hand forgotten. 'What cake, love?'

'Daniel will bin it – you know how evil he thinks fat and sugar are. Her homecoming will be ruined!'

He takes my hand in his and I see him contemplating me afresh. 'Cass, you're displacing your anxiety. Remember how you did that before? The cake isn't important. You're feeling overwhelmed and I'm here to help you. I think you should take something. I could prescribe a small dose or tranquilliser, just to get you through this. You're in severe shock . . .'

'I took trazodone,' I confess. As far as he knows I haven't even got any, but my GP keeps prescribing it and I have a secret supply. 'Last night.'

He removes his glasses, rubs the bridge of his nose where the skin is red. I can see his disappointment that I self-medicated without checking with him first. 'How much?'

'One, maybe two tablets. I keep a bottle in my car for emergencies.'

Before last night, I hadn't taken antidepressants for two years, not since that terrible September when I was confined at the Bartlet Hospital. I've kept well all this time, with only the blood in my body, the air in my lungs, to tell me how I feel and keep me going. Mindfulness and clean food have cured me – Daniel healed me just like he healed you. But yesterday, I couldn't see past my delusions, my grasp on reality slipped and it terrified me.

I'm lying to Clive: I took the whole bottle.

If you hadn't found me, Mum, and made me purge, I wouldn't be here at all. So, yes, I know how suddenly suicidal thoughts can come, just like they did two years ago, and I'm not strong like you. I can't stop thinking about that iced pink cake going to waste.

Clive watches me the way he does the members of Team Talk. I've become his patient once again, and fear grips me. *I won't go back to the Bartlet. I won't let that happen.* The same thought that hounded me last night, that made me swallow those pills.

Clive reaches down to his black hinged bag and brings out a small brown bottle, rattling it towards me, like a tempting toy. He shakes two white capsules onto his palm. Two nubs of narcotic, one swallow is all it takes, and then I can relax, and later my sleep will be heavy and deep.

'I'm going to try you on something different this time, Cass, because we know the trazodone disrupts your sleep. I'm going to monitor you closely, and you must tell me if you have any side effects.'

He uncurls my hand and places the pills on my palm, where I balance the weightless possibility of them. 'What are they?'

'Fluoxetine.'

I know about antidepressants and their names. I've become an expert thanks to Team Talk. 'Prozac,' I say.

'It's for the best, Cass. You're in severe shock and there's no shame in getting help. I'm going to give you something to calm you.'

Clive goes to the café counter and buys a bottle of water. He returns and hands me four pills. I swallow the drugs without thinking and sit quietly like a good girl, because I don't want him to think I'm refusing treatment. Hard down the throat, sugar on the bitter pill, landing in my stomach when it's too late. Too late to stop the capsule breaking apart and dissolving like sugar into my bloodstream, sweetening the pain, blurring the edges of my world which is suddenly so cruel. My hands are so shaky, he has to hold the bottle to my lips and I sip again, letting my tongue swim in the relief of the cold water, as my body sweats and my limbs shiver. I regret it when my mouth is empty, when the water washes away the acrid coating on my throat, and hits my stomach. I want this all to be just a bad dream.

When the rush comes, it's familiar. Antidepressants make feelings – love and pain, nested like sick birds in the heart – become distant, separate. I know they're inside, cawing, but I no longer need to nurture them. This is how the drugs work: I'm able to starve my own heart of feeling. This is how I was healed two years ago.

I want Daniel to comfort me. *Why isn't he here?*

Dad returns, and the stench of cigarettes and despair is overwhelming. He looks blankly at Clive, though I know he must remember him – he was there for the family sessions at the Bartlet too. The three of us continue to wait for news. Finally, a nurse comes for us.

'Mr Hawke, Miss Hawke? I'm Lauren, the ward sister in intensive care. Maya's out of theatre and in her own room. She's in an induced coma, her condition is still critical, but you're able to sit with her. It's best that the atmosphere is calm around her, as she may be able to hear. If you'd like to follow me?'

Clive stops me, a hand on my shoulder. 'Do you want me to come with you, Cass?'

I hesitate, because I would, but it's better if I seem to be coping. 'No, I'm fine.'

'Then I'll say goodbye, but I'll drop in on you tomorrow. Call me if you need me.'

Dad and I follow the quick-footed nurse across the car park to the Garrett Anderson Centre and upstairs to the intensive care unit. She opens the door and ushers us inside. The overheated hospital room is in semi-darkness, the blinds are pulled low.

Oh, Mum, there you are! Propped high on a narrow bed with tubes connecting you to machines, your head in a brace, your mouth and nose covered by a misted oxygen mask. There are dressings on your head and neck. Dad moves towards you without hesitating, his bad hand hanging limply at his side, all bluster and breeze. He's a man who belongs in the open air, not in a small room. He leans so heavily over your poor body that the bed sways.

'Maya! Oh God, Maya, wake up!'

I lean against a nearby chair, unable to move, watching him panic.

'Please lower your voice, Mr Hawke.' The nurse has her hand on his arm, touching the corduroy elbows of his crumpled work jacket. He has no other type of clothes, though he'd normally also wear a cap. It's strange to see him bareheaded, and he must feel this too as he keeps running his left hand through his thinning hair.

'It's better if you speak calmly,' the nurse says. 'It's possible Maya can hear us – when people wake from comas, they often say they could. So please talk to her, reassure her.'

Dad rubs his good hand over his face, then says, 'But when is she going to wake up? Maya!'

He's angry with the nurse, with you, with me. He's a bull in a ring, not sure which way to direct his impotent rage. It's all she can do to coax him into the seat beside the bed. He looks aghast at the array of machines, all connected to you by wires, at the tube coming from your mouth. You're so absent, the idea that you can hear anything seems ridiculous.

'What the fuck does all that beeping mean?'

The nurse gives Dad a broad smile that digs into her thick foundation, and I wonder if the make-up is a mask to help her perform around distressed people. 'All her vital signs are being measured, Mr Hawke. The bullet caused a bleed on her brain, which the surgeon managed to cauterise, and she has a fractured skull. That's why she's in an induced coma. We're also using ice packs to keep her body temperature low to slow her metabolism.'

'Is she in pain?' I ask, still standing back.

Dad looks at me then, wide-eyed, as if he'd forgotten I was there, then he turns back to the nurse.

'Well, is she?' Dad demands, ignoring the nurse's advice, his hand clenched.

Lauren hesitates. Her face is set in a forced half-smile. 'The drip includes morphine, so she almost certainly isn't. We really can't be sure, when someone's in a coma, how much they do feel. But she was lucky, Mr Hawke. If the bullet had travelled an inch to the right she'd have died.'

'You call that luck?' he growls. 'This is a nightmare.'

We sit together in the hot room. Dad by the window, me by the door, you in the bed. I'm so exhausted by all that's happened, I can't fight it any more. I close my eyes and dip into sleep so quickly it's as though I've been anaesthetised.

'Cassandra? Sweetheart, wake up.'

I open my eyes, finally he's here: *Daniel*. His dark hair falls into his brown eyes, he wraps me in his arms, and it feels like medicine. He's wearing his usual outfit – loose navy joggers and a polo shirt with the Samphire Master logo. This is the man who cured you, then me. I've never needed him more than now.

'Oh, darling, you poor thing. I'm sorry I couldn't get here earlier, but I'm here now. Everything's going to be okay.'

I believe him: he cures diseases when doctors have given up hope. If anyone can help us through this, it's him. I sink into him, his minty, freshly showered scent, give in to what is being offered. With his arms around me, the world feels safer.

'Can you help her out of any pain, Dan? Maybe some reiki healing?'

He releases me gently and moves to the bed, reaches a hand and places it on your leg, closing his eyes for a moment. When he opens them, he says, 'I can feel her fighting to stay with us. There was a moment I thought we'd lose her.'

'When?' My question comes from nowhere conscious.

'Hmm?' He lifts his eyes to meet mine, and I repeat the question. '*When* did you think we'd lose her?'

'When she was in the operating theatre, of course.'

'But you weren't even here!'

He frowns, reaches forward so his hand cups my chin and I feel weak at his proximity. God help me, I love this man.

'Your mum and I have a connection, Cass. I've been with you in spirit the whole time. That's why I called Clive and asked him to come – I knew you needed support. But I had things to sort out: I did a pre-record of the radio show so I can be with you without interruption.'

He studies the bruises on your neck, the dressings on your head and throat where blood has seeped through, but he doesn't seem shocked, just curious. Daniel always keeps his demeanour. I've never seen him cry and I've never heard him shout – he has a quiet authority that people respond to instinctively. It's one of the many reasons I fell in love with him: my dizzy admiration for a personality trait I so completely lack.

Finally, he turns his attention back to me. The warmth in his brown eyes is so soothing, it's almost indecent.

'So,' I finally say, 'what was the pre-record?'

'I interviewed a woman who has a brain tumour. The doctors believe she's only got weeks to live, but they're wrong. She's healing.' He says this neutrally, as if it isn't a miracle, but there are people in Suffolk who owe him their lives. Each Christmas, we get gift hampers from his patients. He gets stopped in the streets by grateful relatives wanting to shake his hand. One of the people he saved was the female track cyclist who won triple gold at the last Olympics, one of them was me. 'Then I drove to Norfolk, to see Victoria and explain that she wouldn't be coming home for half-term after all. I thought it best to keep everything as normal as possible, so I took her and Dawn to that American diner they like so much. I hated to think of you going through everything here on your own, but I knew I had to do what was best for the family.'

Even though I'm being unreasonable, given how busy he's been, I still feel he should have been with me. I punish him by saying, 'Clive gave me some Prozac and some other drug. I don't know what.'

Daniel respects Clive, and understands the need for psychiatry alongside his holistic approach, but he doesn't approve of drugs. His therapy includes meditation and herbal remedies – Suffolk recipes that use samphire and go back to the Iceni. He's cured everything from infertility to cancer, that's why he has a regular show on Radio Suffolk, why the Studio is doing so well, and why Samphire Health Spa is such a wonderful idea. You believed that too, Mum, until last night.

'Have the tablets helped, love?' he asks, doubtfully.

'It's too early to say.' Though I'm not crying, so something worked – maybe some trazodone made it to my bloodstream before I purged. 'I feel tired, a bit flattened.'

'I'm going to take you home to get some sleep,' he says with determination, 'then from tomorrow I'm putting you on my Samphire Strength juice programme. You've been through a traumatic experience: you need to heal from the inside out.'

I feel like one of his clients again, swept up in his conviction that he knows exactly what's right for me. His hand covers mine, and I feel steadied.

Oh, Mum, look at you: pale face, half-covered by a mask, black hair matted with dried blood. You don't move, only your eyelids flicker.

'How can I leave her?'

'It's okay,' he says. 'I promise it will all work out just fine.'

7

Cassandra

Back home, in our semi in a cul-de-sac on the edge of Greater Kenley, I wonder how everything can seem so perfect. Cream carpets, white walls, everything neat and in its place. How can the fact that you're fighting for your life in hospital mean nothing here?

Daniel and I moved here when Victoria was a baby, just as a stepping stone. The longer-term plan has always been to open a health spa, so Daniel can help even more people. A dream you shared, and were helping to make a reality, at least until yesterday evening.

But if the house looks the same, the people within it are changed. Dad hasn't spoken once since we left the hospital. He barely seems to know where he is. He sinks heavily into an armchair, his face as grey as his hair, his eyes half-closed with fatigue. He's never seemed old before, as if his sixty-odd years have suddenly caught up with him in a matter of hours, showing in the lines on his jowls, the shadows under his eyes. Even after the stroke he didn't look like this, it was only his right side that was affected, and I notice how he cups his right hand protectively to his chest as though the injury were new.

'Oh, Dad . . .' Unable to stand the tension any longer, I reach out to hug him, because that seems the right thing to do – it's what they'd do in films – but he holds up his left hand to stop me.

'That's enough, Cassandra.'

He never could bear signs of affection – any love in his gnarly heart he reserved for you. He's a man of few words and even fewer touches, but still I ache with longing for comfort. He won't give any and he certainly doesn't want mine. I don't realise I'm crying until I feel the tears on my cheeks.

'Come here, love.' Daniel reaches for me, just as moments ago I reached for Dad, and I fall into his embrace. I catch the scent of another woman on his skin, but that's not unusual. He works closely with women, their perfume is often on his clothes, but I trust him. Daniel works intimately with his clients. In the past, the boundaries got blurred. Like that Olympian cyclist, who he healed so she could go on and win triple gold? She became his lover. They were going through a messy separation when he started working with me. I too was his client and then his lover. So sometimes I wonder about whoever he's curing now, whether he's attracted to them, even though he assures me I'm being silly. Jealousy is one of my demons. I've fought hard to master it, but sometimes I relapse.

'Hector, you're welcome to stay on the futon in the spare room,' Daniel says, 'just until the police finish their investigation at the farm.'

Dad doesn't even thank him, but the spare room is where Daniel meditates every day. It's where he keeps his folk art from India, propped against a wall, waiting until the Spa is open and he can put it on display. Where his golden Buddha lives, waiting serenely for its rightful home. The sanguine room is a small indication of what the Spa will look like, and I know it's a sacrifice for him to give it up, even for a few nights. But Dad must stay with us, no one's allowed at the farm while the police check that nothing suspicious took place.

Then I realise I don't know where the dog is. In my feeble state, I can't even remember his name. 'Where's the spaniel?'

'Jet's fine, love. Ash went to the farm a while ago to check on everything, and there's a policeman watching the house. He told Ash a neighbour had taken Jet.'

Dad looks up. 'What neighbour?'

'Philip Godwin,' Daniel says, and they exchange a look. Godwin is the head teacher at the local school, has been since I attended it. He's also leading the campaign against the development plans, and he was at the farm yesterday, but they're not friends. It would be hard to be friends with a man like Philip Godwin.

'Well, if he knows, so will the whole village,' says Dad. 'I wouldn't be surprised if he doesn't call the press.'

Daniel pulls a disgusted face. 'He probably has Alfie Avon on speed dial. If he gets the notion that Maya's suicide attempt is anything to do with the farm, he'll use it for Save Our Countryside. No scruples, that man.'

Dad bristles. 'It's *my* campaign too, Dan. That's why I'm working with Godwin. To protect the land.'

'Which I always said was a bad idea.' Daniel says it softly, but there's steel behind each word. The farm's future is important to him, we've got a stake in what happens – or at least we thought we did. 'My radio show has a growing following, people need healing and the samphire is a miracle. The Spa is the key to saving our land: that's the future.'

'That land has been farmed on since the Iceni and you want to turn it into a spa! I'm working with Godwin, trying to get the Port Authority to see reason. Godwin invited Dave Feakes to a shoot yesterday, to show him what would be lost if Innocence Lane becomes a lorry park.'

Daniel is irritated. I can see the rising rhythm of his breathing, but he controls it well.

'For God's sake, Hector, the Port Authority want the farm because it's a convenient location. You can't change their minds with a few hot toddies and some dead birds! And Godwin doesn't care about what's right for *you*. I've told you before, Samphire Health Spa would attract a new clientele, and the publicity from the healing programmes would force the council to protect our land and the samphire growing there . . .'

'It don't matter what either of us want, do it?' Dad's voice is raised and his face is flushed with anger. 'Maya agreed to sell the farm over to 'em anyway.'

Daniel breathes out deeply, trying to keep his own fury in check. He knows what happened yesterday. I called him from my car and told him that you'd decided to sell, but this is the first time it's been mentioned.

'A verbal agreement means nothing.' He takes another deep breath and closes his eyes, calming his brain. 'Now isn't the time to talk about this, Hector. We should all get some sleep.'

Sleep. It's a call to another place, somewhere I long to visit. I switch off and let the words float around me, thinking how much I want to lie down and close my eyes.

Daniel carries me upstairs, his strong arms cradling me as though I weigh nothing.

'It's all changed now,' I say, sleepy and confused, my brain leaden with drug-induced lethargy, but trying to remember all that has happened in just a few hours, to make sense of it. Everyone is telling me you tried to kill yourself, but I can't believe that. Yesterday I had an episode, a moment of delusion when oblivion seemed tempting, and you were so angry, Mum, so furious at my weakness, that I can't believe you succumbed to the same flaw just a few hours later. I'm the weak one, not you. I need Daniel to heal me again.

'Please look after me.'

He lays me down on our bed, sits next to me and unbuttons my blouse, unzips my skirt. I'm naked underneath. I move my hand to my chest, covering myself where my old scar sits, trying to explain. 'When I woke, I couldn't find my knickers or bra.'

He shushes me with a kiss, takes my hand and removes it from my breast, kissing the place I was trying to conceal. His other hand comes to rest on my thigh and he moves so he's above me. He quickly pulls off his own clothes and touches me, so we're skin on skin. I want to take his comfort and I move for him, under him, opening myself up, even though I can't stop wondering about all the other women Daniel has loved. My jealous brain torments me with their ecstasies, *oh, oh, oh*. Imagined sounds that I drown out with my own as I cry out, giving in to the overwhelming love I feel for Daniel.

After we've made love, I feel revived, giddy even, as though your being so close to death has made me cling to life and all its pleasures.

Daniel wraps me in his pyjama top, then coaxes me downstairs to eat. It's proper night now, pitch-black outside, and far too late for supper, but suddenly I'm starving. In the kitchen, nothing has changed. It's spotless, except for a solitary bowl on the counter, a plastic container of linseed and nuts on the side, and a teaspoon by the sink. It was a lonely breakfast for Daniel this morning.

And look – Victoria's homecoming cake. Still where I put it on Friday afternoon, beside the glass jars of pumpkin seeds and goji berries. Pink and sticky and sweet, untouched under clear plastic and coloured cardboard.

'If you need some comfort food, what about a bowl of kefir? Or some miso soup?' I shake my head. 'Do you want a piece of *that?*'

The cake isn't mine to eat. 'How was Victoria when you saw her?'

He leans forward to kiss the corner of my mouth. 'She's fine, love. Try not to worry so much – it's not healthy. Dawn's also staying at the school so they're keeping each other company.'

Dawn is Victoria's best friend. She was coming to stay for the week too. It's easier that way, now Victoria doesn't have friends in the area, and Dawn enjoys staying with us. So many plans, ruined.

'They'll be okay. They have each other. You didn't mind me going to see them, did you?'

'Of course not. It's just – I miss her. I'd rather have her home . . .' This is an old argument, one I lost two years ago.

'I don't think that's wise, Cass, under the circumstances. Let's focus on your mum, and see what happens. Okay?'

He saws off some sourdough bread, loads it with cashew butter, and I eat it fast. I wipe the crumbs from my lips and say, 'I want to go back to the hospital to see how Mum is.'

'It's almost midnight, Cass. You're disorientated, you've lost track of time. Go back tomorrow morning, that's soon enough. You need to sleep now.'

I feel how true it is, the heaviness, the thin skin over my eyes weighed down, my limbs leaden, as if I'm already under blankets, already giving in. Sleepiness hits me so hard that I'm not sure I can manage the stairs. I want to be carried again, to be held close.

'I'll check on Hector before I turn in. I saw the light was still on in the spare room, but let's get you into bed first.'

He speaks to me like I'm a child, and pathetic though it is, I like it. Up the stairs we go, Daniel at my side, supporting my weight, as if my pain is physical, though if I slip, his guiding arm won't be enough to stop me falling.

Daniel helps me back into bed. 'In you get!' he says, just like he used to say to Victoria when she was little, opening up the duvet like a doorway. He busies himself with collecting my blouse and skirt from the floor, discarded before we made love, folds them with studied care. He's lost more than one member of staff over his fastidiousness. They thought he was controlling, but really, it's the poise that comes with an ordered spiritual life. Not everyone understands that.

'I'll go check on Hector.' He reaches for the handset to the phone on my bedside cabinet.

'Leave it there, please. If the hospital calls, I want to be the first to know.'

Reluctantly, he replaces it.

When I'm alone, I listen.

I can hear Daniel talking to Dad in our spare room at the end of the hallway, a low rumble with bouts of silence. I know what he's asking, and what Dad will reply: no, he doesn't need anything. Nothing will help.

I'm hot and push the duvet aside, looking down at my body. Pale and saggy. Scarred. The stomach of a woman who had a child and didn't do enough exercise afterwards, despite her partner owning a holistic gym. I was too busy enjoying Victoria.

Daniel could have chosen any woman he wanted. His lover before me was a world-class athlete and in the photos, I've seen how lean she is, how fit. But he isn't superficial – he doesn't just improve people's bodies, he improves their lives. People travel miles to see him. He's a healer, a reiki master, and an advocate of samphire juicing. People call his radio show for advice, doctors refer patients to his gym, people stop him in the supermarket with questions. And he never resents it; he always gives people what they need. Whenever hidden doubts surface, I know it's my insecurity taking over – my fear that a wonderful man like him can't really be happy with me. I never was confident, was I, Mum? Never learned to stand on my own two feet. If you die, I'll have to start.

On my left bicep, I notice a bruise, the dusky grey shade of an unripe grape. I touch it and find it's the length of my middle finger. Why didn't Daniel say anything when he saw me naked?

Then I remember Saturday morning, and Jet jumping up at me, knocking me back against the door frame. I hadn't realised how hard

I'd knocked myself, but the mind blocks out pain when it needs to. It's like those stories you hear of people on mountains, who walk to safety with broken ankles. The body shuts down when the mind has other things to concentrate on.

I close my eyes and hope for oblivion. I don't know when the tears start but they seem like they're not going to stop. *I'm weeping for you, Mum.* I can hear Daniel putting the chain across the front door. It was already there when we bought the house, but we've never used it before. Does Daniel think the same then, that this wasn't a suicide attempt? That bad things happen, even in sleepy Suffolk?

I'm woken by a single 'tring' coming from the handset beside me, meaning the second phone in Daniel's study has been picked up. I stare at it as if to hear through the cream plastic. Through the wall, I can hear his voice, low and indistinct.

I slide from the bed and tiptoe along the hallway to listen.

I hear him say, in a low voice, 'It's difficult right now, things being like they are. She's very sick.'

Then he's silent, listening. Finally, he says, 'I know. I promised, didn't I? It *will* happen. Nothing has changed, Monica.'

Monica. I return to the bedroom and hide under the duvet.

I close my eyes and wait for sleep.

DAY 2

SUNDAY 2 NOVEMBER

8

Cassandra

When I wake, I hear an unfamiliar voice and then an animalistic keening. I dress quickly and, holding the banister for support, go downstairs, bare feet registering cool kitchen tiles. The whining isn't human, it's dog. Jet throws himself at me, bangs his tail on my legs, his black-and-white muzzle pushing between my legs until I shove him away.

'Jet, stop it!' I look up, and Daniel is quickly by my side. 'Has something happened? Is Mum . . . ?'

'Everything's fine, love. It's only the dog being returned.'

'By me,' says a loud, rather arrogant voice. 'I had him overnight to help you out.' There, in a cold waft of air that tells me he's just arrived, is the headmaster at the primary school. Mr Godwin.

'Thank you, sir.'

Even though he hasn't taught me in twenty years, old habits die hard. He's often in the library asking me to put up his posters, his pinched face emblazoned on them, alongside shouty slogans. Since the campaign began, he's been hanging around the farm.

I agree with him – the Port Authority shouldn't buy the land – but I doubt he'd approve of the plans for Samphire Health Spa either.

Daniel guides me to a chair. 'I'll get you a Samphire Sparkle, love.'

Uninvited, Godwin runs a hand over the pine settle as if to clean it, then sits. 'I haven't had a chance to say how concerned I was to see the ambulance at the farm yesterday. The police officer at the gate wouldn't tell me anything.' He shakes his head, as though this is the tragedy, rather than the ambulance. 'How is Hector?'

Daniel turns from the juicer and says quickly, 'It's Maya who's been injured.'

I see a reaction from Godwin, a lift in his lips that looks horribly like relief, until he rearranges his face to show sorrow. 'Poor Maya. Injured, you say? Oh dear, they do say the home is the most dangerous place.'

Daniel turns the juicer on, and the silver blade masticates apple, samphire and ginger.

I feel myself sinking, elbows heavy on the table. I rub my face, feeling dry skin on hard knuckles, even while I flinch at Jet's barking. He pushes his muzzle into my waist and I shove him away but he persists, jumping up and clawing my backside.

'Go away, Jet!'

'I can keep him another night,' Godwin suggests, with some distaste, 'if it would help?'

'Yes, please,' I say. I can't cope with the dog, not now.

'Poor Maya,' Godwin repeats. His beady eyes repulse me. He's hungry for more detail. 'Was it an accident in the kitchen? I believe that's the most lethal place.'

Just then, the back door opens and Dad walks in, bringing with him another harsh gust of cold air and the woody stench of Golden Rush tobacco. Jet is overjoyed to see his master, and bounds towards him. Dad staggers back, looks so pathetic and sad that I want to hug him until I remind myself that we've never been a family for physical affection. He seems older, thinner – is it possible to lose body mass overnight? He strokes his dog, then blinks in unhappy surprise at our guest.

'I heard you took Jet for the night. Thanks.'

'I'll take him for another night, so you can focus on what you need to do.' Godwin stands and grasps Dad's hand, pumping it heartily, though I can see no returning strength from Dad. 'It's no trouble, Hector, really. I'm so sorry to hear Maya's in hospital.'

He's a repulsive man and I want him gone. I try to keep still, lest I say or do something I shouldn't.

Dad drops his bad hand to his side and staggers around the kitchen like a sleepwalker, landing heavily on the wooden bench under the window. Jet's still delighted to see him after a night's absence and he pets the dog without seeming to see him.

Whatever I feel, whatever I look like, Dad is worse. It's like staring into the mirror in a fairy tale that only reveals the ugly and painful. His hair, grey and sparse, is sticking out at crazy angles and I remember how he usually Brylcreems it flat each morning. His ashen face is unshaven. But it's his eyes that disturb me the most. I used to think his eyes were grey, like mine, but now I see they're the colour of dust, the colour of nothing. Any life there is extinct.

Daniel places a glass of the green juice in front of me. 'Well, Mr Godwin,' he says with crisp politeness, 'many thanks for agreeing to look after Jet, that's a real help. But we're actually quite busy.'

It's true: Dad and I have to get to the hospital.

'Oh, of course.' To my relief, Godwin gets up and pulls on his coat. It's one of those green waxy ones that gentlemen farmers wear, though he is neither. 'I'll take the dog for a walk, and he'll be at mine until you want to collect him. Please give my best wishes to Maya when you see her.'

Dad stares at Jet, who is munching on a newspaper at his feet. 'It wouldn't mean anything. She's not conscious.'

Godwin has that eager look in his eyes again, hungry for information, and I remember how he was in the classroom, forcing pupils to stand on their chairs if they got facts wrong. 'I'm very sorry to hear that, Hector. What actually happened?'

He just can't stop himself, it seems, from interrogating Dad. The ground is wobbling beneath my feet. Must be the drugs, stronger than I thought.

'She tried to kill herself,' says Daniel, as if finally facing the fact that this man will persist until he knows. 'Of course, she was raised on the farm, so she knew all about guns and how to handle them. She shot herself with Hector's rifle.'

'Oh my goodness, but that's terrible!' Godwin barely catches breath before adding, 'What does that mean with regards to her decision yesterday to sell to the Port Authority? Did she even sign a contract? If she wasn't of sound mind, it's surely null and void anyway?'

Of course – he was there at the shoot. I can see how much more important saving the land is than your survival and for a creeping second, I imagine him holding a gun to your head. I need him to disappear or I'll not be responsible for my actions. Daniel seems to know this, or perhaps he feels the same, because he practically chucks the man out of the back door.

'Thanks again for having the dog – we'll be in touch. But we need to be left alone now.'

When he's gone, I turn on Daniel, unable to keep my rage inside. 'Why did you tell him that? What you said wasn't even true! Mum never used a gun!'

'Plus, the whole fucking village will know by noon,' says Dad, wiping his left hand over his brow, where beads of sweat have appeared. 'And he's bound to call Alfie Avon. It'll be front-page news this evening.'

'Maybe that's a good thing, Hector,' says Daniel, gently. 'Much as I hate to give Alfie Avon any fodder, at least if he reports that Maya shot herself it will stop people speculating.'

'But everyone will think Mum is mentally ill,' I say from my spot at the table, the green juice clamped in my hand like it's the solution.

I know how devastating that label is: it's like having something stolen from you, something you can never get back. Daniel moves so he's close to me, touches my shoulder which has risen up with tension, trying to calm me.

'It's better if it comes from us. You know how people in Kenley gossip.'

'And they know she was depressed after you was born,' says Dad, grudgingly. 'It's why Janet moved in, to help her cope with you.'

I can't believe he's dragging up the past like this. 'Dad, her parents had both died, she'd just taken on the responsibility of the farm, and she had a baby all within a year. So, yes, she had postnatal depression. But that was over *three decades* ago! She wasn't depressed on Friday. In fact, she seemed very sure of everything she said. Why are you refusing to see what's obvious: Mum didn't shoot herself. Whoever did is wandering around, getting away with it.'

'Now, stop – I'm warning you!' Dad's face bunches up like a red fist. 'No one needs you to play psychologist, girl. Maya was depressed about the farm. It got too much for her. End of story.'

Dad and Daniel both watch me as if I need to be kept in check. I try to find some compassion in Dad's eyes but can't.

No, I don't believe you shot yourself. And I need to find out who did.

9

Holly

Holly woke earlier than she wanted, unused as she was to sharing a bed. The world outside was dark and quiet, except for the occasional sound of letterboxes being rapped as the newspaper boy worked his way along the flats, pushing thick Sunday papers through doors. But not hers – she avoided lurid stories and, thanks to her synaesthesia, red-tops could make her feel sick on a headline.

Beside her, Leif slept on, his handsome face completely relaxed, blond fringe fallen to one side, his body relaxed and warm. Imprinted on him were the marks of the night before: his lips were slightly swollen from their kissing and there was a pink mark on his shoulder from where her hand had pressed against him as they slept. Seeing this triggered the recent memory of sensual touch, and Holly experienced again the urgent need to be close to him. It wasn't just sex. Leif stimulated in her a deep sense of calm, the colour yellow and the taste of honey. Not that she'd tell him this: he'd think she was crazy.

As she turned away from Leif, Holly's brain clicked into another channel and replayed the morbid memory of Maya Hawke's bruised face, her narrow body under that white sheet. She couldn't conceive that the woman had done it to herself – her instinct was that Cass was right, and the violence had been inflicted by another hand. She couldn't stop seeing Maya's dark hair matted with blood. Her own scalp ached in sympathy.

Innocence Farm, a place she had refused to think about in two decades, was now back in her head. *If only I hadn't run away that night, if I'd stopped to help . . .* Holly stopped her irrational thought: she had been a child, just eight years old and powerless. Now she was grown, she believed her synaesthesia was her brain's way of ensuring she wouldn't run away again. And now it was pictures of Maya prodding her to get up, to take action, to *do something*.

Holly kissed the sleeping man goodbye, and with a tug of regret returned to her own flat for a quick cool shower. She washed Leif's scent, the salty tang of sex, from her skin and dressed quickly. Putting on her green paramedic's uniform always soothed her. Glancing at the window and seeing grey marbled clouds, she reached for a raincoat.

Closing her front door, Holly checked for activity from Leif's flat, but there were still no lights on. He had a lazy Sunday ahead, but she had work to do. The November air stole the breath from her lungs. She pulled her coat more tightly around her and thought about her parents in America. In November, they always drove to Lake Tahoe for the start of the ski season, a trip her brother James joined them on. This year he'd be taking his Bostonian girlfriend Kaitlin Burgess, whom Holly had met on her last visit. Kaitlin was as beautiful as she was accomplished; a Masters graduate, she developed exercise programmes for varsity athletes. Full of pep and enthusiasm as only Americans can be, Jamie adored her. They'd recently bought a golden retriever puppy, and Holly predicted babies would soon follow.

Thinking of her brother brought back other memories, unwelcome ones. They had been close once, when they were younger and could play the same games. But then he became distant, he resented her hanging around and would spend his weekends shooting his air rifle or tramping through the woods with Carl. There was no space for her in his life and after that Halloween, they never hung around together again. She had never asked him what he thought had really happened that night. When she was eight, she believed he had killed a ghost, but now she remembered the screams as being all too human.

How could she ask Jamie now, when they were half a world apart and it was twenty years in the past?

Thanksgiving was just three weeks away, and in California her family would celebrate it without Holly. It was a festival their father insisted was important, even when they were living on the airbase in Kenley, where a patch of Suffolk soil had been turned into a quasi-America with a bowling alley and a two-aisle Walmart. Her mother, Ipswich born and bred, had been quick to adopt his traditions since she had so few of her own. She had embraced America with the gusto of the newly converted, as had Jamie. They had exchanged Suffolk for the sun of California and never once looked back. Her family's life in America glowed with success, yet Holly was forever stuck back here, in Suffolk. She was just eighteen when the airbase closed and her father was re-posted to Iraq, his final stint before taking early retirement. She, along with her mother and Jamie, had moved to California. Jamie had excelled at college, made friends quickly. Her mother had made a home for them, never once looking back. Only Holly had felt that she didn't belong and inevitably Suffolk had pulled her back with so much unfinished business.

Now Innocence Farm once again loomed into her life.

She arrived at the hospital an hour earlier than her shift began, and lied to herself that it was so she could get ahead of the assignment she needed to write before Christmas – a case study she had yet to think about that required her to focus on a disorder or disease of her choosing. But instead of going to the library, she walked into the Garrett Anderson Centre, flashed her paramedic ID and told the ward sister she was doing a follow-up from the call-out on Maya Hawke. But in truth, it was Cassandra whom Holly was thinking about; the vision of her sitting on the step with her blood-tinged hair was imprinted in Holly's brain. She paused outside Maya's room, taking a slow breath as she erased the distracting image.

Inside lay Maya in her coma, and either side of the bed were Hector and Cassandra. Both looked up expectantly.

'I hope you don't mind? I just wanted to drop by, to see how Maya is.'

It wasn't entirely the truth. Cassandra had filled Holly's thoughts far more than the mother, with her desperate belief that her mother hadn't shot herself, her need for Holly to believe her. She lifted her face and gave Holly a warmer smile than seemed fitting. 'I knew you'd come back,' she said. 'Thank you.'

Hector Hawke sat stiffly on the opposite side of the bed. He was dishevelled and unshaven, his hair haywire. But he seemed determined to keep his composure, his solid jaw jutted and set, as if his teeth were gritted. He nursed his right hand with his left, as though protecting it from injury.

Holly's senses reacted, sending a numb ache down her own right arm and a tingle into her fingers, his shock so profound she could tune in to nothing emotional except leaden confusion. She tried to find the appropriate words. 'Is there anything I can do to help?'

'Not unless you can wake up my missus!' Hector still had the scent of outdoors on his weathered corduroy trousers and thick green jumper, worn at the elbows. Clothing meant for loading a tractor or carrying hay bales, not for hospitals.

Holly stood, awkward. 'Well, I'll be going then.'

She turned, feeling hot and wishing she hadn't come, when Cassandra's voice called out, 'No, Holly, wait. Do you remember Mr Godwin from school?'

'Of course, he was our head teacher.' Holly wondered if Cass too had been thinking of the past. 'I never liked him.'

'I don't think any of us did,' Cassandra replied. 'But I remember he picked on you kids from the base mercilessly, always banging on about your lazy accents.'

Hector looked up, his expression angry, and said irritably, 'You're rambling, Cass. The nurse isn't here to talk about your schooldays.'

'She's not a nurse, she's a paramedic. And her name's Holly, we were friends at school.'

Holly was taken aback by Cassandra's statement, which was wrong on both counts, given that she was not yet qualified and they had never been friends, but when the blonde woman smiled at her warmly it felt like the truth. Had they even spoken before yesterday? Holly doubted it: Cassandra was older, and more than that she was beautiful and rich. She had suddenly left the local school and Holly's childish imagination had placed her in Europe, maybe at an exclusive boarding school in Switzerland or studying in Paris. Now she wondered what the truth had been – why a teenage girl would suddenly disappear. She remembered this as happening just after that Halloween, but it could be that her brain had worked these two acts together, and they had no link other than the location.

Hector seemed to soften. 'Well, I suppose you need your friends at a moment like this.' He gazed at his unconscious wife, then his face crumpled. 'Maya is the best of me. How can I carry on if she dies?'

He panted, and Holly thought for a moment he was going to cry. Instead, he yanked off his jumper and pushed the sleeves of his shirt beyond his elbow, as if to free himself of their constraint, revealing the muscled forearm of a labourer on his good arm and the narrow vulnerability of his other arm, which he nursed to his stomach. When he spoke, she wasn't sure if it was to his daughter, his unconscious wife, or simply to himself.

'I work the soil, that's all. I was employed by her father to work the farm when I was just a lad, and I've loved Maya since I first seen her. She thought I was too young for her, too rough and uneducated. I promised her that if she'd marry me, I'd make sure she never regretted it. Now I've let her down.'

His face was wormed with broken veins, the complexion of someone who toiled in the wind and the rain. There were beads of sweat at the hairline.

Desperate to say something soothing, feeling his pain so keenly she had a physical ache in her core, Holly said, 'I'm sure you didn't let her down, Mr Hawke.'

No response.

Holly listened to the silence. Nothing in her paramedic training had prepared her for this. She'd been taught how to find a vein, stop a bleed, but Hector's wound was much harder to staunch. 'She's alive, and the prognosis looks favourable.'

This, at least, she could give him. As part of the debrief, Jon had told her that Maya had been stabilised so rapidly that she had a good chance of surviving.

But Hector's gaze remained narrow, as though what she said was a challenge. 'Do you believe in God?'

Holly hesitated, thinking of the night she went ghost-hunting with Jamie. 'I'm not religious, but I feel something is out there. Something bigger than us that we can't fully know.'

'New Ager, are you?' he asked, dismissively.

'I don't know what I am exactly.' This was true. Her childish fear of ghosts had largely gone but the world still felt a confusing place to her.

He softened. 'Count yourself lucky to have any faith, because I know for sure now there ain't no God. We're just animals, just savages, no better than the pigs in my fields or the chickens in my barn. I just work the land, get on with my own business, and thank my lucky stars for what I got. But all that don't mean squit, do it? Not if my Maya dies.'

Cassandra, who had been silent through this whole conversation, said, as if dazed, 'If Mum dies, that would make her shooting a murder. Then the police would *have* to find the culprit.'

His response was immediate. 'Stop that crazy talk, Cass. You know she done it herself. You'll make yerself sick with thoughts like that.'

Cassandra said nothing to her father, but looked at Holly with such a pleading expression that Holly felt as if she were reaching across to her: *Please believe me.*

10

Cassandra

Mum? Can you hear me?

They've told me to talk to you. The nurse – Lauren – said that it might help, but maybe she's just trying to be kind, and wants to give me something to do.

Mum? It's me. Your daughter, Cassandra.

You're in Ipswich Hospital. Dad's just gone outside for a smoke. You fought so hard to get him to stop after his stroke, but what does any of that matter now? The intensive care unit is peaceful, not like the maternity ward in the main building where Victoria was born fourteen years ago, where I could hear women screaming and babies crying all night. Not that I minded, not when I had her in my arms. She was such a sweet thing, so small. I could hardly believe something so precious belonged to me.

Lauren is at the nurse's station with two colleagues, discussing cases. They've all been kind, but she's the one I like best. She's jazzed up her white tunic with a rainbow of pens poking from the pocket, her lipstick is a cheerful pink and you'd say she's wearing too much foundation but then not everyone's as naturally blessed as you. You don't even have any grey hair – amazing for a woman in her sixties. You always joked that marrying a younger man was the secret to keeping youthful. I wish I had a comb, to remove the dried blood from your hair.

My chair is pulled up as near as I can get to the side of your high hospital bed, so I can reach you to stroke your hand, bones slender as a bird's, skin loose as silk, avoiding the place in the middle where a plaster covers a cannula that feeds you with saline. The other side, near the window, is where most of the wires lead to the machine, beeping its mechanical heart like a clock, hypnotising me, keeping you alive.

They don't know if you'll die, or if you'll wake and be yourself, or if something inside has been broken forever. Dr Droste said they can't measure the damage, not yet. Not until they release you from the induced coma and see if you can breathe on your own. He's very direct, German I think, though his English is impeccable. I trust him, or I trust his white coat and expertise.

This ward is on the first floor, looking out onto the car park below. All I can see is darkening sky; it's only just past six and already stars are appearing. No moon though.

Mum? Everyone is saying that you shot yourself. Dad won't talk about any other possibility, and even Clive said that I was in shock, not thinking straight. As if believing that someone else did this to you means I must be crazy.

Only Holly seems to believe me. I felt it at the farm, just after the other paramedics took you away, that she had her suspicions. And today, when Dad tried to stop me from talking about it, I saw her expression: she knows it wasn't attempted suicide. It's true what I said to Daniel: you never handled those guns. It's also true what I said to Clive: you think suicide is cowardly. And I have better reason than most to know that.

If I'm going to find out what really happened, I can't do it alone, I need help. And Holly was there at the farm, she helped save you. I know she's the one.

I lower my head so it rests on your lap and listen to the heartbeat of the machines. I close my eyes and fall. I can smell the starch of hospital sheets, the faded bloom of your jasmine perfume, the sour scent of old sweat which might be mine.

I stand, stretch, go to the window. Does it open? Probably not. There are cars down in the car park, their shiny roofs pocked with bird shit, staff arriving for shifts, visitors for patients, visible to me only as the tops of heads.

Turning, I can see the nurse's station from here. Lauren looks up from her notes. Something she sees in my face makes her get up and come into the room.

'How're you bearing up, love?'

'Okay,' I say. I'm not though. Not by a long stretch.

'Would you like a blanket?' Without waiting for my answer, she opens the bedside locker and takes one out, handing it to me, and I'm so grateful I want to cry. She pats my hand.

'You're going to be seeing a lot of me. I practically live here.' She rolls her eyes, and I'm glad of the chance to smile.

After she's gone, I return my head to the dent in the sheet, the blanket around my shoulders, and begin to cry. I'm crying deep into the bedding when I feel an arm around my shoulders, holding me tight. I think it's Lauren but when I look up, peering through swollen eyelids, it's Holly. She came back, like I knew she would. She doesn't take her arm away, she doesn't tell me it'll be okay and her deep brown eyes are full of concern.

'I've just finished my shift,' she says. 'I thought I'd pop back and see how your mum is?'

I smile gratefully at her. It's as though my silent prayers summoned her back. 'The same. Lauren says talking to Mum will help. I've been doing that.' My nose is running, and I reach for a tissue. 'She says we should try and stimulate all of her senses, and that even though she's unconscious she could still be responsive in other ways.'

'Really?' I can see this interests her and she takes a seat beside me. 'What has she suggested?'

'She said we should play her favourite music, but Mum never listens to any. Then she said I should bring in her favourite perfume, but I can't go to the farm. I've been holding her hand, for touch. I want to do more. I just can't think of what else to do.' I can feel tears rising inside again.

'What about reading to her, from her favourite book?' Holly suggests.

'She always hated it when I read to her, even when I was a child and she was supposed to listen to me. Mum loses herself in a book, but she wouldn't want someone else's voice to ruin it for her.'

'Okay, something else.' Holly probes, 'What does she love to do?'

I think about what gave you pleasure, and remember you seated at the kitchen table, enjoying your afternoon break before going back up to your study to resume work. 'Janet's cakes – she has one every day with a cup of tea. God, I can smell them now.'

'Janet's your housekeeper, isn't she? Ash's mother. Didn't she make the 999 call?'

'That's right. She found Mum when she arrived that morning, ran home to make the call.'

'And your mum loves her baking?'

I'm confused as to where this questioning is taking us. 'Yes, but what good is that? She can't eat anything. The only nutrition she's getting is through that tube.'

I'm no longer crying, I'm watching Holly. I can practically hear her brain working.

'Do you really think your mother was shot by someone?'

I look at her, certain there's a bond of understanding between us. She was there that morning too, she saw you.

'I'm sure she didn't shoot herself. I don't even think she could. But no one else believes me.'

'I do,' Holly says. 'And I've got an idea.'

DAY 3

MONDAY 3 NOVEMBER

11

Holly

Holly's Fiat was still splattered with mud from when she'd travelled this road on Saturday morning, but this time she didn't turn into the farm, she continued further on down Innocence Lane to the house where Janet Cley lived with Ash.

Sooner than expected she saw it, a low-slung thatched cottage in Suffolk pink, the traditional shade resulting from stirring pigs' blood into paint. It looked older than the building the Hawkes lived in, and might even have been the original farmhouse. Ash and Janet had lived here back when she was a girl living on the airbase nearby. He was the grubby boy who never had the right shoes, whose shirt was always frayed at the neck. Kids are cruel, and Holly remembered how Jamie and his mates, with their smarter uniforms and stylist-cut fringes, would push him around. He never seemed to mind though, as if he knew his place wasn't to be with them. He belonged to the animals and the land, and when she saw him yesterday, she saw he was now settled in his skin.

He was ribbed by the boys from the base for having no dad, too. On the airbase, people lived singly or in families. If a marriage failed, the non-military spouse would return to America, so the idea of a parent and a child living alone together seemed unusual enough to attract bullying. Or maybe Ash, being as he was, was simply vulnerable to any taunts and this was just a convenient way to get a reaction. There must have been other kids at the school with an absent parent, but if so, she wasn't aware that they got picked on because of it. Only Ash seemed to suffer. She felt ashamed for her bullying brother, and also for herself, because she had witnessed the bullying and said nothing. She remembered how Janet would sometimes come at lunch and wait by the red-brick wall to sit with her son as he ate his sandwich, since he wasn't supposed to leave the school grounds and no one was playing with him.

Feeling desperately sad, she pulled up beside an old banger, its tyres deep in mud and as flat as the fields opposite, useless to all but the opportunistic magpie who had made a nest on the steering wheel. There was an abandoned tractor on the scrubland around the cottage, and some discarded Calor Gas cylinders.

She closed her car door and walked away without locking it, thinking *There's no one here, not for miles.* That must have been what Maya thought, when she left her home unlocked last Friday night. If Cassandra was right, and someone else shot Maya, danger was close by.

The outside of the cottage was in better shape than the tractor, but only just. The thatch was spiky and dark in places, a bedraggled hat above its raddled face, its eyes unlit. The ground in the yard was uneven, stones and muck rolling freely with no defined border to stop them. There was no grass, just patches of white chalky earth and shingle.

Holly pressed the cracked plastic doorbell but no one came. Noticing a wire dangling loose beneath the casing, she rapped her knuckles on the glass panel and peered through. A small figure was curled in the corner of the sofa, knees drawn up to her chin like a child. When she stood up and came to open the door, Holly recognised Janet Cley, the woman who had sat outside the playground to comfort her son. That was twenty years ago, yet her mousey-brown hair was still pulled back into its usual braid, incongruously youthful against her lined, worried face. Thin legs stuck out from beneath her ugly beige housedress, and she wore tattered slippers.

'Miss Cley?'

'Yes, can I help you?' She spoke in a small, nervous voice.

'You probably don't remember me, but I was at school with Ash and Cassandra. I'm a student paramedic, and I was part of the team that dealt with Mrs Hawke on Saturday morning.'

Janet Cley's cheeks sunk even lower as her mouth turned downwards in sympathy. 'Poor Maya. I just can't get me head around it. I'm so glad the ambulance arrived in time. Thank you for savin' her.'

Holly slid her hands into her jacket pocket. 'I didn't do much, I'm afraid. But I've been visiting her hospital room, and I did think of something that might help. May I come in?'

The woman hesitated. 'Ash ain't here right now. He's workin' with the pigs – allus gets up early, that boy.'

'It's actually you I came to see. I have a favour to ask.'

Her hand fluttered to her neck. 'I wasn't expectin' visitors. The place is a mess.'

'Just for a few minutes, Miss Cley. I promise, I'm not here to judge the state of your home.'

Holly entered the cottage and closed the door behind her.

The cottage stank of boiled meat and the room was so cold that Holly stiffened. Janet lowered herself onto the dusky-pink sofa, which registered her slight weight with a twang. Beside her was a low table on which lay a plate covered in foil, the source of the smell.

'Pheasant, from Friday's shoot,' said Janet, tapping a finger on the foil. 'Ash made my lunch afore he went to work, but I've hardly been able to touch a bite since Saturday mornin'. He says I need to get me strength up, but I'm tougher than I look. He's a good boy. So, you were friends with him at school?'

He wasn't a boy any more, he was in his thirties. School was a long time ago. 'I was a few years younger, so no. He knew my brother Jamie.'

'Jamie the Yank?' she said, her face souring.

'Yes, my dad was in the American Air Force, so we lived on the base.'

Janet Cley coughed into her hand and Holly felt a sharp stabbing pain within her own chest. Her synaesthesia often helped her intuit things, and this woman needed medical attention. The urge to wrap Janet in a blanket and get her to a doctor was almost overwhelming.

'Are you okay, Miss Cley, or would you like me to call your GP?'

She shook her head quickly. 'I don't need no doctor.'

'You must have had quite a shock, discovering Mrs Hawke on Saturday morning. I believe you've known her for many years?'

She waited as Janet caught her breath. She was obviously nervous at being interviewed.

'I were just a girl when I started as their housekeeper, only seventeen. I used to live in, until Ash got older and we needed more space, so then they give us the cottage.' She became suddenly defensive. 'It's not a freebie or anythin', it's part of me contract. I go to the farmhouse, all weathers. I've never had a day off in me life, except for when I had Ash, but soon as I was on me feet I was back workin', seein' to things around the place just like always.'

'Sounds like hard work,' observed Holly, thinking that Maya's accident would have given Janet her first chance for a proper rest. But the woman nudged her chin slightly higher, with obvious pride.

'It's no bother, two babies in the house. S'no more work than one, and Maya had just had Cassandra when I moved in. I'm a workhorse, that's what Hector allus says. We all are – him, me and Ash – the three of us together. We're a good team and we look out for each other.' She was looking tearful again.

Holly thought it was odd that Janet had barely mentioned Maya, and sensed her feelings ran deep but wouldn't easily be revealed. 'Cassandra was telling me how much her mother loves your baking. That's why I'm here, actually. To ask if you'd mind cooking something for her?'

Janet screwed up her features in confusion. 'She's in a coma, ain't she?'

'Yes, but apparently her other senses may still be active. She may be able to smell your baking. The staff think it will help if her senses are stimulated by things she likes.'

'She allus likes what I make.' Janet gave a grim smile. 'Shame if no one eats it, but there you go. I'd be happy to do anythin' for her, just like always. I'll set about it now.'

'Thank you.'

Janet pushed her weak frame up from the sofa and Holly followed her to the small kitchen. As Janet began to crack eggs and measure flour, Holly watched as if hypnotised from a kitchen stool in the corner. Janet seemed lost in a world of her own, talking quietly as if ordering her thoughts.

'I'll make scones, she likes 'em best, and if I put candied cherries in, they'll smell nice and fruity. She likes 'em of an afternoon, with a cup of green tea – though she'd prefer Earl Grey, but the green is healthier so she stomachs it. Maya really belongs to another time: she's a proper lady. But she inherited the farm when she was young and it was failin', so Hector was a godsend to her. He was workin' there, you know, as a farm labourer?'

Holly had picked up on this – he was a working man of the soil, but Maya was educated and owned the farm.

'Do they have a strong marriage?'

'Oh goodness, yes!' Janet seemed shocked that the question was even asked. 'Livin' together, workin' together, for nigh on forty years. I think she thought she were too good for him at first, him not havin' book-learnin' like her, and of course he was younger too – just twenty-three to her twenty-seven years when they met. They was both too young for all that responsibility.'

Janet fell silent, and Holly knew why. This story was common folklore: the farmer and his wife, driving along Innocence Lane, had hit a tree with their car. Just yards from the farm, they had been killed and the story went that their daughter could hear their screams as they died. It was their ghosts that were said to haunt the area.

'That were a terrible time for Maya. So, there she was, all alone with the farm to run. Soon after that, she married Hector.' Janet paused, rubbed the butter between her fingers and worked it into the flour. 'When you live in a place like this and you've lost your kin, you rely on folk near you. We've gathered together at the farm when there's been a leccy strike or flood warnin', or just because there was snow on the way.'

'And you never wanted to move on, work somewhere else?'

'I have my son and the cottage. That's enough for me,' she said firmly. But then she glanced at the door, as if to check no one was listening.

'It's a funny thing,' Holly said cautiously, 'tragedy striking the farm a second time. Her parents dying in that car accident and then this. Did Mrs Hawke seem . . . ?'

'What, suicidal?' Janet's grey eyes flicked at Holly, narrowed. 'Friday weren't a normal day, that's for sure. It was a shoot – we only have 'em about eight times a year, and there's always a lot to do. I make the lunch, and of course the men have their hot toddy in the mornin' and their Sloe Orgasm in the afternoon.'

'Their what?'

Janet smiled, and the years fell away in that moment. 'It's sloe gin mixed with a bit of fizz.'

'Sounds nice,' observed Holly.

'Hmm, well, usually it is. I can't say Friday was much fun though, with that snooty headmaster Godwin. You must remember him?' Holly nodded. 'There was a man from the docks too – Mr Feakes, who seemed very nice and all, but it's added pressure when there's guests. And to top it off, they had that reporter there too – Alfie Avon – takin' pictures and gettin' in everyone's way.'

'Why was he there?'

'Oh, Godwin had this notion that a piece in the paper, all about the farm and how it works and that, would go down well with the locals. Get 'em on side, like. Also, a picture of Mr Feakes havin' fun makes him look like a hypocrite if he bulldozes it all over, don't it? He's canny, is Godwin.'

Holly thought so too. The whole shoot was just a PR exercise for Save Our Countryside. 'So did it work?'

'After a fashion,' Janet said, considering. 'Hector even let 'em kill the low-flyin' birds, which ain't the done thing, but he wanted to keep 'em happy and they weren't used to handlin' guns. Not like Hector and Ash are.' She looked as if she might have said something wrong. 'They have licences, of course.'

'But what about Maya?'

'Well, she wasn't happy on Friday, I'll say that much. A shoot's an expensive thing to put on, and Hector was footin' the bill. The farm's not exactly a gold mine. Cass was there too, and she seemed upset about somethin'. The day just seemed to turn rotten. Who knows what pushed Maya into makin' that bad decision?'

'What bad decision, Miss Cley?'

She frowned, and leaned forward as if divulging a secret. 'The day ended with her sayin' she were gonna sell to the Port. It caused a right to-do. We was all shocked since she never planned on sellin' the farm, not afore then. She can be a bit impulsive, fly off the handle sometimes. But then she's had a lot to put up with, losin' her parents like she did. Such a tragedy. You have to make allowances, don't you?'

Holly noticed that Janet seemed to be struggling with all that had happened, as much as Cassandra. Perhaps she too had her doubts about what had happened. 'What if Maya *didn't* shoot herself, Miss Cley? Could someone else have wanted to harm her?'

'Oh no!' Janet sounded shocked, and Holly felt she'd overstepped an invisible line. The woman seemed to pull herself in. 'Her family have been in Kenley for years and are well respected. Her dad was Master of the Hunt afore the accident, and her mum was president of the WI, as much part of this area as the pheasants and partridges. She shot herself in a moment of weakness. Maybe she felt wretched about all this nonsense with the land, and that pushed her over the edge. I told you she could be impulsive. But she'll be okay, won't she?'

'We don't know yet. We hope so.'

'For all our sakes! Ash is so upset about it, I could hear him cryin' after he went to bed last night. Poor boy, he always was sensitive.'

'I remember he was like that at school. The other boys weren't always kind to him.'

Janet's face fell and her mouth nipped small. She was cutting the dough into shapes now, apparently concentrating hard, though Holly noticed that she reshaped and recut the same dough three times.

'Kids can be cruel, and there's always gossip in a village. Ash suffered on account of havin' no dad.' Janet began to pummel the scone mixture. 'Godwin didn't help, makin' him stand in the corner every time he done summat wrong.'

'I remember. It wasn't fair how Ash was treated.'

Janet looked mollified. 'He were never one for books – kids like him don't belong in a stuffy schoolroom. Since Hector had his stroke, Ash practically runs that farm on his own. Think a halfwit could do that? Teachers know nothin'. But Hector allus believed in Ash, and I won't forget that.'

Janet's face was pink with emotion, and she leaned back to catch her breath.

'Now, these scones need to bake. Why don't you come back in twenty minutes and I'll have 'em wrapped and ready for you to take to the hospital?'

Holly knew she had hit exposed nerves with her questions and Janet needed to be alone.

'I'll come back later, Miss Cley. Thank you for your help.'

Holly had time to kill, and speaking with Janet had reawakened her own memories and her curiosity. If Maya didn't shoot herself, chances were whoever did was someone close to her.

Next to a fenced-off clump of woodland, where maybe the game birds were reared, Ash Cley was working in a field littered with half-domed huts and muddy pigs. The stench of them, rotten and sweet, had been present since she first drove down the lane, but now it hit her nose with force. Beyond the wood lay more farmland, the motorway taking lorries to the Port of Felixstowe, a distant point of civilisation. It seemed a world away from this grim and desolate spot. He was hammering a nail into the side of a hut in the corner, using more force than seemed necessary. Holly had almost reached him when he finally saw her, though he did not stop his angry hammering.

'Hi,' she said.

He gave a final bash with the hammer and stood upright, wiping his sweaty brow with his forearm, his face flushed. He didn't move from his position, the heavy hammer dangling from his hand like a prosthetic. Ash still bore the traces of the boy he'd once been, enhanced by the straggly hair that hung around his face and his intensely blue eyes, which combined to make him seem younger than his thirty-one years.

'You look busy.'

'I've got all these huts to check afore dark. The sows need protectin' from the wind now the weather's turned.'

A cold gust caught Holly's jacket and whipped it against her, forcing her to hold it close to her body.

'I've just been to see your mum.'

Ash threw the hammer into the soil. It landed just a foot in front of Holly, making her step back. His face was twisted and he spoke with barely suppressed anger. 'My mum's upset. You shouldn't have gone there.'

'I'm sorry, I didn't go to cause any distress. It's for Maya. Cass told me what she loves smelling best is your mum's baking. I'm just killing time while the scones are in the oven.'

His face changed, and relief bloomed across his features now he realised she wasn't here to interrogate him. 'Is Maya awake then?'

It struck Holly that this should have been the first thing Ash said. 'Still unconscious. Cassandra and Hector are by her side.'

He dug his hands into the pockets of his worn jeans and tucked his chin to his chest, leaning back on the hut. A young pig came snouting up to him and he pushed its flank with his boot, sending it scurrying away. Then he ran his hands over his face, as if to remove any pain that might be lodged there. 'God, what a mess. I still can't believe she did this.'

Ash's mask of anger dropped completely. She felt his emotions, mirrored in her gut: anxiety twinned with hurt as he struggled to grasp what had happened.

'Your mum showed me the pheasant you cooked for her, from your shoot on Friday.'

'I'm tryin' to get her to eat more. Unless I remind her, she just forgets about food. But she's tough – stronger than all of us.'

Janet didn't look strong, and Holly had sensed she was sick. 'Has she seen a doctor?'

He blew a long breath into the cold air. 'She's not seen a doctor in years – never had a day off. Me and Mum are workers. Doctors are for folk who have time to be sick.'

There it was again, the idea that to be tough meant not seeking help. Holly realised that both of them thought this was a good thing, but how did it serve him when he was a young boy, bullied at school by pupils and teachers? How did it serve Janet, when she discovered she was pregnant after a one-night stand, and the villagers said she wouldn't cope?

'It's none of my business, but I think she really needs to see a doctor . . .'

Ash's face contorted with anger. 'You're right, it's none of your bloody business. It's, what, twenty years since you was here? And now you come snoopin' about, when we've got this stress on us. Why you askin' about Mum anyway? Maya tried to off herself, and thank God she failed, but it ain't that unusual in farmin' circles. This ain't anythin' for you to get involved with.'

His voice suddenly broke, anger giving way to softer feelings, and he rubbed his sleeve over his face. Holly remembered Janet saying she'd heard him crying in the night. As the wind whipped around her, Holly felt herself fighting just to keep upright. The icy blast didn't bother Ash, who huddled into it as if it was a comfort. His weather fitted him like a second skin; he belonged here, and she didn't.

'I'm just trying to help,' Holly said weakly. But even as she said it, she knew there was something else, another motive, pressing forward. Ash had been there that Halloween, she and Jamie had left him to face the fallout when they ran. She wanted, more than anything, to know what had really happened that night. What was that ghostly figure? But Ash had turned from her, and she knew she didn't yet have the strength to hear the answer, in case it was the one she feared most: that it was a human cry. That her brother had shot someone, and they had ran away.

Holly turned into the wind and made her way back to the cottage, where Janet was waiting by the door, a foil-wrapped parcel of scones in her hands.

'Now off you go,' said Janet. 'No need to bring the plate back.'

Holly felt she was warning her away.

Inside Maya's hospital room, it was very quiet.

Cassandra was sleeping on the grey-blue plastic chair beside the bed, slumped uncomfortably to one side. On the bedside cabinet sat an empty cardboard bowl, a plastic jug half-full of water, and tissues – the trappings of hospitals everywhere. On the wall above the bed, a picture with the title *Un Pichet de Limonade* by Nicholas Verrall: a perfect scene, a rustic table and some empty chairs, a jug of lemonade. Was it hung there to inspire patients to recover? Most likely it served as a cruel reminder of what they were missing, though for Maya it was neither of these things. Unmoving and unresponsive, she was oblivious to everything. Whatever her secrets, they were locked inside her. Holly looked at her bruised and swollen face, and had to close her eyes against the pain. Violence had been committed, and she was sure that it wasn't self-inflicted. If only Maya would wake, she could name the culprit. She unwrapped the foiled package, smelling the scones, their buttery scent of warm kitchens and comfort, the sweet tang of sugared fruit. She placed them on the bedside cabinet, and watched to see if Maya responded at all.

But it was Cassandra, still asleep, who reacted. 'Mmm,' she said.

Holly reached to gently touch her shoulder and Cassandra jolted upright, her gaze immediately directed at her mother. Holly experienced it as a surge of sorrow twisted with resentment, an invisible cord running from Cassandra towards the woman in the bed. She removed her hand and the feeling snapped away as if it were a figment of her imagination.

'Oh, Holly, hi. How long have you been here?' Cassandra rubbed her eyes, then noticed the scones.

'I just arrived. I brought some of Janet's baking. Let's hope it helps.'

Cassandra smiled warmly in gratitude. 'Thank you. I should have thought of that myself.'

'You have enough to worry about.' Holly pulled the second chair closer to Cassandra. 'Where's your dad?'

'Downstairs having a smoke, I imagine. He was here when I fell asleep.'

'And Daniel?'

'He can't cancel his Samphire Studio clients – some of them are very ill. They need him.' There was no trace of bitterness, though they could hardly be as 'ill' as Maya.

'Don't you need him?'

Cassandra looked up with watery eyes. 'Yes, of course. But he can't be in two places at once. And you're here.'

Holly was overwhelmed by how openly Cassandra smiled at her, her beautiful face warming like the sun. Her eyes returned to the woman in the bed and the temperature cooled. 'It makes no sense that Mum would have done this to herself. But it's what everyone seems to believe.'

'Not everyone,' Holly said. Discreetly, she reached her hand forward to touch the mound of bedding that covered Maya's foot and tried to tune into her subconscious. She felt a shiver of cold and a dull heaviness, very little life and no emotion.

Cassandra closed her eyes tightly, as if to fight an eruption of tears. 'How can this have happened, Holly? Friday was just an ordinary day. I don't understand . . .'

Holly knew intuitively that Cassandra needed to talk. She needed to make sense of the fact that her mother was fighting for her life. Holly felt her hazy confusion as she struggled to navigate her way through the emotional landscape of recent days.

'You can talk to me, Cass. It might help us to work this out.'

Cassandra bit her thumbnail. 'I don't know anything . . . I wish I did.'

'How was your Friday, before this?'

'I was at the library in Greater Kenley, as usual.'

Holly nodded, remembering that she knew this. 'You're a librarian there.'

'I'm the manager. A therapy group called Team Talk is held there every Friday. I help Dr Clive Marsh run it.'

'I know Dr Marsh,' said Holly, glad of a connection to build on, and wanting Cassandra to talk more openly. 'He's one of the supervisors at the hospital; he's marked some of my assignments.'

Cassandra gave a smile. 'He's a good friend.'

'Do you want to talk about Friday?' said Holly, tuning in to Cassandra's muddled feelings. 'I'd like to help, and I think we need to start there.'

12

Team Talk starts at ten. Around me, a motley gathering, all in the grip of the same sweat: strained faces, bunched bodies, slow movements. These are the foot soldiers of the mentally ill and Clive and I are on a mission to help them.

Roger, in a wide-lapelled suit that would have been fashionable back when he was still a company director, looking at his oversized watch, though he has no job to go to.

Trish, dark roots showing, fumbling in her bag for a box the size of a cigarette packet containing lollies.

Kirsty, milk stains on her jumper, struggling to keep her eyes open.

Alex, passing round the biscuits, ducking his acne-red face when anyone acknowledges his kindness.

An unlikely group, united each Friday. Some by choice, others by obligation.

Supposed to bolster each other up, calm each other down, steady each other to face the brutal world.

'Go on,' says Holly, listening intently.

I'm so tired, every bone heavy as lead, that if I close my eyes again, I know I'll be back there. I want to be back there, to Friday afternoon. I want to be sitting tall on a library chair, wearing my freshly pressed blouse and fitted skirt, hands neatly clasped in my lap. Back to when everything still felt ordinary and within my control.

Across the circle is Clive. Scruffy-collared, his bulging briefcase on the floor, he's the only one of us paid to be here, though whatever he spends his salary on, it isn't his appearance. His beard is daubed with something suspiciously organic. Despite his dishevelled appearance, Clive is well respected. A consultant psychiatrist at the Bartlet Hospital, many of the group first met him when they were hospitalised and now he's working with them in the community. He also gives expert evidence in court and he's often running behind with deadlines: he's either a bad time manager or a workaholic. His wife Ellen wishes he'd take a holiday and he asks our advice on this, sharing his own problems.

I'm his unpaid helper, with the added bonus that I can offer a venue, because on Friday mornings the library is closed, and as manager I can give permission for the group to meet there. I believe in this therapy; I know it works. When Daniel and I open Samphire Health Spa, I'll run sessions like this there, alongside other things to soothe and heal the troubled mind. We'll keep Punch, the horse. It's good for depressed people to be around animals, and Victoria will be home to ride him.

It will all be perfect.

Trish is in the hot seat, and we've heard it all before. Her boyfriend beats her, which she doesn't seem to mind, and screws other women, which she does. A decade ago, when her boyfriend left his wife for her, she thought she'd won, not reckoning that she too would grow old and get replaced. Her latest suspicions involve a neighbour's eighteen-year-old daughter and 'business' trips away, all coinciding with the teenager's visits to a 'friend'.

'Lucky bugger!' says Roger, giving a real belly laugh. Clive throws him a warning glance and he stops.

This week, Trish's best friend saw the girl getting out of the lucky bugger's car. It's tacky and sad and Trish twists her hanky in her lap, making excuses for him, her face swollen with tears.

The story makes my heart throb like a faded and forgotten bruise, newly knocked.

'Now, Trish, no tears.' I hand her a tissue. 'You're a strong woman – don't let this beat you. You have a choice: to be a victim and let life drag you down, or you can make the decision to survive.'

Trish bites her lip, then reaches into her bag for another Chupa Chup. She sucks them almost constantly when she's not smoking.

'I just want to know if he loves her. Is he going to leave me or is it just about sex? She's barely more than a child. Little slut! Why can't she find a bloke of her own?'

Clive shifts in his seat, begins to speak, but I know what he'll say. I've heard his solutions many times over the years: controlled conversation, couples counselling. Some such crap.

I interrupt him. 'Here's what I think, Trish: you don't need to know any more about it. Tell your friend you don't want to hear it. Forget what you know. It may be just malicious gossip and if you confront him, you might lose.'

Kirsty looks up, woken by shock. 'So, she should just let him get away with it?'

I wait for the blood throbbing in my ears to ease off. 'Recovering from depression is a long road, and digging into suspicions isn't healthy. It's best not to feed our insecurities.'

Five pairs of eyes consider me. With situations like this, they respect my advice more than Clive's because I speak from the heart, rather than a text book.

Our silence is contained by the stacked bookshelves, my words of wisdom insulated by all those pages, secret worlds. Our shared secrets.

Trish stops crying. 'I don't think I can do it.' She bends the stick of the lolly around her ring finger. 'I can't let it go.'

'It's the only way to keep your man *and* your sanity.'

When I was eighteen, I dropped out of university. Panic attacks had gripped me, and I was crippled by anxiety. I needed treatment and Mum had just been cured by a healer. She thought he might be able to help me too.

Daniel had just started out then. Because he was kind and gentle, business was thriving. Slowly, he introduced reflexology and then reiki, and I started to improve. No one knew who he was when he saved me. He patiently helped me conquer my demons and we became close. He told me about his girlfriend, a competitive cyclist who had dreams of competing in the Olympics – a beautiful woman who'd been on the cover of *Sports Illustrated* that year. He wanted to end their relationship, he said, but she was very needy and still recovering from a cancer scare. When he left her for me, I knew I was blessed beyond belief. I could hardly believe he'd chosen me, especially over such a superior woman, but he told me I was special.

Two years ago, I began to slip again. I don't know what triggered it, but depressives sometimes have episodes that arrive out of a clear blue sky. The symptoms were the same as back when I was eighteen: paranoia, delusions, believing people were against me. Unfortunately, it's always those closest who bear the brunt of the illness and I began to believe Daniel was lying to me. I scrutinised our bank records and quizzed him on transactions, certain he was being unfaithful. He said it was just work stuff, that the calls he kept disappearing to make were just needy clients, but I didn't believe him. I was certain my luck had run out and I'd lost his love. This is how my illness presents itself: jealousy, paranoia, self-loathing.

I have to be clear on this: Daniel never gave me any reason to doubt him. The doubts were all seeded in my head. Seeing I was ill, he tried to heal me, but this time it wasn't enough. I was admitted to the Bartlet. I really wasn't well and needed to be somewhere safe. I wasn't home, so Mum suggested we send Victoria to my old boarding school, up in Norfolk. It was supposed to be a temporary measure, with Mum paying for the school to help us out. But then Victoria settled so well, and everyone said it would be cruel to remove her. Mum said what a wonderful gift it was, a private education, and who doesn't want the best for their child? No one cared what I thought, or considered what it does to a child to be sent away from home at such a young age. No one ever listened to me.

'Cassandra?'

I've drifted off, back into the past, but Holly returns me to myself. 'I'm listening.'

In ten minutes, the library opens to the public and already a few regulars are milling around outside in the drizzly rain, peering in through the glass door. Clive notices too.

'We need to draw today's meeting to a close. Thank you, Trish, for sharing with us.' A half-hearted round of applause, a ritual of appreciation. 'I'd like to set some homework for next week. Could you each be mindful when a situation affects you? Maybe something frightening, or angry, or something that challenges you.'

'Easy,' drawls Kirsty. 'Try a baby who won't sleep, little sod. If I'm here next week, it means I didn't kill him.'

Clive gives a game chuckle. 'Well, yes, that would be one example. I'm under pressure from Ellen to book a winter cruise, just over Christmas when I get most busy.' He pauses, and we all acknowledge what he means: the festivities are a bad time for the depressed. Most suicides happen in December. 'Plus,' he says, trying to sound more cheerful, 'I hate boats. Please come prepared to share with the group next Friday.'

'Not Friday,' I remind him. 'I won't be here.'

'Ah, yes, Victoria is home for half-term, isn't she? What day are you back at work?'

'She returns to Oakfield on Sunday, but Daniel always drives her. So what about then?'

'Sunday it is, same time. Okay, everyone?'

Roger is pulling on his jacket, Alex has gone to unlock the door. One regular has his nose almost touching the glass, clutching books, desperate to be let in out of the cold. The last Friday in October and already it's winter.

Kirsty helps put the chairs back into the reference section, but Trish remains seated. I take the lolly stick from her lap and pick the wrapper up off the floor.

Clive stands. 'I'll be off then.' He secures his bag, looks again at the clock. 'I appreciated your input today, Cass. As always.'

By mid-afternoon, when I finally leave work, I'm exhausted and I still need to go shopping. I decide to splash out and go to Waitrose. I pass the rows of chickens, their plucked corpses wrapped tight in cellophane, and wonder if any were raised on Innocence Farm.

At Oakfield, fizzy drinks are forbidden, breakfast is nutritious, the food is dull but wholesome. We both approve of this, of course; Daniel spends his life lecturing people on the benefits of porridge and pulses. But I weaken and buy a large pink cake, intended for a birthday. Victoria's homecoming is something to celebrate.

I arrive home around three thirty and Daniel's car is in the drive. He must have finished early. I'm excited about tomorrow, about seeing Victoria, and that makes tonight special. I have ingredients for a delicious tea – a roasted vegetable and garlic timbale with quinoa. I'll ask Daniel to open one of his excellent bottles of red wine, mostly gifts from grateful clients. I'll listen attentively when he tells me the wine's merits, I'll have a bath with that expensive plant oil he bought me, I'll wear that linen dress he likes.

I'm still smiling, the key still in the door, when I hear a woman laughing, upstairs in our home. I freeze, listen.

'*Oh, Daniel!*'

I'm imagining things. I do that sometimes. Clive says it's my brain's default valve in times of stress. I climb the stairs slowly, uncertainly, and it takes a lifetime, but I have to find out: either I'm having another episode or Daniel is fucking another woman.

I'm at the top of the stairs when I hear her voice again.

'*Oh, Daniel, please – just do it!*'

He says something, I imagine him directing her to a new position, a new pleasure.

I'm frozen to the spot, poised ready to fight or flee. Heart speeding, muscles tight, ears pricked. I can't see the bedroom, but in a flash my brain pictures a shapely calf wrapped over Daniel's thigh, painted fingernails digging in his buttocks to take him deeper.

'*Daniel! That's too much, I really can't . . .*'

It's the script of a porn film. Then Daniel's voice booms, as blood pumps in my ears.

'*Please . . .*'

He's giving in to orgasm, as he does with me. I see in my mind's eye the tangle of limbs. My pounding heart prods me on. Fury rises like a tide in my ears. I push open the bedroom door.

The room is silent, our bed is empty. Confused, shaking, my hands turn clammy as my grip on sanity loosens. It was all in my head. This was how it was two years ago, jealousy playing tricks with my mind. My brain was knitted together with therapy and drugs and time, but now the sutures are coming loose.

Then I hear a breathy voice, coming from the study.

'Daniel, I'm begging you.'

I imagine animal positions and ecstasy as they fuck on his desk and I double over, hands on my knees, not knowing what to do or which way to turn. I don't have the strength to go through this. I'd rather kill him.

I remember my advice to Trish. I think of the can of worms I can't afford to open, the violence I'm capable of if I open that door.

I creep away. While my partner finishes fucking another woman, I flee. Downstairs, in the kitchen, I carefully unpack my Waitrose bag, put the vegetables in the fridge, the cereal in the cupboard and the pink cake in the centre of the table.

I leave by the front door, closing it quietly behind me. I start my car, backing out of the driveway, and do a swift turn, driving down the street away from my house. Just two hundred yards along I bump against the kerb, scaring myself with an emergency stop. I'm shaking, unfit to drive, and still catching my breath when, in the rear-view mirror, I see the front door to my house opening and there she is, the other women. I slide down in my seat, but she isn't even looking my way. She cuts a smart figure, in a trim business suit, a tall black woman carrying a briefcase. She has Egyptian features, finely cut cheeks and cat eyes – but her expression is stony.

I watch as Daniel follows her to her car, his hands in his pockets, his face impassive. They say goodbye and they don't kiss, he doesn't even smile as he waves her off with a single raised hand, dismissive. It was just a business meeting, that's all. So, that's how I know my paranoia is back.

I'm ill, and I need to fix myself before it spirals to a darker place, one from which the delusions are so strong I can't claw out.

I stop speaking and open my eyes. Holly has stilled; she's watching me. Between us, a moment is exchanged. 'So now you know,' I say. 'I have a mental illness. It's why no one believes me when I say Mum didn't shoot herself.'

13

Holly

Cassandra stopped talking and bowed her head. Her face was pale and when she touched her lip, her fingers were shaking. Holly felt her distress, how her world seemed to be collapsing around her.

'Come on. You need a break.'

Holly took Cassandra's arm as they walked away from the Garrett Anderson Centre to the main part of the hospital where the café was situated, steeling herself as patients crossed their path. Choosing to help the injured was a conscious way for her to manage her synaesthesia, but it was still tricky being around so much physical pain – pain that she could sense in her own limbs. She'd learned a long time ago that she could only cope with feeling other people's suffering if she could break it down into its individual components. She could then manage it or stop it entirely, like she had in the Poacher and Partridge at Halloween. This was what had motivated her to train as a paramedic, but she'd discovered that it also made her especially responsive to patients. In the emergency room, she had felt the most visceral, immediate pain and been able to respond using her medical training. It worked the same way with emotions too: she could sense what to ask, intuit what someone really felt. And now her attention was focused on Cassandra, whose story sounded in her brain like Morse code, tapping out a message about mental illness and a loosening grip on reality. Connecting with this form of pain felt like trying to hold water or fog – so much harder to fix than a flesh wound or broken bone. She felt Cassandra's vulnerability as a sore bruise in the centre of her body, right where the heart sits, and it spun Holly back twenty years, back to Innocence Lane, back to the night everything changed.

'Why don't you go and find us a table and I'll get us some food?' Holly asked Cassandra, who immediately began looking around for the best place to sit. 'What would you like?'

'Anything that doesn't contain pig or poultry, please. Living on a farm can do that to you.'

'Cheese sandwich it is then. Drink?'

'Green tea, please.' She hesitated. 'No, Daniel's not here, so what the heck. I'll have a double espresso.'

The woman in front of her in the queue had her lower leg in a brace, and with every step Holly was forced to concentrate on the menu board above their heads to stop her own leg from adopting the other woman's pain. The café was masquerading as a Costa, but couldn't overcome the hospital whiff of bleach and industrial-grade handwash, the odour that pervaded all the corridors and wards. Once she had Cassandra's sandwich and espresso on the tray, she chose a bottle of water for herself and held it out to the cashier.

'Could I have a glass for this, please? And a straw.' She never got over her embarrassment asking for one, but straws placed a welcome barrier between her mouth and the glass, which if touched would leave the gritty taste of sand in her mouth. The woman ignored her, moving quickly away, her heavy eyelids and downturned mouth telling Holly she was too busy to deal with whims.

Holly didn't ask again. She took her bottle and glass, with its solitary cube rattling around at the base, and placed it on her tray. She joined Cassandra at the table she'd chosen by the window and handed her the plate. 'You'll feel better if you eat something.'

It was different between them, now Cassandra had told her about her fragility and history of mental illness. A barrier had been broken.

Cassandra chewed her sandwich, gazing into the middle distance. The café was busy. A too-young couple fussed over a baby who was refusing his bottle of milk. Next to where the trays got stacked, a woman with no hair but startling blue eyes stirred her tea for too long and gazed into space. Over in the corner, an elderly couple, straight-backed and smartly dressed, sliced their steaks neatly, dabbing the corners of their mouths on paper napkins as though enjoying a meal at the finest Michelin-starred restaurant. What a microcosm this place was: birth, illness, death.

On the other side of the window was a double-sized black bin that totally obscured any view, and around it gathered a huddle of hardy smokers, not put off by the drizzle of rain that had just begun. Among them was Hector Hawke, standing slightly apart, but smoking with serious intent. He was gazing up at the Garrett Anderson Centre, home to the intensive care ward, where his wife now lay.

Cassandra saw him too but she continued to eat her sandwich with mechanical, sleepy chews. 'It's best to let Dad be when he's angry.'

'Who's he angry with?'

'The world. Me.'

'Why with you?'

Cassandra leaned back in her chair and rubbed her eyes. She looked exhausted. 'Because I was there. Because I'm questioning things, and he's frightened.'

DAY 4

TUESDAY 4 NOVEMBER

14

Cassandra

I sleep, deeply and for too long, on account of the Prozac Clive gave me, and the trazodone I'm secretly taking, waking in a sweaty tangle, strands of hair stuck to my face, my heart quivering. I reach for Daniel, my hand seeks his body, but he's gone. Instead, laid flat on the pillow, is a piece of paper. It's my Waitrose receipt from last Friday, and on the back he's written:

> *Hospital called to say your mum is stable.*
> *Gone to see a very sick client who can't be cancelled.*
> *Back soon.*

The clock beside me says it's almost ten. I should have been awake hours ago. I stagger downstairs, only in my nightdress, hair unbrushed, but I'm so hungry. I want to call Daniel, to check on when he'll be back, but I know I shouldn't interrupt him when he's with a client. Instead, I take tofu from the fridge and pour coconut oil in a pan: comfort food. Eventually, when I can stand it no longer, I call the Studio.

'Hello?'

It's the teenage receptionist, Katie. She's only just left school, unqualified, and doesn't even give the name, Samphire Studio, but Daniel believes in giving people a chance. Plus, he likes that he can train her from scratch, to his standard. He just hasn't achieved this yet.

'Katie, I'm looking for Daniel. Is he still there?'

'Oh, Cass, hi! He's – um – busy.' Something in the way she's pausing between words sounds shifty.

'I need to speak with him, please.'

'Um – he did say I should take a message if you called.' I want to reach through the phone wires and slap her.

'I mean it, Katie. It's urgent. Get him to call me.'

I slam the phone down. The tofu has shrunk from puffy white to hollow black when it finally rings.

'Katie said that you shouted at her and then hung up. Are you okay, love?'

I can't remember shouting. 'I'm fine, just making a tofu scramble.' As if that proves I must be.

'Good, that'll give you energy. Make sure you have a samphire shot too. Look, Cassandra, I'm sorry I had to leave you, but I couldn't cancel my client: she's in crisis. The hospital is pushing her towards chemo and I'm helping her stay fit and well enough to avoid that poison. I just need to write up her case notes and I'll be home, then we'll drive to see your mum. How's Hector?'

I feel tears well up inside me. 'Please come home *now*. I don't want to be alone with him.'

'Cass, he's your dad and you need to support each other through this. I know you don't always see eye to eye, he doesn't always understand us or what we're trying to achieve, but he's your father and he loves you.'

'He's so difficult to talk to.'

I can hear Daniel breathing down the line, as if trying to send me relaxing vibes. 'He's a different generation to us – no one helped him to open up. Why don't you go back to bed for an hour? You were tossing and turning all night. Did you have a bad dream?'

'I don't remember sleeping at all.'

'I'll ask Clive to pop round. Maybe he needs to adjust your medication?'

I know that for Daniel to suggest drugs therapy, he must think I'm bad. My hands tighten on the phone and I feel like tossing it on the floor. I don't want Clive to come. I know what will make me feel happier: my daughter.

'Please can Victoria come home?' I add quickly, 'She should see Mum in case . . . in case it's the last time she can.'

There's a pause then he says, so gently I want to scream, 'The doctors haven't said that, Cass. If they do, of course I'll go and fetch her. If you call Tori while you're feeling like this, you'll only upset her and we don't want that, do we, love? We agreed on this, remember? You just try to rest.'

I can hear someone speaking in the background, a woman. I don't think it's Katie.

'Will you come home now, Daniel? Please.' I hate myself for begging, but I need him.

'I'll be back as soon as I can, I promise. It's okay, don't panic. Try meditating. If you let me crack on here, I should only be a couple of hours writing up my case notes. Look, why don't you go and collect Jet from Mr Godwin's house? The walk would be good exercise.'

He hangs up on me, leaving me with this task that I know is beyond me. I can't bear to see that man. I'll ask Holly to do it. I text her, and she replies straight away:

I'll go after I finish my shift. See you later, H.

I stare at the phone for a long time before dialling the number for Victoria's dorm. I picture the communal phone on the wall ringing insistently to an empty hallway. Oakfield has strict rules about the pupils having only limited access to mobile phones, so this is the system we must use. It hasn't changed since I was a pupil. That perpetual ringing used to drive me crazy but to pick up the phone meant running to fetch whoever the call was for, so we all ignored it.

I didn't turn the gas off, so the tofu is now charcoal.

Still with the phone wedged under my chin, I make toast instead, and have time to butter and eat it before the damn phone is finally answered by a student whose grasp of English is poor.

'Victoria Salmon. Can you get her, please?'

She keeps telling me to slow down and repeat myself so it takes a lot of explaining to make her understand. Finally, she goes to fetch Victoria, but when a girl's voice comes on the line it isn't her.

'Hi, it's Dawn. How are you, Cassandra?'

I've never told her she can call me by my first name, she just assumed, and I never corrected her. Whenever we meet, she kisses me on both cheeks, takes the initiative. That confidence is the private school cultural capital people pay for.

'Hi, Dawn, is Victoria there?'

'Tori's still playing tennis but we're going into town to see a film this afternoon. She should be here.'

Dawn is wrong: Victoria should be *here*, at home, not playing tennis, not going to the cinema. This was supposed to be our week. 'Is she okay?'

Dawn hesitates. Teenagers are like this, always cautious with parents in case they say something that'll get their best mate in trouble. 'She's great, we've been having a real laugh. Most of the girls have gone home for exeats, so we've had the run of the place. It's just us and the overseas students.'

Dawn's mother is a single parent; she lives further up the Suffolk coast. I've never met her because Dawn comes to stay with us rather than Victoria going there, and Daniel always does the pickups. The set-up works. I want Victoria here for every day of the too-brief holidays, but she doesn't know any kids locally, so it's good for her to have Dawn to stay. Daniel's always been keen on this – he's a great believer in the power of friendship.

Dawn is polite and very pretty, but there's something I can't warm to about her. Maybe it's that sense of entitlement she exudes that irritates me. I can't recall what her mother does for a living, but she must be well paid, or her ex-husband is, to afford the school fees. We certainly can't afford them. Victoria's only there because you pay, Mum.

'Hang on, Cassandra, I can see her coming across the yard.' I hear the sound of iron on wood, the window in the hallway being opened, and then Dawn shouting down, 'Tori! Telephone! It's your mum.'

Tori. I wish I could call her that. Abbreviated names are so affectionate. But when your daughter hasn't lived at home for two years, it's inevitable the closeness goes. She's had to face things alone: homesickness, bullying, her first period. I don't blame her for the emotional distance between us – it's what happens when a child is sent away.

I can hear Dawn closing the window with several bangs and then listen to silence. Finally, a breathless voice says, 'Mum? Are you okay?'

'Hi, love.' I force cheeriness. 'Dawn said you were playing tennis. Did you win?'

'Nah. I'm shit at tennis.'

I bite back the temptation to scold her for swearing. 'I'm sure that's not true.'

'So, what's up?'

Everything. 'Nothing. I just wanted to explain about half-term. I'm sorry you aren't here . . .'

'It's okay, I understand.'

'I was looking forward to seeing you, love. And Dawn, of course. I'd got you girls your favourite cereal.'

'Don't worry, Mum, really.'

'And this lovely cake. Pink. Large, full of sugar, but I thought what the heck. And you could have taken some back to school. Shared it with your friends.'

'I said it's okay. Dad explained when he called.'

This stops me in my tracks. 'When he *called*?'

'Yeah, on Saturday. He rang to say you were sick. Are you feeling any better?'

'*Me?*'

'Dad said you were having another . . . y'know, like before . . .'

'What?' I demand, suddenly feeling cold.

'Jeez, Mum, I don't want to upset you! But if you're having another *episode* . . . Hang on.'

I wait as she says something to Dawn and then comes back on the line. 'I've got to go, the minibus leaves for town in half an hour and I need to take a shower. We're going to see the latest *Fast and Furious*. I don't want to miss it.'

'Of course. Victoria?'

'Yeah?'

'Did you *see* your dad on Saturday?'

'How could I *see* him? He was with you, wasn't he?' Another pause, longer this time, and she lowers her voice. 'Mum, are you sure you're okay?'

Daniel lied to me. He said he'd driven to Oakfield and taken the girls out. Where was he, when I was watching the paramedics save your life? When I was waiting for news at the hospital?

'Mum?'

'Sorry, love, it's just . . .' *I miss you. I love you.* Words I never say, left hanging in the air yet again. 'Don't miss the film.'

She's already gone. Another failed connection.

I call Katie again, who is less friendly this time. She tells me in a terse voice that Daniel isn't at the Studio, that I should call his mobile if I need him. I do, redialling every time I get his voicemail until he finally picks up.

'Cassandra, I'm driving.'

'Why did you tell Victoria I was sick?'

'I'll be home in twenty minutes. I need to concentrate on the road. This is dangerous and illegal.'

'Don't you dare hang up on me!'

I hear him sigh. 'What would you have me tell her, love? That her grandma shot herself and could die?'

I freeze. 'She *didn't* shoot herself.'

His response is so urgent it makes me jump. 'Cass! Your mum attempted suicide – why can't you just accept that? I'm really starting to worry about you . . .'

'Don't talk to me like I'm crazy, Daniel!' I can hear the noise of a motorway in the background, the distance in his voice. 'Answer me! Why did you tell her I was sick?'

'I didn't want to worry her. It was the first thing I could think of.'

'Why couldn't you have told her it was *you* who was ill?'

'For pity's sakes, Cassandra!' I can hear him muttering and cars are beeping. 'I'm never ill. If I said I was, she'd be *really* worried.'

He wasn't with me on Saturday morning – he lied to me about going to Oakfield. *And he's refusing to believe that you didn't shoot yourself.*

If I'm going to discover the truth, I need help. But it's clear I can't ask Daniel.

15

Holly

Philip Godwin's home was easy to find. The lights were ablaze in the flat at the top of the school building and Holly could see him moving around up there. The doorbell was next to the main entrance to the school with a gold sign importantly announcing HEADMASTER'S RESIDENCE.

She rang and waited, and soon the door was opened. If asked to envisage a headmaster from the nineteenth century, this is the man she'd think of. He looked exactly the same as he had when he'd taught her, twenty years ago now, with his narrow squirrel-like face, brown beady eyes and orange-tinged bushy hair. He was dressed eccentrically in a long-collared burgundy shirt paired with a red cravat and formal trousers.

'Mr Godwin? Cassandra asked me to come and collect Jet. You may not remember me, but I used to be one of your pupils: Holly Redwood.'

He scrutinised her, then his eyes gained intensity. 'You were the girl from the base. You speak much more clearly now you've lost that American drawl. Come on up! Mind the stairs, they're steep.'

Steep and narrow, so she followed him carefully up to what must have once been the school's attic, but had been boarded over to provide bijou living quarters for the head teacher. The ceiling was low, and the windows looked down onto the school playground and the road beyond. She understood now why the lights were on even in daytime, as any light they provided would be scant.

Hearing activity, a black spaniel bounded forward, pushing his nose between Holly's legs.

'Hi, Jet, I'm here to take you home.' She ruffled his fur, trying to push him back as she did, and surveyed the flat. It was open plan, a kitchen area with a small table and chair that led directly to an area with a sofa, and as they walked, their feet clomped on the wooden boards. It was a bit like being in a treehouse, although instead of nuts, he had piles of books against the wall, and on a low coffee table a stack of glossy A4 posters, all bearing the logo HANDS OFF OUR COUNTRYSIDE!

'Drink?' he asked, a congenial host. 'I have a pot of filter coffee already brewed.'

Holly wasn't thirsty, and she had no wish to spend time with this odious man, but he had been at the farm on Friday and might know something valuable. 'Lovely, thanks.'

The dog still twirling at her feet, Holly bent to read one of the posters, noting with her senses the pervasive feeling of being up high, the whiff of loftiness and arrogance.

'This,' he said, returning with the drinks, 'is my passion. Protecting our land from the fat cats at the Port who would turn our countryside into a car park.'

Holly took the cup from him, and without wishing to alert him to the real subjects she wanted to discuss, asked, 'The disagreement over the farmland has been going on a while, hasn't it?'

'Since your lot abandoned the base, it's been derelict. No one wants to move to the empty houses – it's like a ghost town. No one knows what to do with it,' he said, sitting on the sofa. There was no armchair and she imagined he had few guests. 'Things have heated up recently with the Port Authority upping their offer, but they can't do anything without the farmland surrounding the base. And Hector would rather cut off his arm than sell, so he's always been our first line of defence.'

'The farm isn't his though,' Holly said slowly, sipping her drink so Godwin couldn't see just how much she needed to say this. 'It's Maya's. I heard that on Friday she'd decided to sell.'

Philip's eyes darkened and he webbed his hands together in a gesture that looked as though he was planning something clever. 'The thing with women wanting equal rights over property and wages when they're married to the breadwinner, is that it cuts both ways. Hector has rights, even if his name isn't on the deed. He's married to Maya, and he works the land. We've instructed a solicitor to clarify the legalities, given she wasn't of sound mind, and to challenge any contract she might have signed.'

'You've done this since Friday,' Holly asked, 'even though Maya's in a coma?'

Philip's head moved to one side, as if quizzical. 'Of course, that's unfortunate, but the big picture is the land. Individual feelings are really neither here nor there to me.' His voice gained resonance, bouncing around the tiny flat like he was speaking to a class, spinning Holly back so she felt like a ten-year-old again. He was the teacher with all the answers, and she had a question. 'Did Maya not seem of sound mind then, when you saw her on Friday?'

Philip sighed now, lifting his laced hands behind his head, affecting weariness. 'Well, she's always been an odd creature, rather rude I always thought. Traditionally after a shoot one eats at the host's table, but Maya made us eat in the barn. The housekeeper had put on a good enough spread, a sort of afternoon tea, but the environment was hardly conducive for a pleasant meal. Cassandra had arrived, and my impression was that there was some trouble. Maya declared the house was out of bounds. We ended up sitting on hay bales, with plates on our knees. Most embarrassing, especially given Dave Feakes from the Port Authority was our guest. And then Maya topped it all by declaring she'd sell to him, and with Alfie Avon listening. It was complete sabotage!'

'But did she seem suicidal?' Holly asked, irritated by his condescending tone, his lack of compassion.

'Not at all!' he said, his small sharp teeth showing. Jet, as if sensing the change in atmosphere, gave a yelp and moved behind the sofa. 'She seemed to me like a woman very much determined to live as she saw fit, and the rest of us could go to hell.'

Holly left the Headmaster's Residence with the spaniel and a strong sense of Godwin's anger at Maya. There was no question that all he cared about was the land, and it gave him a motive for wanting her dead.

16

Cassandra

I'm glad to see Holly, and she's got Jet, which means Godwin has no further reason to call on us. But the dog's full of energy. I can tell Godwin hasn't walked him today, though he promised he would.

'Shall we take him out?' Holly says, as the spaniel jumps up at me, then her. 'A walk might do you good. Plus, I want to talk to you about what he said.'

I'm glad of the suggestion. Glad of her company. Glad that I'm not alone in trying to find out who shot you.

And it *is* good to get out of the house, out of the smoky kitchen and away from the dark thoughts about why Daniel is lying to me. Why everyone wants me to think you shot yourself. Why no one, except Holly and me, is prepared to see the truth. I need fresh air to snap me out of it so I can think clearly. I pull on my winter coat and shout into the empty hall that I'm going out, but no one answers. Dad is either still asleep in the spare room or unwilling to come out. Cold air catches in my throat and I see from the low sun that it's going to be a gloomy day. We pass houses and cars I know so well, though I feel lost.

Jet pushes through my legs to sniff the ground with his black snout, yanks on his lead. He doesn't know this area. He's an energetic spaniel used to roaming free through farmland and I let him pull me to the end of the road, Holly by my side, the two of us breathing in the November air. Jet finds a long stick that drags on the ground, and he dances at my feet, twisting around his lead, barking at me to throw it. I free him, throw the stick into scrubland and he barks madly when the hedge stops him getting at it.

'Cass, you're not alone in thinking Maya didn't shoot herself. Godwin agrees that she wasn't depressed on Friday.'

How ironic, that the only other supporter for my theory should be him.

'But he's angry with your mum for agreeing to sell the farm. He's seeking legal advice, to see if her decision to sell can be challenged. It's also clear that there's no love lost between him and your mum.'

This makes me feel sick. 'You think he could have shot her?' I ask.

Holly pauses, then sighs. 'I think he's a very unpleasant man, but to shoot a woman in cold blood would take someone evil, wouldn't it? I wouldn't rule him out, but I don't think him having a motive and being a horrible person makes him a potential killer. We should consider other people. Who do you think it might be?'

I shake my head – the task seems too huge to contemplate. There is a name that springs to mind, but I can't say it aloud: *Ash*. I touch my collarbone, feeling the old scar, wondering if I really am sick or if I'm the only one thinking clearly. Holly doesn't push me, but each time she looks my way I feel she understands. For now, that's enough. We walk side by side in silence, but this respite can't last. We'll be back at my house and the reality of what has happened will once again take over everything.

We arrive back, wet and tired. I'm pulling off my walking boots by the back door, Holly is unclipping Jet's lead, when we hear men's voices, bickering loudly, coming from the front room. Jet, unclipped, scrambles to his water bowl, spraying it over the floor as he laps it up.

'Who's here?' Holly asks, alert to the possibility that something has happened.

I stand still to listen. 'Daniel and Dad . . . and someone else.' At first I think it's Clive, but then I listen closer. It's him, here in my house. 'And Ash.'

Jet lifts his head, ears pricked. He barks and runs through to find his master.

All three men fall silent when Holly and I walk into the room. They look at us as if we've discovered their dirty secret. Daniel stands in front of the unlit fire, leaning against the mantel as if for support. Dad sits close beside Ash on the sofa. Ash fusses over Jet like a boy with his favourite puppy, his lanky hair dangling over his eyes as he scruffs Jet's head, but he doesn't fool me. I know what he's capable of, despite his feigned naivety. On the coffee table is an open bottle of bourbon and Daniel is nursing a tumbler as he rocks on the balls of his feet. I've never known him to drink in the daytime before.

'Ladies, hi,' says Daniel, regaining his poise. 'Where have you been?'

The men are wary of Holly. None of them have started to relax around her like I have. 'Walking Jet,' she says. 'We walked to the marshes – I haven't been there in years. I'd forgotten how dramatic this part of Suffolk is.'

No one responds to this. We're like actors who've forgotten our stage directions.

'We were worried about you, Cass,' Daniel says. 'You didn't take your phone.'

I slide my hand into the back pocket of my jeans and there it is. But when I check, it's not switched on. 'Why, is there news from the hospital?'

'Dr Droste said they're slowly reducing the barbiturates, and taking out the tube to see if Maya can breathe on her own. I said we'd be there this afternoon, so Hector can sign his permission as her next of kin.'

I hate that phrase and all that it means. What it could mean, if you don't start breathing on your own and a machine has to keep you alive.

'Love, you can't just go out without telling anyone. Promise me you won't do that again?'

'I'm not a child, Daniel.' I won't promise him anything. He lied about visiting Victoria. He told her I was sick. He lied about where he was – and I don't know why.

I drop into the armchair nearest the sofa and Ash lifts his head from Jet's fur. His eyes are red and watery, making him look even more sorrowful than usual.

'I wanted to visit Maya yesterday, Cass, but the nurse said only family are allowed in.'

Daniel finishes his drink, clinks the glass down on the mantelpiece. His usual poise is gone, his normally neat hair is ruffled and there's stubble on his chin. 'Can I get you a cup of tea, Holly? Cass?'

'I'm fine, thanks,' says Holly, who's standing discreetly by the door, deciding whether she should stay or leave. I can see that her curiosity will win.

'We'll both have one of those.' I nod at the bourbon.

Daniel hesitates, and I dare him to say I shouldn't. 'I'll fetch some glasses.'

Dad pats Ash's knee with his good hand. 'I'll speak to 'em at the hospital, explain that you're as good as family. And don't worry about the police – it's just routine, that's all.'

'What's routine?' Holly asks, then blushes at her own pushiness.

Daniel returns with two shot glasses from the drinks cabinet then fills them with stingy portions from the bottle, handing one to Holly. 'When there's been an attempted suicide like this, the police have to go through the motions, just to be sure there's nothing suspicious about it. Of course, as Maya's in a coma they can't ask her, so they've interviewed Ash and Janet, because Janet discovered Maya first, and they both live closest to the farmhouse.'

Holly glances at me, and I know we're both thinking the same thing: *If I'm right and someone else shot Mum, it could be either of them.*

'They recorded my interview on camera.' Ash shifts in his seat, casts a wounded glance at me then looks away. 'I felt like a criminal.'

He begins to cry but Dad pats his arm and he stops. I try to remember when Dad last touched me. 'Don't fret, son. I'm sure you didn't say anythin' wrong.'

Dad's concern for him itches under my skin like a rash. Ash isn't his 'son'. Ash's mother isn't lying unconscious in a hospital bed with a bullet hole in her head. I finish my drink in one, reach for the bourbon and refill my glass to the brim.

'The police wanted to know how well we all got on.' His face flushes pink, and he glances at Holly. I sense he's hiding something, afraid to say it because she's here.

'Don't worry, you can talk in front of Holly. She's my friend.'

'You think so?' He chews the inside of his mouth. 'You haven't seen her in twenty years, Cass. Me and you, we've grown up together. That's real friendship.' He looks at me hopefully, those wide eyes of his so like those of a desperate child, but he's deluded. 'I told 'em how we used to bunk off lessons sometimes, Cass – go to the barn and build houses with the bales of straw.'

I'd forgotten that. It can't have happened more than a few times, and that was before I went to Oakfield. It was *before*.

Ash grows desperate. 'Then they wanted to know about your Anschütz, Hector, askin' if I ever used it. I said no, on account of havin' me own guns that you bought me.' He puts his head in his hands and moans. 'They found my prints on it.'

'On the rifle used to shoot Mum?' My breath catches, my hand clutches the glass. Holly moves beside me, sits on the edge of the chair and I feel her support. It gives me the strength to ask, 'How could that have happened, Ash?'

'That's what I said!' he says, as if I too am doubting the police's expertise. 'I never touched the gun, Hector, I'm sure I didn't . . .'

'Ash!' Dad says sternly. Ash shuts up and blinks at Dad in mute surprise. 'It must have happened when you were puttin' my shotgun away on Friday afternoon – you went to the gun cupboard, didn't you?'

Ash's eyes roll up into his head, as if trying to remember this, but his face remains doubtful and I think: *It's a lie. Dad always puts his gun away himself.* Then another thought follows: *Ash shot Mum, and Dad is trying to cover for him. Just like before.*

'Where were you on Saturday morning, Ash?' I ask.

He gazes solemnly at me through blond lashes. 'You know where I was, Cass. I was with you at the farmhouse. Holly saw me too – we were all there.'

'I mean *before* that – when Mum was shot!'

'When she *shot herself*,' Dad corrects. 'He was workin'.' He's angry. I see his good hand clenching his knee to keep it steady.

'That early? They say it happened just after six.'

Ash scratches his scalp. 'Six ain't early for me. I were in the copse when Mum came runnin' across the field, screamin' about Maya. I ran straight to the farm – I wanted to help. You remember, I wanted to help *you*.'

I do remember him being at the farm, but that was much later, after Holly and the other paramedics had arrived. His timings seem wrong and he keeps looking from Dad to Daniel as if to check he's saying the right thing. Finally, his gaze lands on me and whatever my face reveals, he flinches back from it. He stands, wipes his hands on his trousers, his face still flushed with anxiety. 'I need to get home to Mum.'

'I'll drive you if you like,' says Holly, casting me a knowing look. She's sending me a message: *I'll try to find out what I can.* 'I'm going that way anyway.'

'I'll see you both out,' says Daniel.

An icy silence follows. It's just me and Dad. He sits ramrod-straight, his breathing heavy, and shoots me a dark look, making me feel as if I've done something wrong.

As soon as Daniel returns, he too accuses me. 'That was unfair, Cass. You can see Ash is devastated by what's happened.'

'What was unfair?'

'Grilling him. Asking where he was, why his fingerprints were on the gun. And in front of Holly too. You may think you can trust her, but you haven't seen her in twenty years.'

'Those are good questions!' I can't believe this is being twisted back on me. The injustice stings.

Daniel shakes his head as if he doesn't understand me. He runs a hand through his fringe and it falls back lopsided. 'He's on our side, Cass. So is Janet.'

I bristle at this, hands clenched by my side. 'The police don't seem to think so – they've interviewed him *on camera*. That must mean he's a suspect!'

Dad erupts then, as if he's finally lost his will to control his anger. He curves his spine back as if to pounce. His voice is directed at me and penetrates like a bullet. 'That boy loves this family and this is very hard for him. Janet practically raised you when Maya was too sick to do it!' His face is puce with indignation.

'For God's sake, Dad, that's a bit of an exaggeration.'

'You know nothin'.' He's standing now, pointing down at me from his full height. 'We'd be lost without that pair. And Maya's taken to Ash like he's her own son. She's seen him *every* day of her life for the past thirty years.'

I want to move away from the tip of his accusing finger, but the damned armchair is keeping me wedged in. 'Of course she has, for fuck's sake – he works for you.'

'See what you know. He doesn't just work for me, he's workin' for himself!' His lips curl into a slight smile of pride. 'He deserves to inherit. You don't need the farm, Cass. You and Daniel already have the Studio, and this fancy idea of a spa is a fantasy. And it's not fair: the Spa would mean Janet and Ash losin' their home and their jobs. I'm fixin' for Ash to take over. It's what he deserves and what the farm needs.'

Daniel takes a step forward, his muscles flexed. I see how powerful he is, and how angry. Dad sees it too, and suddenly looks sheepish.

'Hector. What have you done?' Daniel demands.

Dad sits back down, creating more distance between himself and Daniel. Again, he nurses his right hand into his chest as though it pains him. 'Godwin's found a solicitor. I'm gonna fight Maya for my rights.'

'If she wakes up.' Daniel's voice is steady, though I can hear the tension beneath, and I know he's very close to breaking point. 'And if you win, what then? The farm isn't viable – you'll go bust. You still need to look at alternatives.'

'Like your fancy spa? Look, Daniel, me and Ash've sweated our guts over that land. Whatever the deeds says about who owns it, it belongs to us!'

Daniel is gripping the mantelpiece now and his face has turned deathly pale. 'What about Cassandra's rights? She's your only child and this spa is our dream, the culmination of all we've been working for, all these years. People *know* me, Hector. I've cured people – this is a gift to the sick.'

Dad looks daunted. Daniel intimidates him, but still he stands his ground. 'I told Maya and now I'm tellin' you, that farm is Ash's livelihood and it's not right to steal it from him.'

I'm thinking about Friday. I'm finally realising something obvious. 'This is why you slept on the sofa, isn't it, Dad? You told Mum you were going to fight her in court. Did you tell Godwin to do it, that very afternoon?'

Now he's the one under scrutiny, and he can't see how to get away. And it's so obvious, so fucking obvious, that this is why Godwin called the solicitor on Saturday. That Ash and Dad are in alliance, just like always, when they should be on my side. *They should be thinking about you!*

I push myself from the chair, propel myself from the room and out to the back door, only breathing when I'm on the pathway at the side of the house, leaning on the brick wall and feeling sick – sick to the core with the injustice.

My fingers tingle, I've been unconsciously grazing my knuckles against the brickwork at the side of the house, and now they're cracked and bloody. I'm standing with no shoes, no coat, on a cold November day outside my house because I'm afraid of what I know. I breathe in cold air and try to clarify my feelings, but the Prozac is making it difficult. It's like trying to decipher a code.

I can't go back inside that house, not when I have these dark thoughts. I can't stay here either. Shivering, I shove my hands in my jeans pockets, forgetting my key fob is there. The sharp edge of a key digs into my right hand. It's the key to the farmhouse.

If I'm right, if someone else shot you, it's because of the farm and your decision to sell it. But no one's listening to me. I need proof. There's only one place to look.

I walk quickly to the driveway, where my car is parked. My feet are now so cold I can't feel them, and I know I must look crazy, trying to drive in only slippers. Daniel would stop me if he realised what I'm doing. He's already told me I shouldn't drive while I'm taking a cocktail of sedatives, always thinking he knows what I need.

I start the car, foot heavy on the accelerator, motoring on autopilot back to the place that was my home until I was sent to boarding school. It wasn't until I dropped out of university that I finally returned. I returned to you, Mum, because I was wounded and wanted comfort. As recently as Friday, I was back in my childhood bed, asking for your help. But I can't do that any more. I need to grow up. I need to be the one in control for a change.

A mist lies like a thick blanket over the tops of the trees. Innocence Lane is shrouded by a canopy of blowing branches. The farm is hidden, but I know it's there. Waiting. No lights along the road – the only illumination is the dashboard, and the red flashing bulb on the petrol gauge alerts me that I'm running on empty. I must keep driving.

I've never seen Innocence Farm look more desolate. There should be light from the kitchen, where Janet should be bustling around, warmth from the oven, tea in the pot. And you, Mum, working in your study or reading a book in the sitting room. Instead, Janet's at the police station and you're in the hospital. And I'm here, searching for proof that you didn't shoot yourself – something that would count as evidence and make the police take this seriously.

Around the back, by the barn, the bitter wind plays with strands of straw, flicks at the hedges, swoops through the outhouses. Dad should be working there, but it's empty except for the chickens. They're hungry, squabbling over sodden straw. I find my way to the back door, squelch mud beneath my feet, seeping through my socks, and sink into puddles I can't see to avoid. I finger the key in my pocket then open the back door.

The kitchen reeks of sour milk instead of the delicious aroma of Janet's homemade bread. I have to feel my way for the switch, ridiculously pleased when I flick on the light. I kick off my muddy slippers and climb the stairs to reach your study, pushing the door wide to survey the mess before I enter.

I look down at my bare feet, feel how my body is shaking. I can't do this alone, I need a friend, and I fumble for my phone knowing there is only one person I can call.

I'm doing this for you, Mum. Dad may feel he has to protect Ash, but I don't.

Solving this is the key to my sanity.

17

Holly

'Cass?'

There was no answer, but Holly saw her car parked outside so she opened the kitchen door. Stepping inside the farmhouse, she felt the stark atmosphere keenly, as though the walls were too tall, the rooms too wide. The farmhouse would once have been grand, but it was unloved, like an ugly antique that can't be thrown away because of its value. The coving and fancy details around the light fixings suggested money hadn't been a problem once, but now the wallpaper was peeling and the wooden floor below her feet was scored with ancient gauges. Dusty curtains hung in tatters at dirty windows and the storage heaters looked inadequate to heat such lofty rooms. The long hallway would once have been impressive, but the paint was flaking away like an old lady's face powder, while the carpet runner had come unhooked from its pinning and curled back to reveal tarred wood beneath. The front door, through which Maya Hawke had exited on her stretcher, was flanked by an ebony coat stand to one side, a scuffed mahogany table on the other, with a large silver platter forlorn in its centre, presumably a relic left over from the days when people left calling cards, now tarnished and dull. On the platter lay a set of keys and some junk mail – a takeaway delivery leaflet, though Holly didn't believe any pizza driver would come out this far for free.

'Cass?'

Still no answer, and Holly found herself shuddering. When she was a child, she'd believed this place was haunted, and she certainly felt that something unpleasant had happened here and the house was not at peace. *Just leave. You don't need to be here. You're overstepping your role and you aren't Cassandra's friend. Just go.* But she'd left before, run from this house to the sound of screaming, and it had haunted her. She was an adult now: she wouldn't run away. She owed it to Cass to stay, she owed it to Maya.

Holly walked carefully but with purpose along the hallway until she reached the back of the house. Here, the ceilings were plain plasterboard, the floor uncarpeted, the rooms narrow and dark. These must be the old servants' quarters where, in the past, maids and a butler would have moved up and around the house without disturbing the more distinguished residents using the grand main staircase and large rooms at the front. It was at the base of this rear staircase that she, Jon and Hilary had worked on Maya. There was a splatter of blood on the floorboards, possibly urine, given how close she had been to death.

Holly thought of a gun's power, the damage it can do to flesh, muscle and bone. Even a small gun, something as toy-like as an air rifle, could have a devastating effect. Her father, an American and an ex-military man, had no problem with guns and kept several in his house in California, but Holly detested them. They filled her with a sickening feeling of dread. Even the thought of firearms was enough to make her heart beat fast like that of a rabbit caught in the sights, causing a helter-skelter of panic as she re-experienced the fight or flight she had first felt that terrible Halloween when she was eight.

When she visited California, her dad was forever trying to cajole her into joining him on one of his hunting trips into the mountains.

He'd complain that even Jamie had lost his boyish enthusiasm for the sport, and Holly wouldn't even give it a try. He had no idea that they both had very good reason.

Hearing movement upstairs, she felt her way up the steep, unlit staircase to the first floor. The hallway landing was oddly shaped, so that the three bedrooms seemed to have mock corridors and secret corners before their doorway was reached. There was little light, just one tall window above the stairwell, with speckled rectangular panes of glass set in a leaded arch. Holly gazed out onto the distant fields of pig huts and white plastic wind tunnels that from this distance made it look as though snow had fallen. The sickly sweet stench of pig shit was pervasive – it had been in her nostrils since her arrival, but seeing the huts intensified her sense of the smell, one she'd been accustomed to when she was a girl. Now it made her want to retch.

Beyond the fields was a wooded area, circular and very dense, where Jamie had led her and Carl that night, seeking ghosts. And beyond that, the perimeter fence of the disused airbase, within which she had once lived, an innocent. It seemed so long ago now. This was the land that the Port Authority wanted to turn into a lorry park. The banners outside the farm and the school had shouted HANDS OFF OUR COUNTRYSIDE!, yet no one loved it enough to buy one of the old military houses. They would all be razed to the ground, and she couldn't say she was wholly sorry. Better that than another group of children should wander too far from home and get mixed up in danger they didn't understand.

'Holly, is that you?'

She stepped back from the window. 'Yes, Cass. I'm just coming.'

She pushed open the door to the study and there was Cass, barefoot and dishevelled, adrift in an alarming sea of scattered papers. On the desk beside her was an assortment of randomly sized family photos, the largest ones of Maya and Hector on their wedding day. There was no question that Maya had been lovely to look at, as lovely as her daughter, and also older than Hector by a few years. Her dress was elegant, her tiara looked like real pearls.

There was a smaller picture of Cassandra with Daniel, on a beach somewhere exotic-looking. A golden couple, he was as dark as she was fair, and their matching perfect smiles said that everything was good in their world. Then came a baby photo. Holly picked it up to look more closely at the image of Cassandra cradling the pink-swaddled bundle. 'That's Victoria,' she said sadly.

In the photo, Cass looked exhausted, her eyes sunken into her skin, which had lost its glow, and Holly wondered why Maya would have chosen to have this picture framed. Finally, above all of these framed snaps and nailed to the wall, was an A3-sized publicity shot of Daniel. He looked perfect: his skin almost glittered with health and his hair was lusty. He stood flexing a bronzed muscular arm as he held a glass of green juice as if it were the elixir of life itself. A slogan ran across the bottom of the picture:

Join The Samphire Master on Radio Suffolk
every Friday evening at 9.00!
Because Health Matters.
www.samphirehealth.com

'Mum is so proud of Daniel,' Cass whispered, as if they were in church, looking up at the graven image. Then she looked around, as if bewildered by the disarray she was seeing for the first time.

Everything in this room was open – the curtains pulled back violently, torn from their hooks at the side, and every drawer in the desk ransacked, papers scattered everywhere. Even a box of pens had been upended.

'What is it we're searching for?' Holly asked, kneeling beside Cass and picking up random papers.

Cass looked around helplessly. 'Anything.'

'You'll need to be more specific.'

'I think Mum was shot because of the farm. If she actually signed a contract, it would give any number of people a reason to be angry with her.'

'So we're looking for something official relating to her decision?' Holly clarified, suddenly uneasy. They shouldn't be doing this, it should be the police, yet she knew she couldn't stop now. 'Something her assailant too may have been seeking?'

Holly peered at one of the papers and saw it was a bank statement. A cursory glance showed long lines of numbers in the debits column, and very few in the credits. The Hawkes were in serious debt. She recalled Janet saying *The farm's not exactly a gold mine.*

It looked as if all official correspondence was addressed to Maya. One letter had a familiar banner across the top, *Hands Off Our Countryside!* It was signed by Philip Godwin and its tone was both angry and demanding:

> If our farmland is sold to the Port, they'll rip the heart from our community. 3,200 lorries EVERY DAY and 600 cars EVERY DAY. Local schoolchildren will be in GREAT DANGER from the INCREASED TRAFFIC and the value of local homes will plummet!

Holly noticed that Cassandra had hardly moved. She was still gazing up at the publicity photo of Daniel. Directly behind her was the open gun cupboard. Empty, of course; the police had seized all the weapons, the spaces like empty sockets of missing teeth.

'Cass, where was the rifle kept?'

Cass turned, and pointed immediately to the thin central space. 'This is the home of the Anschütz.'

'It seems very long,' Holly said, standing. Her senses pricked so she knew something was coming, a taste or a smell, but not what.

Cass trailed her hand, with its broken fingernails, along the groove. 'The rifle is always stored with its silencer attached.' Holly's nose filled, as if with the scorched scent from the gun. She felt renewed energy, as if a hand were at her back, pushing her. 'Find me something as long as it would have been.'

Wide-eyed, Cass did as she was told, leaving the room. Alone, Holly closed her eyes, let her senses tingle alive. *Tell me something useful*, she begged. When Cass returned, she was carrying a length of bamboo cane, the type used for supporting plants.

'It's only an estimate, but I'd say this is about the length.'

Holly took it. 'And your mum is how tall?'

'She's very petite, just five foot.'

Three inches shorter than Holly, yet as she held the cane away from her, imagining it was a gun and she was trying to point it at her head, she found she physically couldn't. Her arms simply didn't have the reach, the gun would have been too long.

She breathed in sharply, feeling the synapses in her brain make connections as though piecing together a jigsaw.

'Maya didn't try and kill herself, Cass. I don't think it's even possible.'

18

Cassandra

The relief is immense. I hug her, so grateful that not only does she believe me, she's found something to prove it.

'How did you even think of that?' I ask, staring at the cane.

'I sometimes intuit things. It's hard to explain.' She rubs her head with her fingers. 'I have a bit of a headache now. Could I get some water?'

'Oh, of course. Come on.'

Holly takes a seat, and places her arms on the kitchen table, resting her head there. She gives a light groan.

'Are you okay?'

'I'm just feeling a bit . . .' She looks up, and right then I see a child. Like when Victoria's ill, I just want to take care of her. 'Overwhelmed. Your mum, it's like she's here.'

Spiritualism, I understand that. Daniel talks about karma and I know the world is a mysterious place.

'Can you think of anything else?' I say, tentative because Holly looks so ill. But she thought of something I'd never have considered, and Janet's cakes . . . I realise what a gift it is, her coming back into my life like this.

'When I was in the study, I could feel your mum's pain, Cass. How serious was her cancer when Daniel cured her?'

'Bad enough that the hospital wanted to operate, but Mum . . . Well, she's vain. And losing her breast was something she wouldn't agree to. She tried lots of things, so many strange therapies, but it was Daniel who saved her. She went into remission, she kept her breast and became his cause célèbre, the star of his radio show.'

Holly lifts her head, but only slightly. Her cheeks have lost their colour.

'Mum survived cancer, against the odds, only to get shot in her own home. What are the chances of that?'

'I'm so sorry, Cass.' I can tell she means it. I trust her, feel I can say what I've been thinking, though only to her.

'Holly, I think it was Ash who shot Mum. We know his fingerprints were found on the rifle . . .'

'But the police let him go. Surely they wouldn't do that if they had any suspicions.' Holly rubs her temples, making circular motions. I push the glass of water closer to her and she sips it. 'And your dad seems very close to him.'

'Dad thinks the sun shines out of him. He's thinking of him more than he is of me right now, that's for sure.'

'Why do you say that?'

I don't want to talk about this. 'Besides, Ash isn't close to Mum. Neither is Janet, for that matter.'

She looks at me in surprise. 'You can't think Janet is involved? She made those scones for your mum . . .'

I prickle with defensiveness. 'She's our housekeeper – she's just doing her job! She's like a table or a chair or . . . What I mean is, she's always here but that doesn't make her *family*. Mum and her have lived on top of each other all these years, but they're not friends. Mum is educated and cultured. She got saddled with this place, so she married Dad because he could work the land and she needed him.' I can't help but shiver.

There's a pause. I can feel her eyes drilling into me. I know what she's thinking: *It's usually the husband.*

'Do your parents have a good marriage?'

'I used to think it worked, despite their differences. But Dad seems more concerned about Ash than Mum right now. Which isn't right, is it?'

Holly sips her water. She seems to be reviving. 'Maybe not.'

'Mum wasn't happy on Friday and I was too wrapped up with my own problems to ask her why. But now I think I know. Dad told me today that he wants Ash to take over the farm, but Mum didn't want that. She was in his way.'

'Ash seems heartbroken by the attack on your mum,' Holly says in a measured tone, so neither of us loses sense of where this conversation is leading. 'And very shocked.'

'That's what he'd like you to believe.'

'You don't think it's true?'

My thoughts are muddled again. It's hard to say what I think, but I have to try. She's the only person I can tell. 'People always think Ash is slow but he can be manipulative. Living with just his mum all these years, he sees the world in a very narrow way, as if nothing exists beyond the farm and the handful of people he cares about.'

'In what way is he manipulative?'

'He plays on his limitations, pretending to be less intelligent than he really is. Like he did when he assaulted that boy who just wanted to put up a tent for the night. Once the police arrived, he played the dumb card and walked away with a caution.'

'You've seen Ash do this?'

'Many times. When we were at primary school he was a pest, hanging around, and if I tried to distance myself, Janet would be here, telling tales to Dad about *poor Ash*. Maybe if she'd had a husband she wouldn't have been so over-protective – it's not normal. Dad always said I should be kind to Ash, but he didn't understand that being friends with Ash meant being called "weird". No one wants to be an outsider, do they?'

There's a moment, a space in the room. I think Holly understands everything I'm trying to tell her – she knows what it is to be different.

'I had . . . an accident.' My hand strays towards my collarbone, but I pull it back into my lap. 'It was thought best I should be sent away. I hated Oakfield but at least, I thought, I'm away from Ash and all his strange stalking. Then he started helping Dad around the farm and I couldn't get away from him again. He was here every holiday, every half-term. As the years have gone on, he's become more and more involved in the business and I've become the outsider. Now it's like I'm a child again, forced to play with someone I have nothing in common with, just to please our parents. I used to think Janet wanted us to marry.' I laugh at this thought – it comes out as a mad cackle. 'I jokingly said that to her once when I was about twelve, and she looked so horrified I realised I was wrong. She just wants him to have the farm.' I wait while Holly registers this.

'Did you ever tell your dad how you felt?'

'He wouldn't have listened – he was just glad to have someone to help out. People round here want to work down the docks or at British Telecom in Ipswich. There's no money in farming.'

'What about your mum?'

'I didn't need to tell her any of this, she knows, but Dad will never see any wrong in Ash – he's blind to his faults. But I'm not. And I want to make sure that the police aren't either.'

Holly pushes her empty glass aside and leans forward. 'What is it you're really saying, Cassandra?'

'I'm telling you what happened on Friday.'

Holly's face is frowning with attention, and I realise she could be my only hope of discovering what really happened. 'Tell me,' she says, 'what happened on Friday after you came home.'

19

Cassandra
Friday 31 October

'Mum?' I wander through the farmhouse, calling your name. My brain is slipping again, the delusions are back. I need help.

I find you in your study, seated at your desk before a pile of papers to one side and an account book. You don't look up: you're too engrossed in your sums to notice my tear-soaked face, but point with the nib of your pen at the numbers.

'The copse isn't bringing in much rent and the supermarkets are always trying to get the lowest price they can, despite the quality.'

'Mum?'

You throw your pen on top of a glossy document that has the Port Authority logo on the cover.

'They're offering a lot of money, Cass. More than its market value.'

'You can't sign that,' I say, slowly tuning in to what you're saying. 'What about the Spa?'

Finally, you properly see me. You frown, suddenly concerned. 'What's happened, Cass? You look terrible. What on earth is wrong?'

Downstairs, you make a pot of tea.

I sit obediently, trying to keep my spine straight, though it wants to crumble. Inside my head is foggy, a sensation I identify as the beginning of depression, when thoughts slip and slide in my mind like fish. When you finally sit down opposite me and take my hands, you feel them trembling.

'Cass, has something happened? You don't look well.'

'I think . . . I think I'm starting to get sick.'

'Is it the delusions?'

Oh, Mum, you always understood me so well. My shaking intensifies now we're talking about it aloud. I'm afraid to ask for help, but more afraid of being alone with this. Last time I hid my symptoms, I waited too long, and then the illness took me over completely. I was sectioned to the Bartlet and Victoria was sent away to boarding school. 'I don't want to be ill, Mum.'

You move, coming to sit with me on my side of the table. 'Is it the same as last time, Cass? Tell me the truth.'

'I think so, I . . .'

I falteringly describe hearing a woman's voice, then opening the bedroom door and finding it empty. How I then heard noises in the study, and once again I thought Daniel was having sex with another woman.

'I left the house, and then I saw her,' I say, 'fully clothed, with a briefcase. Oh, Mum, it was just a business meeting. It's all in my head.'

Just like before.

Then you say something that shocks me – the last question I expected: 'Could she have dressed quickly?'

'No, Mum!' God, are you going crazy too? 'It's just jealousy, my old demon. I wanted to come here and get my head straight.'

I wait, for your assurance that you can help me. That we can fix this together and I can go home and everything can be okay.

'Cass, I'm really sorry to hear this.' You speak so carefully that it scares me. Something is happening, something I don't understand.

'It's okay.' I try to stand, but I stumble. I try to smile, but my face won't co-operate. I can feel the fogginess is in my muscles now. And still you watch me, so carefully, and I can tell that something is coming that I can't stop.

'Look, love, there's something I've been keeping from you. But, given this, you need to know.'

You reach into the pocket of your skirt and remove a piece of paper, folded into squares. My hand won't move to take it from you, so you unfold it on the table. The paper is so worn from being refolded that it's torn almost in half. It's an appointment letter, from the oncology department at Ipswich Hospital. My jaw releases and I take in air quickly, panting like a puppy. No, this can't be happening, not again.

'I found another lump, bigger this time, and went for a mammogram. This is my second appointment with my consultant, to discuss treatment options. There aren't many.'

'You can't get ill!' I feel the panic like a cold wash: you could leave me. My voice is shrill, uncontrolled. 'Daniel cured you.'

You look concerned, for me rather than you, and this more than anything breaks my heart. 'Daniel isn't God, he isn't even a doctor. It's leaving things so long, trusting him, that has left so few options for me.'

'No, you're not ill! Doctors, they make mistakes all the time.' I'm shaking from toe to tip, cold all over. You try to still me, but I'm gone too far for that.

'Cass, love, this is why I didn't tell you. Please calm down . . .' Through the window, I see a group of men in the distance, guns broken over their arms, voices loud. You notice too and run a hand through your hair. 'Look, love, there is a new treatment that's available. But it's only available for high-priority cases and at my age . . . Well, the bottom line is, it's only available if I pay privately.'

'What treatment?'

The men are outside now, in the yard. I see Dad speaking with Ash. There are other men, who I can't identify.

'Proton therapy.' You sigh. 'And out there is an official from the Port, Dave Feakes. Your Dad and Phil Godwin are trying to show him what the countryside means to us, trying to make him withdraw his offer for the greater good.' You laugh then, harsh and ironic, and it scares me.

'Mum, I don't understand.'

'Don't you, Cass?' you say, so gently. 'That little PR stunt out there has come at the perfect time. What with me needing treatment, and Daniel up to his old tricks . . .'

'Mum, no, Daniel's done nothing wrong. I'm sick, it's me who needs help!'

'We've all been sick, Cass. It's time we started to get better.'

I hear a honking voice outside, and lift my head to see a distinctive ruddy face. 'That's not Alfie Avon, the journalist?'

You grimace. 'Phil Godwin thought of everything, didn't he? Get the Port Authority on our side, and get it covered in the newspaper at the same time.'

'I can't believe you've let that man on our land – you really have gone crazy. You know he has it in for Daniel.'

'Well,' you say coolly, 'this isn't Daniel's farm, it's mine.'

'But it will be his,' I say, still struggling with all the swirling in my brain. 'When the farm becomes Samphire Health Spa.'

Your face is stony. You take the appointment letter from the table and carefully fold it back into squares, returning it to your pocket. A shiver of fear runs through me.

'Haven't you been listening to anything I've said, Cass? Samphire Health Spa was just a fantasy.'

'What the fuck does that mean?'

You try to reach for me, but I shove you away so violently that the sugar bowl falls from the table with a crash. I stand up, knowing I should leave, but too angry to move. My future, all our plans, feel as though they're slipping from me. Samphire Health Spa isn't only a career ambition, it means Victoria would come home to live. No, Mum, you can't be ill, it's not fair.

'Cass, calm down . . .' You try to reach for me again, but I won't let you touch me.

'You can't change your mind!' I'm shouting now, but I don't care. 'You promised Daniel the farm.'

'And he promised me my health,' you say, so coldly that it freezes me to the core. 'Don't you see, Cass, I'm going to save myself, but I'm going to save you too. Do you really think you can run a business? Look at you, stood shrieking like some lunatic!'

Lunatic. 'I have rights! My daughter, my future . . . Why, you bitch . . .'

The back door opens.

Janet stands still for a moment, staring at us: me standing, you seated, the hard words still in the air. Ignoring the tension in the room, she scampers over to the kitchen worktop and says, 'Don't mind me, I just need to get the afternoon tea ready for the men.'

Poor Janet, she looks frail and scrappy, so different from you. You're defiant. Proud, chin up, with your dark hair and clever eyes, your smart shirt, so smug. You don't look ill, Mum, not at all.

Janet pauses to cough, her dull hair comes loose from her ponytail and hangs down the sides of her face. Ignoring us, she melts into the background, sets a saucepan to boil for the eggs and starts to butter bread. It's mesmerising, comforting too, to watch her continue on like a wind-up doll when my world is imploding.

'You can serve the food outside, Janet,' you tell her decisively.

She looks up, obediently, at your order. 'Won't the men mind?'

'I don't want them in here. Tell them they can eat in the barn if they want a real taste of the countryside.'

Janet begins to wipe her hands on her apron, the eggs are boiling noisily, and I'm suddenly desperate to be out of the oppressive kitchen, and away from your scrutiny.

I need to get away and make a dash for the back door.

But at the farm there is no respite from suffering. Outside, stood in the cold October air, I hear the noise before I see anything. The screams of birds dying.

Dad is in the barn, alone, reaching into a squabble of hens who are corralled together by a metal grille. His hands are encased in thick black rubber gloves up to his elbows and he grabs for a bird. When I was a child he'd tease me, prod me with a rubber finger until I screamed. He thought it was funny, but I knew what happened when he wore those gloves. I always hated those gloves, but since his stroke they're necessary, to give his right hand the support it needs to wring birds' necks.

Jet runs towards me, jumping up and barking as I pat his ears and scruff his neck, and then he finally lets me pass. Dad is bent over, a hunched man, but between his legs are feathers, a moving shape. The black gloves hold the shape fast, despite its desperate struggles, and I see the black rubber twist, the gloves turn against themselves once, hard and sudden. I marvel he can do this when, without that glove, his right hand is useless. He tosses the bundle of limp red feathers out of the pen and onto the pile of carcasses, all feathers and flesh, but no life. His daily work, the chicken order for the supermarket.

In a second pile are dead pheasants with green and purple feathers and useless wings, the spoils of today's shoot. The bloodied mass of slack bodies makes me want to heave.

'What you doin' here, girl?' he shouts at me, without looking up, already reaching for his next victim.

'I came to see Mum. Dad, did you know she plans to sell the farm?'

Now he looks at me, the live chicken caught by the glove, its beady orange eyes glittering with fear, wings flapping. 'Over my dead body. What do you think this whole day has been about?'

I hear the distant voices of the other men returning from the copse, and start to walk away. 'Janet will bring food out to you soon.'

He looks back at the terrified bird. And with a deft move, he breaks its neck.

Back in the kitchen, Janet has almost finished preparing the food.

She's put cream and jam on scones and is mixing gin with prosecco for the boozy drinks. You've disappeared. I climb the backstairs to find you. The door to your study is closed, so I know you're in there. I wonder if you're phoning Clive, right this minute asking him to come and assess me for admission to the Bartlet. I wonder if you're looking again at your letter, thinking about all the money you'll need. After all you said, Mum, about natural treatments. Publically, on the radio. You'll make Daniel look a fool – worse, you'll make him look a fraud. I open the door.

You're on the floor, knelt in front of the safe. You look up, startled. 'Get out!' you scream. And I turn to go, but as I do, I see that you're sliding something into the base.

The men are now assembled in the barn, high from the murder of pheasants. Godwin's voice is booming, 'Ah, Cassandra! Come and meet Dave Feakes, from the Port Authority.'

'Hi, I hope you've had a good day.' I shake the man's hand. Does he know how much rests on his offer?

'Excellent, thank you.' His face is flushed from the adrenalin of the shoot, but he looks kindly, with soft white hair and gentle eyes huge behind bifocals. Alfie Avon is watching, hunched like a vulture over his swollen notepad. He gives what may be a smile but is really a show of teeth and pink gums. 'Evening, Cassandra. How are you?'

I don't reply. I can't bring myself to be civil to him. He's hounded Daniel ever since he took over the Friday-evening slot on Radio Suffolk – before that, it was *Alfie All About Town*.

Ash is collecting dead birds – no doubt each man will leave with a gift of a brace and the rest will go to the butcher.

Dad reaches for a scone and I see how without the black rubber glove to add strength to his right hand, he can't grip the plate properly. I try to eat too. I take a morsel in a bid to look normal, but I can't even swallow for thinking about Victoria, who will be packing for her trip home. I want to turn back time, pretend I never imagined I heard Daniel fucking another woman, pretend I never heard you say that your cancer has returned.

I want my life back, the one I had just two hours ago. I shouldn't have come to the farm. I've ruined everything.

'I'm going to fetch something from my car,' I say, excusing myself from the boozy gathering.

In my car, I rummage for my mobile phone in the glove box, among tissues, a half-eaten bag of sweets and hidden bottles of trazodone. I call home and Daniel picks up after the first ring.

'Cass?'

'Yes.' My voice is uneven, as though I've been silent for a long time.

Then, quickly and too loud, he says, 'I've been so worried – where the hell are you?'

'The farm.'

Daniel pauses. 'I saw the cake.'

'It's for Victoria and Dawn . . .'

'When did you bring it home?' I can hear the beginnings of suspicion in his voice.

'I popped home at lunchtime.' Lie.

'When will you be back, love?'

'I don't know. Look, Daniel, it's Mum. She acting so strange, says she's sick . . .'

'Tell her to go back to the juices for twenty-four hours and I'll give her some reiki healing. Samphire and wheatgrass shots and we'll get on top of it in no time.'

'No, Daniel, you're not listening. She changed her mind. She's not giving us the farm, she's going to sell it to the Port. There will be no Samphire Health Spa.'

The pain of the moment snaps me back to the kitchen.

'Samphire Spa? What's that?' Holly asks. She's listening so intently, and I need her to understand what a terrible thing it was, for you to change your mind. How it triggered everything that came later.

'Daniel has cured many people, but Mum is the one everyone knows about. When she went into remission, she became his most famous success story. She's been on his radio show loads of times. I let him believe that her health was the problem, when really it was me.'

'I'll come over straight away, talk some sense into her.'

'No, I don't think you should. It's best to let her calm down.' I can hear him moving around, maybe collecting his keys. 'She's gone to lie down anyway – she'll probably sleep right through. There's no point in you coming over tonight.'

I don't want to see him. I need time to recover, to get the bad thoughts out of my head.

'Well, if you're sure that's the best thing to do,' he says, doubtfully. 'I'll come over first thing with a Samphire Sunshine for her breakfast and I can give her a reiki treatment. Hopefully she'll have seen sense, but if not, I can talk to her before we drive to fetch Victoria. Can you be ready for me?'

I say I can and hang up. But I've ruined everything: Samphire Health Spa won't happen, and it's my fault. If only I hadn't come here, with my doubts, opening up a can of worms . . .

I take a bottle of trazodone from the glove box and open it. For the first time in two years I swallow one, and hope it works fast. Then I tip the rest of the bottle onto my palm. Suddenly this feels like the only option open to me. There's a bottle of water on the passenger seat, and I grab it, bring it to my mouth and swallow the tablets.

Time passes, minutes, I'm not sure how many. I close my eyes and sleep comes quickly.

Then, in an abrupt jolt of violence, the car door swings open, and there you are, Mum, your face purple with rage.

'What have you done? Cassandra!'

The empty tablet bottle is in my lap. All business, you yank me from the car by my arm, and haul me back inside the farmhouse. We walk past the men, still drinking in the barn and eating Janet's scones, oblivious to the drama going on just yards away.

Upstairs, to the bathroom. I see the white porcelain of a toilet bowl and feel your fingers scratch my throat. There is no softness, no tears.

'What a stupid thing to do! You're so selfish, Cass. And you think you could run a business? There's no way. Simply no way you're capable.'

After you've made me empty my stomach of the foaming tablets, you tell me again that there will be no more Samphire Health Spa, and Victoria won't be coming home.

You saved me, Mum. I'm not sure I wanted you to.

Holly breathes deeply, taking in everything I'm saying to her. She's started making notes.

'You tried to kill yourself, Cass?'

'I panicked, don't you see? I'm not strong, I have a history of illness. It's why no one believes me about the shooting. It's why I need you to help me.

'After Mum had made me sick, she went to the barn and told the men she was selling the farm. Godwin was livid, of course. Dad was angry, and Ash cried. He could see his life, everything in it, being ripped away by Mum's decision. I believe that on Saturday morning her attacker was searching for that contract, but Mum wouldn't say where she'd hidden it. Don't you see, her hiding it means she was afraid of someone close to her?'

Holly says slowly, 'Then that contract is what we need to find.'

I kneel on the floor, and realise how crazy I must look, with my bare feet and bedraggled appearance, like a mad Alice trying to get into Wonderland. The place you were crouched, that afternoon, when I disturbed you.

I look around for the heaviest thing I can see, and there you are, staring back at me in your wedding dress. I grab the wedding photo in its heavy oak frame, praying this will work. Holding it like a hammer, frame against the panelling, I begin to bash, hard and repetitive, until the frame cracks and the panelling falls away. There's a hollow space inside the clever mock cupboard you had made years ago. I pull out a white folder containing a thin but official-looking document with a company logo on the cover.

I pass it to Holly, and wait, your crumpled wedding picture clasped in my lap.

DAY 5

WEDNESDAY 5 NOVEMBER

20

Holly

When she arrived at his office, the door was open and Jon was at his desk, bent over some notes. She tapped lightly on the door and waited for him to look up.

'Hi, Holly,' he said, smiling. 'Everything okay? You're not on shift until this evening, are you?'

'That's right. I just wanted to have a word, if it's okay? Something's bugging me.'

'Of course, take a pew.' He put down his pen and leaned back, waiting for her to take the seat on the other side of his desk. 'So what's the problem?'

Jon had been on the interview panel when she got accepted as a trainee. He was her supervisor, and she moved into the room, his presence enveloping her in a powerful sensation of calm and safety. Jon wasn't much older than her, maybe in his mid-thirties, but he was steady in a way that made him seem of a different generation. Married, with kids, the photos tacked to his noticeboard showed a family growing together, travelling a bit, enjoying life. As his children grew into teenagers, Jon's brown hair had got sparser and the glasses appeared more frequently, but the smile was the same. She had seen, with every patient, how he always took such care. That was why she was here: because he was a good man, with good sense. And she needed some perspective.

'It's about that call-out we had on 1 November.'

'The suicide attempt?'

She hesitated. 'Well, I suppose you've just cut to the crux of it. I told you that the daughter, Cass, has doubts about that. Do you know if the police have found anything conclusive?'

Jon scratched his scalp and leaned back in his chair, his fingers lightly tapping the edge of the desk. 'Since I submitted my report, and passed on what Cassandra said to you, I haven't heard anything. Maya's stable, that's all I know.'

Holly had seen Jon's report. It detailed the time they had attended the scene, the medical attention they'd given Maya. It didn't give any opinion, just facts. She wanted to tell him that she'd been at the farm with Cass, that at that very moment she had the contract Maya signed in the glove box of her car and she didn't know what to do with it. No, she couldn't tell him the full extent of her involvement.

'I told you that I used to live near the farm, that I went to school with the victim's daughter? Well, since the shooting I've sort of become friends with her again. I've been supporting her.'

Jon removed his glasses, wiped them on his green tunic. 'Okay, and how is she?'

'She's troubled, convinced that her mum was shot and that the police aren't taking it seriously.'

'Well, I doubt that's true,' he said reasonably. 'The police are trained to be thorough with this kind of thing, and they cordoned off the farm straight after we took Maya to hospital.'

Holly knew he was right. Leif had been the officer guarding the place. And the police were certainly investigating – they'd interviewed

Ash. Away from Cassandra, things seemed so much clearer: the police were doing their job, Cassandra was being paranoid. But then there was her own belief that the gun was too long. More than that, there was the contract. Maya was signing away the farm and several people would have been very angry indeed about that. Both of them had understood this, and there had been an intense discussion about where to keep it while they decided what to do. Cassandra was adamant she couldn't take it, and though neither explicitly acknowledged it, Holly knew this was because Daniel and Hector were two of those people, hence it being in her glove box. She was in deep, and she knew it.

'You know, Holly, you really handled everything well on Saturday. I saw how sensitively you dealt with Maya, and the family. You're going to be a fine paramedic.' He gave her a warm smile, then looked back at his notes. She sensed his need to get on with his work.

'Jon, can I ask something else? I'd like your professional assessment of Cassandra.'

He kept his gaze neutral, but she sensed his surprise. 'Why is that?'

She hesitated. 'Because, as I said, she's my friend. And I'm worried about her.'

'Well, I was really concentrating on Maya – all I saw of the daughter was a woman in shock. Understandable under the circumstances.' He paused, she could feel him pondering something. 'You know, if you think she needs psychiatric help, that's really out of our sphere.'

'I know.' She could see that this conversation wasn't going much further. 'She's been involved with Clive Marsh. They run a therapy group together at the town library. Maybe I could ask him?'

Jon frowned, then said, 'Remember patient confidentiality, Holly. You're in danger of overstepping your professional remit here. Our work is done: you've done your duty as a paramedic. If you want to support

Cassandra as a friend, of course you can, but please don't confuse the two. Why don't you go home and rest, so you're fresh for this evening's shift? You look exhausted.'

Holly walked along the hospital corridor, knowing Jon was right. But still her feet took her to Clive's office, which he used just half the time, his main base being at the Bartlet Hospital. From here, he supervised placements, worked alongside the university to mark student assignments, and provided a counselling service to staff in need of support. Clive's door was known always to be open to normally stoic medical staff, where a case had got under their skin.

'Well, Holly,' he said, tapping his pen on his knee as he leaned back, 'you did the right thing to seek help. What you witnessed was traumatic – it's bound to affect you in some way.'

He removed his glasses, which had misted in the overheated air of his office, and Holly saw deep compassion in his eyes before he slid them on again. 'So, what is it that's bothering you?'

Now Holly knew she had to be careful.

'I think it's processing the idea that Maya shot herself. I've been spending time with Cassandra and she doesn't believe that, but I'm not sure if she's in the soundest of minds. I'm worried she's ill, and by supporting her theory I'm not helping her.' As she said it, Holly realised this was the complete truth. She needed someone to tell her that Cass was sane, that their quest was legitimate, because this would mean that her own instincts were sound. She had hidden her synaesthesia for many years, and she didn't know if she could trust it. She looked hopefully at the sage man for reassurance.

'Cassandra woke on Saturday morning to find her mother almost dead. She's going through the stages associated with a grief response:

shock, anger, denial. She's still trying to process what happened to Maya – she's very confused. But why would you share that feeling, Holly?'

He was good, she had to give him that. Kindly eyes, warm voice.

'I suppose I'm not as objective as I should be. I used to live near the farm. I went to the same school as Cassandra, though I was several years below her . . . Everyone used to say the farm was haunted, and us kids would tell each other stories about it. I think seeing Maya, shot like that, in that place may have brought back all those fears.'

'I see,' he said, making a bridge with his fingers as he contemplated her. 'So this call-out has resurrected some deep anxieties.'

His tone was almost hypnotic, lulling her into agreeing. 'Yes . . . no! Clive, Cass doesn't believe her mother shot herself and I don't either. I sense it very strongly – the violence in the farmhouse. It's why I'm helping Cass.'

Clive cocked his head to one side. 'You *sense* it?'

This wasn't a subject she could talk about with most people. But Clive made her feel she could open up, that in this room she could say anything. 'I have synaesthesia, Clive, so I see personality as colour. I can also, and I know this sounds weird, feel touch when I see it. I call it my curse and sometimes my gift.'

'Oh, that's very interesting,' he said. She felt herself under his intense scrutiny. 'So what colour am I?'

'Salmon-pink,' she replied without hesitation.

'Oh. Can't I be blue? Something more masculine?'

'It doesn't work like that,' she smiled, enjoying the chance to talk about this without being made to feel like a weirdo. 'Colours aren't gendered, not for me. Salmon-pink is comforting, homely. It's a colour I trust.'

'You make me sound like a human version of *hygge*. Can someone's colour change?'

Holly thought about this. 'Mm, it can modify. Like, this Swedish guy I'm seeing, Leif. The reason I agreed to date him was because he was such a nice creamy colour, like butter. Only now I know him better I can see the most perfect yellow, like a sun. It's so powerful to me – I experience it every time we're together. I could fall in love with him, just because of that damn colour!'

She laughed, but then realised what she'd said. The thought terrified her.

'I see,' said Clive, with all the objectivity of a clinician, although his face remained friendly and approachable. 'Your synaesthesia is intrusive: it could cloud your judgement. And what did you say about experiencing touch?'

'When I see someone being punched or kissed, either in real life or in a film, I actually feel it. Like it's actually happening to me. So when I'm in Maya's study, I can feel her pain, and I'm not sure that's simply my synaesthesia. I think it may be my imagination. Sometimes it scares me – when I was younger and before I knew the word, I thought I was simply strange.'

'In my experience, strange can often be marvellous.' Clive leaned forward to get a better look at Holly, as if studying her for the first time. 'Synaesthesia has always been around. It's a trait that affects about four per cent of the population – something that was first described by the ancient Greeks, but in more recent times has only been subject to rigorous study since the 1980s. You have a form called mirror-touch synaesthesia, though you seem to have signs of other forms too.'

'You've heard of this before?' Holly breathed deeply, relieved. This was the first time she'd spoken to another human about it: before now, her only confidant had been Google.

'Why don't I refer you to the research team at Sussex? They'd be delighted to meet you. It could help others, to discover more about this trait. Most importantly, it could help you.'

'I don't know if I'm ready for that. I think I should go – I've taken enough of your time and I'm working this evening, I need to go home to rest.' Talking to Clive in the sanctuary of his office was one thing. But for others to be told was something she couldn't contemplate. She began to gather up her work bag to leave.

'Just one thing, Holly. You said when you arrived that you're worried Cassandra isn't thinking clearly, and that you may be feeding her delusions, so I'm going to ask you something, in confidence.' He scanned her face, eyes blinking behind his glasses, and she felt immediately alert. 'Do you know that Cassandra was previously sectioned?'

'Sectioned?' Holly came closer to him and felt his unease as teetering on a ledge. 'No, I didn't know that. Just that she's suffered from paranoia, that she dropped out of university . . .'

'Two years ago, she suffered a serious psychotic episode: she was a risk to herself and possibly others. That's why her daughter was sent to boarding school. She was having delusional thoughts, a great deal of paranoia directed towards her partner. We had no choice but to section her.'

Something dawned on Holly. 'So, that group you run at the library – she's not your colleague at all then? She's your patient.'

'A bit of both,' Clive said, raising his shoulders in resignation. 'After she was discharged, she attended Team Talk, then, about a year ago, I told her she was recovered enough to stop attending. She had a crisis of confidence, so we came to an arrangement.'

Holly was blinded by colour then, one she associated with deceit: a shrouded grey. Cassandra had seemed to be opening up and trusting her, but she'd lied. She gathered her coat around her and turned to go.

'Thanks for your time, Clive.'

'You're welcome,' He waited until she was almost out of the room before adding, 'Holly, I've told you this in confidence because I'm trying to warn you. Cassandra isn't a well woman – a trauma like this makes her very vulnerable to relapse. Please don't do anything to encourage her delusions. If there is anything suspicious about the shooting, then we must trust the police to do their jobs.'

Holly drove home and felt the murky grey colours recede, as though every mile she placed between herself and the hospital gave her greater clarity. She needed distance between herself and Cass. She'd been pulled into a conspiracy theory and hadn't been thinking straight. How could she judge the potential of a gun by holding a length of cane against herself? Why should she assume Maya had been shot because of a contract? No, she needed to stay away, to concentrate on her career.

She arrived at her flat with just a few hours to go before she had to return to the hospital for her evening shift. She needed solitude and space to think. Her flat was exactly that: a room with no colour, simple furniture and only a few photographs for decoration. Her brain buzzed, overloaded.

She staggered through the small lounge to the kitchen, all white and cool surface, a space that soothed, and slid onto the stool at the breakfast bar, placing her head on her folded arms, breathing deeply. All she saw in her mind's eye was Cassandra, the only colour was grey, and it was getting in the way of doing her job. She took the contract Maya had signed and placed it in her desk drawer, not sure what else to do with the damn thing.

I should never have got involved. I haven't seen Cassandra in twenty years. She wouldn't have even known who I was if I hadn't told her. And now the past is snapping back at my heels – nothing good comes from Innocence Lane.

Holly had known since primary school that she was different, since the night in the wood outside Innocence Farm with her brother. It was only later, when she was seventeen and struggling, that, thanks to the internet, she'd learned that the word for her condition was synaesthesia. Today Clive had told her she had the mirror-touch form. But her senses had tricked her with a mirage – she had colluded with Cassandra. Her senses had told her that Maya hadn't shot herself, but she had overstepped the mark and now she had been sucked in to a false friendship with a woman with severe mental health issues. Just when she was getting her life together, and embarking on a new career, this was pulling her right back to where all her problems had started: Innocence Lane, the ghost, the shooting.

That was where this all led back to, that Halloween night when she was eight years old. She'd avoided it for too long. She logged on to her laptop, and loaded Skype. There was her brother's name, Jamie Redwood, and the tiny picture in which he and Kaitlin pressed their faces close together, but the icon was closed: he wasn't online. She looked at her watch and worked out that Jamie would be at work. Instead, she typed a message: Jamie, can you make sure you have Skype open when you're home, please? We need to talk.

Frustrated, she stared at her laptop screen for answers.

There was only one other person she could think of who was as obsessed with Innocence Lane as she was: Alfie Avon. And he had been at the farm last Friday, so he'd seen Maya just hours before the shooting. Did he think it was an attempted suicide? If he too had doubts, then maybe her senses weren't misleading her after all. But she couldn't just rely on Cassandra's version any more, not without seeking some other perspective. She needed clarity, and she wouldn't get it from anyone in the Hawke family.

Finding Alfie online wasn't difficult – he had Facebook and Twitter, as well as his own website. She sent a message via the latter: I'd like to talk to you, in confidence, about Innocence Farm. She left her mobile number, but no name. Even as she pressed 'send', she wondered what the hell she was doing, delving deeper rather than backing away.

A tapping on the front door interrupted her thoughts. It could only be Leif – no one else called on her unannounced. When she opened the door, he acted bashful, his head lowered, blond hair over his sea-blue eyes, grinning cheekily and cradling a massive flan dish.

'I'm sorry, Leif, but I'm due at work later.'

'But you need to eat first! And I have here a taste of my homeland for you: *Västerbottensostpaj.*'

She saw he was wearing police uniform: he'd been working today. Immediately, her reluctance to see him vanished. 'Visitors bearing gifts are always welcome,' she said, standing aside so he could enter, catching a waft of warm pastry and cheese, so delicious she almost groaned. How could she be hungry, when only minutes ago she'd felt sick? Her body was different to her brain: it functioned normally and needed sustenance.

Leif went straight through to the kitchen, where her laptop was still open at Alfie Avon's website. He began to find plates and cutlery, making himself at home in a way that made her heart soften. This is what it would be like to live with someone, something she hadn't done since she'd left her parents' home in California to return to Suffolk, drawn by echoes of long ago. She envied Jamie for having settled into American life without a backward glance, and for the first time wondered how he managed this.

'Bonfire night,' Holly said, after she heard the crack of a rocket coming from a garden nearby. 'We'll probably see a few burns this evening.'

Leif frowned. 'This is a tradition I do not understand, the celebrations of burning this man, Guy Fawkes. When I came home from work some children were pushing a man-doll in a pram and asking for money. Why is this?'

Holly shook her head. 'Remember, I'm not a native. It's a mystery to me too, all I know is we'll be hearing fireworks all night.'

Seated side by side at the breakfast bar, they ate in appreciative silence. A light tapping of rain began to fall at the kitchen window.

'Rain again,' Leif said, pleasantly. 'Always it rains in this country.'

Together they watched the drops patter on the glass, and she realised that she was feeling much better than earlier.

'So, here's what I know about Sweden: Abba, snow, and lovely cheese pie. Why on earth did you leave?'

He finished his mouthful and raised his eyebrows. '*Ja*, being lovely is important, but so is being exciting. And England is that for me.' He slid a hand onto her thigh. 'My mother was in love with the idea of Hollywood, but for me it was always London.'

'Ipswich isn't London. Did you get lost?'

'Ha! No, I submitted my Bergman thesis idea to several universities in the big city, but Ipswich liked it best. And for that I am most happy, because I like my colleagues, I like this town and now I have met a woman I like very, very much.'

He leaned over and kissed her, forcing her to swallow her mouthful of cheese pie quickly.

'What about you, Holly? If you think Ipswich is so unlovely, why are you here?'

She shrugged. 'I think loveliness is a bit overrated too. I moved back to California with the rest of my family when I was eighteen, but I couldn't settle. Too much sun.'

'They're a long way off,' he said, glancing at the computer screen, where Alfie's red face gazed out. 'What brought them to Ipswich?'

She stood to clear away the plates, and closed the lid of her laptop. She pointed to a small photo attached to the fridge, which showed her father at a Giants baseball match, wearing an oversized T-shirt and holding a huge beer. 'My dad was an Air Force man. He arrived here in the eighties and met my mum in a local nightclub. She said it was love at first sight, and my dad would have made an impression. A black American in Ipswich is going to stand out.'

'You must miss them?'

'Yeah, but I visit every summer. And we have Skype.'

It did pain her to be away from her parents and Jamie, but the arrangement worked for her too. The solitude suited her and through the new job, she was learning to manage her synaesthesia. If it hadn't been for the shooting at Innocence Lane, life would feel very good indeed. She wanted to ask Leif about his day, what he'd been doing with the police, although a voice in her head told her to let it be. Jon's voice, warning her she was overstepping her remit. Clive's warning her not to be taken in by Cassandra's delusions. 'Tell me more about Sweden,' she said, wanting to be transported away from all these nagging thoughts. 'What about your family?'

'My *morsa* got pregnant when she was having an affair with my father, who was on the town council and married. She got support, but she was still a young single mother. Her only role model for behaving immorally was Ingrid Bergman. Do you know Ingrid's story?'

Holly shook her head.

'She was an idol – everyone loved her. An actress, a mother, a wife. Then she ran off with her lover and was hated. She wasn't even allowed to see her daughter for many years. *Morsa* used to watch her films obsessively, as if to find answers to her own life. When I was a boy, she'd take me to the old cinema in Malmö whenever a Bergman film was showing. It was a special time.'

'Is that when you got your interest in films?'

'For sure. And my love of Ingrid Bergman. And older women!' He kissed Holly, and leaned in for a deeper kiss, but she pushed him back, slightly affronted.

'Hey! I'm only a couple of years older than you. What are you, twenty-six?'

'Twenty-four,' Leif smiled. 'But, so what? I think you're delicious as cheese pie.' And then, wiping her mouth with his thumb to remove a pastry crumb, he leaned in and kissed her again.

She tugged at the navy shirt lapel of his uniform, unable to keep it in any longer. 'So what were you up to today? Still guarding Innocence

Farm?' She asked the question, knowing there was no longer any guard placed there, but she couldn't think how else to ease him into the subject. Luckily, he didn't need coaxing.

'Not at the farm, but I'm still involved. More of us are, now they think it wasn't suicide.'

Holly's breath caught. 'They're sure?'

'Not certain, but the man who works for her has a record for gun crime, so he has been questioned.'

'Do you mean Ashley Cley?'

Leif raised his eyebrows. 'Wow, this really is a small town.'

'And he's actually shot someone before?'

For the first time he looks uncomfortable, pulls back slightly. 'This is confidential, Holly. I shouldn't really . . .'

Two routes flash before her, the second one wins and she moves closer to him, kisses his cheek. 'You can trust me,' she says. 'Who did he shoot?'

'Look, I don't know any details. But it shows he's used a gun before, that he has some tendency . . .'

Holly's heart was beating fast. 'Are they going to arrest him?'

'It's possible, what with that, and his fingerprints being found on the rifle. But they're also interested in his mother, they've taken her in for questioning.'

'Janet?' Holly pictured the poor woman, baking scones for Maya. 'But why?'

'Because she was the one who called 999. She swears she never went beyond the kitchen that morning, yet they found her blood on the gun.'

21

Cassandra

'It's a horrible drizzly evening, Mum, and the rain is getting heavier. All of the parents and children, waiting in Christchurch park for the firework display to start, how disappointed they'll be. Their sparklers will fizzle out, they'll be cold. Younger ones will want to go home before the show is over. It's such a shame. Do you remember taking me to the display in Felixstowe? How we cried "ooh" and "aah" at the colours blooming in the sky, the explosives as bright as flowers? I have flowers for you now. I wish you could see them.'

I hold the bunch of freesias close to the misted mask covering your mouth so you can catch their scent, and place one flower in your cupped hand. I'm doing what Nurse Lauren told me to, trying to stimulate your senses, though it seems pointless. You've already left me, I'm sure of it.

'Not so close to her face, love, you're smothering her,' says Daniel, taking the flowers from my tight grip and placing them on the bed-sheet covering your inert body. I can't help thinking that you look like a corpse awaiting burial. 'You're shaking like a kitten, Cass – why don't you sit down?'

I take the seat, gripping the rim. Dad sits, then stands, then sits again. He hates this – he wants to be outside where he belongs but the rain is stopping him.

Lauren arrives to check the machines. 'Now then, Maya, I'm just going to move this pillow, love, so you don't get stuck in one position. There we are.'

She talks to you as if you're awake, but I'm losing hope. As if she can hear my thoughts, she turns, beams broadly and says, 'Now then, family! Why don't you talk to this lovely lady about a happy holiday memory, or something you all enjoy watching on TV?'

Her suggestions are endless and exhausting. I'm mute, there just seems no point, but Daniel sits on the edge of the bed and leans over you.

You and he, always so close. He'd saved you from the knife, from the indignity of hair loss and nausea. He cured you gently with meditation, massage and nutrition so pure and healthy your body healed from within. He was the son you never had, so gifted. It was your idea that you speak on the radio together, which was such a success that afterwards he was offered his own show – though to be fair, Alfie Avon's listeners were already dwindling and Radio Suffolk was looking for someone new. The Samphire Master was a hit. How could you lose your faith in him, Mum? Please wake up so he can cure you again.

'You've missed a big twist in *Broadchurch*, Maya,' Daniel says, taking your hand and stroking it. 'All my clients are talking about it. There's this character, he's managed to convince everyone that his wife is imagining things when really he . . .'

'Maybe something else,' Lauren interrupts in her sing-song voice, heading for the door and raising a wagging finger. 'Positive and cheerful, that's the ticket.'

I hear her shoes squeaking along the corridor, then they stop. She's talking to someone and the sing-song has gone. 'No, sir,' I hear her say, 'I'm sorry but there are already three family members in with Maya . . .'

'I've got to see Hector!'

Ash, demanding to be let in. How dare he come here, now he's a police suspect? He has no right.

Dad lifts his head, registering. 'In here, boy!'

Ash doesn't need any further encouragement, he's through the doorway in a flash, face red. At first, I think it's from anger, then I see his puffy eyes and realise he's been crying. Dad immediately stands to comfort him, his bad right hand finding awkward purchase on Ash's shoulder. 'What's wrong, son?'

Ash mumbles something. The only word I can make out is *Mum*, and Dad has his arm further around him, saying, 'Tell me what's happened. Whatever it is, we can fix it.'

I think I see your eyelid twitch, Mum. I want to tell you it's okay, but I don't believe that. Ash shouldn't be here, he's dangerous. Why can't Dad see through the snivelling schoolboy routine?

I don't know what Daniel makes of this – he looks concerned, but he keeps that detached air he's so good at. 'Has something happened, Ash?'

It takes Ash a few swallows and a bit more coaxing before he can speak. He's in the grip of panic. 'They've arrested Mum. They came to our house, and took her away in a police car.'

Despite my suspicions, I'm stunned. Janet. All those hours and weeks and years she's spent at the farm with you. Her, arrested?

'Why would the idiots do that?' Dad says, his voice rising in anger.

Ash wipes his cheeks with the back of his hand and says quietly, 'They found her blood on the rifle.'

Dad clears his throat and looks at Daniel, as if he might be able to explain it, but Daniel puts his hands in his pockets and turns to the window. I want him to fix this, I want him to make sense of it, but he remains silent.

'Shit,' Dad says.

I can't believe his reaction – anger pushes all other emotions away. 'Is that all you can say, Dad? *Shit?* They think Janet shot Mum!'

Daniel doesn't turn around. He quietly says, 'Calm down, Cass, and let me think about what to do. We need to help Janet.'

Dad is reassuring Ash, blind to the possibility that Janet might actually be guilty.

'That don't matters, a spot of blood can be explained away, son. Janet cleans our house, she cooks for us, 'course her blood could get on my gun!'

This is such bullshit – she didn't clean in the gun cupboard! It was kept locked.

'Or maybe she shot Mum,' I say, bitterly. Already I'm thinking I was wrong to focus on Ash: Janet is the obvious suspect. Cooking, cleaning, skivvying . . . Who knows what resentment builds up? Two women, living out in the sticks with only each other. And if you sold the farm, Janet would lose her home, her livelihood . . . her life. Who could deny that as a motive for murder? A spontaneous act, then she panicked, ran from the house, called 999.

Daniel tries to pull me to him, a silencing move and nothing about giving me comfort. 'Shush, love.'

Ash is crying hard now, his hands pressed to his eye sockets. 'She only ever wanted to help.' Tears roll down his nose.

No, I won't be silenced. I turn to my father and my lover, desperate for one of them to listen to sense. 'Janet and Ash are the only ones with a motive. If Mum dies, the farm won't be sold, they keep their cottage and Ash takes over!'

I see the full force of Dad's rage in his grey eyes, he steps towards me and in that moment I know that he wants to hit me, that the only thing stopping him is Daniel's presence. In that splintered second the door opens, shocking us all, and Holly stands in the doorway in her green uniform, her face registering the violent atmosphere in the room. She looks from me to Dad.

'Hector, what's wrong? What's happening?'

I'm euphorically happy to see her, close to hysterical with relief.

'Janet's been arrested, Holly. The police have finally woken up to the fact that this isn't attempted suicide. Don't you see, I was right!'

'You bitch!' Dad's anger makes me flinch, and Daniel moves a protecting arm around my shoulder, and Holly moves between us, alert to the possibilities of violence.

Nurse Lauren marches in. 'What *is* all this shouting? Please, if you want to talk like this, go outside! It's not fair on Maya.'

I can't stop now, even if it's disturbing you. I turn to Daniel, pleading. 'You can see, Dan, can't you? The police wouldn't have arrested Janet without evidence.'

'You're crazy.' Dad jabs a finger at me and Daniel holds me tighter. 'If your mother can hear you, God help her!'

'Mr Hawke, really,' says Lauren. She reaches past me to press the call button on the wall by your bed. 'I'm calling for assistance.'

'Lauren, please don't. I'm afraid Cassandra isn't well.' I can't believe Daniel is making this about me, about my health. Why is Holly the only other person who can see the truth? 'Where are your tablets, love?'

'I don't want tablets. I want you to be on my side!'

Daniel seems desperate to pacify me. 'Cass, look at the facts: the police let Ash go. They didn't charge him with anything. They don't think he's guilty.'

'But they still have Janet! And we found the contract, didn't we, Holly? Mum had signed away the farm.'

Daniel's fingers squeeze my shoulders. 'Where is it, Cass? It's best if you give it to me.'

'No, Dan.' I move away from him, closer to Holly. 'It's best if we give it to the police.'

Holly's face remains neutral, though her dark eyes are assessing everything that's going on. I want to know what she's thinking, what she's making of this, when Ash starts blubbing again. He wipes tears and snot with the back of his hand.

'This is a witch-hunt,' spits Dad. He lifts his damaged hand and points a gnarled finger at my face. 'And I forbid you to show the police that contract. It will only make things worse for everyone!'

Lauren has had quite enough. She turns to leave in a squeak of rubber soles. 'I'm fetching Dr Droste. This shouting has to stop. We have a very sick patient in the room.'

Daniel is trying to manage the situation, trying to calm Dad. 'I'll call Jackson's Solicitors and get someone down to the police station straight away to help Janet.'

There's a bang outside, a firework exploding, and I think I hear you moan softly, but when I turn, you're still inanimate, still unaware of anything.

'It's me who'll need a solicitor. I'm going to end this.' Dad stands, bones cracking as he does so. 'I'm off to that police station to sort one or three things out.'

Daniel stands too. 'Hector, you can't go alone,' he says.

And then both men walk out of the hospital.

DAY 6

THURSDAY 6 NOVEMBER

22

Holly

It had been twelve hours of focused hard work, but as the sun rose, her shift was finally over. As she worked, Holly tried to forget about Innocence Lane, she made herself not wonder what Hector and Daniel had said to the police, and what had happened about Janet's arrest.

Jon said nothing about Holly's tardy arrival for the night shift, though she felt his questioning gaze. She set her shoulders back, kept her face neutral, keen to show him that she was the professional he believed her to be. She was shadowing him and Hilary again, and their first call came just after seven; a home birth that wasn't progressing, where the midwife had asked for assistance.

They found the woman pacing the hallway, breathing on an Entonox mouthpiece for dear life. Her husband, deathly pale and banished to the corner of the lounge, pleaded with his eyes for them to fix this and Holly went to speak with him. The whole house reeked of lavender, and scented candles burned on every surface. 'First-time mum,' the midwife whispered to them when they arrived. 'In her thirties. Wanted to do it the natural way.' She held up her index fingers to show them the quote marks she was putting around 'natural'.

'Leave it to me,' said Jon.

As it happened, the woman didn't need any persuasion – she was quite ready to abandon her plan and get a spinal block at the hospital. The husband was already blowing out the candles in relief.

Around eleven there was an inevitable call-out to a bonfire party. They treated a man for third-degree burns; he'd been hosting a display for his teenage grandchildren and had foolishly returned to an unexploded firework only to have it detonate in his face. His reddened skin would heal quicker than his pride.

In the early hours of the morning came one of the more common calls, a suspected heart attack, and luckily they were in time to stabilise the man, who was in his seventies and had already had a bypass.

As she clocked out at 7 a.m., Jon told her what a good job she'd done that night. She'd felt it too: in control and calm, she'd managed to keep her synaesthesia at bay. It was only as she was driving home that thoughts about Innocence Lane once again began to intrude. She saw the sign for Kenley and slowed down.

Leave it alone, she told herself. *The police are on it now, there's nothing for you to do. Go home and sleep!* But their focus on Janet felt instinctively wrong to her, how could they think that a woman who had devoted her life to the Hawke family could suddenly turn on her employer so violently? Hector had certainly implied that he had some new information for the police, and in the twelve hours since they left the hospital something would have happened. She needed to know what.

Minutes later, she pulled up outside Janet's cottage, not thinking through her actions, not even sure who would be here. There was a light on downstairs, so someone was awake. She parked her car and went to the front door, tapping lightly.

It slowly opened a crack and Holly saw Janet's pale face. She was home then.

'It's only me, Janet. I know it's early but I wanted to check you were okay? I heard what happened.'

The door opened further and Holly went in.

In the small front room, Janet returned to one end of the sofa, curling her small frame over as if her spine was broken, her face almost hidden on her chest. Holly sat beside her.

'Janet . . .' The woman may have been allowed to leave the police station but she had the haunted look of the condemned. Holly touched her leg, as if in support. Janet's fear was strong enough for Holly to feel it crawl beneath her skin. 'Where's Ash?'

'Still asleep,' she said, in a quiet voice. 'After he drove me home we stayed up talking, and he only fell asleep at about four. Poor boy, he's worried sick. We both are.'

'But the police have released you, so that's good?' She was fishing for information, and Janet moaned softly, not giving anything away. 'Ash said you were arrested because the police found your blood on the gun.'

Janet pulled her knees up, looking like a schoolgirl who'd been caught shoplifting, not someone capable of a violent shooting. 'I don't know – I can't remember ever touchin' it. When I arrived at the farm, Maya was at the bottom of the stairs. I didn't go any closer, I never went further than the kitchen.' Janet looked sheepish. Her voice was so low, Holly had to lean forward to hear.

'Did you see anyone with her?'

Janet hesitated, and Holly knew that whatever she said next was being revealed reluctantly. 'It's not a clear view from the kitchen to the back hallway, and it wasn't fully light. Maya was cryin', I could hear her. I couldn't see properly. I was afraid to get any closer. What could I do against someone with a gun? I ran and got Ash.'

Holly felt a wave of understanding wash over her: Janet knew exactly who was holding the gun. She was protecting somebody.

'Ash and me ran back to the farmhouse. 'Course, Ash is faster than me, so he ran ahead. He went straight in the house, regardless of who might be inside or if they was armed.' There was a flicker then of pride for her brave son that Holly felt to be completely genuine. Was she protecting her son, surely the most natural instinct in the world?

'And what did you see, inside the house?' Holly nudged her back to the story.

'Maya was lyin' at the bottom of the stairs, bleedin' from her head. So much blood . . . I was afraid she was dead, but Ash said she was breathin' – he was so much more with it than I was. And there was Hector's rifle, next to her. Ash went to pick it up, to get rid of it. I've seen it on TV, on *Broadchurch*, you shouldn't touch anythin', and I started shoutin' at him, pullin' it away, and the top of the sight, where the metal's rough, scratched my arm. It bled a bit – that must be how my blood got there.'

Holly watched the woman as she spoke, the way her eyes flicked up – the way they do when people are remembering something. Something true.

'So you're saying that Ash touched the rifle?' Holly asked, realising the significance of this: *his fingerprints.*

Janet sighed deeply, to the very bottom of her soul. 'Ash loves that family. He'd do anythin' for 'em.'

There was a hush in the room.

'Did you tell the police this, Janet?'

Janet blanched. 'I don't want to get my boy in trouble, and we just panicked. But they needed to know how my blood got on the gun, and this is the God's honest truth. I called the ambulance straight after – I just wanted to get help for Maya. My blood may be on that gun, but not for the reason they think.'

'I believe you, Janet. But what you're saying is that Ash wanted to remove the rifle. Was this to protect whoever did shoot Maya?'

A flush of colour rose to Janet's cheeks and something occurred to Holly, a premonition of sorts, a gut feeling she'd had before. Yes, Janet was protecting someone, but it wasn't her son.

'Janet, when I was at the hospital last night, Hector said he was going to the police station. Do you know what he told them?'

Tears welled in Janet's eyes and Holly saw love there, and fear. She remembered that Janet had fallen pregnant after a one-night stand and for the first time she wondered if Hector was Ash's father.

'Janet? What do you think Hector told the police?'

The housekeeper looked up, and her face revealed such protection and fierce love that Holly knew she wouldn't get an answer. Janet jutted her chin towards Holly.

'I don't need to tell you anythin'. You have no right to be here, or to ask me any questions. You left this village twenty years ago – you don't belong here no more.'

23

Cassandra

I can smell the flowers.

I can hear the air coming through my mouth, into me. A whoosh of freedom like, oh, like breathing.

I'm breathing, and I hear it, and it's wonderful.

And then I feel the shot, sinking into my flesh just above my heart. I'm just twelve years old and someone has shot me. I tell myself it's a memory, that it's over, but the pain is intense and my breathing isn't easy any more.

'Cass!'

There are hands on me, someone is talking from a long way off. It's me, the voice is talking about me. I'm awake and in a bed and I can breathe.

I fall down the stairs, the gun under my neck. I have to tell them. I open my eyes, but I can't speak. I'm on the wet grass, I'm cold. It's not safe and I begin to scream.

'Cass! It's okay. You were dreaming.'

Daniel. Pale yellow light is cast from the morning sun and I can make out his face, I smell him. He's fully dressed, but dishevelled, and then I remember: he left me last night, he went with Dad to the police station.

'What's happened, Dan?'

'You need to be strong, love. Your dad won't be coming home.'

It was just a bad dream. No, it was a memory.

And then Daniel tells me what's happened. What Dad has told the police, that he's been locked up.

I am awake and the nightmare isn't over after all.

24

Holly

Holly was woken by an insistent rapping on her front door. She reached for her alarm clock and saw it was midday, she had only slept for four hours. She pulled herself from the warmth of her bed and padded to the front door. Leif stood there, in his police uniform.

'I know who shot Maya,' he said, before he'd even got inside her flat. 'I've just done a morning's shift and it's all anyone is talking about.'

She needed to breathe, space to think through all that Janet had told her, but here was Leif with more news, any fears he'd had of breaching confidentiality gone with his enthusiasm.

'He confessed. It'll be in the evening papers so I don't tell you anything that you won't know in a few hours.'

'Okay,' she said. 'Tell me.'

Late yesterday evening Hector and Daniel had arrived at the police station, determined to see the officer in charge. Bedraggled and bowed, his left hand nursing his right, Hector had waited patiently for the police detective to find him and lead him down to an interview room. Gone, Leif said, was the farmer's physical toughness. Without his bluster, he simply looked like a man out of his mind with worry.

Leif said that the room had been crowded, everyone watching the screen as the interview played out.

'Would you like to speak with a solicitor, Mr Hawke?' he was asked.

'Nope. You can just listen.'

'First, I'm going to read you your rights.'

As he was cautioned, Hector seemed to straighten up, to push his shoulders back, as though preparing himself for battle.

'Okay, Mr Hawke,' the detective asked. 'What is it you'd like to say?'

Hector crossed his arms on the table and leaned forward, pushing his bad hand into his chest as if hiding it. Leif said Hector hadn't looked like he'd had much sleep recently.

'You interviewed my boy and you've had Janet in here too – you think one of 'em shot Maya. But you're wrong. Janet keeps the farmhouse goin', as she allus has, especially back when the kids were babies. The blood on the gun *is* Janet's. But not because she's guilty.'

'How did it get there, then?' the detective asked.

'Janet and Ash, they both held the rifle that mornin'. There was a struggle and Janet got scratched. That's how she came to bleed. But she was protectin' Maya from *me*. I pushed Maya down the stairs, then I got the rifle from the cupboard, which was already open on account of me not lockin' it after the shoot. I went down the stairs, loadin' the gun as I did. Then I put the muzzle under her chin and I shot her. And I didn't know what I'd done until Daniel woke me.'

The detective, Leif said, was puzzled. So was everyone watching.
'Until he *woke* you?'

'I was sleepwalkin', see. I shot Maya, but I was asleep.'

Having told her his burning news, Leif moved into her kitchen like it
was his own. 'Shall I make us some lunch?' he asked, then noticed her
pyjamas. 'Or, in your case, breakfast?'

'That'd be great,' she said, trying to sound normal, though her
thoughts were reeling. Hector shot Maya, but in his sleep. She certainly
hadn't seen that coming, but her instincts with Janet had been right:
she and Ash had worked together to protect someone they loved. It was
over then, the mystery was solved.

Relief made her giddy, lack of sleep made her impulsive. As Leif
stood at the hob scrambling eggs, she wrapped her arms around him,
wanting to lose herself in the moment, relying on only her most basic
human senses and forgetting all else.

Later, physical appetites sated, they lay together on the bed, arms
and legs entwined in the relaxing aftermath of sex, Holly felt content-
ment calm her senses like balm. She stroked the side of Leif's face and
snuggled closer to kiss him. It was his acceptance of her, the ease she
felt with him, that made her open up in a way she never had before.

'Leif, there's something I need to tell you, something that's wrong
with me. You might want to run a mile . . .' she began, as his eyes registered alarm.

He sat up, so he could see her face, and said so tenderly she wanted
to cry, 'Are you ill, *Sötnos?*'

'No, nothing like that. It's more a way I have of seeing things.'

She told him, as well as she could, of how the world seemed to her;
how he was the colour yellow. She felt lighter, as if a burden had been
removed from her shoulders.

'For certain you're lucky!' he said. 'Your senses are completely attuned – this is what I try to do with films. I try and engage all my senses, but often I fail.'

Although she knew her synaesthesia could sometimes be a gift, she was still surprised at how positively Leif viewed it. 'It's not all roses, Leif. I sometimes can't stand it . . . I avoid the news, and TV. Some days all I want to do is sit in this flat and stare at a blank wall.'

'*Ja*, you need some time off from it, of course. It sounds intense,' agreed Leif. 'But this also makes you very special, *Sötnos*. You could be an artist or a film-maker, seeing the world in such an extraordinary way.'

She was silent for a moment. 'One of my supervisors at work said he could arrange for me to have an MRI scan so they can look at how my brain reacts to stimuli. I've said no.'

Leif sat up on one elbow. 'Why, Holly? It's exciting to know more about ourselves. And you are a rare specimen. Let them study you.'

And he began, then, to study her himself, with his gentle hands and warm lips, and all she saw was the colour yellow.

When Leif left, Holly switched on her mobile and saw she'd had several missed calls, all from the same number. She listened to her voice messages, and realised they were all from Alfie Avon. He too had heard about Hector's confession – the police had just released a statement. And he wanted to know what more she knew, what she could add. Unsure herself, given the police had his confession, she sent a text saying she would come to his office.

Alfie Avon led Holly through a room packed with reporters, their desks divided off by screens. Now Hector had confessed and been charged, the atmosphere was electric with hard-won sweat and the sweet anticipation of success. Small groups of adrenaline-fuelled journalists huddled together, their urgent conversations buzzing around the room. For a town like Ipswich, a case like this was big news.

Alfie's cubicle was lined with clippings about the shooting on Innocence Lane and, she saw with surprise, features on Daniel when he'd been discussing Samphire Studios or his radio show. Alfie was as obsessed by the case as she was. On his desk lay a line of photos. 'Bit of a surprise, this,' he said, his hands deep in his pockets as he leaned back on battered Converse baseball boots, 'but then it usually is the husband.'

Holly edged into the cubicle, and Alfie slid a buttock onto the one part of the table that was clear of papers, gallantly offering her the only chair. He watched her sit, then said, 'I've seen your face before. You were one of the paramedics at the farm that morning – one of the team took a snap of you as you drove away with Cassandra.'

Whatever criticisms people might level against Alfie, inattention was surely not one. 'That's right, though I'm only a student. Not qualified yet.'

'Still,' he said, leaning forward and showing too much teeth and gums, 'you were actually in the house with the victim. What was that like?'

'Bloody,' she said, not thinking this was giving too much away.

From where she sat, she had a direct view of the information tacked to Alfie's noticeboard, which also served as a divider between desks. Everything on the board, all six feet square of it, related to Innocence Lane. Dominating it was a line of photos, presumably taken by Alfie or his colleagues. The first showed Janet emerging from the police station: her brown hair was scraped back and her face was pale; she looked like a startled mouse. Next came a distance shot of Ash, driving his tractor, blissfully unaware he was being photographed: lanky hair, brown puppy eyes, slightly vacant. In this photo, Hector and Cassandra were walking together towards the hospital. Together, maybe, but they weren't talking, and their bodies were slightly turned away from each other. It was like seeing a picture of two people heading to the same meeting, yet they were father and daughter – surely they should have been supporting each other?

Her eyes drifted to the next image, which wasn't a photo at all, but a postcard – one designed to hand out to fans with an autograph; it had the Radio Suffolk logo in the corner. Here was Daniel, handsome and confident, local celebrity and healer. Daniel had groomed hair, skin that glowed from many facials, a smile that was warm and generous. She'd been in close proximity with him many times now, yet the photo shifted something in her thoughts. Fixated by that smile, she was aware that her body temperature was cooling. She wrapped her arms around herself, wishing she'd worn a jumper over her shirt. Her senses crowded in on her, rotten smells and unpleasant static in her ears. She just wanted it to stop.

Alfie followed her gaze. 'That cunt. Have you met him?'

She nodded, unwilling to be drawn into conversation and be distracted from her chattering senses. She tried to rationalise her growing unease, which made no sense.

Breaking into her thoughts, Alfie said, 'So, what is it you have to tell me? In strict confidence, of course. Think of me as a very badly paid doctor.'

She didn't answer, couldn't: she wanted to feel the relief she had experienced earlier, when she first heard that Hector had confessed. But somehow it had ebbed away and instead her senses were pinging with doubts, what she felt about Daniel especially couldn't be articulated. It was her synaesthesia guiding her, not evidence.

'Come on, love, you know something or you wouldn't be here. You don't think the old man did it, do you?'

He gave himself an indulgent moment to study her face, though she steeled herself not to reveal anything. She shouldn't have come – what did she think she was playing at? Contacting Alfie Avon, the most notorious reporter on the local paper, relentless in his quest for news, and vicious with it. He was something of a local hero, and prided himself on exposing scandals.

'Okay,' he said, with a theatrical sigh, 'since you can't bring yourself to talk, I'll tell you something. Hector Hawke didn't shoot his wife, I'd stake my life on it. I've been onto The Samphire Master for three years now, and I think he's as crook as they come. Claims he can cure people, persuading them to quit conventional treatment – and no one else seems to see through him. But now there's this shooting of his mother-in-law, the very woman he uses to prove what a miracle-worker he is.'

Holly couldn't help seeing the photos as a badly shuffled deck of cards – with Daniel's photo as the joker in the pack. 'Why do you hate him so much?' she asked.

Alfie fell silent, the anger around him evaporated and sadness took over. Stronger, harder to control, she felt him buckle under its weight as he tried to locate his fury, where he felt happier. Then he pointed to a photo she hadn't noticed before: an old family picture, dog-eared at the corners but lovingly straightened and pinned to the board. It showed a toddler taking early steps. She was reaching out as she walked, gummy-mouthed, but with the most gorgeous mass of black hair springing around her sweet face. Behind her, a pretty black woman was poised to support her daughter, her face lit with happiness at the special moment that the camera had captured.

'Because my wife was one of his clients.'

The door to Clive's office was open. He acknowledged her with a warm smile. 'Afternoon, Holly. Everything okay?'

She took the seat opposite him, and folded her arms on his desk, desperate for some clarity. 'I want you to explain to me, how can someone fire a gun in their sleep?'

'Ah, so you've heard the news too?' Clive said. 'Well, the legal definition is non-insane automatism, when someone has no conscious knowledge of their actions.' He was wearing a slightly smarter jacket than usual, in brown tweed, but it was still baggy at the elbows and his red-and-yellow-striped school-style tie had what looked like a toothpaste stain. Behind his round glasses, his eyes were bright with intelligence and understanding. 'Sleepwalkers have been known to commit violent attacks – there are several documented cases – but whether that's happened here would need to be assessed.'

'Oh.' Holly appraised him anew: not only did he look smarter, there was an energy about him. 'Will you be doing that?'

'Hector Hawke has been remanded into custody and it's likely court will ask for a medical report. I'm the duty psychiatrist for the court. So, Holly, does this bring you some peace?'

She almost flinched, it was so far from the sensations she was feeling. 'Why would it?'

'Because yesterday you were worried that the police weren't doing their jobs. They obviously were.'

Holly wished she could find peace, but her synaesthesia wouldn't let her be. First it had told her this wasn't a suicide attempt, now she wasn't convinced by Hector's sleepwalking explanation. She felt that the only way to control her senses, and to find relief, was to find answers.

'Clive, you're right: this case really has interested me. I was thinking sleep disorders may be what I choose to focus on for my final case study. I'd like to know more about it.'

'That seems a good idea. If Hector Hawke's report comes my way, you could shadow me. Would you like that?'

What could she say, but yes?

DAY 7

FRIDAY 7 NOVEMBER

25

Cassandra

I don't want Daniel to leave me, especially after what's happened, but he has to go to work. I'm still trying to make sense of Dad's confession when the phone makes me jump.

'Miss Hawke?'

The voice is unfamiliar, plummy and exaggerating every vowel and consonant. I'm immediately wary.

'Speaking.'

'This is Rupert Jackson, your father's solicitor. As you probably know, your father has been remanded to custody. I've got a slot on Monday for a hearing, so I'll be asking the court to bail him so he can attend the necessary sleep tests. It'll be damned awkward if they have to take him to hospital in a prison van, cuffed to an officer. I can rely on you to attend, to support his bail application? I don't think I have a hope in hell without you.'

Even if he was asleep, he's still guilty of shooting you and he was prepared to let everyone think you'd tried to kill yourself. 'No, I won't be there.'

'Hmm, your father thought you'd say that. The old boy wants to talk to you, wants you to go to Norwich Prison today. A visiting order is waiting at the gate.'

Norwich Prison. To see that bastard. I remember him sleepwalking, moving around the house at night, him walking in the woods in only pyjamas. But loading a gun, firing it, and all while asleep . . . I don't believe it's possible. 'No. I won't do it. He shot my mum – he could have killed her.'

'Miss Hawke, if I may? Your parents have been married for a long time. I've met a lot of cold-hearted men who hurt their wives and, believe me, I don't think your father is one of them. A man like him doesn't belong in prison. He'd be best at home with you. Please go and see him. He's on the hospital wing at Norwich Prison.'

'Why isn't he on a normal wing?' He didn't seem ill to me when I saw him marching out of your hospital room. He's strong and fit – even the stroke didn't slow him down.

'He's a good three decades older than the average inmate and he had a stroke last year, plus there's the strain he's under. Oh yes, he gave me a message to pass on. Could you take in a suit for him to wear in court? And some money for cigarettes.'

Norwich Prison is ugly.

A Victorian building, surviving sibling of the workhouse and asylum. Tall walls made from brick the colour of burning coal, an outsize doorway wedged into a daunting portcullis. How many people have walked through here, abandoning faith or hope? I ring the bell and a small door opens within the massive one, like the entry to some hellish wonderland. Only there's no white rabbit behind it, but a burly man with a shaved head, wearing a white shirt with service epaulettes.

'Yes?'

'I'm here to visit Hector Hawke.'

He turns back in to the prison, closing the door on me without a word. I'm not sure what to do and begin to walk away, when it reopens and he calls, 'Wrong side, love. You want the hospital wing, over there.'

I follow where his thick finger points, across the car park.

This part of the prison is newer. It's a lower-roofed building with a fence topped by barbed wire. This time, there's no massive door, but instead a Portakabin office. Inside, it's cramped, and behind a glass screen two uniformed guards are chatting over a copy of the *Sun*. I spy a wall of keys on hooks, rows of black key fobs, each with a number. I speak through a grille, and one of them turns; he's young, barely twenty, still spotty.

'I'm here to visit my father, Hector Hawke.'

He comes to the window. 'Got your VO?'

I shake my head in confusion. 'What's that?'

'Visiting Order, love.' He shouldn't call me love, not at his age, but he's enjoying his power here. 'You got one?'

'No. My dad's solicitor called me. He asked me to come.'

He pulls a clipboard from its hook, and I see it's a list. He runs his index finger down it. 'Name?'

'Er, Jackson. Rupert Jackson.'

The guard looks irritated, but really, he's showing off to his colleague who's stopped looking at the paper to watch. '*Your* name.'

'Cassandra Hawke.'

His finger stops. 'Got some ID, have you?'

The guard reluctantly stamps the clipboard, his moment over. He releases the first door so I can walk through and, like a rat being forced into a maze, I'm buzzed through a series of locked doors, taken down one way, then another, at each corner a camera eyeing my progress. Finally, a female prison officer with spiky purple hair waits to usher me under a detecting arch like they have in airports, and I'm stroked with a probe, which beeps and flashes red.

She asks dully, 'Got any money, keys, a phone?'

I have – all three – and she sighs wearily as she takes them from me and puts them into a metal locker, handing me the key. I imagine all visitors disappoint her like this. She leads me across a square of grass and into the squat hospital unit. It's like a game, where each stage takes you to another level, but you're not quite sure what the rules are. She doesn't say a word as she unlocks doors by a key attached by a chain to her belt. I walk past, then she locks it behind us. I understand that I'm barely visible to her, like a car being directed around a car park by a bored attendant.

Finally, we're in the hospital wing. The name is a lie: hospitals have white walls, plastic floors, clean antiseptic smells. Here, the entrance is a barred gate, opening onto a dark corridor, leading to another gate. Along the corridor, two inmate-patients in poorly fitting denim jeans and dark-red T-shirts – they must be freezing – are half-heartedly sweeping with brooms. The younger one, who looks about eighteen and has arms like pipe cleaners, scans me up and down and whistles, and finally the officer becomes human. 'Quit it, Smith,' she says. Smith clamps his mouth shut, but his eyes still appraise me.

The next room is for visits. It's a large, cold room with bars at the window. Several tables are set in lines. Fixed plastic chairs in dull green and grey face each other across the desks – in a nicer setting, they could be picnic tables. On a platform is another desk where an officer sits, making notes in a ledger. As I walk towards it, my shoes stick to the filthy floor, making a peeling noise. The officer looks up, barely sees me, looks down at his list. He has a shaved head, developed biceps and a bored expression. 'Who are you visiting, love?'

'Hector Hawke.'

He points with his bitten pen to a table in the middle of the hall and a grey plastic chair. 'That seat there. He'll be brought down.'

The purple-haired officer who escorted me shares a joke with her colleague – I think it's about Smith and me, but I could be wrong – then she disappears without a word. Job done. The chair is fixed too low and moulded for a larger body than mine. I scan the room, but there's nothing to look at but tables, chairs and the bored officer. Nothing to do but wait.

'Did you bring the suit?'

Dad has the words out before he's even taken his seat. I look him square in the face and wonder how he can be so unchanged. I'd expected him to look like a monster, at least have thought his first word would be *sorry*. But he's the same, just Dad. I can't believe he shot you, no matter how angry he was about the farm. He loves you – I've never doubted that.

'Cass, you listenin'? Where's me suit?'

'I didn't bring it.' I've driven for over an hour, been searched and escorted through this maze like a convict, and all he wants to know is if I ran his errand. As if his confession hasn't rocked my world on its axis.

The officer on the raised platform glances over, lifts his pen and notes something down, then folds his arms and settles his face to a blank, his eyes fixed on the far wall. This must be how the officers cope with being paid to sit, watch and listen, trying not to look too interested. Perhaps if he pulled up a chair and sat beside us, it would make the meeting between Dad and me easier.

'I hope you at least brought some cash – I'm all out of smokes.' He glances up at me. 'Don't say it, girl! You'd smoke too, in here.'

Do you remember, Mum, how you nagged him to give up smoking after he had the stroke, but it was the consultant who really put the wind up him, telling him he'd be dead in a year unless he did. If he'd been right, you wouldn't have been shot.

He keeps his bad hand close to his body and nods to the officer. One thing about Dad, he's a survivor.

The purple-haired officer returns with another escort, smirking at the visits officer as though she's won a prize. The woman beside her wears a painted smile, her blouse is silky and scarlet, she gives her name in a small voice. The visits officer is charmed, winks at his colleague, not even bothering to hide it from the woman, whom he directs to the table next to ours. As she sits, I breathe in her heady floral perfume. My father leans in, and I think, *Finally, he will explain.*

'You came, at least. I wasn't sure you would.'

'I didn't want to.'

The woman is removing something – a bit of fluff? – from her cleavage. The visits officer behind the desk has noticed too. I lean forward, and look Dad in the eye. Those same eyes – all my life I've been able to read them. And I can't see any malice there, nothing different that tells me this man shot my mother.

'Is it really true, Dad?'

He stares back at me with his flat grey eyes. 'Why would I lie? You think I want to be here?'

'Is it true that you were *asleep*?' I can't believe he shot you, but I find it even harder to believe he did it in his sleep.

There's a pained silence. The woman and the officer have heard my question, but I don't care. I just need an answer. His face slackens, and I see weakness for the first time. He didn't have to confess – doing so cost him his freedom. Since that morning, I've been the only one to say that you didn't shoot yourself, and no one believed me. Only Holly, everyone else told me I was in shock, that I was wrong, that I was crazy: Clive, Daniel, even the police. And Dad let this happen, only confessing when his beloved Ash, and Janet, came under scrutiny.

'Are you really doing all this to protect *them*?'

He reacts to that: colour comes to his cheeks. He breathes deeply, then says, 'Sleepwalkers aren't responsible for what they do, Cass. Don't you remember one Boxin' Day, I went out with the hunt? That night I dreamed I were still ridin' a horse over a very high hedge? I jumped out of the window, fell straight down, almost killed meself.'

I do remember – more than once he was found wandering around the farmland, unsure of how he got there. 'But that was years ago, Dad.'

'It was a few times, I fell from the window. 'Sides, that don't matters how rare it happen, do it? Fact is, you can't blame someone for what they do – they're not responsible if they're asleep.'

'How fucking convenient,' I hiss, and he catches his breath. I can see he's about to swear or say something vicious, and then he stops himself. If we were at the farm, he'd be storming off towards the barns to vent his frustration on the chickens. Then he reaches for my hand, grabs it. He's squeezing, stopping the blood flow, his eyes boring into the very heart of me.

'I love your mother and I love you. And I'm sorry this has happened, but I can't go turnin' back the clock. So let me fix it, okay?'

I pull my hand free. It's not us he was thinking about when he confessed, it was Ash and Janet, I'm sure of it. 'If it's true, what you say, why didn't you tell the police that morning? Why now?'

An inmate arrives, dazed, like he's woken from a long sleep. Even without the burgundy T-shirt and poorly fitting jeans, he has the defeated gait of a prisoner. His shoulders are hunched and his eyes rove in their sockets. He shuffles towards us, sniffing the air as if pulled onward by the woman's perfume. He stumbles as he passes my father, and I'm surprised to hear him mumble, 'Hector, my man.'

'Toby.' My father nods in recognition as Toby lowers himself to the chair, seemingly surprised to find his weight supported. He's impervious to the lipstick kisses of his visitor – on his cheek, not his lips. They resemble each other: brother and sister.

'Place is full of lunatics,' my father says, not quietly.

'Aren't you one, then? Shooting Mum in your sleep sounds pretty crazy to me.'

I can't sensor myself, I'm so fucking angry. This is what's crazy: to be told you're delusional, then to discover that the people closest to you lied. My dad in prison, my mum in a coma. I don't know who to turn to. Even Daniel's treating me like I'm unwell. Only Holly listened.

'You can call it crazy if you like. But what it ain't is cruel.' I think for a moment he might cry.

Beside us, Toby places his hands on the desk and his sister cups them, steadies them, and in that moment our eyes meet. She smiles sadly, reaching out for a female connection in this dreadful place. To feel less alone. She's a healthy, fleshier version of her brother – how he might be if he weren't here, drug-addled and criminally inclined. They have similar mouths. Hers is smiling at me and I want to smile back, but my face muscles ignore me. Her eyes go cold and she turns back to her brother.

Dad taps my wrist with his cupped right hand and I flinch. 'You met my solicitor then?'

'I spoke with him on the phone. It was him who made me come.'

'I reckon if Rupert Jackson can't get me out of here, no one can. 'Course, you pay extra for the plummy voice, but that's what these judges respect. Daniel found him.'

The sister has started to cry, mascara running down her cheeks. Her brother is slumped into his seat, oblivious. 'You need help!' Her voice is shockingly loud after all the whispering.

The officer's body engages faster than his eyes, and he pulls himself up. The woman shouts at him, 'Do you hear that? Toby shouldn't be in here! He should be in a hospital. A proper one. Anyone can see he's sick.'

The guard, assessing the situation as safe, relaxes again. 'Him and everyone else in here, love.' He returns to reading the *Daily Mail*. He's obviously heard it all before and it isn't his problem.

'So you gonna get me out of here then, girl?' Dad's voice is strung low, but his eyes fix me hard. The fingers of his left hand, thick and strong, cradle his weakened right arm. 'I need to get my bail on Monday, but that rests with you. So you gonna be on my side?'

'Is it true, Dad, you really shot her?' I ask, but weakly now. My fire has gone. All that remains is sadness. 'You tried to kill Mum?'

'No, of course not! How can you even ask that? I love Maya! And you, Cass.'

I never heard him say that word before today and now he's said it twice. He leans forward and says it again, as if it's the only thing that makes sense.

'I was *asleep*. Do you get that, girl? *I love you.*'

Once I'm out of the prison, I know I can't go home. Not yet.

I've gone from confusion to anger to sadness and I feel dangerously vulnerable, emotions pulling me in different directions. When Dad said he loved me, it should have been a precious moment – it was something I never thought I'd hear – but instead it feels like a responsibility. Like he was trying to tell me something.

Because it's where I always go when I'm hurt, like an animal retreating to its burrow, I drive to the farm. Even with the car windows up, I can smell the clay earth seeping in through the vents, the scenery is flat and the sky is huge and this is where I belong.

The farmhouse door is unlocked. Janet is here. I want to be alone, but she's on her knees, scrubbing the wood at the bottom of the stairs, a bucket of soapy water next to her. My mind reels back to Friday, and I feel again the desolation of that day – how alone I felt, how you didn't comfort me. I want all trace of that day removed.

'What are you doing here, Janet?'

She yelps at my voice, twists to see who's there, eyes wide with fear. 'Oh, Cass! You gave me the fright of my life.'

'Why did the police let you go?' My voice is harsh and accusing, but I don't care. And Janet has the decency to look ashamed.

''Cos of your dad's confession and how I'm co-operatin', they give me bail.'

I don't respond, don't know how to. Did Dad confess to protect Janet? The police have shifted their focus, of course, but I'm not sure that I have. Her blood was still on the gun – his confession came only when the police became interested in her.

'I need to collect something for Dad.'

'Oh, have you been up to the prison?' She stops her work, and sits back on her heels. Her face is full of concern. 'How is he?'

'Coping. He wants a suit to wear at the bail hearing.'

'Oh, well, Ash can take it to the courthouse first thing on Monday, that would be no bother. It's important Hector is smart.' Janet looks hopeful, as if this is just a mix-up that will be sorted out soon. 'Then your dad'll be back where he belongs, and so will your mum, and I'll look after 'em both, just like I always have.'

Everyone is at pains to tell me how they're trying to help, how their intentions come from a place of love.

So how did you end up being shot?

Upstairs, I run a hot shower and scrub the stench of the prison from my body, leaving my skin a satisfying red. Finally clean, I don't want to put my clothes back on. They stink of incarceration.

In your bedroom, the bed has been made with fresh sheets, and the room smells of air freshener and Pledge. Your pale-blue quilted dressing gown is hanging behind the door and I put it on, buttoning it down the front as you used to. You're slimmer than me and there's a pull around my hips, small differences that went unnoticed, but now seem important.

I want to know everything, Mum – all our similarities, all our differences. I'm clinging to that, because everything is changing around me and I don't know what the truth is. Was Dad really asleep when he shot you? If so, why not say that from that first moment when he awoke – why work so hard to conceal it?

I approach your dressing table. I remove, lift, examine. Learn about you as a woman, as a wife. I should have paid more attention. I discover you're on HRT tablets and that you're the same bra size as me. I find a box of hair colour and realise it isn't true that you don't have any grey. I discover jewellery I've never seen you wear, and all the time I try to make sense of how Dad could have shot you in his sleep.

Finding no answers, I pad across to your study. I see that Janet has been busy here too, there's no longer any sign of disturbance. It looks ready for you to walk in and start work; I half expect you to. This is where you spend most of your waking hours, running the farm like a general. I sit in your chair, gingerly – this would be forbidden if you were here. I open the drawer, a further transgression, the long one directly in front of me. It's empty, but this only spurs me on. I begin to search all of the drawers, and then I move to the filing cabinet and begin again. I know the police have searched, I don't know what I'm hoping to find.

There's the box file entitled *Samphire Health Spa*.

It was your idea originally. You were so thankful that Daniel had healed you, the farmhouse would be your gift to him. I open the box, and there's the planning permission that was granted. Beneath it, the folded design, drawn up on architect's paper in thin black ink. I open it, and see the sketch of the front of the farmhouse, with a new glass extension to the side. Also on the drawing, where our barn stands, is a swimming pool complex with palms and sunbeds and a gym area. I'm holding an idea, a dream, one that united the three of us. We could all have been so happy, but no, you went and changed your mind.

I see the name and details of the architect and pick up the phone extension on the desk to dial the number. He deserves to know.

'Ross King Designs.' It's a male voice, friendly.

'Hi, I'm calling about the design that you drew up for Samphire Health Spa on the Innocence Farm estate in Kenley?'

'Ah yes, I worked on that myself. This is Ross speaking. How can I help?'

'I'm Cassandra Hawke. My partner is Daniel Salmon.'

'Ah yes. Mr Salmon commissioned the plans, so I'm afraid I can only discuss the details with someone else if he gives me his permission.'

'It's okay, there's nothing to discuss. I just thought you should know it won't be going ahead. The farm is being sold to create a lorry depot for the Port Authority.'

'I'm sorry?' There's a pause, a rustling of paper.

'The farm estate belongs to my mother, Maya Hawke, and she's agreed to sell it to the Port Authority.' I wonder how I can sound so calm, saying these words aloud, when this is the end of my dream.

'I'm afraid there must be a mistake. Mr Salmon has authorised us to proceed and even paid a significant deposit. We've already instructed builders that work on the barn will commence later this month.'

'That must have been before last Friday, when everything changed.'

I can hear him taking a sharp breath in surprise. 'Mr Salmon didn't mention anything changing when I saw him on Saturday.'

'*Saturday?*'

'Yes, he came in to finalise the plans and to pay the retainer on 1 November. Is Mr Salmon there – perhaps I should speak with him?'

'I'm sure it's my mistake. Please forget I called.'

I disconnect the phone and see something clearly, for the first time. A realisation, something that's been festering inside me, but I can finally articulate: I've struggled to believe Dad's story that he shot you in his sleep. Even the timing of his confession looks like he's protecting someone else – I'd assumed it was Ash and Janet. What if I'm wrong? What if the person Dad is protecting is Daniel?

The phone rings again, and I stare at the handset, startled. It's as though someone has heard my thoughts, and is calling to chastise me.

The ringing continues, then stops. Then I hear Janet's voice, a distant murmur, and realise she has picked up the extension downstairs.

There's a cry, my name is being called. Quick feet on the stairs, coming up, and I know that whatever she's going to tell me, I don't want to hear. A premonition, a correct one.

Janet stands there in the study doorway, her hands still gripping the handset. Her eyes are wet, and her mouth is agape.

'It's Daniel,' she says, before I can silence her. 'He's at the hospital. Oh God, Cass. Your mum is dead.'

DAY 8

SATURDAY 8 NOVEMBER

26

Holly

Since dawn, Holly's shift had been taken over by one case: a seven-year-old with asthma.

She and Jon had arrived in the ambulance to find the boy puffing on his blue inhaler, anxious grandparents bickering nearby over whether or not to call his parents, who were enjoying a weekend break to the Lake District – their first trip away without their son.

'The cat got in the bedroom last night and slept on the bed,' said the grandmother, clearly blaming herself. 'We gave Ethan a Piriton as soon as he woke up wheezing. Oh God, what will his mum say? She warned me about his allergy.'

'I wouldn't call them yet, if I was you,' Jon said, clipping the mask of a nebuliser to Ethan's face. 'Wait until things are calm, which they will be very shortly.' The grandparents looked visibly relieved, and their smiles returned as the asthma attack ebbed. But Holly knew that the paperwork generated by a case took as long as the medical process, and she'd only just finished writing up the notes when it was time to clock off.

She was still logged on to the main hospital computer. The search box blinked at her invitingly. It was a sackable offence to use the computer to search for information you had no right to access – there could be serious problems if staff chose to look up neighbours and relatives at whim. *But*, she told herself, *I'm just checking on Maya's progress. I'm already involved: I was on the initial call-out. I have a right to know.*

It was a lie – she knew it even as she sent the name MAYA HAWKE into the depths of the computer system, and especially when she opened the returning file from the oncology department. There was the scan picture, and the radiographer's report: stage-three cancer. And the opinion of the specialist: *Cancer has now spread to the lymph glands. Prognosis is not favourable.*

Holly closed down the computer, feeling ashamed of herself, but still her interest was unsated. So much for The Samphire Master and his miracles. No wonder Maya had changed her mind about the Spa.

She decided to stop by Maya's room, but when she arrived on the ward, the door was shut, the blind discreetly down, and Lauren approached quickly.

'Oh, Holly, sad news. I'm afraid we've lost her.'

Holly hadn't expected this – it hit her in the gut. 'I thought Maya was off the critical list?'

'She was: we'd classified her as stable. But with head injuries, the prognosis can change quickly. She went into cardiac arrest and we couldn't save her . . .' The nurse tailed off and looked back towards the nurses' station. If an asthma attack caused a mound of paperwork, Lauren must be facing a mountain.

'Was anyone with her?'

'Just Daniel. He's been so good. I heard him on the phone to Cassandra, telling her, and I've never heard a man be so comforting. I wish I had that knack. I dreaded phoning the prison to tell Maya's husband, but he had to be told.'

'How did Hector take it?'

'No idea, they wouldn't let me speak to him directly. They said they'd pass on the message. Can you imagine anything more cold?'

'Well, this is now a murder case, which changes everything,' Alfie said.

The newsroom was quieter today, with just a few reporters finishing off features for the Saturday-evening edition of the *Daily Post*. Alfie was perched on the corner of his desk in his cubicle, his sleeves rolled up to show his tattoos, munching a sausage roll and spraying crumbs all over the table. He grinned, showing where food had caught in his teeth.

'I don't think you should be celebrating. A woman has died,' she said softly. *When does a woman's death cease to be tragic? How many wrinkles, how many years does she need to live before her passing no longer garners any sympathy?*

Alfie had the decency to look abashed. 'I know, it's tragic. But the public have a right to know what's going on in their backyard, and if I'm quick I can get this on this evening's front page. The police have Hawke's confession, but things could change now Maya's dead. The stakes are higher.'

'Alfie, you've covered a lot of crime, are you certain Hector isn't telling the truth?' Holly asked, genuinely curious. 'The psychiatrist at the hospital says it is possible for him to have shot her in his sleep. And the police believe it, or he wouldn't be locked up.'

'Ah well, now, that's not exactly true. The police will be waiting to see if the CPS are happy to proceed to trial. Given they have a bang-to-rights confession, they'll be hoping to close this case – neater stats, less heat from the press, cheaper budget. And he's got a bail hearing on Monday so he may not be locked up for long. You want my personal opinion? I don't think it's the old man. I think The Samphire Man stinks to high heaven, and I'm sick of the way no one else can see it.'

He dusted crumbs from his trousers, a gesture that said he was done. But Holly wasn't.

'Alfie, I'm beginning to think you could be right. I've found something . . .'

'Evidence?'

'Not exactly. And I can't go to the police with it: I've broken my code of ethics to get it.' What she was doing now was her act of karma, a desire to do the right thing. This was her curse – her senses would forever stop her from doing an uncomplicated job. She would forever feel layers and implications that would at best distract and at worst derail her. And that was why she couldn't go to the police with this. She needed Alfie to take the information she had no right to have, and do something with it. 'Alfie, I looked up Maya's hospital medical records. If I was found out, I'd lose my training position for certain.'

'Tut tut,' he said. 'Naughty girl. Okay, so what did you find?'

'You were right, Daniel hadn't cured Maya. A recent scan confirmed her cancer was level three. She'd only just been told.'

'Level three, in her lymph nodes,' said Alfie, no longer with any glee. 'His career would be down the pan with a revelation like that. I owe you one, Holly – you've just given me a scoop.'

'And it's a perfect motive, isn't it,' she said, 'for murder.'

27

Cassandra

Can I still talk to you, now you're gone?

Oh, Mum. Can you hear?

You didn't always hear me when we were in the same room – it was always your voice that dominated. Now you're dead, mine is the only voice. I imagine you listening and feel closer to you than ever.

Daniel's back at the hospital, organising everything that needs to be done, whatever that means. Undertakers, I assume, though this is a criminal case so maybe he's speaking with the police too. I don't want to be there, with your lifeless body. Your spirit has left its shell, it's with me now. Dear Mum.

I need to be where there is life and warm love.

I need my child and she needs to be home.

At the Shell garage just before the Orwell Bridge, I pump the car with petrol, then settle into the journey to Norfolk, not to the prison this time but to the coast, though my hands are slick on the steering wheel. My palms are sweating, my heart is palpitating – grief is getting to me. I try to fill myself with your strength. You were always so sure of yourself, and I'd love a dose of your resilience now.

I'm dressed in what's become my daily uniform: a denim skirt from Fat Face and a thin jumper – comfortable clothes for a vigil beside a hospital bed in an overly warm room, but not suitable for Oakfield. I should go home and change into a dress and heels. I know you'd do this in my place, but I don't have the energy.

Warm air spews from the vents, the only sound the ticking of the indicator as I overtake the car in front. Clouds scud low over orange fields, puffy as cotton wool, wet at the edges – like the dampened balls I used when Victoria was a baby, piled into an igloo by the side of the top-and-tail bowl as I washed her. The clouds hold weight, I can see that, dark with rain that will surely come.

I drive on in the warm silence of my own company. I can't cope with the inane chatter of local radio: I usually have it tuned ready for Daniel's show, but I switch it off and listen to the rumble of tyres on tarmac as the clouds close in. Norfolk has never seemed so far away. I sweat in my jumper, unable to turn the heating down or take my eyes from the road for fear that Daniel is right and I'm not capable of driving because medication is dulling my senses, or grief is.

Time drags, even as the miles pass. The same speed, second by second, minute by minute. I'm headed for Victoria. I know now, more than I've ever known anything, that she needs to come home. You understand that, don't you, Mum?

Finally, I'm standing at the base of Oakfield's stone steps, extravagantly wide, with the domed school building looming above me, as impossible and unavoidable as a boulder in the road. What if they don't let me take her? But one advantage of private schools is that you can do things like this: you can take your child out of school for a day of tennis at Wimbledon or for a family holiday in Capri. Or for her grandmother's funeral.

Daniel usually leads the way here. I simply can't stand to return, and he's good at smooth talk and handshakes and they all know him. But today I'm on my own.

I ring the bell and wait, then speak into the intercom when asked. 'It's Victoria Salmon's mum.' Finally, the door is released, and I can enter. The entrance is like no school reception anywhere: it's like a five-star hotel, all polished oak and red carpet. I can hear the whisper and giggle of girlish voices as feet scamper along the first-floor landings, heading for the prep room or library – grand spaces where ladies once took morning tea and received callers. The dormitories are in an ugly modern extension, but in the main building are the dining hall and the long ballroom they use for assemblies and prize-giving at the end of each term.

I feel small and nip the back of my hand to remind myself that I paid for this polished floor, the red carpet beneath my feet, at least a tiny piece of it. I long to stand on the stairs and yell, 'Victoria!' or even 'Tori!' until she comes to me. I want to grab her hand and run.

Behind the wooden door, marked SECRETARY in gold paint, is a startled spinster. Not the same one who worked here when I was a pupil, but of the same type. I ask, politely, if I can see the headmistress, who's seated in the adjacent office. The headmistress, Mrs Hollingsworth, is not a replacement. She saw me through four years of secondary school, and she welcomes me stiffly, offers tea.

'Cassandra, how lovely! Earl Grey or Darjeeling?'

The secretary shuffles off to make it and Mrs H, as we always called her, takes her seat behind her massive mahogany desk, smooths the velvet lapels of her dogtooth jacket and flashes me a glimmer of overbite.

'So nice to see you, Cassandra, though next time perhaps you could inform us in advance, so we can be better prepared. This weekend is always busy, with the pupils returning from exeats.'

The secretary makes a trundling return, head lowered as she hands me a bone china cup half-full of milky tea.

'Thank you.'

It clatters in the saucer as I take it.

Mrs H peers at me, like she did the day I first arrived, and I feel fourteen again. 'Nothing wrong, I hope?'

Courage sweats out of me, leaves me with a dry throat and no voice to say the terrible words, *My mum died.* As if saying it aloud will finally make it real.

'Of course, Victoria's trip home for half-term was cancelled and Mr Salmon did call to explain. I was sorry to hear you've been unwell. Are you recovered?'

'I'm fine, thank you.' I shuffle in the warm leather chair, hemmed in by its steep sides, and wonder what he told her about me.

She places her hands into a bridge and peers at me, waiting. She's an important woman and her time is precious. 'So, how can I help you?'

'I want to take Victoria home.'

Mrs H crinkles her brow in a way that is disapproving and makes me quake. 'You mean for the night? Lessons start in earnest on Monday, and Victoria is now on the GCSE syllabus. She'll have to be back tomorrow.'

Time to be strong. 'I'm taking her home for good.'

The bridge of her hands collapses. 'This is rather sudden. Victoria is doing so well here. She's an exceptionally bright pupil, a real asset.' She pauses, smiles silkily. 'Just like her mother was. I do understand that you are in the process of opening a health spa, so if it's a question of extending the holiday on the fees . . . ?'

'No,' I say, trying to hide the fact that this is news to me. I wonder how long we've not been paying. Money must be tighter than I thought – no wonder you were worried about the farm, Mum. 'It's not related to that. But if we can't afford Victoria's fees, then that's even more reason for me to remove her.'

She looks affronted. 'As I told Mr Salmon when we spoke last week, we're happy to make concessions for our alumni. We can give you leeway on both girls' outstanding fees for this term.'

'*Both girls?* What are you talking about?'

Mrs H flushes pink, recovers. 'I'm sorry, I must be getting muddled with another family. But please, don't remove Victoria from the school without due consideration. Why not take her home for one night and reconsider?'

'There's nothing to reconsider, I want her home.' My voice sounds small.

Her face pinches thin. 'Victoria is very happy here – she's quite inseparable from Dawn. Have you actually talked this through with your daughter? As you know, teenagers get very attached to friends and those girls are more like sisters.'

I'm sick of hearing about people being like family when they aren't. As if *family* were a sign of closeness, given the secrets and lies that have been kept from me. 'But they *aren't* sisters, and Victoria should be with her family. I'm taking her home today.'

She stares at me in the same way she did when I'd failed to hand in my homework. Pushing away her cup and saucer, she sighs. 'I'm afraid that you can't simply remove Victoria from the school. You aren't the guardian named on her records: your mother is. She would have to be informed.'

Rage fills me. I can feel it running in my blood, rising to my face. I want to slap her smug expression.

'I'm taking Victoria home, she's my daughter and you can't stop me. Or are you going to say you need my mother's permission? Which would be rather difficult, given that she's dead.'

Mrs H's hand hovers up to her chest. 'Oh my,' she says.

'She was shot last Friday and died yesterday. That's why I need to take Victoria home, to attend her funeral. Any problem with that?'

I know I'm being cruel, that none of this is her fault, but I'm glad to see her face mottle.

She picks up the phone to speak to her secretary. 'Lucy, could you fetch Victoria Salmon, please? Straight away.'

The phone is replaced with both hands and we wait. After a few minutes of awkward silence, she begins to flick through the papers on her desk and I sit on my shaking hands, for fear they will betray me.

'Mum!'

And there she is, the light of my heart: *Victoria*. My little girl looks all grown up, in skinny jeans and a cold-shoulder jumper that bags around her wrists. Her maple-coloured hair, so very much like yours, has grown long. In the seven weeks since the summer holidays, she's changed from pretty to beautiful. It pains me that I haven't seen this transition.

'What are you doing here?' Her face is full of emotion and glowing with health, her cheeks are pink and her eyes have that lively lustre. She's never looked more like her grandmother than at this moment, as if the genes skipped a generation and here you are, as a fourteen-year-old.

'Where's Dad?'

Maybe it's the way her eyes narrow as she waits for my answer, or maybe that slick of red gloss on her lips, but she's no longer a child.

'Dad's busy, love.'

She frowns. 'Then why are you here?'

Mrs Hollingsworth watches with interest, but her lips remain sealed. Now is not the time to tell Victoria about your death. I decide to play it safe with my answer, though I hope to never see this place again.

'I've come to take you home, love. Because I missed seeing you at half-term.'

'But lessons start on Monday. Am I allowed?'

'Of course.' I open my arms to Victoria, holding my daughter in a grip that feels unnatural and forced despite my love, my fierce love, for this teenager who's as tall as me now. She kisses my cheek and I'm grateful for the stickiness of her lip balm.

'Can Dawn come?'

'No, she has to attend her classes, I can't remove her from school.' Her look of disappointment stabs my heart.

Victoria and Dawn's room is small but full of light, two beds on opposite walls with identical desks, tossed Hollister hoodies and teddy bears, a life-size poster of Ed Sheeran, his freckled face covered in lipstick kisses the girls have added, and lots of photos – two years' worth of selfies: the girls in various places and poses. I'm not just taking Victoria home, I'm removing her from one too.

'If I can miss classes, why can't Dawn?' She's still sulking about this, still trying to push me into giving in. 'I bet Dad wouldn't mind.'

'Well, I would. There's something I need to talk to you about, something's happened.'

She pulls a sports bag from under her bead and begins to pack. 'Are you and Dad splitting up?'

I feel like I've been slapped, and I wonder if she's intuited something that I've missed. 'Of course we're not! Why would you say something like that?'

She pushes a few more items into the bag. 'It was what I thought of when my half-term trip home got cancelled. And now you're here, taking me out of school – you never collect me.'

I busy myself with trying to help, folding up some pyjamas bottoms from her bed. 'They're Dawn's,' she says, snatching them from me just as the door flies open and Dawn comes rushing in, dark hair springing from her head and her eyes already moist with tears.

'Tori!'

She flings herself at Victoria and they cling to each other like monkeys. They talk quickly, panicky about the few days they'll be separated. The girls are getting older and changing – Dawn's voice has more depth, she's lost the girlish pitch. My eyes light on her bedside locker, and the framed picture, presumably her mother, whom I've never met. Still though, her face is familiar to me.

I pick up the frame to get a better look. She's a beautiful woman, striking, with skin like mocha and dark silk-spun hair, Cleopatra-like. Then I know: she's the woman I saw leaving my home on Friday afternoon in the business suit. The one I thought I heard fucking him, until I told myself I was being paranoid. I was the only one who could see the truth about the shooting, now I wonder if I was right about this too. You certainly thought so, didn't you, Mum? 'Could she have just dressed quickly?' you asked. This woman is beautiful, slim, athletic-looking. I bet she works out; I bet she looks after herself. She reminds me of his ex, the Olympic cyclist. So much more his type than my slovenly, scarred self.

It's only when I realise that Dawn is watching me that I hastily replace the frame. 'Hi, Dawn. How are you?'

'Fine, thank you, Cassandra,' she says, politely, though her eyes are full of tears and she's still clutching Victoria's hand.

Like Victoria, Dawn has transformed since I saw her last: her face has narrowed and her lips are fuller. She's an early vision of the woman she will become – the beautiful woman her mother already is. I stare at her face, and wonder what other secrets are being kept from me.

We're on the A140, just past the boundary where Norfolk ends and Suffolk begins. The car's speeding now. I've merged into the fast lane, fizzy with euphoria now my girl is by my side. But I know I need to tell Victoria what's happened; it's not fair to keep it from her.

'When Dad said you couldn't come home for half-term because I was ill, it wasn't true, love. It's Granny.'

'What's wrong with her?' she asks, so lightly that she can have no idea of what's coming.

Somehow the fact that I'm focusing on the road makes it bearable to say the words.

'She's gone, love. She died yesterday.'

'*What?*' I know she heard me and I can't bring myself to repeat it. She turns to face me, twisting in the seat. 'Granny's *dead?*'

'I'm sorry.' And I am. For both of us.

'What happened?'

The inevitable question, still it throws me.

'She had an accident.' I'm trying to soften the blow, but Victoria's face twists sharply in horror.

'Mum! What accident?'

'Grandad shot her. He says he was having a nightmare, love. He didn't know what he was doing.'

She doesn't take her eyes off me, I don't take my eyes off the road.

'How can Grandad have shot her?' She's asking me as if I have the answers, as if it doesn't sound crazy to me too. I want to pull over, so I can at least hug her, but there's no rest stop coming up and a lorry is tailing me, very close.

'He was sleepwalking. You know how when people sleepwalk, they can move around and do things?'

'Yeah, of course I know about that.' She flings herself back in her seat. 'Fuck, poor Granny.' Her breathing has quickened, but she's too stunned to cry. That will come later.

'I know, love. It's a hard thing to understand.'

Especially for me, now I know Daniel paid the architect that very morning. Is it possible Daniel shot you because you'd changed your mind about Samphire Health Spa? Or did Dad do it, in his sleep? Either scenario is crazy. Give me a sign, Mum, because I don't understand any of this.

'So Grandad didn't know what he was doing?'

'Not until he woke up, by then Janet and Ash had arrived. Janet called the ambulance and Granny was rushed to hospital.'

'But they couldn't save her?'

I frown at the road. 'They did – she was in hospital. We thought she was going to be okay, but she never woke up. But then, without warning, she slipped away.'

Dark clouds break above us and rain spits on the windows. The fields become more familiar, the road now leads only to the sea, with a turning off that could easily be missed, to the isolated flatness of Innocence Lane.

'Where's Grandad now?' she asks.

'He's in prison, love.'

'But that's not right! He was sleepwalking – it's not his fault.'

How easily she's accepted his explanation. It doesn't even occur to her that it could be a lie. The heavens crack open and raindrops hammer on the windscreen, fat tears obscuring the way forward. As we drive on, another thought buzzes in my head: the woman in the photo. Why was she in my home?

'Where does Dawn's mum live?'

Victoria snivels, and takes a moment to answer. 'Reydon, near Southwold. You know that!'

I ignore the tone of her voice, and allow her to be angry with me, though I don't know why. None of this is my fault, but she's confused and needs to direct her feelings somewhere.

'She's a single mother, isn't she? What is it she does for a living?'

'Dunno. Sells things around the country.'

'What things?'

'God, I don't know, Mum. Water coolers, office equipment, boring things like that. Why?'

'No reason. I just saw the photo of her on Dawn's bedside cabinet and thought I recognised her. What about her dad? He's white, I take it?'

Victoria looks at me, checking I'm not insulting her friend. 'Dawn's mixed-race, yeah. Just makes her more beautiful.'

'Yes. I see that. What's her mother's name?'

'Why the third degree?' she demands.

I search for an answer. 'I was just thinking how often we have Dawn to stay with us, and how nice it would be to get to know her mother better. And I can't even recall her name!'

'It's Monica,' she says.

Monica.

Daniel was speaking to her, on the phone, the night of the shooting. I told myself that my fears were delusional, that my jealousy was a sickness. Everyone has lied to me, everyone wants me to think I'm crazy, but I was right about the shooting.

Now I think I'm right about him having a lover.

28

Holly

Lying in Leif's arms, Holly found herself talking about Maya's sudden death.

It would be in the evening papers anyway. Alfie Avon had covered the Innocence Lane shooting each day since it happened with tabloid prurience, and the ante was now upped. If anything, there would be even more interest in the case.

'This is so sad, *Sötnos.*'

'Tragic,' she agreed. 'Especially if Hector did it in his sleep, though it seems incredible.'

'You doubt his story?'

'My senses do.'

Clive had sent her an email. His prediction had been right: the court wanted a psychiatric report and because a bail hearing had been scheduled for Monday, Clive would be assessing Hector tomorrow at Norwich Prison, driving there after he'd finished running Team Talk at the library. Hector had been told of Maya's death, and had been placed on suicide watch by the prison; her role would be as an observer. Clive had said in his message:

Come and observe. I checked with Jon and he's taken
    you off Sunday's rota.
It'll be good experience for you. Meet me at the library
    at 10 and we can drive up together.

'I just don't believe Hector did it,' she said, tracing Leif's clavicle with a light finger. 'What about Ash – are the police really sure it isn't him? What about that previous offence you told me about, the shooting? You said it showed a tendency.'

Leif was sleepy, his eyes half-shut. 'Hmm? No, it was nothing, just something that happened when he was a little kid.'

A shivery sensation like premonition made her feel cold. 'How old?'

'Oh, eleven or so. He shot someone by accident with his air rifle. Just an accident . . .'

Holly felt herself start to shake. She knew what Leif was about to say, she felt as though she were in a dream where she needed to scream but couldn't. *Don't say any more, please!* But the words wouldn't come.

'*Ja*, it was a Halloween game that went wrong. Teenagers spooking each other out, playing in the woods, pretending to be ghosts. A girl got shot, but she didn't want to press charges so he just got a caution.'

Holly moved closer, trying to steal warmth from Leif's body, seeking comfort from the world outside, but knowing it wouldn't be enough.

The past had found her.

DAY 9

SUNDAY 9 NOVEMBER

29

Cassandra

Just eight days ago I woke to discover you'd been shot. So much has happened since then, but still I haven't got the answers I want: I need to know if Dad really shot you in his sleep, and I need to know if Daniel is having an affair.

Your death, Dad's confession, they can't overwhelm me. I've been down that road before – it leads to weakness and madness, and being locked in a hospital against my will. I have to keep strong, if I'm going to find my answers. I know that Clive's been asked to visit Dad at the prison today, but he has to run Team Talk first. That's where I'll start.

The library's unlocked but deserted, just stacks of books and the hum of the central heating kicking in. The circle of chairs has already been set up and I look around for Alex, hear a scuttling sound from the staff room. When he appears, his face is bright tomato, hands flapping high near his neck.

'Hi, Alex.'

'Cassandra! I read Alfie Avon's article in yesterday's paper. I'm so s-s-sorry.'

I'd seen it too. The headline had lit up on my iPad when I switched it on this morning – *Tragic Maya Dead: Cured of Cancer, Shot in Her Own Home.* I hadn't read on.

'W-w-what are you doing here?'

'I'm here for the meeting. I see you've already got the chairs out. Have you got the mugs ready for break time?'

He's completely thrown by my response, relieved too. No one wants to talk about death. 'Just did it. And I've p-p-put the kettle on.'

'Well done. How's this week been?' Because other people have had a normal week, unbelievable though that seems.

'Good. B-but . . . how are you?'

I can see he's still thinking of that hideous article, all the lurid details of your death.

'I'm okay. Or I will be. Don't worry about me, Alex – let's just think about getting everything ready for Team Talk.'

I'm in control here, a library manager, not a grieving daughter. I take the nearest chair, exhausted by my performance, mouth dry from the extra Prozac I popped this morning, but determined to show everyone that I'm a survivor.

The front door opens, then shuts, then opens again, banging awkwardly against the dented prow of a Silver Cross pram that's seen better days. Squawks of protest erupt from within and then, as the pram's pushed forward through the resistant door, Kerry appears, a dummy clasped in her mouth, a grubby rabbit in one hand as she tries to steer with the other. The wailing noise ceases abruptly when she removes the dummy from her own mouth and rams it into the baby's.

'My bloody sister was supposed to have him, but when I turned up at 'er flat, she's still in bed with that shifty boyfriend of hers and the place was a tip. I wasn't gonna leave him there!'

The infant spits out the dummy and howls. Kerry pushes the pram into the circle, between two chairs, wiggling it wildly, which I'm certain will only make her child cry more. 'And I couldn't not turn up, could I? It's a condition of my probation.'

She looks at me imploringly, as does Alex, both glad I'll make the decision.

'We can't have a baby disrupt the group,' I say. 'It's not fair to the others.'

'If I can just get him to sleep . . .' Kerry jiggles the pram manically.

'If he sleeps,' I tell her, 'he can stay.'

The door opens again. This time it's Trish, who's bleached her roots since the last meeting and is wearing carnival-pink lippie. She makes an instant beeline for the crying baby, picks him up and nestles him into her, cooing into his blotchy red face.

'Ah! What an angel!' She's obviously deaf, but I'm glad no one's focused on me. Maybe only Alex reads the papers.

Kerry collapses into a chair and the baby begins to settle, sucking on Trish's finger and watching her animated clown-like smile in fascination. Alex takes orders for tea or coffee, carefully writing them on his pad before heading to the kitchen.

I can do this. I'll help with the group then go home to spend time with Victoria. Then I'll start planning your funeral.

Roger's next to arrive in his threadbare suit, smelling of last night's booze. He takes the chair furthest away from Trish and the baby, and looks at his watch.

'Well, this makes a change from going to church. Where's the chief? Time we got started, isn't it?'

When Clive walks through the door, the baby's sleeping peacefully and the group's ready. He looks surprised to see me, we exchange smiles, but I can't ask him anything with everyone else already seated and waiting for him to begin.

'Okay, everyone, first of all thank you for coming in on a Sunday. Last meeting I asked you all to make a mental note of a situation that troubled you, something that scared or angered you, made you sad.' Clive pauses, and his gaze falls on me again, as if apologising for the irony. 'Something that would normally unsettle you, but that you dealt with positively. Who'd like to go first?'

'I will!' says Trish. 'My hubby came home on Friday practically swimming in cheap booze and tropical perfume. Well, I wanted to scream at him – I wanted to go at him with a knife, to be honest! At least tear the crotch from his trousers.' She takes a breath and Roger crosses his legs. 'Then I remembered what Cass said about not opening up cans of worms. So, I got a bottle of Baileys and locked myself in the bathroom. I was in that bath for the rest of the night, getting drunk, and when I was wrinkled like a pickled walnut, I got out. He was asleep. I'd almost forgot how angry I was, I was so pissed and tired. I just got in the bed and went to sleep next to him and in the morning the stink of her perfume was gone!'

Trish looks triumphant and gives me a wink.

When we met last time I still believed it was best to keep things hidden, but now I've changed my mind. All the secrets that surround me are like sickening boils that need lancing.

Kerry says, 'The prick got away with it then', glancing at the pram. 'Men always do.'

Trish juts out her chin. 'But he's still mine. That's the main thing, ain't it?' She's seeking my approval, is confused when I don't give it.

Roger coughs. 'I guess I'm next.'

Then, to everyone's surprise, Clive says, 'Actually, I'd like to share, if I may? I won't give any specifics because of confidentiality, but it concerns a one-time patient of mine who's had a very bad time recently. He had something of a breakdown recently and I wanted to help as best I could. I went into work mode and dealt with it objectively and coldly.

I persuaded him to take antidepressant medication, when he said he didn't want any. I was a doctor, but now I'm wondering if I should have just been a friend and listened, and offered emotional support. I'd like to ask the group: was I right?'

The room is silent. Even the baby seems to be thinking.

Roger speaks first. 'You're the psychiatrist, why're you asking us?'

'Because you've all been there, to that dark place, and you know what helps most: a friend, who listens with his heart, or a professional, who responds with his head. What's better – a hug or a pill?'

He doesn't look in my direction, but I can feel his attention straining across the circle, that mine is the only response he really wants.

'I think,' I say carefully, 'you did exactly the right thing.' My only answer, and a lie. But I want to keep him on my side. He'll be useful to me now he's going to be assessing Dad.

In the corner of my eye, I see someone arrive. It's Holly, and I assume she's here for me, but then she catches Clive's eye and waves. She gestures to the stack of books, indicating that she isn't going to disturb the group, she'll wait. Interesting – the two of them are working together then.

'Can I tell you about my week?' I say, knowing Holly must be listening.

They all lean forward. I gather from this that I was wrong about them not reading the paper.

'You all know that my daughter, Victoria, is at boarding school in Norfolk. She was sent there when she was just twelve, because I'd had a breakdown and I was sectioned to the Bartlet. My family felt it was best if she was away from my madness, and once she'd gone, nothing I could say would persuade them she should come home. These past few days I've realised something: it *wasn't* my fault that I was ill two years ago. I've always thought my illness was because I'm weak, but I'm not going to feel guilty any more. I'm not letting anyone take my girl away from me again. I'm not simply going to accept that other people know better.'

The group are silent, then spontaneously they begin to clap. They cheer me on, because I'm like them, because they know what's happened to me and I'm talking like a survivor. I was alone in saying you didn't shoot yourself, and I've been vindicated in that at least. I have to be certain of who shot you, and I'm not going to be silenced any more.

Whatever comes next, I will survive.

30

Holly

Holly arrived at the library to find Team Talk still in session. She hadn't expected to see Cassandra among the group, given her mum only died two days ago, but then she revised this thought: *That's even more reason for her to come. She's getting support.*

Not wanting to intrude, she lost herself among the shelves of books. She could sense the discussion had been disturbed by her arrival – the conversation became quieter, but then Cassandra was speaking, fairly loudly, and the group erupted into applause. Holly saw that Cassandra was smiling bravely, looking a different person from the woman who had sat beside a hospital bed, anxiously waiting for her mother to wake up. Maybe Maya's death had come as a relief, after a week of uncertainty.

Clive drew the meeting to an early close and people began to make their way out. Holly took the opportunity to speak with Cassandra, who was collecting up used mugs.

'Cass, I was so sorry to hear the sad news. How are you?'

'Bearing up. Considering my mum's dead, and my dad's in prison.'

Holly didn't know quite how to respond to the baldness of that. 'If there's anything I can do . . . ?'

She smiled sadly. 'Just keeping on being my friend, Holly. Can you do that?'

'I'm sure I can.' As she said it, Holly felt herself being boxed into a corner: she knew she shouldn't promise friendship when she was secretly speaking with Alfie Avon, and when her own obsession with what had happened at Innocence Lane was nothing to do with friendship, and everything to do with her unresolved past.

'Actually, Cass, I'm going with Clive to interview your dad.'

'Oh?' Though her smile didn't falter, Cass crossed her arms.

'Just as an observer – Clive suggested it,' Holly said, disgusted with herself for sounding so passive.

'Well,' said Cassandra, turning to collect more mugs, 'please tell me how it goes. As for me, I have a funeral to organise. Do you know if the hospital would have an issue releasing the body, anything that might delay me?'

'There'll be an autopsy. I can find out how long that'll take, if you like?'

'Thanks. I want to arrange things as soon as possible.'

'Cass, when I see your dad, I could pass on a message?'

Cassandra straightened her spine, and Holly saw a chrome colour radiate off her like armour. She was keeping herself protected with this show of strength.

'I have nothing to tell him. But . . . can you tell me . . .'

'Yes?' Holly reached out to touch Cassandra's arm, seemingly as a comforting gesture, but really so she could tune in to her feelings. Her emotions ran through Holly's veins like molten tar, heavy and dark.

Mistrust and doubt were clearly there. Holly just couldn't tell if she was experiencing Cassandra's mirrored feeling or simply her own.

'Tell me afterwards if you believe him.'

Holly waited as Clive clicked himself into the passenger seat of her Fiat 500, then they set off on the winding drive to Norwich. They chatted about Leif's obsession with Ingrid Bergman, about Ellen's obsession with going on a Christmas cruise. As they trundled up the A140, they fell into comfortable silence and Holly's thoughts drifted to Hector, this blunt instrument of a man, who would have just learned that his wife was dead.

Her inclination was that he wasn't cold-hearted, yet for him to shoot his wife while sleepwalking seemed bizarre and – frankly – unbelievable. 'What's your gut feeling, Clive? Do you believe Hector was asleep when he shot Maya?'

He breathed out, slowly, and ran a hand through his dishevelled hair, probably the nearest it had come to being brushed today. He was like a scruffy hound, one that was so loyal its ragged looks only made you love it more.

'It's not about gut feelings, Holly. It's about evidence and scientific analysis.'

Clive was saying the right things, but she knew that he was holding back on her. His battered leather case was half-open on his lap and he began to sift through his notes as if they might hold the answers.

'But the opinion of a consultant psychiatrist like yourself counts hugely, doesn't it? Especially when the main suspect says he was asleep when he shot his wife. The jury will struggle with it.'

Clive abandoned his case notes and sat back in the passenger seat. The road before them wound around villages, with flat fields in-between. The A140 was notorious for being slow, and heaven help any driver stuck behind a tractor.

'I think you're confusing my expertise with that of a psychic. I can't say if Hector was asleep or awake.'

Holly stared ahead at the crooked road, the fenland's marshy scent in her sinuses, its dusty taste in her mouth. Norfolk's wide-open spaces dizzied her senses.

'What if Hector was fully awake and he's trying to get away with this?' Holly said. 'Do we know for certain that Hector even has a history of sleepwalking, apart from what he and Janet have told us?'

'It will only be documented if he's seen his doctor about it. And Hector doesn't strike me as the sort who'd make much use of his local surgery,' Clive agreed. 'Luckily, we have the facilities to run sleep tests on him, so long as he gets bail.'

'And would they be conclusive?' Holly asked.

'The EEG will analyse his brain waves. We'll be looking for unusual activity during the non-REM phase, and trying to establish if the part in his brain that should disable movement while he dreams is faulty.'

'You make him sound like a car, the brain like an engine.'

Clive liked that and chuckled. They had reached the outskirts of Norwich quickly, the roads being fairly empty, and were just minutes away from the prison. 'I suppose, to me, that's how it is. What about you, Holly? What does your synaesthesia tell you about Hector?'

'That's not an exact science either.'

'Still,' he said, smiling, 'I'd like to know.'

Holly thought about Hector when she saw him last. His stubble, his grey eyes, his battered skin. And she pictured an ancient tree with twisted branches, standing alone on a desolate plain. She could sense its proud roots under the earth, and she could hear the movement, the life, hidden between the branches, the wild creatures who sought sanctuary there, to whom the tree, ugly and gnarled though it was, offered protection.

'Okay, I'll tell you: I sense that he loves his wife and that he didn't shoot her. But that he knows who did.'

When the prison officer brought Hector Hawke to the windowless interview booth, he looked a haunted man, with hunched posture and bloodshot eyes. He tried not to falter as he took the empty seat, but Holly felt him weakening, like a tree swaying in a storm, vulnerable to any harsh gust. Grief had taken him over.

'The police have got my confession. What more do you people want from me?'

Clive slid a jotter and pen from the briefcase. 'I'm here at the request of your own solicitor, Hector. Holly is a trainee paramedic, and is simply here to observe me. Unless you'd prefer she didn't?'

Hector shrugged, looked at her. 'Can't see what difference it makes. She was there at the beginning of all this – she might as well stay.'

'Thank you,' Holly said. 'I'm so sorry about Maya.' She took the seat furthest back from the desk in the small room, and waited as Clive placed his briefcase on the floor and sat down directly opposite Hector, the small table between them.

'Okay, Hector, so I'm going to be preparing the psychiatric evaluation. Shall we begin?'

Despite Hector's weather-beaten face, his rolled-up sleeves revealed thick arms and he had a neck like a bulldog. 'Psychiatrists are for mental folk. Is Jackson makin' out I'm mad?' He looked towards Holly and she could see he was agitated, and his bloodshot eyes looked damp. He was an old man and beaten by all that had happened, he'd lost his wife, but he was still fighting.

Clive clicked the end of his pen, scribbled on the jotter to make the ink flow. 'That's a good question, Mr Hawke. Sleep disorders are indicators of mental illnesses in some cases, although not in every case. The last time I met you, you claimed to know nothing of how or why Maya was shot. I understand that you're now saying you shot her in your sleep?'

The old man pushed his damaged right hand so that it was held fast in the other. He looked at Clive closely, as if measuring his weight. 'Yup.'

'I'm afraid you're going to have to say more than that, if I'm to write this report.'

'What's in it for me? I've lost everythin' now she's gone.' He lowered his head.

'Your freedom, Hector,' Clive said. 'If you were sleepwalking when you shot your wife, you can't be held responsible. It's non-insane automatism: you acted without conscious awareness.'

Holly watched this sink into the man's understanding, saw his strong brow crease further under its weight. If no sleep disorder were found, any jury would be likely to convict him on the strength of his confession, in which case he'd be looking at a mandatory life sentence. Hector had a lot to lose, if he didn't co-operate.

'I can't tell you anythin'. Only that Maya's dead and it's my fault.' He hung his head, and the tears he didn't shed seemed to be dammed up inside his hunched and shaking body.

A shiver of premonition went through Holly: he really did feel guilty. Her question came unbidden. 'How do you *know* you're responsible?'

He looked at her with wild, angry eyes. 'Because I woke to find Maya shot, with my gun at her side.'

'And yet you let everyone believe Maya attempted suicide,' Holly replied, thinking: *everyone but me and Cassandra.*

Hector slumped, as if all his weight were in his shoulders. 'I should have confessed from the off, I see that now. We thought if it looked like attempted suicide, then no one would ask no more questions. Daniel said with his radio show, people knowin' who he is and that, it was for the best. I suppose none of us was thinkin' properly that mornin'.'

'Wait,' said Holly urgently, leaning forward. 'You're saying Daniel knew all along too? That he was at the farm that morning?'

Hector's face paled. 'You're just here to observe, aren't you? So why not keep your mouth shut. In fact,' he said, turning to Clive, 'I've changed my mind. I want her out of the room.'

Holly arrived home to find her flat cold and empty. She made herself a very large cup of coffee, cradling it for warmth while she studied the photos of her family on the fridge. So, Daniel was colluding with Hector all along. He'd known Maya hadn't shot herself. But why lie, why go to such lengths to pretend it was attempted suicide if Hector had really been asleep? And Holly, along with the paramedics, had been at the farm just after the shooting. They'd entered as soon as the police had declared it safe, and there was no sign of Daniel. Why had he stayed away all that morning, only coming to the hospital hours later?

She sent Cass a text: I'm back from the prison, if you want to talk? Then she waited.

Sipping her coffee, Holly felt desperately sad. Maya's death had brought it back to her, the fragility of life, and she wanted more than ever to be with people who loved her. She booted up her laptop, thinking she'd Skype her parents if they were awake. Then she saw that Jamie was online at last. When was the last time she'd spoken to him, without her parents being there? She couldn't even think of a time: Christmas, summer vacation, it all revolved around mealtimes and her parents' chatter. In truth, her brother was largely a two-dimensional presence in her life, and had been since that Halloween. She needed to talk to him about it, a conversation that was years overdue. She pressed 'video call' and listened to the sound of a non-connection, reaching across time zones and miles. *Come on, Jamie, pick up.*

He didn't. So she typed a message in the vacant box below: We really need to talk about Innocence Farm. Google it, you'll see why.

She was about to close down her laptop when she saw an email had just arrived from Clive. It read:

Holly,

In the car you shared with me your thoughts on the case, so now I'm sharing mine. Like I said, I'm no mind reader, but these are the facts as I understand them. You may also be interested in the case comparisons: they could be useful references for your assignment. I don't think Hector is lying. And that's what you really wanted to know, isn't it?

Clive

There was a file attached, marked confidential. Holly clicked it open.

Preliminary notes on Hector Hawke.

Age: 62

Status: Currently remanded to HMP Norwich, hospital wing.

Background:

Hector Hawke was born in Kenley, Suffolk, and married into the family who owned the farmland there, taking it over when he was still in his early twenties. Innocence Farm predominantly rears chickens and pigs, sold exclusively to a high-end supermarket. There is also an area of woodland used for game shoots. He has had help managing the farm for a number of years from a local man, Ashley Cley.

Hector Hawke shows some reluctance to talk, although it must be noted that when I first met him, shortly after Maya Hawke was shot, he was in a state of shock. His recent arrest was as a direct result of Hector Hawke's confession, and since his remand, Maya Hawke has sadly died.

He now states that on the morning of November 1st, he shot Maya Hawke, his wife. Although he has repeated this claim to me, he's unwilling or unable to provide further details, saying he has no recollection of what happened. A point to note is that Post Traumatic Stress Disorder (PTSD) provokes memory loss, and this is a not uncommon result of witnessing violence, even for the perpetrator.

This is my first case of somnambular violence, but I have come across other sleep disorders during my 30 years of practice. Of all sleep disorders, sleepwalking is the least well researched as it does not have the same clear pattern that accompanies better understood sleep disorders such as sleep apnoea or narcolepsy, which can be more clearly identified during standard clinical sleep studies. I intend to conduct a sleep study (with EEG and overnight monitoring) on Hector Hawke at the Bartlet Hospital.

Maya Hawke was fatally injured. A jury will struggle to accept that someone can load, aim and fire a gun while asleep. In cases where sleepwalkers have committed murder, the verdicts have been unpredictable, resulting in either full acquittal or prison sentences.

Current estimates place the rate of sleepwalking at around 4 per cent of the population – and the percentage is higher in children. It is documented that sleepwalkers can drive, cook, operate machinery, have intercourse; and yet the brain receptors for – say – recognising a loved one, are dormant.

It would seem that Hector Hawke's first experience of sleep disturbance took place when he was a child. This is not unusual. In fact, sleepwalking in children is relatively common, though the onset of sleepwalking can happen at any age. Hector Hawke recounts several specific incidents worth relaying here:

He tells me that his parents were disturbed by his sleepwalking, and discouraged him from discussing it.

Once he left his teenage years, these incidents did become less pronounced, and Hector Hawke believed he had 'grown through it'. However, he still had what he called 'night terrors', when he would sit bolt upright, believing himself to be in danger. This was such a common occurrence that, after her daughter left home, Maya Hawke sometimes slept in her daughter's bedroom, although on the night of the attack this was not possible as Cassandra Hawke was staying at the farm overnight.

Hector Hawke knew Maya Hawke when they were young, living as they both did in a small rural village. They were married shortly after Maya Hawke inherited the farm, following her parents' tragic death. Hector Hawke was in his early twenties at the time, Maya Hawke a few years older. Their only child, Cassandra, was born just seven months later. When asked about the nature of the marriage, Hector Hawke was reticent, and seems a man uncomfortable with, and unused to, discussing his emotions. This is not uncommon for a man of his age, and he was visibly agitated when I tried to probe further.

What we know about sleepwalking crimes, or more specifically, non-insane automatism, derives largely from a few sensational cases that have challenged and redefined the way we see the sleeping brain. In 1997, in America, Scott Falater, a quiet family man, dedicated to the Mormon faith, was seen by a neighbour stabbing his wife over 40 times and pushing her into the family swimming pool. Seemingly asleep, he changed out of his bloodstained clothes, and put them – along with the knife – in the boot of his car. When police arrived, he said he had no idea what was going on. This lack of memory is a key feature of automatism.

Although it looked as though Falater had attempted to conceal the murder, Falater's children testified that he always kept his work clothes and tools in the boot of his car and the prosecution argued he was acting out of habit. The neighbour also gave weight to the case, saying he was glassy-eyed during the attack and unaware of his surroundings. His mother confirmed he had a history of childhood sleepwalking, and his sister testified that as a girl she had tried to disturb him while he sleepwalked, and he threw her across the room.

The jury still found him guilty of first-degree murder.

So, how can it conclusively be proved that the accused was sleepwalking? In short, it can't. It can only be concluded on the basis of probabilities, weighing up past behaviours and evidence of disturbed sleep.

Another example: In 1992, in Canada, Kenneth Parks drove several miles to his in-laws' home, strangled his mother-in-law and stabbed his father-in-law, then drove to a local police station, saying, 'I think I've just killed someone.' His own wife believed he was asleep and this must have helped the jury's decision to find him not guilty. He was under a great deal of stress, and had lost his job due to his gambling addiction.

He was acquitted because of his highly irregular EEG results.

Here the notes finished.

It sounded as though things were clearer for Clive than they had been earlier that day. Holly leaned back in her chair and rubbed her eyes wearily. When she opened them, her father's gaze fixed on her from the baseball photo on the fridge. If only she were still a child, and under his protection.

But she had been a child that night when everything changed, and she hadn't confided in him then. It was foolish to think that now, as an adult woman and living thousands of miles away, she needed someone else to help her.

Her phone buzzed, and she picked it up. 'Cass?'

'I just got your text. How did it go?'

The words tumbled out. 'Clive believes your dad – I've seen the start of his report. He's quoting other cases, to back up the theory that Hector was asleep.'

There was a long pause. 'What about you: do you believe him?'

Now Holly hesitated.

'Holly? Please tell me.'

'Cass, did you know that Daniel was at the farm that morning? He's known right from that first morning that this wasn't an attempted suicide.' She strained to hear Cass's reaction, but through the phone wires, her senses had nothing to go on.

'Are you sure?'

'That's what your dad says. And yet Daniel wasn't at the farmhouse when I arrived. He stayed out of the way while the police and paramedics did their work . . .'

'It wasn't Daniel, Holly. It was Ash.'

There had been a time Holly had believed this too, but now she wasn't so sure. Ash and Janet both seemed devoted to the Hawkes. She asked softly, 'How can you be so sure, Cass?'

'Because Ash is violent. He's shot someone before, when he was just a boy. I have a scar to prove it.'

Holly hung up, feeling wretched. She was a coward: she knew Ash hadn't shot Cass, but she'd kept quiet to protect Jamie. She was still protecting him, after all these years. Still running away, just like she had that night.

So Ash had taken the blame, back then, and he could be wrongly accused a second time. She owed it to him to discover who had really shot Maya, and it was Daniel she suspected. If she could only get close to him, use her synaesthesia to pick up any trace of guilt . . . Tomorrow was Hector's bail hearing – maybe she'd have her chance then.

But tonight, she needed to forget.

After a quick change into sweat pants and a comfortable jumper, she knocked on Leif's door to be welcomed by the smell of cumin and a warm kiss. A selection of curry cartons were already being heated, the beers were chilled and the DVD was ready to roll. Holly was usually wary of films, knowing they'd risk intruding on her thoughts and feelings, causing what she now knew to be a mirror-touch reaction. But the films Leif showed her, they made her think and – maybe because they were in black and white – they didn't rattle her senses. She was curious to see what he wanted to share with her this time.

She leaned into Leif on the sofa, bottle of beer in hand, and felt her breathing deepen as he placed an arm around her, her body sinking into the cushions.

'How was your day, *Sötnos?*'

'Uneventful,' she said, taking a swig from her bottle. The microwave pinged and he jumped up to fetch their food. 'What have you been doing?' she called, as he dished up.

'I wrote eight hundred and five words on this film I want to show you, so I'm quite pleased with my considerable progress.' She couldn't tell if he was joking or not, but he sounded sincere.

'So this isn't a date, then?' she teased, taking the plate of food from him, and settling down to enjoy it. 'It's a seminar.'

'Now, Holly, this film *Gaslight* is a classic. It's important, for film history but also for its psychology. You'll see, there is a type of abuse here that is I think very interesting.'

'Sounds just up my street.' She smiled, happy to be his student and for *Gaslight* to be her evening class assignment. If Leif filled her head with film theory and the talents of Ingrid Bergman, she didn't have to think about Innocence Lane, which was a welcome respite. They sat together on the sofa, but he gave her enough space to curl her legs up, close enough so she could feel his warmth. This Swedish student seemed to know how to play it just right.

Gaslight was an unsettling film, and it absorbed Holly, although the monochrome somehow made the creepy sensations bearable.

The premise was that the young bride, played by Ingrid Bergman, was being persuaded by her husband that she was going mad so that he could incarcerate her in an asylum and thus have free reign over her money and assets. *Gaslighting*, Leif told her, is a word sometimes used to describe the process of persuading someone that they're insane.

It was as if Leif's films held a dark mirror to the Innocence Lane case, where a woman was most at danger in her own home, most at risk from her own husband. But Holly wasn't thinking about Maya, she was thinking about Cassandra, remembering how Daniel fawned over her, telling her she was unwell, telling her she was wrong about the shooting. Yet he had known all along that Cassandra was right.

The Samphire Master, who healed people, who was revered locally. Could he be Maya's murderer?

31

Cassandra

I've put the phone down on Holly. No, she's wrong. Daniel isn't involved, that would make no sense. He was so close to you – he saved you.

Oh, Mum, you always spoke for me, told me what to do. Now I'm having to learn, for the first time, how to stand alone.

This evening I'll go through the motions of being okay, for Victoria's sake. There'll be food on the table and the fire going in the front room: it'll look like I'm coping. When the delivery of Chinese food arrives, Daniel's still not home and he isn't answering his mobile. I call the Studio. Katie seems surprised when I ask for him.

'He said he had to be with you,' she whines, not even offering her condolences. 'I had to cancel all his healing sessions – everyone's so upset! You know how they depend on him.'

Everyone, it seems, needs Daniel. I wonder if he's with Monica. I wonder if he's going to leave me, even as I spoon the pieces of duck onto Victoria's plate and tip a container of plum sauce over. 'Eat up, love. I bet you don't get anything like this at Oakfield?'

'No.' She lifts her fork, but just pokes around the meat, hardly touching it. 'I miss Dawn. Can't she come and stay?'

I know she's sad. I know she misses her friend, but I've lost my mother. We need to support each other through this.

'It wouldn't be appropriate, love. We have Granny's funeral to plan. I've booked the crematorium in Ipswich, but we need to order flowers and talk about hymns and eulogies. Do you want to read something?'

She shakes her head. 'I'd be too nervous. But I'll pick out some music.'

'That would be lovely.' I reach and squeeze her hand in mine. 'Thank you.'

I want Victoria to stay longer, but after she eats a few mouthfuls of food she asks to be excused, and I know she wants to go and FaceTime Dawn. I let her go, and then I'm alone.

Daniel still isn't home.

I go up to the bedroom without turning the light on, and look down onto our empty driveway, as if wishing will make him appear. This conflict, my love for him balanced against righteous anger that he should be here supporting me, is very present for me in the dark room. But even here, now, I don't believe Holly's right. Ash shot you, I'm certain, just like he shot me when I was twelve. An accident, Dad called it, comforting the snivelling boy even before he came to me, though I was bleeding. He made me tell the police I didn't want to press charges, then you sent me away to boarding school. And this is your reward, Mum – this is what happens when you welcome foundlings into your house and treat them like kin.

Every time a car turns into our road and its beam falls on our front path my heart lifts, then sinks as the light dips and the car turns away. The longer he stays away, the more the doubts take hold. Could it be that the man I sleep beside each night is a killer? I can't believe that. But that he's a cheat, that he's fucking someone else? Yes.

Daniel must be with her, with Monica. I should never have doubted myself two years ago: my suspicions were right. He's going to leave me. Oh God, he doesn't love me any more. I've already lost you – how can I cope if I lose him too?

There's only one way to keep him, and that's to forget what I know. I won't say anything when he arrives, I'll act normally. His dinner's saved on a plate in the oven – the smell of charred flesh, bird meat brittle from waiting too long. Will he say he was with a new client, one who desperately needs his help, maybe someone with terminal cancer? I'll nod and watch him eat, pour him a glass of wine and say nothing. My fear of him leaving me is an invisible scold's bridle.

But then another thought. Oh – God forbid – maybe he's not coming home at all. Maybe the phone will ring instead, from Monica's house. '*I don't love you, Cassandra.*' Is this how it ends?

Car lights. Coming down the road. Coming up the drive – his car. I practise smiling as I run downstairs, to the kitchen. By the time he opens the front door, the food is out of the oven and on the table. The purple sauce covers blackened duck meat, a large glass of wine to cover the taste. Pathetic, I know, but I've decided to keep the lid on the can of worms, because I love him.

'God, it's freezing out there.'

Daniel takes off his coat, tosses it over the banister, and then disappears into the downstairs restroom. Running water and a refilling tank. Finally, he's with me in the kitchen. His face is yellow-grey, like there's something leaking under the surface and polluting it. I pour myself a glass of dark grape and slug it down, already swallowing more than I should.

'How was your day, love?' He sounds weary and I hand him his wine, checking his face for signs of deception.

'I'm coping. How was work?'

'Busy. Last month's radio programme on treating ME with reiki has brought in another three clients.' I can see the deceit on his face.

'That's great news, Dan.'

He can't even look at me as he picks up his fork. I watch as he chews.

I can't resist asking, 'So that's why you're late?'

Then he makes himself look at me, his eyes blinking heavily, hidden meaning in pools of blue.

No, don't say it! I don't want to hear.

'Cass, I didn't go to work this afternoon.'

I'd prefer him to lie. This is my fault. I shouldn't have pushed him with questions.

'I didn't want to deceive you, love, but I didn't want to upset you either. It's a tragedy, what you're going through, and I don't want to make your burden worse.'

'Then don't,' I say weakly.

'I have to, love. I visited Oakfield. Mrs H was so concerned about you, what with you just turning up and collecting Victoria with no warning. I saw Dawn too. She's missing Tori. And then I went somewhere else . . .'

'No, don't tell me,' I say. 'Do what you like – as long as I'm ignorant it can't hurt me.'

'That wouldn't be right, love. There should always be honesty between us.'

Oh God, here it comes. I feel my spine curve out, my body already giving in. The lid being peeled back from the can of worms.

'You'll be angry, but hear me out first. I want you to know that I only ever do what is best for our family.'

'Daniel, please shut up.' I don't want to know about his lover; he can fuck her so long as I don't have to hear it. Keep the lid on the can, push it down hard. 'Just eat. We can talk another time.'

'You know we shouldn't eat processed foods.' He pushes his plate away. 'Cassandra, I went to Norwich Prison to see your dad. Look, love, he needs our help. God, that prison is truly hideous. All those bloody criminals. Hector looked like a trapped animal. I mean, he's a farmer – he belongs in the open air. Seeing him in there, locked away like that. And the stench!'

He takes my hands in his, holding them tight and waiting till I look at him. Every instinct tells me to run away, but his eyes hold me.

'To attack someone while sleepwalking isn't a crime, Cass, it's just sad and unusual. If you're not conscious while you act, you're innocent.'

I look at him hard to see if he really believes that, and I think that he does. His blue eyes are clear. He's trying to make me understand something.

'Hector needs to come home for Maya's funeral, love. We need to support him at the bail hearing tomorrow and if he's released, we need to look after him. And we need to do everything we can to show medical evidence of a sleep disorder.'

'Why are you doing this, Daniel?'

He holds my fingers fast, and in that moment, he looks entirely truthful. 'For you, Cass. Because I love you.'

DAY 10

MONDAY 10 NOVEMBER

32

Cassandra

It's a macabre family trip, with the three of us dressed in smart black clothes, as if for a funeral.

Victoria can't hide her nervous excitement. Going to court is an adventure for her, and she's sure her grandad will be coming home. Daniel's been silent since he woke – strange for him. I wonder if he's brooding over the possibility that Dad may not be released, or if his lover is occupying his thoughts.

At the courthouse entrance, we're accosted by Alfie Avon, all jowls and pinpoint eyes, wagging a notebook at us as he shouts, 'Remember me, Cassandra? I was at the farm the day before the shooting?'

As if I could forget. This man who has tenaciously tracked Daniel's career for years, the parasite who is feeding on our family tragedy. I put my head down, not acknowledging him, but he jumps around me like a bulldog at my ankles. 'Do you believe your dad's confession? Was it assisted suicide on account of her cancer?'

'You bastard!' hisses Daniel, lunging towards him and making the bilious man grin in satisfaction. 'You know she was cured of that. This was an accident!'

'Mr Avon, I must ask you to stop harassing my client's family,' calls Rupert Jackson, jogging down the steps and moving us away from the reporter, 'or I shall file a motion to have you banned from the court vicinity. How would your readers like that bit of news?'

Avon shrinks back, his thick lips curled into a sneer over his stubby brown teeth. 'Only doing my job, mate, same as you.'

Once we're out of earshot, Jackman's hand still on Daniel's elbow, he says, 'Please don't speak to the press, Mr Salmon, especially not *that* man.'

Jackman is smart in his pinstripe suit, dark hair like an unruly ruff that he keeps brushing aside, only to have it fall back over his eyes. Victoria stares at him like he's an actor, which in a way he is. Once we reach the privacy of the solicitor's room, he turns to Daniel. 'I was hoping we could turn the media to our advantage, with you being a local hero, but now I think it could go against us. I gather from reading his articles that Alfie Avon doesn't like you very much?' His voice seems able to project only at high volume.

'He's jealous,' Daniel says. 'He had the Friday-evening slot on the radio, before it was offered to me. He's obsessed with the idea that I'm a fraud, always trying to dig dirt on my Samphire Master programme.'

Alfie Avon has been a thorn in Daniel's side for two years, snidely having regular digs in his 'All About Suffolk' column at Daniel's radio show, and his juice programme. In Suffolk, any celebrity is coveted highly, and Avon can't stand that Daniel gets more media attention than him. His reportage is always vicious.

Jackman adds, 'On the plus side, my wife swears by your juices. They helped her through the menopause, which was a relief to everyone, I can tell you. She listens to your radio show religiously – I may have to get your autograph later.'

Daniel manages to look bashful. 'Shame she can't testify for me.'

'Well, of course, you aren't the one on trial. Now, to the matter in hand. Miss Hawke, if the court asks you, you should say it will be better for you to have Hector home, yes? Less travelling to and from Norwich, and of course you want him home for the funeral. Do you have a date?'

'Next Monday,' I say.

It was the earliest Ipswich Crematorium could do. I just want it over. You understand that, don't you, Mum?

'Good. Now, this medication Hector's on is very important, it's to control the sleepwalking. It will be monitored by Dr Marsh, so he must take it, and you can tell the court that you'll make sure he does. Daniel has said he'll take Hector to the sleep tests at the hospital, but the big bonus is that if he's bailed home a longer sleep test can be set up. It's a sensible arrangement all round. We'll need to argue that there's no risk to you or yours, not now Hector is being medicated and his sleepwalking is controlled.'

This is the first time that I've thought about this: if Dad is telling the truth, he's a risk to me and Daniel and – worst of all – to Victoria. If the stress of the farm pushed him to this violence, what might the stress of the court case do? But I'm not frightened, because I don't believe any of it. Dad is protecting Ash – don't I know more than anyone what Ash is capable of? Don't I carry the scar? As soon as I can prove it, this madness can all end.

Daniel gives me a long blue stare. I know what I have to do.

'I want him home, Mr Jackson. He needs to be with us, especially now we're all grieving, so please make that as clear as you can to the court.'

Daniel places a concerned hand on my shoulder. We're a united front, and I lean into his body. 'This is a terrible time for all of us, but Hector has our full support.' Just then his mobile starts to ring, and he glances at the screen. 'I have to take this, I'm afraid: it's a very poorly client. Won't be a minute.'

Rupert Jackson watches him go. 'Remarkable man. Now, Cassandra, there's already been some developments in the case. Dr Marsh has a colleague at the Bartlet Hospital who can run the sleep test later this week, which is great news, and he'll also need to set up overnight monitoring in your home. What do you know of your father's behaviour when asleep?'

'He has done strange things in his sleep, I won't deny that, like the time he jumped through the window, but that was years ago. I had no idea he still sleepwalked. My mother never mentioned it.'

'She did, Mum! I remember the story of him driving the tractor and not waking up till he reached the motorway,' Victoria chips in, unable to suppress her nervous excitement. 'We all do it – you bake cakes in your sleep, don't you, Mum? Dawn says sometimes I get up and move things around our room, but only when I'm anxious about a test.'

I turn to her sharply. 'Hush, Victoria, Mr Jackson isn't interested in our family anecdotes. Why don't you go and get us some drinks from that machine in the foyer – make yourself useful.' I hand her my purse, and Mr Jackson watches her go with amusement on his face, rocking back on his patent shoes.

'Sorry about that.'

'Not at all, Miss Hawke, your family are quite charming, which will help immensely with the trial. And the housekeeper, Janet, also confirms his sleepwalking from when she lived at the farm, so we're in a strong position.'

I glance across to where Daniel's leaning on a wall beside the main entrance. He's facing away from me, so I can't see his expression, and still talking on his phone. Victoria's pushing coins into the vending machine, too far away to hear me.

'How do you know Dad's not lying though?'

Jackson doesn't even seem shocked, as though my disloyal question is simply philosophical musing.

'Truthfully, I don't.' He raises an eyebrow then removes a yellow pad from his bulging briefcase, flicking rapidly through his notes to find the right section. 'What I present is an argument, and ultimately, the jury decide if it's a convincing one. Everyone deserves a defence, Miss Hawke, and that's my motivation. Now I'm off to the cells to see Hector. I'll come back and get you when it's time.'

Daniel is agitated when he returns.

He slides his phone into the pocket inside his jacket as if it's something he wants rid of. I wonder if Monica is making demands he isn't happy with. He places a hand on my shoulder and squeezes.

'Poor love, you look awful. I think once your dad is home, after the funeral, you should take a break. Spend some time relaxing.'

'You mean a holiday?' All of our money has been earmarked for the Spa: we haven't had a break in years. My pathetic heart lifts, because he wants to spend time alone with me rather than his lover. 'Where would we go?'

'*We?* I can't take time off work, love, not with my growing client list, and the radio show is getting so many listeners. I meant you could get signed off from work.'

'Signed off?' The phrase is a chilly one. It takes me back two years, to the last time I wasn't coping. Bad times.

'It might be a good idea, Cass. Give yourself a chance to recover.'

He thinks I'm sick. I watch as a group of teenagers kick a paper cup between them, despite the usher's warning look. There's a weepy woman across from me, clutching the hand of a man wearing a suit and trainers, speaking to his solicitor. Life's outcasts, but right now, I feel more kinship with them than with Daniel and his successful life.

Rupert Jackson returns. 'We're up next,' he says, as if we're about to get on a stage and perform. He places a hand on my elbow and guides me through a dark wooden door with gold script announcing its name: Court I.

Among the faces up in the public gallery are people from Kenley who knew you, Mum, most of your life. This is an event: a family tragedy worthy of prime-time television, played out in front of their eyes like the best kind of theatre. I imagine them muttering behind hands, '*He shot her, you know. Said he was asleep.*'

'*Likely story. They should bring back hanging!*'

Alfie Avon is up there, of course; I can hear his rasping voice from here. He's hounded this case since the start, and now he's looking around to see who might have some tidbits for him. In the front row, leaning over the balustrade, is Philip Godwin. He'll be thinking only of the farmland, and the question mark that looms over it now you're dead and Dad's been accused. Criminals can't benefit from crimes, I know that much, so any decisions will now fall to me and Daniel.

Godwin catches the reporter's beady eye and Alfie Avon moves to sit next to him. He must be enjoying this, feasting on our tragedy.

I sit as far back as I can on the bench, so they can't see my face. Wedged between Daniel and Victoria, I feel myself swaying, like I'm in a dream and can't wake up. Victoria is subdued now, her nervous energy evaporating into the intimidating atmosphere. I slide my hand over hers and feel sweat, whose I'm not sure. She's only fourteen, it wasn't fair to bring her, but Daniel insisted it would show the magistrates that Dad is a family man.

Daniel. In his smart suit, with his dark looks. So handsome, so controlled, and I see women in the public gallery pointing him out to each other, wondering if they dare ask for a selfie with him later. But what they can't see is that his leg is shaking, jiggling up and down.

There's movement, a door is opened and Dad is led to the witness box. He slides into the wooden seat, head high and I notice the web of broken veins across his nose and cheeks that redden his skin. His nose, prominent on his face, is fleshy and broad. A weathered face: no mistaking that this is a man who works the land in all seasons. Whatever grief he feels, he's keeping it held in.

The excited chatter in the public gallery gathers momentum, and I see Alfie Avon exchange a few words with Dave Feakes, who looks sullen, seated on the end of the row. Whatever Alfie's asking, no doubt seeking some sensational headline linking this case to the Port Authority's desire to buy our farm, Feakes isn't inclined to answer.

Victoria fidgets, shuffles her black skirt lower over her knees. She's wearing her school uniform, but without the tie, the only suitable clothes she had. She'll probably wear the same outfit at your funeral. She watches the activity in the gallery.

'Look, Mum,' she says, tugging my sleeve, 'it's Ash!'

I look up, see him take a seat in the back row beside the woman who runs the Spar shop in the village. Dad has noticed too, gives him a sorrowful nod. An intimate moment passes between them and I feel a pang of envy, then anger. *He* should be in the witness box, not Dad. My scar itches under my blouse, as if sending confirmation.

Then I notice Holly, taking a seat in the public gallery, but in the corner. She gives me a small smile, which I return. She's here for me, sending me support across the room.

Rupert Jackson appears, like an actor stepping onto a stage, striding to the front desk – in his element here. In seconds, the usher says, 'All rise, please', and from a door at the back of the room, three magistrates appear: two men in suits and one lady in pearls. We all stand, waiting for them to take their seats beneath the crest and Latin motto, the woman in the middle.

Dad's poise deserts him, his face pales and even from here I can see him shaking. I notice he's wearing the checked shirt he's worn to farmers' conventions and a badly fitting navy jacket – an expensive one I don't recognise.

'Where did he get that jacket?' I ask Daniel, in a hushed whisper.

'It's mine. I took it when I went to visit.'

I turn and stare at him, thinking again how little I know this man. How many more secrets does he have? He keeps looking ahead, to where the action has begun.

Dad watches Mr Jackson as he would an untested bull just released into a field of cows: everything depends on his performance.

Rupert Jackson begins, his plummy, over-loud voice, punctuating every sentence with *Your Worships*, and *Madam*, referring exclusively to the woman in the middle, who I gather is the most important. She's the only one who looks up; the men are writing with their heads bent. He points me out as he explains the bail application, using more words than needed, enjoying the moment.

I realise that I won't have to say anything. My very presence, the fact of me sitting here, is enough to suggest that I want Dad home and that I'll look after him.

Dad holds himself still, looking ahead. Only his gnarled right hand moves, shaking hard until he grips onto the balustrade to steady himself.

The magistrates don't even retire to decide their course of action. The two men whisper to the woman, she speaks to each, nods, then finally she asks Dad to stand.

'Hector Hawke, you will be bailed to your daughter's home. Bail conditions are that you must attend all appointments with Dr Clive Marsh, take any medication prescribed and co-operate with the sleep tests both at home and the hospital. Your case will be committed to the Crown Court for trial, and you will await notice of this date.'

Just like that, it's over.

And then it isn't. We're outside, on the court steps, and there's a circus around us. Dad's in the centre of our family circle, hands bunched into fists, blinking in the daylight, but so is Alfie Avon.

'How does it feel to be free?' he shouts. 'What will happen to the farm now?'

Cameras click, people push, there's too much noise.

Holly's trying to catch us up, but the crowd are seeping around us, a human barrier. Alfie Avon turns to her. 'What do you make of what just happened, Holly? Any comment?'

She catches my eye, shakes her head at Alfie, but it's enough for me to understand: he knows her, they've spoken. Why didn't she tell me this?

I'll follow you home, she mouths, over the heads of the crowd.

Then Avon turns to Daniel, his voice raised above the chatter of other reporters. 'If it isn't The Samphire Master himself. Is there any truth in the rumour that Maya wasn't as well as you said on your radio show? That your claims to cure cancer are just a big con?'

It's too much, and Daniel lunges forward, ready to punch Avon. Jackman is quicker though, pulling him back, just before Daniel's fist meets Avon's jaw. Avon pulls the ugliest, most joyous grin and I see that he wants Daniel to hit him, how perfect that would be for his next article.

'Temper, temper!' he crows. 'Doesn't that meditation work either, then?'

Daniel turns to me, his face is ashen with rage and regret. I shout across to him, 'It's okay, just get out of here.'

I reach for Victoria and for once she allows my arm to circle her, pressing against me. Then Holly is with us, guiding us both away from the crowd. I have never felt more grateful.

33

Holly

Daniel drove away at speed, so fast his tyres screeched on the road. Holly watched the car go, and turned to Cassandra, who was holding Victoria close.

'Can you take us home, please, Holly?' she said.

It was Alfie who'd provoked this reaction with his jibe about Maya's cancer, and Holly had given him that tidbit, revealing confidential information from the hospital files. Daniel had shown his sore spot, and hadn't Alfie said his own wife had been one of Daniel's patients? There was something there, she knew it, but she also knew she was overstepping her remit and risking her career to seek it out.

They arrived at the house and Cass remained seated in the car, staring out of the window.

'Come on, Mum,' said Victoria, jumping out of the back seat. Cassandra began to move, as if going inside her home was the last thing she wanted to do. Holly sensed it was because of Hector, the tension between them was palpable, but Cass had been deceived by both of the men. And Daniel had just revealed his violent side.

When they were inside, Hector and Daniel were nowhere to be seen, and Victoria disappeared upstairs; she could already be heard talking on her phone. Holly followed Cass to the front room, where she sat on the sofa like a soldier returned from battle. She looked tired but elegant in her court outfit of a simple cream blouse and navy trousers. She'd pulled off her heels so her feet were bare, and Holly noticed that her toenails had newly been painted pale pink. Her blonde hair had been swept up and clipped out of her face, enhancing her even features, her mouth was slightly pulled down, and her eyes looked bruised with fatigue and grief. Even so, anyone could see that, like her mother whose picture had been on the front page of the *Evening Star* every night that week, Cassandra was beautiful.

Holly reached out to touch her arm, squeezing it in a gesture of comfort. 'Are you okay? That moment outside the court was a bit tense.'

She could feel relief seeping into Cassandra's marrow that the ordeal was over. 'I will be. I don't know about you, but I need a drink. Bourbon?'

Like a stunned animal Cass stood, staggered slightly, then made her way towards the kitchen. Holly followed, leaning against the kitchen counter as Cass found some glasses and poured from a bottle of Wild Turkey.

Victoria came back downstairs and grabbed an apple. 'Are you hungry, love?' asked Cass, but the girl just shrugged. What an ordeal for a fourteen-year-old. Holly had the impression of a young rabbit who'd just made it across a very busy road. The decision to let her attend the court hearing seemed strange to Holly.

'Do you want some juice?' Cass asked her.

'Please.'

Cass busied herself at the fridge and Holly took a moment to study the daughter. Victoria had a similar beauty to her mother, except she had dark hair like Maya. When she left the room, she took ninety per cent of its energy. Cassandra looked ready to collapse, she leaned on the kitchen table as she downed her bourbon in one smooth belt.

'Was it a hard decision, Cass, to let Hector come back here?'

'It's the right thing to do, and what Mum would've wanted. Besides, I think he's innocent.'

She reached for the bottle of Wild Turkey, poured another shot. Holly wished she'd sit down, relax, talk. She wanted to help, and it seemed that in order to do so she'd have to probe.

'Even though he says he's responsible?'

'He says he was asleep. Holly, you interviewed him in the prison. Do you believe him?'

Holly waited a beat, and in that moment she heard movement upstairs, quick but heavy footsteps that she knew must be Daniel's. Her mistrust surfaced like the scent of sulphur in her nostrils. Unpleasant, a warning: tread carefully. 'No, I don't. But the police do, and a court date has been set. So that's it.'

'Not for me,' said Cassandra. She seemed to have grown in resilience, as if her mother's death had forced her to take a stronger role within the family. Holly saw how, since that first morning at the farm, Cass had gained confidence. Warmth spread through her, maybe the bourbon, maybe friendship, and she reached to clasp her hand.

'You're coping so well, Cass.'

'Not everyone thinks so,' Cass said drily. 'Daniel suggested I take time off work, compassionate leave.'

Daniel, again, telling Cass she was ill. Gaslighting her. Once again, Holly had the sensation of smelling burning matches, her senses alerting her.

'I think he's wrong, Cass. Some people would be struggling to get out of bed after all you've had to deal with. And you've still got the energy to want to solve this.'

'Yes, but I have other things to do too. Victoria is home, and I still have the details of the funeral to organise. I've booked a humanist to do the service – Mum didn't believe in God so it seems appropriate. To be honest, having so much going on around me helps me get through this. I have to get through this, but Daniel says I'm not strong.'

Holly thought that the person coping least well was Daniel, whose calm demeanour had broken when he raised a fist to the reporter. This was the person she most wanted to know about; being in the same room as him would give her senses a chance to work. 'What do you think Daniel and Hector are doing?'

'Dad will be resting and Daniel will be upstairs, meditating. It's what he does when he's agitated and that scene with Alfie Avon really shook him. That's why I told him to leave; I knew that was the safest thing.'

'He has quite a temper, doesn't he?' Holly said, pushing the conversation back to where her interest really lay.

'Alfie Avon provoked him – he never usually loses his cool. He takes everything on, and tries to fix it. Daniel thinks he can heal the world, but this is outside of his control.'

'I suppose everyone deals differently with trauma.'

Cass finished her drink and looked at Holly coldly. 'Please don't try to suggest Daniel has anything to do with the shooting, Holly. You're my friend, and you've been the only one who believed me when I said Mum didn't shoot herself. I want us to help each other, but please don't turn on my man. Ash is the guilty one, not Daniel.'

DAY 11

TUESDAY 11 NOVEMBER

34

Cassandra

Stepping from my shower, I catch my reflection in the mirror, the dark bruises under my eyes. *Oh, Mum, what's happened to me?*

Thank God for the Prozac, for that medicinal veil that covers all my emotions. Despite it, every feeling I've had since that Friday, the betrayal and anger and confusion, it's all there in lines around my mouth and the deep shadows under my eyes. I look tired and faded, the events of the past week etched on my skin like worry and not wisdom. I try to fix it: rub in concealer, blush my cheeks bronze, paint my lips pink, and tell my smoothed reflection that from now on things will be different.

Yawning, exhausted to my bones even though I've just woken, I go downstairs to the kitchen. There, on the table, all along the kitchen tops, are trays and plates of cakes, cool to the touch and ready to be iced. *Oh God, not again.* I wrack my brains, and locate a dull memory of coming downstairs in the night with a furious need to do something.

You taught me to cook, Mum, and muscle memory must have kicked in as I sleepwalked, because here are cakes of my childhood: buns, flapjacks, scones. I'd forgotten I even had the ingredients – the flour and sugar have been at the back of the larder for months.

The dream comes back in a fuller form. I dreamt I was a girl again: you were here too, flouring the kitchen top, rubbing butter between my fingers, the warm smell of sugar and fat. You let me lick the spoon afterwards, the floury prints on the bosom of your apron from where you'd lifted me down from the stool. How impatient I'd been to open the oven, to taste the too-hot cakes, but you warned me I'd only get burned. Just a dream, but here are the cakes as if to prove it was real.

'Tori!' Daniel calls, as he comes down the stairs. 'Time you got up! It's not healthy to get more than seven hours' sleep.'

He brings a masculine, woody smell into the kitchen, hair damp from the shower, buttoning his designer polo shirt, but not all the way. He kisses me on the lips, then notices the baking. An intake of breath, then he forces a smile.

'Wow, Cass. Are you opening a cake shop?'

'I couldn't sleep so I cooked all Victoria's favourites. I thought I'd take some to the hospital, as a thank you for what they did for Mum . . .'

He rubs my shoulder and I lean into him, his delicious smell, and want to weep. How could he have betrayed me, when I love him so much? *It isn't fair* . . .

'The cakes look delicious. I'm sure we can give some to the neighbours.'

I know that concerned look, that careful tone, and it chills my blood: he thinks I need treatment. Last time I felt this unstable, I ended up being sectioned. Last time I became suspicious about all the calls he had been taking, all the money missing from our bank account, and I became convinced that he had a lover. He said that the calls were clients, that the money was spent on the gym. He convinced me that I was paranoid; that I was sick, not seeing straight. Now, the same thing is happening again: frequent calls, unexplained absences. But this time I'm certain I'm right: I even know her name. Monica.

I hear light steps on the stairs, then Victoria is in the room, wide-eyed at the cakes. 'Oh yum!' She reaches for a bun, saying with a mouthful, 'This is *so* good.'

Daniel's eyes turn stony. 'Not very healthy though, so just have one, please. Why don't you go and get dressed, Cass? And take off some of that make-up. You look like a clown.'

After I've sorted myself out, the day gets moving, as it will do. Daniel goes to work, and Victoria promises to do schoolwork and not spend the entire morning watching Netflix. Dad wants to go to the farm. He was only away from the land a few days, but that's still more than ever before, though I understand that he wants to be at home to grieve. He's desperate to be back in a place he belongs after being in a hospital, a prison – places where he's a fish out of water – though he could wind up in either after the trial. I agree to drive him as his medication means he can't operate machinery. I also want to go to the farm, maybe there's evidence there, something that will directly implicate Ash.

Dad is silent the entire journey. There's discomfort between us as if words can't bridge the gap caused by your death, so the eight-minute trip seems much longer. When I'm parked, we both stare up at the farmhouse, as if it might have something to say about all that's happened. But the farm keeps its own counsel: it knows it will outlast us all, in some form or another.

Dad leaves the car without a word, striding off to the pig field where I can see Ash is working, a dark solitary shape in the distance.

I'm about to go inside the farmhouse when something stops me – a memory I can barely grasp forces my feet towards the barn.

Pushing open the black wooden door, I see the chickens are roaming free, pecking in hard earth or roosting in triangle houses of mesh and wood. It's true what Ash told the police: we did play here when we were kids, hiding in stacked straw bales, pretending it was a den or another world. The earth dips where it's been trodden down by Dad's heavy boots.

Last time I was in the barn was that terrible Friday, around six, with the shooting party. That evening, the floor lay littered with a pile of dead birds, the spoils of their sport; now only a rusty bloodstain remains. I notice a left-over wine glass, half-hidden behind a bale of straw. Next to it are Dad's black rubber gloves, the ones he uses to finish off any birds only half-dead.

One of the gloves moves on the straw, fingers flapping in the wind like crows' wings. I kneel down closer to look at them. What do I expect to see? Blood? But the stains aren't red, they're black, the colour of oil or fertiliser. The glove is large and open-mouthed, long-necked and waiting to swallow a hand, an arm, whole. I touch it, and the rough slipperiness curls between my fingers. I slide my hand inside the loose rubber. It swallows my forearm, but still the glove almost fits. My fingers find the grooves worn by his; the moulded shape of regular use as comfortable to me as my own. Could he have pulled the trigger, like he says he did, without the glove to strengthen his right hand?

No, I don't think so.

I enter the farmhouse, needing to be away from that place of death. But here, the atmosphere is even darker because you aren't here in the kitchen, nursing a cup of green tea, talking to Janet as she stands at the sink, hands wet with soap. I can see her apron strings in a knot behind her, flat shoes solid on the brick floor. I can hear your voice, Mum, low and confident as you tell her about something you read in the paper that morning; you always had an opinion on everything, didn't you? The scene is so real I can smell the Harrods soap you asked for each Christmas, the scent of winter walks and fresh snow, as if you were here with me.

I hear something, noises overhead. I stand and listen.

It's a scraping sound – mice? No, too big for that. Rats? Could be. I gingerly go to the bottom of the stairs: I hate rats. Outside, in the distance, the rumble of the tractor tells me I'm the only one who's going to fix this. I climb the backstairs, and reach the landing, your study to the left, your bedroom to the right. The scratching is coming from your room.

Mum?

Your bedroom door creaks on its weary hinge, just enough to let me in. The bedspread is pulled tight over the pillows, coral-pink washed to blush, the scent of winter faded here but lingering still. It draws me in, to you, a place I could never normally go. I perch on the edge of the bed, run a hand over the place you last lay. Tiredness falls over me like a blanket, weighs down my back and shoulders. I can't fight it, I have to lie down. I breathe the familiar scents and imagine you're in a better place. I close my eyes.

Scratching wakes me, claws on wood. I jump up, braced to see a rat run over my leg, across the pink sea of covers. The sound comes again, louder, from inside the wardrobe. Walnut wood, handles smooth with wear. I open the door, careful and slow, even as the scratching becomes moaning and I smell pine trees, thick like a forest.

Mum, are you here?

I step inside, knowing it's no rat, not any more.

Then I see you, curled like a dormouse at the bottom of the wardrobe. The only perfect thing is your red silk nightdress, but your face – oh, Mum, your poor face! The bruises, the blood broken in the whites of your eyes . . . I scream and try to shut the door, but it won't budge because of your body. I push, and you push back to be free, you look at me with your intense brown eyes and say my name, 'Cassandra!'

Someone is shaking me, touching me, and I'm so frightened I put my hands to my face and scream.

'Cassandra!'

35

Holly

Holly arrived at the house in Greater Kenley to find the only person home was Victoria, who answered the door with earphones in her ears, wired to her phone.

'Mum and Grandad have gone to the farm,' she said, lifting just one pod from her ear so Holly could hear the thudding bass of music. 'They left an hour ago.'

It was a short drive to the farm, and Holly found Hector in the barn, mucking out the old straw as the chickens pecked at his feet. 'Morning, Hector. I wanted to drop by to see how you're getting on.'

Hector was pulling a straw bale apart with his pitchfork, his right hand serving as a wedge to stop the bale from slipping. 'I've got work to do.'

'Are you sure you should be exerting yourself so much?'

'I may as well work. I can't see much point in anything else.' He spat on the ground.

The chickens scrabbled around Holly's feet and she stepped back into something wet. Her trousers gathered dirt at the hems. 'You're on strong sedatives and you're grieving. Be kind to yourself.'

'Work's the best cure for grief.'

Hector turned his attention to raking the mucky straw into a steaming pile and Holly noticed how he was avoiding her gaze, just as he had always avoided her questions.

'I can imagine the farm is very demanding.' She thought of the case studies Clive had told her about, how the stress Scott Falater was under had caused his sleep to be disturbed, though the jury didn't believe him. 'Were you experiencing any pressure, something that caused you to sleepwalk?'

'No more than usual,' he said defensively. 'The Waitrose order for the chickens hasn't been so good – seems people have got it in their heads that they shouldn't eat chooks on account of this bird flu nonsense. I told 'em, my birds ain't sick. See?'

He pointed at a rooster, high in the rafters, its plumage an obscene red, orange feathers ruffling, orange claws clinging to the beam. It was watching the clutch of nervous hens, who scrabbled in the straw below. He was boss here.

'Were you worried about orders being down?'

'Nah – we'd bounce back. People worry about factory birds, but they sure suck up organic, which, being a small farm, we can provide. Allus have been, though they didn't have a fancy name for it afore.'

Free-roaming chickens were something Holly was discovering first-hand, as they pecked around her feet, watched by the vigilant rooster. 'What about your financial worries?'

'My solicitor keeps bangin' on about that, but we get by. We're not rich, course.' Hector shooed the chickens away, and threw his rake onto a pile of straw. 'We have food in the larder and fire in the grate, so it's not so bad. Any cross words we had over the farm didn't make any difference how I felt about Maya. So, don't go tryin' to make out I was angry with her, 'cos I wasn't.'

His eyes looked moist and his breath plumed in the cold air like a feather, then he looked at Holly with such steely force in his eyes that she felt herself jolted in the gut. The weary man shook his head. He was on the verge of tears.

'You should go on inside to see Cassandra. You're supposed to be her friend, ain't you? Happen she needs you more an me.'

Holly turned to leave. Hector needed a moment, and she was glad to be getting out of the barn. The acrid smell of chicken mess was making her nostrils itch.

Holly knocked at the farmhouse door, but couldn't make Cassandra hear. Tentatively, she opened the door and called her name. As soon as she stepped within the farmhouse walls, she could hear panicky sobs echoing down the hallway. Hesitating no longer, she followed the sound up the stairs and into the main bedroom.

Cassandra lay in a foetal position inside the wardrobe, weeping hysterically.

'Cass!'

Holly tried to reach for her, but she didn't seem to hear. Cass had a confused look, as though she was drunk, and she was wobbling too.

'Cass, what's wrong?'

She shook her head, but her eyes began to focus as if she was becoming aware of her surroundings again. She rubbed her eyes, confusion replaced by fear, then she pulled her top down, exposing her collarbone. 'I was shot!' she said, as though it had just happened.

It was an old scar, white where the skin had been stitched. Holly shivered. 'Did you see who shot you, Cass?'

'No,' she said, groggily. 'I was asleep. But Ash admitted it was him.'

Once she'd settled Cass on the sofa in the front room with a glass of water and a blanket over her legs, Holly sat beside her. She wanted to help this woman, who was so distressed that she sensed it as utter black despair.

'How did you end up falling asleep in the wardrobe?'

'The rats . . .' Cass tailed off, looking around in confusion.

'Were you having a nightmare?'

'Mm,' she said, which Holly took as a yes. 'It's being here, thinking about Mum, I suppose. Then I fell asleep and woke up here.'

Holly took her shaking hand, and they sat together like that for some time. Holly thought of the ghostly figure who had approached them in the barn that Halloween, the white gauzy image that could have been a child in a nightdress.

'You're a sleepwalker, aren't you, Cass?'

'No.' She looked down at her fingernails, which Holly could see were torn and bleeding. 'I sleep like a baby.'

36

Holly

Holly should have driven straight to the hospital to start her shift at 7 p.m., but instead she drove home. After seeing Cassandra at the farm, and the scar on her chest, she simply couldn't bring herself to go in. She called Jon, and said she was sick. 'Food poisoning,' she said. 'I'm so sorry.' And she was sick – sick with guilt.

She lay on her bed and curled around herself, moaning gently as the forgotten memory returned.

Twenty years too late, she realised that what she, Jamie and Carl had seen that night wasn't a ghost at all, but a sleepwalking girl. She'd wondered what had happened after Jamie fired his gun, and now she knew: Jamie had shot Cass, and Ash had taken the blame.

It couldn't go on: Jamie had to take responsibility. She opened up her laptop, determined to reach her brother one way or another.

After that Halloween, other than when he was at school, Jamie mostly stayed in his room. Their dad was worried about him, he kept telling him to go out and get some fresh air, but to no avail. Holly too had hung around the house, waiting for Jamie to appear, yet whenever he did actually make it to the kitchen, he'd grab a sandwich or a drink and then disappear again. It was the start of a pattern that didn't end until the family relocated to California. As if the distance from Suffolk absolved Jamie of his guilt.

With Jamie avoiding her, Holly had looked for Carl, but he too was elusive, and she was scared of him. The only other person she could seek out was Ash.

Though she knew where Ash lived, and also that he spent most of his time at the farm, this was a problem for her, as it meant returning to the scene of the crime. Even though it was daylight, and a watery sun yellowed the sky, she still felt nervous when she stepped under the shaded cloak of the copse. Branches broke under her trainers, and she kept swinging round, sure someone was following her, and then equally frightened to discover that she was alone.

Ash wasn't in the copse, or in the fields. She found him in the barn, perched on a bale, tossing handfuls of grain at a bevy of disinterested chickens. He looked up through his fringe, saw her, and tossed the grain at her feet.

'What you doin' here?'

She pushed her hands into her pockets and jutted out her chin, desperate not to seem afraid. 'Came to see you.'

'Me?' He stood, wiped his hands on the front of his jeans, and stepped towards her. He was tall, although not as tall as he'd seemed on Halloween night. Then she saw he had a black bruise circling his left eye.

'Who did that?'

'My dad,' he said.

This surprised her; Ash was bullied at school for not having one. Then she whispered, 'Because of what we did?'

His face twitched, and he looked at her as if she were a piece of grain he'd like to toss to the birds. 'What *you* did, you mean. I didn't do nothin'.'

'You showed us the ghost! You brought us here.'

He kicked the ground, sending a balloon of dust into the air.

'Did we kill someone?' she asked, still whispering. Afraid of the answer, but needing to know anyway.

'She didn't feel it,' he said. ''Cos she was asleep.'

Holly had known the truth all along, but had somehow misunderstood and pushed it away. She'd carried on telling herself she didn't really know what had happened that night. But her senses had protested, raining down their reactions, making her feel everything threefold.

Denial, deeply rooted. But not for any longer. She got up, and went to find her laptop.

'Jamie?'

His face came into view on the screen. He was chewing – she could see she'd interrupted his lunch but she didn't care.

'You're persistent, know that, sis?'

So he had been avoiding her. 'Did you do what I asked, and google Innocence Farm?'

He yawned again, and this time she noticed the dark circles under his eyes. She hadn't woken him – he looked like he hadn't slept in days. 'I did, but how's it concern us? The farmer's wife got shot. It was the husband, wasn't it?'

'Not everyone thinks so: another man is under suspicion, and I think he's innocent. Ash Cley. You remember him?'

She waited, watched as his smile dropped and he looked more awake. Yes, she could see it in his face – Jamie remembered Ash all right.

'He took the blame, Jamie, he has a police record for a gun crime when he was innocent. We can't let that happen a second time.'

He didn't speak, just rubbed his eyes wearily. 'I can't talk now. I have work to do.'

'Jamie, you *shot* someone!'

'So what, you want me to confess?' he spat. Across the miles, through the wires, she could feel his venom. 'What would that do to my relationship with Kaitlin, to my career? It was *two decades* ago, Holly. You can't just expect me to destroy my life over something I did when I was a kid.'

And then the screen went blank. The connection had been severed, and Jamie was gone.

37

Cassandra

Holly wanted to drive me home – she said she was worried about me.
It seems that everyone is. I'm determined not to seem vulnerable, so I
drove myself home, though in truth I did feel groggy. Dad wasn't ready
to leave yet, so I told him Dan would pick him up later.

I can hear the drilling before I even open the front door, and once
inside, it's deafening. Sharp bursts, the horrible sound of metal being
threaded into wood. I climb the stairs and reach the source. Daniel's
stood in Victoria's doorway, the drill in his hand.

'What's going on?' I say, though I can see. He's putting a lock on
Victoria's door, one that can only be used from the inside. He puts
down the drill and picks up his screwdriver, finalising the twists so the
lock's in place.

'Tori's a young woman now, love. She needs her privacy.'

Inside the room, Victoria's cross-legged on her bed, eyes focused on
the screen of her iPad.

'Hi, Mum.'

'Hi, love. Did you ask Dad to put a lock on your door?'

She shakes her head, not really listening. I move to see the screen that has her attention, and there is the face of her best friend, gazing out at me. 'Hi, Dawn.'

Victoria raises her eyebrows at me as if to ask, *Well?* Daniel's right: she needs her privacy. Teenagers don't want an adult hanging around, earwigging.

The grogginess pervades. Just walking is like pushing through treacle. I need to lie down, though it's dinnertime, not yet time for bed. Probably it's because of all the baking I did last night: I've had two sleepwalking incidents in the space of twelve hours. It could be the drugs causing it – I should tell Clive. But I won't.

I didn't tell Holly either, though what else was she to think when she found me in the wardrobe? I don't want to be under her scrutiny, or anyone's. I need to keep well, to get through the funeral and court case, find out what Daniel's up to, bring Ash to justice for killing you.

He killed you.

I can't run to you any more, Mum. I'll finally learn to stand on my own two feet, and your solutions weren't always what I needed anyway. When you sent Victoria to Oakfield it broke my heart, but you always thought you knew best. Now all the decisions will be mine.

I only meant to close my eyes for twenty minutes, but when I open them again, it's quiet and dark. I have the sick sensation that I've missed part of my life. Under the duvet I'm fully clothed, sweaty, and through the open curtains a disc of pure white shines down on me. The moon knows everything. I'm hot and heavy and my head feels like lead, weighted to the pillow. I listen greedily for Victoria's voice. I only need a few words, just enough to know she's still here and hasn't been spirited away from me. But she'll be in bed by now, asleep. I didn't even say goodnight.

My bladder demands that I get out of bed. My stomach grumbles for food – my body's completely out of whack with its usual rhythms.

Downstairs, there are signs that a meal has been cooked and eaten. There's an almost empty bottle of wine and the parmesan is still on the table, the spiraliser's on the draining board. Why didn't anyone wake me?

I check the fridge, but there are no leftovers for me. There's only the buns and scones I cooked last night and one quarter of Victoria's home-coming cake. I dig my fingers into the hard sponge and take a huge bite. It's soft and sweet and I grab more, a handful this time, stuffing it in my mouth as if it's the very thing that can save me. Guiltily, mouth still chewing, I check no one's watching. The door to the front room is shut but I can hear voices in conversation. Dad, who hasn't spoken to me properly since the bail hearing, who hardly said a word in the car on the drive to the farm, is talking plenty to Daniel. Curious, I move to the door, careful not to make any noise. I swallow the last of the cake and bend my head to the gap.

Daniel says, 'We need to protect her, Hector, for the sake of the family. She's such an innocent, like a child in so many ways.'

Is he talking about Victoria? It's true – she may seem grown up, but she's only fourteen.

'Yup,' agrees Dad, 'and that's what I'm doin'. Don't be lecturin' me, boy.'

'I'm not, I promise. I'm just worried she suspects.' Daniel sounds desperately weary.

'All of us, we're doin' it for her, 'cos she's not strong enough to know the truth. But, by God, sometimes I could just whack some sense into her.'

I straighten. I no longer think they're talking about Victoria. Only I can inspire that level of anger.

'Hector, I know this is hard on you, but speaking like that helps no one. It's natural you're anxious about the sleep test . . .'

'Sod that! What do doctors know? They weren't there that mornin', so whatever that test says, it proves nothin'. I know what happened, and so do you.'

His voice is muffled then, and I imagine him fighting back emotion, pushing it down as always. Then Daniel says, 'Nobody is responsible for what they do while they're asleep, Hector. We just have to hope the jury understand that and then this will all be over. We have to stick to the story . . .'

Dad mumbles something I can't catch, but my mind has latched on to that word: *story.*

I'm certain now: Dad's lying, and Daniel's colluding with it. I'd understand Dad protecting Ash – he loves him. But why would Daniel?

This man I love with all my heart has secrets I don't understand.

I creep back upstairs to Victoria's room, and have to wait for her to unlock and open the door. 'What's up, Mum?' She resumes her place, cross-legged on her bed in shorty pyjamas, listening to music on her earphones and tapping on the screen of her iPad.

'I just wanted to say goodnight.'

Her small room's cosy, a little girl's room in pink and white with bunting around the walls. There seemed no point in decorating it after she left.

I was so angry with you then, for taking her away from me, even though I believed I was sick. Now I don't think I was, I think I saw things clearly: Daniel was cheating on me. It was you who couldn't see that. And he's doing it again, deceiving me.

I want to curl up next to Victoria and listen to the music, lose myself in it. But that would be hiding from the truth, and I've done that for too long.

'You shouldn't still be awake, love – it's very late.'

'I'm messaging Dawn.' She quickly types another line, adding in a sad-faced emoji. 'I miss her, she hates being at Oakfield without me. Can she come here for the weekend? *Please*, Mum.'

She's used to Dawn coming to stay each holiday, and I want her to be happy. God knows this has been a tough enough week for her. I'm ashamed of feeling jealous too – why can't being here, with me, make her happy?

'It's not a great time, love. We have Granny's funeral on Monday, and there's still details to arrange.'

'Dawn gets that, she's been supporting me,' Victoria persists. 'We'll just stay here while you're sorting everything, and do prep. Please, Mum. I'm so lonely, and it's just so sad about Granny and everything else . . . If she comes, she'd cheer me up. I know Dad would say okay.'

'Would he?'

'He loves Dawn,' she says, so simply there can be no doubt.

I think again of Dawn's mother, Monica. Daniel seems so willing to believe I'm ill again: could he want me out of the way to be with her? Is he planning on having me sectioned, once the court case is over, so the farm will be all his? And Victoria's right, Daniel does always seem keen to have Dawn to visit. His motivation, I see now, isn't just to keep Victoria happy. He's doing it for Monica, preparing the way for when they'll be a happy family, without me.

It seems so drastic a conclusion. Maybe I am sick after all.

I need proof. I need to know for certain what the hell is going on, and this could be a way to get it. I need to know I'm not crazy.

'Mum? *Please?*'

'Okay,' I say, though the word comes out reluctantly, 'Dawn can come.'

Victoria jumps up, and throws herself at me, hugging me tight. 'Thanks, Mum, you're the best.'

'But check that Dad agrees. He can collect her on his own. I want you here to help me.'

She's already leaving, happy with the deal I've offered, running downstairs to ask him.

'I love you,' I say to her empty room.

I pretend to be asleep when Daniel finally slides into bed next to me, anger rising off me like heat. If I open my mouth, the accusations will boil over and spew out of me. *We just have to stick to the story . . .*

Daniel's breathing deepens but my suspicions keep me awake, tangled up with the other feelings. Since the shooting, he's lied to me about where he's been, what he's been doing, he's been whispering to *Monica* on the phone, speaking to someone in the courthouse. As paramedics fought to save your life, he was instructing architects to move forward with his plan for Samphire Health Spa.

I sweat the night away, watch Daniel as he sleeps, thinking how much I love him and how easily I could shoot him dead.

DAY 12

WEDNESDAY 12 NOVEMBER

38

Holly

'Morning, Holly, you're up with the lark! Got me another scoop, kid?'
Alfie said. 'I'd offer you a seat but . . .'

But there wasn't another. He was in his cubicle, the desk piled high
with notepads, a laptop and bitten pens, while the floor was a sea of
photos and torn newspaper articles – a clutter that seemed to have some
order, judging from the way he was studying it.

Around the room, in neater cubicles, some reporters chatted about
the Netflix saga everyone was watching, others bemoaned ITV for
showing Christmas adverts already. Alfie seemed oblivious to all of this,
he too was obsessed with Innocence Lane.

Holly stepped gingerly into his space and saw that the surrounding partitions were layered with information. Alfie himself looked even
more radioactive than usual: his flushed face toned with his ginger hair,
not helped by the red shirt he had chosen. Holly wondered how the
shop assistant had let him make this error of judgement.

'How's the reporting?' she asked him.

'I'm trying to find a new angle to please the punters, keep Innocence Lane on the front page, but my editor's thinking it's old news. If I don't come up with something soon, it'll be relegated to page five.'

'Will you go to Maya's funeral?' she asked.

Alfie grinned. 'It would be negligent not to. Though I doubt I'll make it inside the crem', not if The Samphire Man has anything to do with it. You?'

'Cass has asked me to go,' Holly said, 'as her friend.'

'And does she know you're here?' he asked, sickly sweet. 'As her *friend*?'

He grinned at her, and Holly was reminded of the red-crowned cockerel at Innocence Farm, lording it over the hens. But who was she to judge – at least his interest in the case was driven by something pure. Alfie's wife had gone to Daniel for help, and turned her back on conventional treatment. He hadn't said what had happened to her, but his obsession told her that the outcome hadn't been good, and the only family photo on his wall looked at least a decade old, judging by the clothes. As for her, she was motivated by something far less wholesome. Twenty years ago, she'd watched her brother shoot a sleepwalker and she'd kept her mouth shut, letting Ash take the blame.

'No, she doesn't. Alfie, can I tell you something in confidence?'

He raised one bushy eyebrow. 'You know this is like a confessional box – only without the hope of salvation. So go ahead.'

'Yesterday, I found Cassandra at the farmhouse. She was curled up in her mother's wardrobe, shouting, like she was in the middle of a nightmare. It was . . . strange.' This wasn't the best word to describe how unsettling it had been to see a grown woman so terrified while locked within her own dream. 'I think she'd been sleepwalking.'

Alfie raised an eyebrow. 'What are you telling me, Holly? That you think it was the daughter, not the husband?'

To hear it said so baldly made Holly catch her breath – was that what she thought? She had been with Cass many times, and her senses hadn't sung out.

'No, I don't think that. I think she's very vulnerable, and I'm worried about her. I think she needs protecting.'

Alfie took a broken biro from his desk and pointed to one of the articles pinned to his cubicle wall. It was about The Samphire Man. 'Do you mean from that jerk?'

'Yes,' said Holly. She hesitated, then realised Alfie might be the one person she could really confide in. 'I'm beginning to think Daniel could be guilty.'

Alfie leaned back suddenly, a muscle near his eye twitching as he spoke. 'God, I'd love to see him arrested. But he's watertight.'

She felt nervous then, as nervous as she had been in the barn, that terrible Halloween. 'You promise anything I tell you is confidential?'

There was a moment, a silence in the cubicle, unpenetrated by the hubbub around them.

'Holly, you and I, we're on the same side here. If there's any way we can expose The Samphire Man, we have to do it. What is it you have for me?'

She knew it was time. For twenty years she'd kept her condition secret, but now she'd told Clive, it seemed the floodgates were opening. 'Alfie, I have this special trait. I can pick up on what other people feel, their deep emotions. It's a form of synaesthesia.'

Alfie's biro had made its way to his mouth, and he now had black ink on his chin. The skin around his eyes crinkled as his smile widened. 'I did an article on that a few months ago, interviewed this guy who tastes words. His wife's name tasted like Cornish pasties – he said it's why he married her.'

'Yes, well, it takes different forms. Me, I feel touch when I see it, and I feel emotions as if they're mine if I'm close enough to someone. It works best if I touch them.'

He was chuckling now. 'That's fucking brilliant, I love it. So if you got close enough, you could tell if Daniel's the crooked charlatan we think he is?'

'Or if he shot Maya. Yes, I think so.'

'Then what are you waiting for? Go see Daniel. Just you and him, close enough so you can sense the guilt. He'll be stinking of it.'

Holly shook her head. 'How would I do that, Alfie? I have no reason to see him alone.'

'That's easy,' he said, an ironic smile on his lips. 'Do the same as my ex-wife – go to him for help. You're young and pretty: that bastard would never turn away the chance to cure you.'

Samphire Studio was located in a small industrial park, in a blocky building set between a kitchen designer's showroom and a pet store, the pathway was flanked with storm lanterns inside which red candles had burned flat. The gym had darkened glass windows so the interior was hidden, and Holly pushed open the door with a certain trepidation.

The vibe was boutique-hotel-cum-brothel, with massive black leather sofas and displays of red roses on glass tables. The underpinning aroma was rubberised flooring and sweat. To the left was a huge window, on the other side of which an exercise class was taking place with two ladies suspended from loops of coloured cloth. They looked to be engaged in some sort of yoga. Holly tried not to stare, her own sinews straining in sympathy. Daniel was leading the class, his toned physique arching in the straps.

Opposite the door was a long reception desk, with chrome bar stools at one end. At the other, with a laptop open in front of her, was a young woman with spiky pink hair.

'Can I help you?' The receptionist squirrelled away the graphic comic mag she'd been reading and smiled at Holly in a slightly crazed way. Her blue eyes seemed covered with a layer of fluid as if she were very bored, and had been for some time.

'I'd like to speak with Daniel Salmon, please.'

'Oh.' Now the blue eyes looked more alert. 'Are you a new client?'

Holly bit her lower lip. 'I hope to be. I haven't made an appointment . . .'

'Oh, that's fine, he has plenty of spaces. He's teaching right now.' The girl pointed a pink talon at the large glass window. 'Aerial Fitness finishes in seven minutes.'

'Thanks, I'll wait.'

The sofa sagged beneath her, taking Holly lower than the square table, which had a tastefully displayed fan of magazines: *Your Health, Positive Energy, Vogue.* No tacky chat mags for this crowd, only the best for Woodbridge's finest. The wall in front of her was flanked by a huge glass-fronted fridge with rows of juices, green and purple and orange. A price list was taped to the glass under the heading *The Samphire Master suggests.* Each juice was listed, not only with its price, but with all the ailments it treated. She leaned forward and read the notes, fascinated: these magic potions were said to treat everything from psoriasis to melanoma. The juice that caught her eye was crimson, called Dragon's Blood, and according to the description *restores your mental equilibrium and cures emotional overwork.* Something she was experiencing, especially given the task in hand. *Well, Holly,* she chided herself, *you suggested this, so woman up and stop whingeing.*

Beyond the glass, Daniel remained oblivious to what was coming. He was focused on two women, whom he was tying up like origami with red bands that hung from the ceiling. Holly was unable to hear a word but still followed everything that was happening. A smooth operator, Daniel didn't have a dark hair out of place. His taut frame was clad in tight black running clothes, and both women contorted at his command like fluorescent parrots. One woman in a bulging electric-blue unitard found this harder than the other, but he was there to push her generous bottom along the narrow band until she had achieved the position, grinning at him as she did so. Holly felt the mirrored touch on her own backside, and shifted in her seat to make it go away.

Daniel tapped his client on her bright-blue thigh in congratulation, looked at his watch and then began a spontaneous round of applause, which neither of the women could join in without risking a fall. He untethered them, and the class was over, the women collecting their water bottles and snazzy sports bags, eyeing Daniel appreciatively as he exited.

Arriving in the reception area, he spotted Holly on the sofa. His features froze and his eyes turned steely, then as the receptionist told him she was here as a client, he adjusted his face to be more welcoming.

'Hi, Holly. What a surprise to see you here – welcome to Samphire! How can I help you?'

He actually looked sincere, and she thought how easy it must be to trust this man.

Holly smiled sweetly, aware of the twitching ears of the receptionist. 'It's rather delicate, so if we could talk somewhere private . . .'

She saw him hesitate, and feared he was going to say no, despite the receptionist saying he had loads of spaces. 'I'm very busy right now. Christmas is such a stressful time that my clients always like a bit more attention.' As he said this, the two women from the class appeared, now with brushed manes and glossy lips, chatting together and looking curiously at Holly as they made their way to the juice fridge, and he called, 'Try the new Christmas Samphire, girls – it's got cinnamon and turmeric to help you get through the shopping madness!'

They both smiled, and keenly grabbed the snot-green bottles as though they contained the elixir of health.

'I'd really appreciate just a little of your time,' Holly said. 'I've heard such good things about your cures.'

'Then please come up to my office.'

Upstairs was no match for the luxurious ambience of the lower floor. The corridor was narrow and dark, paint peeled from the walls, the restroom door hung open, as did the door of a cleaning cupboard, revealing anti-bacterial sprays and tall rolls of paper. Daniel's office was a room of similar size, barely large enough for the MDF desk he had wedged against the wall and the single kitchen stool. He appeared not to register the incongruity of this, and showed her into his office with the same flair as if he had managed to find a space on Murray Mound at Wimbledon.

'Voilà! I'll go get another chair. Would you like a juice?'

'I'd like to try the Red Dragon, if I may.'

She wasn't thirsty, but asking for a juice bought her a few minutes as he'd have to return downstairs to fetch it, and who could turn down the promise of emotional peace?

Once he'd gone, she looked around properly, surprised by the mess and clutter, when the man himself was so well groomed. It was like cracking open his handsome skull and peering inside to the ugliness within. Stacks of paper flooded the desk, old mugs bore tea stains on the porcelain, a calendar tacked to the wall had a mess of scribbles next to different dates: *Flora*, *Gabby*, *Linda*, *Victoria & Dawn*.

He was soon back, brandishing a bottle and a camping chair.

'Red Dragon, my own secret recipe.' He passed it to her, and as she took it, their fingers touched. She felt his need to keep control of this interview, as well as his underlying fear that he wouldn't be able to.

'Madame,' he said, opening out the camping chair for her to sit on and perching on the desk.

'Thanks.' It had a low seat, so she was looking up at Daniel. 'Looks like you're in the middle of something?'

'Ah, I'm playing catch-up. Most of this stuff just needs filing, and Katie's been too busy on reception to sort it out. I'm getting ready for the end-of-year returns and all that nonsense.'

'How's the gym doing?' she asked, opening and sipping her juice, waiting for the Red Dragon to kick in.

'Woodbridge is a great town for a healing studio – lots of educated people who care about their health and their bodies.'

Holly involuntarily pulled her stomach in. She couldn't remember the last time she'd worked out, unless sex with Leif counted as aerobic exercise. The juice, though, was tasty and she could almost feel it doing her good.

'And, of course, we offer far more here than exercise – there's a whole host of alternative therapies. And the juices. Enjoying it?'

'It's delicious,' she said, honestly.

'This is just the start. When the Spa opens, we'll offer a raw-food programme, tailored to specific needs. We'll have more space, a better ambience . . . Think of all those people we'll be able to help. I'm only scratching the surface at the moment.'

Daniel's ambition sickened her: he was able to enthuse about it so soon after Maya's death and Hector's arrest. And none of it would be possible if Maya were alive – she'd have sold the farm to the Port Authority. Holly glanced again at his calendar, with its scattering of names. 'Are your customers always women?'

'It's a female-only studio. My clients would feel inhibited if there were a man around. It's a safe space for them.'

'But you're a man,' Holly pointed out, taking another sip of her juice to hide her bemusement.

'I'm a professional,' he replied curtly, 'so I don't count.'

Holly thought back to his two smitten customers. Daniel counted very much, and he liked it that way: the only male in an exclusively female environment.

'So,' he prompted, 'how can I help you?'

Holly took a breath and dived in. 'I have synaesthesia. I can sense people's emotions, feel touch when I see it. And it's driving me crazy – I'd like you to cure me.'

Daniel's face lit up with intense curiosity. 'Well, that's a new one. Let me see what I can do.'

He came towards her, and Holly tried not to flinch when he placed his hands on her shoulders, pressing down. *This proximity is what I need, to sense any guilt.* 'Breathe deeply and close your eyes, please.'

She did, and she found her breathing matched his, that his hands warmed her arms, moving up her neck. And then she saw him, lifting the boot of his car and bundling something inside. She smelt blood in her nostrils as surely as if she were back again with Maya's body.

'Breathe, Holly. You're tensing.'

Her body betrayed her: she was relaxing, her mind seemed to be uncoiling and laying itself flat. Daniel was chanting now, a strange humming sound that made her think of dark places, warm spaces. *No, tune in to his senses, don't let him take over.*

She tried to get back to that place, to see Daniel once again bundling something into the car, but the moment had gone. The smell had left her, and all that remained was the sandalwood of his aftershave. Her body was moving, swaying to his command, and she felt heat travel through her limbs, a healing balm. Then he stopped.

Her eyes clicked open like shutters. She was back in the room.

'Okay, Holly,' Daniel said, crouching in front of her, 'you can relax now.'

She realised that she wanted him to cure her, that if he told her he could, she'd believe him. *Please,* she inwardly begged, *make it stop.*

'I'm so sorry. Your disorder is so hardwired, I can't reach it. I don't think there is a cure.'

Two miles out of Woodbridge, she pulled into a lay-by and, hands sweating, called Leif. She didn't know if he'd understand, didn't understand it herself, but she had to speak to someone.

'*Sötnos*, where are you? Are you coming home?'

Home. It was where she longed to be, not hunched in her car in a rest stop, shaking like a kitten. 'Leif, something happened.'

'Holly, are you crying? Tell me where you are – I shall come.'

'No, just listen. Leif, I can't tell you how I know this, but it was Daniel who shot Maya. And I think he bundled something with her blood on it into his car. Can you get the team to examine it?'

'To seize a car we need proof, Holly. Do you have that?'

She really was crying now, for the career she was giving up. She had to do this though. Like Alfie said, people's lives were at stake. 'Leif, I looked at Maya's medical records and her cancer had returned. I think Daniel shot her to stop her exposing him and because she wasn't going to give him the farm. I have the contract she signed, agreeing to sell to the Port Authority. And I have reason to believe her blood is in his car.'

39

Cassandra

Daniel arrives home late and in a taxi. He's pale and looks upset.

'Where's your car?' I ask, but he shakes his head, gesturing to where Victoria's curled up on the sofa, her phone in her grip as she furiously types messages and takes selfie snaps.

'Dad! Come and see this clip Dawn just sent me,' Victoria says, oblivious to his pallor. 'It's a kid who somehow got into a gorilla's enclosure at a zoo. Hilarious.'

It doesn't sound hilarious to me, it sounds terrifying. But it's good to see her so happy, all because Dawn is coming tomorrow. Daniel organised it, with Mrs H and Dawn's mother, who collected her from Oakfield today so he doesn't have to make the long trip to Norfolk and she can spend one night at home. She's going to miss a few days of school, but she'll be here to support Victoria. And I agreed, for my own reasons. Tomorrow, Daniel collects Dawn from her mother's. He'll be seeing Monica.

Daniel gamely watches the clip, though I can tell something's bothering him. He asks me, 'Where's Hector?'

'Gone for a lie-down. What's wrong, Daniel? Why did you come home in a taxi?'

He runs his hand over his face and for a terrible second I think he's going to cry. 'I'll tell you later.' He casts a glance at Victoria, and I understand that whatever has happened is bad.

'There's some halloumi salad left,' I tell him. 'Come eat something.'

'I'm not hungry, I just need a drink.'

'There's some Cabernet open.' I stand, obedient. 'Do you want some juice, Victoria? Green or red?'

'Green, please,' she says.

In the kitchen, I replay my daughter's voice in my mind – confident and clear, with the enunciation of a public-school education; her accent isn't a place, it's a class. This is the gift you bought her, Mum, when you paid for her to attend Oakfield. A bonus to the larger gift of a sanctuary away from my madness.

Back in the front room, I hand her the juice and pass Daniel a large glass of wine. He's acting like everything's okay, but he's tense. I'm trying to be normal too, though it's a stretch. The only thing left of 'me' is on the outside: my stiffly smiling face, my trembling hands on the glass of juice. Inside is a liquid mess, a flood of incomprehensible feelings. Maybe the drugs I'm taking, the Prozac and trazodone, are making me dissolve as well.

Finally, Victoria yawns and takes herself off upstairs and Daniel begins to clear away the napkins and empty glasses.

'She's barely said a word today that wasn't about Dawn, she can't wait to see her tomorrow.' I laugh, as if this weren't something that cuts my heart in two.

'Mmm, that's boarding school, I suppose,' he says. 'Strong friendships that last for life. Your mum said that's why it's such a wonderful experience.'

So much for that: your so-called friends, Mum, have sent cards but none have offered to help with the funeral. I keep that thought inside. It's a battle I've already lost.

'Please, Daniel, now will you tell me why you came home in a taxi? I can tell something bad has happened.' I'm frightened of what he'll say but I've been waiting since he came in, and I can't wait any more.

'The police came to the Studio an hour ago,' he says. 'They've seized my car.'

'So how will you collect Dawn?' My first thought, rather than the obvious question. This is how obsessed I am with Monica.

'I've got a hire car arriving in the morning. I didn't want to change our plans, especially when Dawn's mum has already collected her from Oakfield.'

'But why do the police want your car?' Finally, the right question. 'What reason could they have?'

'That's what I'd like to know,' he says, taking a deep slug of wine.

DAY 13

THURSDAY 13 NOVEMBER

40

Cassandra

As a watery sun appears, I abandon sleep and take a cold shower in a punishing attempt to wake myself up. I need to be prepared, I can't be slow today. I have to concentrate.

Daniel comes downstairs an hour later, dressed in his work outfit: a navy polo shirt and jogging bottoms. I see a spot of blood on his chin where he cut himself shaving, and touch it. He holds my hand and kisses my fingers and I realise that for once he's the vulnerable one. I let him cling to me, and when he pulls away he looks pale. I wonder if it's because the police have seized his car or guilt because he's about to betray me. But after today, there will be no more wondering. I'm going to know for certain: I'm going to follow him to Monica's house.

I have eggs boiling in a pan, the spelt bread is toasted, green tea is poured. It would look like a normal morning scene in an ordinary house, something from a TV ad, unless you could peer inside my suspicious mind.

'You're looking better today, Cass.' He kisses me again, on the lips this time, and I lean into him. He's resilient, my man, he'll bounce back quickly. He's already organised a hire car so he can fetch Dawn, and he's said nothing more about the police taking his car.

I sneak a glance at him as he begins to eat. 'What time are you setting off?'

'Soon. I want to fetch Dawn and drop her back here before lunch. I have clients to see for the rest of the day.' He takes the toast from me and begins munching. 'What are you up to?'

'Oh . . . I'm seeing the funeral director for the final arrangements, choosing the flowers. Lots to do today.' I keep my head lowered, pass him a glass of orange juice. 'You don't mind going to fetch Dawn? Given that the police . . .'

'I'm not letting them change our plans, Cass. We carry on as before, okay?' He downs his juice in one gulp. 'The least we can do is let Tori have her friend to stay.' He kisses me goodbye. 'Look after our girl,' he says.

We agreed Victoria isn't going with him, that she'll stay home to help me instead. That's my story, but the truth is I don't want her to be there when I don't know what will happen, and anyway, her presence would change Daniel's behaviour. If he's guilty, I need to see it. And if he's innocent, then I'll know I really am sick.

Aware of the seconds passing, I go to the window of the front room to study the hire car. A Pacific-blue Mazda. I can't see the number plate, but the car has a distinctive fin antenna on the roof. Then I dash upstairs to see Victoria, but she's still asleep and her door's locked. I push a message under it, already written, along with a ten-pound note:

I'll be back later. Call if you need me. Mum xxx

The truth is, I don't know how long I'll be gone, but I need to see for myself what Daniel is up to, because of seeing a woman in my home that Halloween, because it was the woman in the photograph on Dawn's bedside cabinet, because of hearing the name *Monica*. Because of Daniel's conversation with Dad about their *story*.

The can of worms is going to be opened today, whatever it reveals.

By the time I leave the house, the blue Mazda is gone, but there's only one road out of the cul-de-sac and soon I'm on it, driving fast towards the A12. I glimpse the car tail light, lit on account of the dull day. I keep my lights off, though it would be safer to use them, desperate to go unnoticed. My hands slip on the steering wheel and it's an effort to keep my breathing steady. I'm frightened of what I'll discover, but I've taken the first step now and I'm not stopping. I pray Daniel doesn't need anything; if he pulls into a garage, I'll have no chance of tracking him without being seen, but onwards he drives, so far ahead of me that there are several cars between us. This could be a fool's errand. I may discover nothing today that helps me.

It's tricky to remain unnoticed after we hit the B-road, inland from the coast that leads to Reydon, where I remember Dawn and her mother live. It's just his car and mine on the road now, so I hang well back and see we have arrived at the town. I almost miss him when he takes a sudden turn left into a side road. I pull over, the risk of him seeing me is just too great now we're driving in a 30 m.p.h. zone. I wait two minutes before I drive on again, scanning the tops of cars along the street for the blue fin. Then I see it, parked directly outside a red-brick end terrace.

I pull over sharply, breathless, pulling on the handbrake just as he gets out. My heart hurts. He looks so very much like my Daniel, but if my suspicions are true, he isn't. He doesn't even look down the road as he locks the car. He has no idea I'm watching as he walks up the path, stands on the doorstep and reaches forward to rap on the door. At least she hasn't given him a key.

He collects the single bottle of milk from the step: it looks like she lives alone then. The front lawn's uncut and the curtains hang uneven at the windows, as if she pulled them back in a hurry. This isn't how I'd expect his lover to live – I'd imagined manicured perfection.

Finally, the door opens. I can't see her face, she's standing too far back in the porch. He walks in, hands her the milk. I can see her better now: yes, that's the woman who was in my home that day, *Monica*. Dark bobbed hair, dark skin, an elegant profile like that of Cleopatra. The door closes and whatever is going on inside remains a mystery. What did I expect, full sex on the front porch?

I'm disappointed, it's not enough. I can't have come all this way for nothing.

I wait. Time passes.

The postman arrives, whistling as he walks up Monica's path. He leaves an envelope sticking out from the letterbox; it hangs there, like a taunt. It's a large envelope, white and official-looking. A gift, too golden to resist, despite the risk. I try to look casual as I walk up the paved path, trampling weeds and grass that have forced their way through the cracks.

I lift the letterbox slowly, silently, pulling the cream-vellum franked envelope free. As I'm easing the flap back, I hear a voice inside, Daniel's voice. I want to scream through the letterbox. Then, through the glass, I see someone coming down the stairs: Dawn. I let go of the flap – slap – shove the envelope deep into my pocket, jump away and move briskly, purposefully, down the path. I run, not turning, until I'm safe. Even when I reach my car, I don't slow down. I pull away with such force, the wheels skid under me. I make my hands loosen their iron grip on the steering wheel and wait for my heart to return to normal.

I drive fast out of the street and a hundred yards further on I pull into a cul-de-sac, circling around until I reach a dead end. No one followed me, I'm safe. After I've parked, I take the crumpled envelope in my shaking hands and read it:

Miss Monica Ray

4 Runnels Way

Reydon

Monica Ray, are you my husband's lover?

I thought my relationship was okay. I believed that my jealousy was baseless, a sign of my suspect mental state. Two years ago, I believed Daniel when he said there was a good explanation for the missing money from our account, for all those calls that came at odd hours, for his many unexplained absences.

You persuaded me too, Mum, that I was paranoid, that Daniel wasn't doing anything wrong. A stay at the Bartlet and I'd be fixed.

I want to be well, I want Victoria to stay home. Nothing can stop me now; I tear open the envelope. I need to know everything.

Inside is a letter on paper as thick as card, creamy coloured with black type, and on the top is the Oakfield logo. It's a bill for an outstanding payment of £3,000, a final reminder. I read the typed message, feeling the thick paper between my fingertips and imagining the scent of Oakwood's oak panelling in my nostrils.

> We have liaised with Mr Daniel Salmon regarding the fees, but if no payment is forthcoming by the end of term we will have no alternative but to ask that Dawn is removed from the school.

The tone, the signature, is all Mrs H. My skin turns cold on my bones as I try to decipher the lines on the page. These are the hieroglyphics that slowly become clear to me.

Daniel is paying for Dawn to attend Oakfield. When I collected Victoria, Mrs H referred to *two* lots of school fees and though she said she'd made an error, I don't think a woman like her makes errors with money. I see it all now, the secret that he has kept from me.

Daniel and Monica are having a relationship and this is the only logical reason for him to pay for her education: Oh God, Dawn is *his child*.

I can't go home, not now. I need to keep going, to know the whole truth. Arriving back at Monica's house, I see that the blue Mazda has gone, and I park in its place. Hands on the steering wheel, I realise this is a moment of choice, just like when I thought I heard them having sex in my house that Friday. That day I chose to flee, but I'm not going to do that any more.

My finger shakes as I press the doorbell. No answer, no movement, so I rap my fist on the glass. Monica Ray opens up then, irritated, fixing an earring in her lobe.

'All right, where's the fire?'

Her expression is closed, her eyes are hard; she thinks I'm here to convert her or to sign her up to save children, either way she wants me gone. Despite her face being nipped with irritation, she's striking to look at: café au lait skin with shaped, angular cheekbones and dark eyes. She'd turn heads anywhere and, with those fierce eyes, she's not a woman to be messed with.

'Monica? I'm Cassandra Hawke.'

Now her face alters, the eyes soften slightly. 'Oh, did Dawn forget something?' She looks behind me, expecting her daughter to appear.

'No, Daniel's driving her back to Kenley. I'm here alone.'

The flint returns, though I also see she's puzzled. 'Well, I'm due out in twenty minutes.' She's wondering what I'm doing here, but she's not panicked. I have my first flutter of doubt: if she's his mistress, why is she so calm at my turning up?

'That's plenty of time. Can I come in?'

Monica holds the door a little wider and I cross the threshold.

There's no emotion in the house: scuffed pink walls, a dark green carpet belonging to another decade. There are no pictures or photos hanging on the walls. It feels temporary, like a place you'd stay because you needed a roof, but it's not a home.

Monica leads me through to the front room and I perch on a sofa I recognise from the Ikea catalogue, but from several years ago. It sags under me, and to the side is a bare shelving unit that must have been bought at the same time as the sofa.

'So when Dawn's at school, you live here alone?'

'I mainly live in hotels,' says Monica, sitting at the far end of the sofa, adjusting her other earring and fluffing her hair. She's dressed for work, in navy trousers and a cream fitted jumper, simple clothes that you'd have found in the high street a few seasons ago. 'I sell office equipment so I travel a lot. This place is just somewhere for me to shower and change my clothes.' She pauses. I can see it's an effort for her to be civil – she's really irritated I'm here. 'I appreciate you having Dawn to stay. It's a big help.'

'My pleasure.' Which *was* true, but how can it be now, if she's Daniel's daughter? If she's a secret he's kept from me for fourteen years?

'I was surprised you still wanted her to stay, what with all you've got going on, but Daniel said it would help Tori. I'm sorry about your mum.' Monica says this casually, as if your death is an inconvenience rather than a tragedy. There's a coldness about her that makes me wonder why Daniel chose her, beautiful though she is. His ex, the Olympian athlete, was vivacious and passionate, but Monica is an ice queen. His tastes must have changed.

'Thank you.'

'Do you want a drink?' It's an offer made in the hope I'll refuse. Monica's going through the motions of civility, but really I'm an inconvenience.

'I'm fine, thanks.'

There's a hesitation, then she looks at her watch again. 'I'm sorry, but – what do you want?'

I can imagine this woman in her business meetings. I bet the men she works with describe her as *a ball-breaker*. I bet she doesn't have much time for the women.

'Are you having an affair with Daniel?'

To my utter surprise, she lets out a massive snort. 'What? Are you *crazy?*' She starts to laugh – loudly, as if the very idea is preposterous.

Now it's my turn to be confused. 'But you did then? Fourteen years ago?'

She looks at me like I'm something the cat dragged in. 'I wouldn't touch that man with a bargepole, not now or anytime. What has that wanker been telling you?'

'Nothing! He has no idea I know that Dawn is his daughter.'

Her reaction hits a new low – she looks as though she's bitten something unpleasant. 'You must be mad saying something like that.'

I feel exhausted by this. 'Please, Monica, just tell me the truth. I know he's paying for Dawn to be at Oakfield.' I bring the crumpled envelope out of my handbag, because I can't bear her lying to me.

'You stole this from my letterbox?' Monica snatches the envelope from me, reads the letter and grimaces. 'Fuck. So, as you see, he's *not* paying. That is exactly the problem.'

'But why would he pay for Dawn's education, if she's not his?'

Something happens then, her haughty face clears and I see a realisation dawning. 'That bastard never told you then? I assumed you knew, but Alfie always said you didn't. Like he said, The Samphire Master's a sneaky fucker.'

I'm now completely in the dark – what has Alfie Avon got to do with this? One thing is obvious, Monica isn't a woman in love. She clearly despises Daniel and she's warming to her theme.

'I used to be one of Daniel's clients, did you know that?' I shake my head. 'Breast cancer. God, I was such a fucking idiot – so vain that when the doctors said they needed to cut the tumour out, I was easy meat for

Daniel. I'd heard him on the radio, of course. It was your mum's case that convinced me.'

She glares at me, and I feel guilty, though it was never anything to do with me. After Daniel cured you, it was your decision to be so vocal, crowing on the radio about the miracle of his healing. It was then that you agreed to give us the farm.

Monica doesn't care about my reminiscing, she's got memories of her own: bad ones.

'So Daniel prescribed a regime of juices, reiki, meditation. I was a zealot: I didn't deviate from anything he suggested, I just wanted to keep my tits. He warned me how the medical profession would try to sabotage the programme, explained how his treatments were older than time itself or some such crap. And because I wanted to believe him, I did. Alfie warned me I was vulnerable, but I thought he was just being bitter because he'd lost his radio show . . . It cost me my marriage.'

Here she tails off, gazing into the middle distance and suddenly I understand the unloved house. She doesn't want to be here – she had a better life that was taken from her.

'Did the cancer come back?' I ask, hardly daring to hear the answer.

'Of course it fucking did!' She pulls down her vest top, revealing a padded post-surgery bra. I can see an ugly red scar on each side of her chest. 'What could have been treated had been left to fester and grow. A double mastectomy was the only option by the time I finally woke up to how I'd been conned and went back to the hospital.'

Her voice cracks, and I see how broken she is by this.

'I'm so sorry.'

'Oh yeah,' she snaps, 'sorry does a fat lot of good. Two years ago, it all blew up. I told Daniel I was gonna sue him for every penny he's got, called him, turned up at his work, did everything I could to make him pay attention! Alfie wanted to put the story out on the front page, but I was too proud. Didn't want the world to know what a fool I'd been.'

The dreaded name makes me flinch. 'Alfie Avon hates Daniel.'

'And with good reason. We'd been married thirteen years – ironic, isn't it? But the stress of my cancer, then this . . . it broke us apart. I was *sick*: I didn't have the energy to fight for my marriage. I'd finally agreed to Alfie exposing Daniel, and it was lined up for the front page, when Daniel made me an offer: private education for my girl and private treatment for my breast reconstruction.'

'And this was two years ago?' I knew nothing about any of it. Daniel had kept it from me. The calls, the missing money: there was no affair. 'I didn't know anything about it.'

'Yeah, well, Alfie always said Daniel was protecting you and that you were his Achilles heel – the reason he feared exposure so damn much. Frankly, as long as he paid Dawn's fees and for my reconstruction, I didn't give a fuck if you knew or not.'

'But how can Daniel afford it?'

'Well, clearly,' she says, snapping the envelope in my face, 'he can't. I've had it with his empty promises. This really is his last chance.'

'Last chance?'

'He's told me about the Spa, what a gold mine it'll be. So I've given him six months and he's promised me – promised me! – that he'll see me right. And if he doesn't, Alfie will get his scoop and I'll sue him to high heaven.'

When the door slams closed behind me, I take in a lungful of cold air, then another. Monica's unhappiness filled the whole house, but out here in the cold air it's gone. I feel released, and so grateful. I was wrong, Daniel's not having an affair. Oh God, I'm almost delirious with it. He doesn't love Monica – it really is just a business arrangement. She said it herself, he was protecting me – that was why it was kept secret. I'm dizzy with relief, I feel a stone lighter.

He's still mine, and he loves me.

DAY 14

FRIDAY 14 NOVEMBER

41

Holly

It was a cold afternoon, and colder in her car where the air seemed to have set at a low temperature. She'd managed to get a few hours' sleep that afternoon, in preparation for her night shift at the Bartlet. Tonight, with Jon's approval, she'd be shadowing Clive at the hospital, watching as the sleep test on Hector was conducted.

Holly's breath travelled around her as she turned the key in the ignition and willed the heating to kick in. The windscreen hadn't yet cleared when her phone rang. It was Leif, and as soon as she heard his hushed voice, she knew he was about to tell her something he shouldn't.

'Are you sitting down, Holly?'

'Not comfortably, but yes,' she said.

'Okay, this is confidential, *ja*? There is much excitement at work, and I think you should know.'

'What's happened?'

She could hear his rapid breathing. 'I shouldn't tell you, you know this . . .'

'But you want to. You know how much it means to me.' She hated how coaxing she sounded, using his feelings for her to win him over, but he had called her. Whatever had happened, he wanted to tell her as much as she needed to hear.

'Okay, *Sötnos*.' His voice lowered, although she knew he was calling from his flat – the number was on her screen. 'The forensics team used a Crime-lite on Daniel Salmon's car, and the boot lit up. *Blue as Portman Road when Ipswich are actually winning*, the man said. He is very humorous, despite the science.'

Holly tried to process this. 'A blue light? What does that mean?'

'It means Maya's blood is in his car. In the boot, just like you said.'

Holly didn't want to get excited, but she couldn't help her heart breaking into a trot. Her synaesthesia had been spot-on. 'I don't understand though – Maya was found inside the farmhouse.'

Leif patiently explained, '*Ja*, but whoever shot Maya would have been splattered in blood. If it was Daniel, he'd have had to take off these bloody clothes before he drove away.'

Holly closed her eyes and the image returned of Daniel balling up his outer clothes, shoving them in the car boot. And he'd disappeared for hours that Saturday, presumably getting rid of the evidence.

'Is he going to be arrested, Leif?'

'Now this is completely confidential, you understand, *Sötnos*? Daniel will be brought in for questioning tomorrow, but the SIO wants the sleeping test on Hector to go ahead as planned. He's still the main suspect.'

Holly disconnected from Leif, already hearing in his voice that he was regretting his indiscretion. He had called her in a state of excitement, but he had breached every code of ethics by telling her the police's plan. Not that she was one to judge.

So, Daniel was now implicated, but Hector was still in the picture – could the two of them have colluded to murder Maya?

Clive's office was in the main part of the Bartlet Hospital – the same side as the locked ward, but towards the middle, thus benefitting from a large bowed window that looked out over the North Sea. Unlike his office at Ipswich Hospital, this was a huge room with very minimal clutter.

'That's some view,' Holly said, walking to the window, and spying the container ships in the distance. The night sky was an inky blue, the moon shimmering a path across the black water.

'Some mornings I watch the swimmers going to the pier and back. They brave the North Sea even at this time of year.'

She hugged her jumper more closely around her. 'You'd have to pay me, weather like this.' She sat in the Lloyd Loom chairs in front of the window, looking around. 'This really is a grand place, isn't it? It must have been amazing when it was a hospital for convalescents.'

He chuckled. 'Oh yes, time is and time was. I found that chair in a store room – remnants from the glory days here, and you should see some of the furniture stacked in there: Edwardian turned-leg tables, daybeds for sitting in the sun! It must have been another world.'

Now it was a secure psychiatric hospital, and Cassandra had been incarcerated here two years ago. Holly wondered how that must have felt, locked away in this house on the hill, with the sea crashing down below like something from a Gothic novel.

'Tonight feels important,' Holly said, the room and enveloping night sky making her wistful. 'By morning we'll know if Hector has been telling the truth.'

Clive collected up his briefcase and looked at his watch.

'Let's hope so, Holly. We should be going across to the lab to see the patient. It's almost bedtime.'

The sleep lab was on the opposite side of the hospital. Holly followed Clive down corridors and across the poorly lit central courtyard to the more modern part of the building. Their feet echoed, and Holly shivered, thinking that this weekend she really must fish her winter coat out from storage under her bed. She was glad to get inside again – the newer part of the hospital was warmer. They arrived at the double door with the sign SLEEP CLINIC to be greeted by a cheerful, chubby nurse at the reception desk, who told them to wait a moment. Minutes later, a lanky man with a broad smile and thick glasses strode down the corridor, calling jovially, 'Evening, Clive! Good to see you. And who is this young lady?'

'Francis Block, meet Holly Redwood, student paramedic. She's here to observe, as part of her clinical case study assignment. Francis is the sleep technician here at the Bartlet.'

Francis took her hand in his long bony grip and shook it vigorously. 'Hope you enjoy the show.'

'Me too.'

'Has Hector arrived?' Clive asked Francis, as they walked down the long corridor towards the Sleep Clinic.

'Half an hour ago, his daughter brought him. He's completed the paperwork and he's already wired up to the EEG machine; she's gone to get a drink in the café. He now needs to relax in order to get the best sleep possible.' Francis threw open the double doors at the end of the corridor and said, 'Welcome to our Sleep Clinic, Holly. It's very impressive.'

He was right. Once through the doors, it was like stepping into a different world from the rest of the hospital: calmer and more opulent, with dimmed lighting, a cosy space against the battering winds outside. Here, the usual antiseptic smell of hospitals was absent, there was lavender in the air. The sleep unit was a six-bay ward, but each bed had been partitioned so it was in its own small area with soft lighting and crisp linen in pastel colours, a side lamp with a simple shade, and enough homely touches to make the space inviting. Each had a vase of gerberas or wild flowers, a woven rug and some art books on a low shelf. She saw the plug-in air freshener that must be the source of the lavender.

'It reminds me of an Ikea showroom,' Holly said, 'with all the touches to make it seem like a real home.'

'It's a good imitation, isn't it?' agreed Francis. 'The flowers are plastic, and the books are just empty cardboard, but it looks good.'

Francis showed them into a tiny surveillance room, from where the bay could be seen through one-way glass. There was also a bank of six cameras, each showing a bed. Five beds were empty, so only one screen showed movement as Hector shifted on his mattress. He was lying on top of the sheets in pyjamas, his feet crossed casually at the ankle and his hands rested in his lap. His seemingly relaxed pose was betrayed by his tense frown. He had contact pads stuck on his temples, forehead and chin, with wires leading to a nearby monitor.

'I'm not sure I could sleep with that on my head,' Holly said, thinking about Clive's offer to contact a research team for her, 'and knowing I was being watched.'

'You'd be amazed how quickly the brain forgets details like that,' Francis told her. 'I've slept in one of those beds myself, wearing that cap, so I know.'

She'd heard how therapists and doctors often specialised in subjects where they had a personal history, and knew how her own trait had dictated her career. 'Do you have a sleep disorder, Francis?'

'Nothing so interesting,' Francis grinned. 'But it's good practice to experience first-hand what we put our patients through.'

On the monitor, Hector could be seen shifting position. He looked towards the camera, his eyes weary, his jaw tense.

'This bit always takes a while, waiting for patients to fall asleep. Go grab a bite to eat if you like.'

'I'm happy to wait here,' said Clive, studying the screen.

But Holly was hungry, and knew it would be a long night. More than that, she wanted to find Cassandra. 'I wouldn't mind getting something.'

'Here – take this beeper. If it buzzes, you'll know the show's started.'

Sliding her tray onwards to the cutlery stand, Holly saw Cassandra, hidden in the corner of the café, nursing a chipped mug.

'Can I join you?'

Cass looked up, and Holly was immediately struck at how different she seemed. Her hair looked freshly styled, and her face was dewy. She looked well rested and healthy, and even her clothes were smarter than the ones Holly had become accustomed to seeing her wear.

'Oh, Holly!' She smiled warmly. 'Of course you can.'

Holly sat beside her. 'You look well, Cass.'

'Thank you. I feel it.' She touched her empty mug lovingly, as though it contained a genie who had just granted her wish. 'I've just sorted a lot of things out today: my head feels much clearer.'

'I'm glad,' said Holly. Though she was perplexed too – the last time they'd spoken, Cass was convinced Ash had shot her mum and that Hector was covering for him. She must know Daniel's car had been seized by the police – how could she be so calm?

'Do you think this sleep trial will give us the answers we need?'

Cass smiled. 'The truth has to be the best thing, doesn't it? Whatever that may be.'

It seemed to Holly that whatever Cass was thinking about, it wasn't her mother. She was lost in a daydream.

'Cass,' she said gently, touching her arm. 'If your dad's sleep test doesn't support his confession, what do you think will happen?'

Holly felt how unwilling Cass was to be pulled away from her happy place. 'Then it will prove he was covering for Ash.'

'Or Daniel.' Holly hesitated, just long enough to acknowledge that she knew she was betraying Leif's trust. 'Cass, the police found your mum's blood in the boot of his car.'

As soon as she said the words, she wanted to snatch them back. She was alerting Cass to the police's new evidence, she had no right, and Cass could tell Daniel.

But, to her great surprise, Cass didn't react. She didn't seem shocked, or even angry at Holly for suggesting that Daniel could be guilty. In fact, her expression was one of pity.

'Daniel is a good man. He loves me: he'd never do anything to betray me, and whatever the police have found there will be an innocent explanation for. Don't you recognise true love when you see it, Holly?'

DAY 15

SATURDAY 15 NOVEMBER

42

Cassandra

I fall asleep in the cafeteria, my head on my folded arms, still seated in the chair. It seems like just minutes later that Holly shakes me gently awake.

'The results are in, Cass,' she says. 'Your dad and Clive are waiting for us.'

I lift my head, yawn. 'What time is it?'

'Half six,' she says. I don't know if she went home to sleep, or if she's been here all night, but she looks alert, sympathetic too. We both know that whatever we're about to be told is critical.

I let Holly lead me across the courtyard to Clive's office. She links her arm through mine and I feel a solidarity between us. When this is all over, I'll miss her. It's cold in the courtyard, the early sun is watery and it feels like we're the only people awake in the world. My breath carries on the air and seagulls watch us from the rooftop. I lean into Holly for her warmth, for her comfort, and I feel her leaning back as if we're friends. Something we can never truly be, not meeting like this.

I don't like being here. The Bartlet haunts me, set in a cliff facing the sea, red-brick visage and dark glassy eyes. Rigid and angular and symmetrical, just like the regime inside. The council wanted to turn it into luxury flats, but the locals protested: the hospital was a gift from Dr Bartlet to Felixstowe, in perpetuity. They demanded the town honour this.

I'd like to see it burned to the ground.

Lording over the town like a fortress, its red-brick walls a prison for patients too sick to have rights. Two years ago, I was one of them. This isn't the convalescent hospital Dr Bartlet imagined when he gave the building his name – gone are the glamorous but ailing women languishing in bath chairs, no shell-shocked gentlemen in panama hats stroll the gardens any more. Those people are ghosts, and now everything that happens here is ugly.

'It's just along here,' Holly says.

I don't need her to tell me this, I know this place; it features in my nightmares. Clive has his office in the wing at the far end that houses the locked wards, where people arrive screaming and leave mute. Last time I was here was two years ago, my discharge meeting.

Do you remember, Mum? I was told I was finally sane but still you wouldn't let Victoria come home.

Inside the office, they're waiting.

Dad doesn't look like he slept a wink, though he must have or they couldn't have conducted the test. I take the empty seat by the window, and wait for Clive to tell us what the test shows. He fumbles with his paperwork, though I can tell it's more from nerves than anything else, and this worries me: I've never seen him looking this uncomfortable.

There's a clock on the wall, an old-fashioned one with marquetry in the mahogany, that's probably an antique. It keeps the seconds, along with my heartbeat.

Holly takes a chair at the back of the room. I know she doesn't want to be intrusive, but also she's watching and monitoring everything. I'd rather she were sitting beside me.

'Go on, then,' says Dad, leaning back and sighing deeply, 'tell us.'

In the silence that follows I can hear seagulls screaming outside.

'Hector' – Clive clears his throat, glances at the floor, then back at Dad – 'your sleep test indicates no evidence of sleepwalking at this time. The home monitoring also confirms a regular sleep cycle. Neither test shows any sign of sleep disturbance.'

I knew it: Dad lied. 'Now's the time to tell the truth, Dad. You were protecting Ash, weren't you?'

'No, I'm not protectin' Ash.'

Dad lowers his head, I can see the vein throb in his forehead. A seagull lands on the windowsill, taps its beak on the glass. I feel trapped, back in this place of insanity. Why won't he tell the truth? The game is over now, he must know this.

Holly finally breaks the silence. 'Could Hector's medication have skewed the results, Clive?'

Clive sighs deeply, in and out. 'Medication masks the symptoms but not the brain patterns. There were simply no markers for a sleep disorder – nothing that would suggest a sleep disorder so profound it could lead to non-insane automatism.' He finally pushes his paperwork aside. Now he's empty-handed, as if wanting to absolve himself from any involvement. 'Sleepwalkers may not have disturbed sleep every night, but their brainwave patterns would be erratic and there would be indications. But there were none. No reading at any point to support the idea that Hector could have shot Maya in his sleep.'

Dad keeps his head bowed, and nurses his bad hand. I move to him, kneel at his feet and take his bad hand in mine. His is shaking and he won't look at me, but now turns his head towards the window. I know him – he wants to be outside, where he belongs.

'It's over, Dad,' I say. 'Time to tell what really happened. You can't protect Ash any more.'

'I'm not, Cass.' He's breathing heavily. The seconds mount. I imagine the clock ticking faster or maybe it's just my heart. Still, he won't look at me. The seagull flies away. The North Sea is an expanse of cold dark water and I long to be there, beside the water, and out of this place. Just like the first time I was here.

'You're protecting him just like you did back when he shot me, defending him even when I was injured. But he shot your *wife*, for fuck's sake. How can you still be on his side?'

'Ash wouldn't hurt Maya.' Dad reaches for me, a rare thing, his good hand feels like a weight on my shoulder as he pulls my face closer to his. 'I had to lie, Cass.'

'Why?'

Dad says, so softly I have to lean in to hear him, 'Your sleepwalkin' has got worse, hasn't it?'

The sharp twist in the conversation takes my breath. 'What's that got to do with anything? You lied!'

'I lied to protect you,' he says sadly. 'We all did.'

And there, it is said. It feels like a trick; they're going to keep me here, aren't they? I'm going to be locked away like last time.

'No, I'd never hurt Mum!' The words hang in the air. I begin to shake, turning desperately to the other people in the room. 'I don't even know how to use a gun, Clive. You believe me, don't you, Holly?'

'Cass,' she says, walking slowly towards me as though I'm a cornered animal that might escape. 'When I saw you in the wardrobe, at the farm, you had no idea how you'd got there . . .'

'No . . .'

'There's something else,' she says, coming to my side, kneeling at my feet as if she needs my forgiveness. 'It wasn't Ash who shot you when you were twelve. It was my brother.'

'What?' I can't understand how this has changed so suddenly, how I'm now at the centre of things. And Holly is looking up at me, crying.

'I was there,' she says, her voice wet. 'I ran away, and I'm so sorry I did. But Ash can't take the blame any more. I should have told you right from the start about that Halloween. I kept it back and that was wrong. We were just kids, out ghost-hunting. And I wasn't sure what

I saw, not until I saw you in the wardrobe at the farm. Then I realised you're a sleepwalker, and that I've seen you do it before.'

I undo the buttons on my blouse, move the opening aside to show her the scar on my collarbone. '*Your brother* did this? And all these years, I've thought it was Ash.'

'I'm so sorry. But if I can make it up to you, I will.'

My spine is a puppet string and no one is in control. 'I don't understand,' I say. Though I do, oh God, I do. *Oh, Mum.*

'Cass,' says Clive, who's moved to stand by the window, 'it sounds as though your father was protecting you.'

'No, it's another lie, just another trick! Wire me up to that fucking machine, if that's what it takes to prove I'm innocent.'

Holly looks hopeful. 'Could Francis do that, Clive? It would at least prove it. Or would you need a court order?'

Clive pauses, then he finds his mobile. 'Not if Cass is giving her permission, but do you think you can fall asleep, love? Would we be better to wait until things have sunk in a bit?'

I shake my head vigorously. I can't wait, the test has to be done – there is no other option. 'I'm exhausted. I'm sure I can do it. And I want it over with. Please, Clive?'

'I'll call Francis and see if he can do it now.'

He walks away to make the call, out into the corridor.

Dad is still breathing heavily. I know he has more to say and I want him to stop. I prefer his silence. He's barely spoken in days or years, but it's as though a dam has burst and it must all come out now. As though, now you've gone, he's had to find a voice.

'I was never protectin' Ash, or Janet. You had that all wrong. It was just me and you in the house that night, Cass, and I was asleep the whole time. As you've heard, I don't sleepwalk, haven't done in years. When I made that confession to the police, I was protectin' *you.*'

'I don't believe it, it's a lie. You say you were asleep! Who told you that I was guilty?'

His face doesn't change. For him, there are no more secrets to be told. 'Daniel,' he says. 'He found you, just after you shot Maya. You were still sleepwalkin' and he led you back to bed, then he woke me.'

I close my eyes, my brain desperately searching through its back files. I slept deeply that night, I hadn't heard a thing. I woke naked and covered in sweat. *Could it be true?*

'I need to see Daniel,' I say, looking at Holly. 'Before I have the sleep test, before I say anything else. And I want you to take my father home, I don't want him near me.'

43

Holly

Parking her car in the driveway, Holly had a view of the cosy breakfast scene she was about to destroy. In the front room, Daniel was seated on the sofa, dressed casually in jogging trousers and T-shirt, with Victoria close beside him in her fleece onesie. Next to her, knees drawn up snugly, was another teenager who could only be Dawn. The three of them were watching something, laughing together, and the girls were sharing a plate of toast.

Beside her, Hector stirred, unclicked his seatbelt.

The old man had been silent all the way from the hospital, and he just grunted now. Holly rolled back her shoulders, straightened her spine, and opened the car door, then went to the passenger side to help Hector out. Maya's death had broken him, and as she touched his elbow to support him, she felt his emotion: deepest despair. He'd tried to help his daughter, but in the end, he wasn't able to. Cass had to face what she'd done, even if she had no knowledge of it.

The front door opened, and Daniel stepped forward. 'Hector, how did it go?' Then he looked back at the empty car and said to Holly, 'Where's Cassandra?'

Hector made a sound, muffled and distressed.

'She's still at the hospital,' Holly said. 'I'll drive you there.'

It didn't take long to explain, and within a few minutes Daniel had gathered up whatever he needed, and they were driving back to the hospital. In all the scenarios she'd imagined, never had Holly thought Cassandra might be the guilty one. She'd been blindsided by her synaesthesia. Aided and abetted by Alfie, she'd followed the wrong scent.

Back in the sleep unit, Francis had wired Cass up, and she was lying on the bed, just as Hector had been twelve hours earlier. When she saw Daniel, she opened her arms to him, and they locked in an embrace so fierce Holly had to look away. She wasn't needed here any more, she could go home.

Home.

Innocence Lane had been an ever-shifting landscape beneath her feet, but now it was seemingly over.

As she approached the landing, Leif opened his door and stood waiting for her. She hadn't even reached him when she began to cry. It was tiredness, of course, but also what she had witnessed. The love Hector had for Cassandra, enough to make him lie about shooting his own wife. And Daniel's love for her too. She'd seen how Daniel had taken Cass in his arms and started whispering to her, a monologue of calm and comfort that changed Cassandra's expression from fear to focus, as she leaned into him and he held her tight.

Holly had doubted Daniel – she had sensed him to be a liar, a charlatan who played on the weakness of others to make his living, and she had suspected he might be guilty. But in that hospital, she had felt only his love for Cassandra.

Leif held her, still on the walkway between their flats, and let her cry herself out. Only when she had caught her breath did he ask what had happened.

It was hard at first to explain. Holly didn't exactly understand herself, why seeing Cassandra and Daniel locked together had overwhelmed her to such an extent. Perhaps it was mirror-touch again, and she was experiencing their emotions?

'I want to tell you about a Halloween, back when I was eight. My brother shot into the dark, and hurt someone.' She hadn't even known the words were coming until they were there, hanging in the cold November air. Leif moved closer, sharing his warmth.

'Do you know how many times I've thought about that night, and the fact that I left without even looking back. Leaving someone, I didn't know who, screaming in pain?' She pulled back slightly, to see Leif's reaction. 'I feel I've been trying to make things right ever since, that it's why my senses are now so alert, why I'm training to be a paramedic. But now I have a real chance to fix things.'

She freed herself from Leif, leaned over the banister and looked at the streets below, doors concealing hidden lives.

'I'm going to call the police tomorrow and make a statement about what I saw that night. I'm going to have to tell them that my brother shot Cassandra.'

Leif moved behind her, pressed into her body. They were cold, they should go inside, but she knew that if they did, the moment would be lost. Leif seemed to understand this too, as although his hands on hers were cold, he said, 'It was a long time ago, Holly. You were all just children.'

'But still, Jamie needs to face any consequences. Just like I must. I can't keep hiding from things, from the damage that happened that night.'

'So this is why,' he said, so softly that his words were almost like a thought, 'you don't open up, why you hold back your emotions?'

'Yes. Because my senses give me an emotion, but not the reason or thinking behind it. And the feelings are not always my own.' She turned, facing him. They were nose to nose. 'I'm frightened, Leif.'

'Don't be, *Sötnos*,' he reassured her. 'Everything will be fine, I'm sure.'

She fell silent then, her head to Leif's chest, listening only to the wind and the beat of his steady heart. She hoped he was right.

44

Cassandra

So, I've ended up back here at the Bartlet Hospital, just like you said I would. Are you happy, Mum? You always liked to be right.

Daniel's with me. He'll stay until I'm asleep and the machine begins its job, monitoring the rhythms of my sleep-world.

'I won't leave you,' he says. His lips find mine and I kiss him. 'I'll be with you all the time. I'll keep you safe.'

I love this man – I always have, but I wasn't sure he loved me. Now, after meeting Monica, I know the truth, and I trust him.

'Are you going to tell me?' I murmur, already beginning to drift away. 'Holly told me the police found Mum's blood in your car. What did you do, Daniel?'

He releases me slightly. His eyes have a faraway look and I know he's thinking back. He tells me everything then, and I listen. It's as though I'm hearing a story I already know, I've dreamed it before, or I'm experiencing déjà vu.

'She was going to ruin everything, Cass. You see that, don't you?'

DAY 16

SUNDAY 16 NOVEMBER

45

Holly

Holly was woken, still wrapped tightly in Leif's arms, by a knock at her door. Wrapped in a blanket, she was surprised to find Daniel waiting there.

'I'm sorry to come to your home, Holly. Cass gave me your address. We need to talk.'

Holly returned to her bedroom, and pulled on some jogging bottoms and Leif's jumper that was lying on the floor. He was still asleep, so she closed the bedroom door carefully behind her, not wanting to disturb him. Daniel had already perched on one of the stools in the kitchen.

'Can I get you a coffee, Daniel?'

'No thanks, it's carcinogenic. But don't let me stop you.'

She boiled the kettle, made a cup of tea instead, and slid onto the empty stool beside him.

He looked very calm, and totally in control. Holly waited for whatever he needed to say, not breathing for a moment.

'As you now know, I was at the farm on the morning of the shooting. What I've just explained to the police is that when I arrived, I saw Maya struggling with someone who was holding a gun. I was too late to intervene: I heard a shot and Maya was already on the ground when I got to her.'

'Who was struggling with Maya?' Holly asked the pertinent question.

'I think you know the answer to that.'

The silence in the room was palpable. 'And where was Hector?'

'He was asleep in the front room. I had to wake him, to tell him his daughter had shot his wife. Can you even imagine how terrible that was?' Daniel's face was pale, and he clasped his hands together as if for self-support. 'And poor Cass, she was still asleep – she had no idea what she'd done.'

Holly remembered finding her in the wardrobe, how disorientated she was. Hector saying to his daughter, *There was only you and me in the house.*

'When Cass sleepwalks,' Daniel continued, 'she's strong. It took all my strength to wrestle the gun from her. She was only wearing the clothes she'd slept in, her underwear, and they were covered in blood, as was her skin. Maya's blood. I led her upstairs, and stripped her, then I showered her. All the time, she remained asleep – she had no idea what she'd done.'

Holly was playing the scene in her head, although what she was picturing was the scene Daniel was painting for her, not one she was sensing.

'What happened next, Daniel?' she asked.

'By then, Ash and Janet had arrived and the bloody dog was going crazy. Of course their first priority was Maya, and Janet called 999, but she did it from her cottage so she could say she hadn't entered the house beyond the kitchen, so she wasn't implicated in any way. Then Ash and I made it look like a suicide, placing the gun so it looked like Maya had shot herself. We wanted to protect Cass from what she'd done. We knew she couldn't handle it.'

'What did you do then?'

'I took Cass's blood-spattered clothes and hid them in the boot of my car – that's why the police found those traces. I drove to Rendlesham Forest, where I took a long walk and buried the items in a remote spot. They aren't deep: I didn't have a spade, I just used my hands. We just wanted to protect Cass. You understand that, don't you?'

'Yes,' she said, thinking of how she'd protected Jamie for twenty years, 'I do.'

She thought of the first film Leif had shown her, *Murder on the Orient Express*. All of them had conspired to conceal a crime, all had guilt on their hands. This was why she'd been so confused by their emotions, by Ash, Janet and Hector as well as Daniel. They were all lying, and she'd sensed that.

The only person who hadn't been lying was Cassandra.

'The reason I came here, Holly, is because Cass needs you. You were her friend, and you hurt her.'

'I was eight,' Holly protested. 'I wasn't Cassandra's friend, we'd never even spoken. It was a horrible accident.'

Daniel looked irritated and Holly's senses prickled with alarm. 'But you were there when she was hurt, and you said nothing. And now you're her friend, or so you say. It's time to prove it.'

After Daniel had left, Holly examined her heart for a reaction, and found only sadness for Cassandra, who was now facing the terrible fact that she had shot her own mother. Yes, she'd help her, but first she wanted to be with someone who loved her: *Leif*.

She opened the bedroom door, and he was still asleep. She removed her clothes and slid in beside him, needing his touch.

Leif opened his eyes. '*Sötnos,* what is it? You have been crying again?'

She shook her head. 'Go back to sleep. I'm okay.'

He touched her chin with his finger. 'No, you aren't. You know you can trust me.'

He listened, and she told him what Daniel had said. How she finally had the chance to right the wrong her brother did.

Later, while he was taking a shower, her phone beeped and she saw she'd received a new email:

> Holly,
> Here is my updated and concluded report.
> Clive

She skimmed down the page, for the final section:

> Following careful analysis of the sleep trial data, and after extensive discussion with the somnambulistic polygrapher (see his attached report), my conclusion is that Hector Hawke does not suffer from non-insane automatism and, therefore, there is no evidence that he's capable of violence while asleep. Indeed, the tests indicate he's a sound sleeper with no disturbance at all.
>
> I additionally interviewed his daughter, Cassandra Hawke, and a sleep trial was conducted on her immediately afterwards. Her brainwave patterns show clear evidence of brain activity associated with sleepwalking. It is evident from what Hector Hawke says that his daughter has been a sleepwalker for many years. The family largely view Cassandra as vulnerable and in need of protection, especially since an episode of severe psychosis resulted in hospitalisation to the Bartlet psychiatric hospital two years ago. I was the consultant responsible for her case and can confirm it

was feared she would take her own life. As Cassandra was not married, it fell to a parent, her mother, as next of kin to sign the sectioning order.

Hector Hawke tells me that, fearing his daughter would relapse if she discovered the devastating knowledge that she shot her mother, he decided to say he was guilty. Cassandra's partner Daniel, together with Ashley and Janet Cley, all colluded in this deception out of concern and love for Cassandra.

This is an unusual case, and a very sad one.

Cassandra's actions are a clear example of non-insane automatism. She needs medical care and, in my opinion, she does not belong in prison. But that, of course, is a matter for the court.

Reading Clive's report, something struck Holly: Daniel wasn't Cassandra's next of kin, Maya was. It was she who had signed the sectioning form, effectively locking Cassandra away, and she who paid for Victoria to board at Oakfield. Two strong motives for Cassandra wanting her mother dead. But sleepwalkers don't have motives, only conscious people do. Holly shivered, felt a warning in her psyche – one that would do her no good. The case would be built on evidence, and there was now plenty, that this was a somnambular murder. It would be a jury that would decide, and not her. But she intended to tell them what she'd seen that first Halloween night, how Cassandra had remained asleep even after she'd been shot, and stand as a witness for her defence.

DAY 17

MONDAY 17 NOVEMBER

46

Cassandra

The sky is grey on the day we bury you, full of rolling thunder.

I pull on a black wool dress and wander around the house, making sure everything looks tidy. Not that it matters: there won't be much of a wake. We couldn't risk anyone looking for an angle, a story to sell, so it'll be just family here afterwards. I run my hand along the bookshelf, tweak the cushion on the chair, feeling a wave of love for the house, for everything in it, now I won't be here much longer. It's just a matter of time until I'm arrested. The police haven't charged me yet, but they will. I'm officially a suspect, and they're gathering the evidence. The sleep trial; Daniel's statement. But it's Holly's statement that she saw me sleepwalk when I was a child, how she saw me remain in that state even after I was shot, that Rupert Jackson says will save me from a life sentence.

Victoria moves around upstairs, getting ready as she talks on her phone to Dawn, who's back at Oakfield. Victoria won't return to Oakfield: she's home for good now, and it hurts like a fresh cut that I could be sent away from her again if I go to prison.

Dad's in the kitchen. I make us a cup of tea and place it in front of him. There's nothing more to say – he tried his best, but in the end, he couldn't protect me from what I did while I was asleep. Or rather, what he believes I did.

In seconds, Daniel is beside me, pulling me into his arms. My face is against his chest, the smell of him is so familiar and comforting that I can hardly breathe.

I'm the strong one now – I have been since the day of my sleep trial, when he told me everything. He's fighting back tears, and I kiss him quickly on the cheek.

'The car will be here soon. Go and put your shoes on, love.'

The rain begins to fall as we sing 'Morning Has Broken'. It's not a funeral song, the celebrant told me that, but I insisted. The service is simple and quick. We sit at the front: Dad and Daniel, me and Victoria. Ash and Janet are behind us. Further back are people we didn't invite, but who came anyway.

Neighbours, a handful of people who called themselves your friend. We all watch your coffin slide behind the curtain. This is goodbye, Mum.

Afterwards, people mingle under the wooden gazebo, reading the notes on the flowers: *Dearly beloved, In deepest sympathy, To my wonderful mother.* The rain starts a drumbeat on the roof, a sound so startling I fear it could collapse. From the shelter of the gazebo I watch as Victoria, my beautiful girl, hurriedly crosses the car park to the woodland, where the ashes from the cremations are buried, where you too will be soon. She finds shelter under a holm oak. Under the canopy of trees are commemorative benches, and stakes with names, some surrounded by flowers, some with photos. The oak is just beyond these, on the edge of the wilder wood where no plaques stand to remember the dead. She turns to its trunk as if it's a person, places her arms around it as if it could hold and comfort her. Maybe it *is* comfort – that tree will outlast us all and our daily struggles are as nothing. Though her expression is hidden, I can tell by the way her shoulders shake that she's sobbing.

I long to step out into the rain, to be with my girl, but around me people are waiting to kiss me and shake my hand and say how sorry they are for my loss. Then I see Daniel, striding across the lawn, a soldier marching onwards with head up despite the downpour. He opens his arms to Victoria long before he reaches her, and she leaves the tree's comfort to find his. My man, my girl, hold each other tight and fast.

'Cassandra, I just wanted to offer my condolences,' says another voice, a face I don't recognise gives a good impression of sorrow and I shake a cold hand. She turns away, her place filled by yet another stranger.

'I'm sorry, I need to go to my daughter,' I say. For who can argue with the grieving?

'Of course, of course' ringing in my ears as I follow where Daniel leads.

I pass the memorials, some with an abundance of trinkets, candles and wind chimes, but saddest of all are those names with nothing. Don't worry, Mum, there will always be fresh flowers for you.

My family open up, letting me into the embrace and I'm not sure where tears end and the rain begins. The three of us, drenched as if heaven itself is crying and all the time I know, in my heart, that it is going to be okay. To live is to love, and to love is to lose – this is always the way it ends, sooner or later. And I lost you, Mum, long before that Saturday morning. I've lost you for good now, but I've found something else.

Daniel and Victoria have been returned to me.

We walk back, through the woodland, to the crematorium, where the dry group awaits us. We don't hurry, the rain doesn't bother us; we have each other. Our arms entwined, I am central, flanked by the two people I love most in the world.

'Let's speak to everyone,' I say, 'and thank them for coming. Then let's go home and plan Samphire Health Spa, just like Mum would want us to.'

Back under the gazebo, I release Victoria and she goes to comfort Dad, who's standing nursing his bad hand, looking lost. This will be hard for him, I know, but he still has us. I turn to Daniel and we exchange a moment that is all ours. I say, so softly only he can hear, 'I forgive you.'

He kisses me deeply, and a line comes to me from my favourite book: *like guilty lovers who have not kissed before.*

After most people have left the crematorium, I find Holly. She has been present through all of this, and I'm grateful. I have one last favour.

'Holly, please can you drive me to the police station? I think we both need to make a confession.'

NINE MONTHS
LATER

47

Cassandra

Courtroom Number One is oppressive with the smell of polished wood and starched collars, the glitter of dust on wood, sweat on skin. Many people have sat on this hard bench before, hearts tight, hands clenched, just like me. It's a comfort that others have survived this.

The circus of activity in this ancient and pompous room seems to be happening to someone else. Each day of the trial, reporters and rubberneckers fought for seats in the public gallery. It's over now: only the verdict remains.

The large empty chair is where the judge will sit to give his verdict. The space below is where the barristers, in their monochrome costumes, have already acted their parts and are now punch-drunk with the euphoria of the final bow, crowing about their plans for Christmas. This is their final case before the party begins.

The audience, the jury, have gone out to deliberate. The two rows where they sat are empty, have been for two days, but we've had word that they'll return at any moment and the mood is lifted because of it.

Tonight, they can return to normal life. I keep looking at the door, tall and wide, deep brown wood, so thick I couldn't smash through it. It lets others in, but wouldn't let me out. Where would I run to?

Oh, Mum. Why didn't you love me? If only you'd protected me instead of sending me away to boarding school, locking me away at the Bartlet, things would have been different. You loved Daniel, when you thought he'd saved you, but your love was a fickle thing.

Upstairs in the public gallery, faces peer down. Just seeing Victoria's heart-shaped face, her long hair that is so much like yours, gives me courage. Poor Victoria – she's strong to be here. She leans on the balustrade, kisses her fingers and throws me a greeting. I try to believe in her faith, but she has the advantage of innocence.

Beside her, Daniel looks handsome, smart in his suit. When he was in the witness box, I saw how the female jurors looked at him and felt a stab of anxiety before I told myself he's mine, he's been faithful to me all along. I never need to worry about him straying – I know he won't leave me now.

Of everyone, Dad looks the most worn down. Ash and Janet have taken turns to sit beside him, faithful as ever. He catches my eye and smiles stoically, but I can tell he's not sure this will all work out well. How can we trust twelve strangers to affirm the truth when it's so obscure? Guilt or innocence aren't as straightforward as lawyers would have us believe.

But Rupert Jackson says Holly's testimony will swing it our way. She cried when she told the story of that Halloween, of how I was shot by her brother. How, even then, I didn't wake. No one could doubt her testimony. I catch Daniel's eye and we share a moment. There's honesty between us now, and trust.

Our relationship has never been stronger.

As I waited to fall asleep in the hospital bed, he told me everything. How he arrived that Saturday morning in the blurred dawn, a lone car crossing the plain, headlights strafing the far field, before he pulled into the farm, bathed red by the spreading glow of the rising sun. The door was, as always, unlocked.

Everyone else was asleep. He paused at my door, then continued to yours. You were shocked to see him, but he calmed you.

'It's me, Maya. It's Daniel.'

But you were angry: 'Get out of my bedroom! What the hell are you doing here?'

He just wanted to talk, just wanted you to see sense and destroy the contract I'd told him you'd signed. You wouldn't listen, so he went to the study, where he knew the contract must be. He didn't even notice the gun cupboard was hanging open.

You pounced out of bed, still in your red silk nightdress, furious. I can imagine this – you hated anyone going in your study.

'Please, Maya,' Daniel begged, 'let's talk about this. Think about how the Spa will help people . . .'

'Help?' you taunted him. 'You're a quack! I'm going to expose you for the fraud you are.'

Even hearing the story second-hand, I was shocked that you'd said this – so unfair of you. You know how hard Daniel works to help people. It was the hospital results, of course, that turned your mind against him. But how could Daniel be blamed for the failure of your body to fight the cancer cells? You always believed that other people were responsible for anything bad that happened, didn't you, Mum? But you were just unlucky.

Another shock was coming: you weren't alone in blaming Daniel for a returning cancer. You said her name: Monica.

Daniel could barely speak. 'How do you know about her?'

'Alfie Avon told me,' you said. 'She's his ex-wife – their marriage was destroyed by the stress you and your false claims caused. It's over, Daniel. I'm not going to let you ruin anyone else's chance for survival.'

You took the gun from the cabinet. A farmer's daughter, you weren't afraid. 'Now get out of my house, you fraud!'

You forced him down the stairs. It was then that I appeared at the top. Still asleep, dressed in the clothes I'd gone to bed in. Who knows what my somnambular brain made of my mother pointing a gun at my lover. I was dreaming, and in that barely conscious state I protected the person I loved most.

I tried to grab the gun from you, and there was a struggle. The gun was in Daniel's hand when it fired the fatal shot, knocking you into a coma from which you'd never wake. It was an accident. But who would believe that? He'd arrived at the house to confront you; he had a motive. He had to think quickly.

I was no good to him, I was still asleep, so he walked me back upstairs, stripped me of my bloody clothes and returned me to bed. Then he woke Dad, and told him I'd shot you in my sleep. Janet and Ash arrived and were told the same story, and they all agreed to say you'd attempted suicide. Everyone was willing to lie, to protect me.

But really, Mum, they were protecting Daniel. And now I'm protecting him too.

A buzzer sounds in the courtroom, and Rupert Jackson throws me a quick look, the barristers tug their wigs straight and everyone looks attentive. A wooden door swings open, and the twelve jurors enter in a long line. Some look at me, others definitely don't.

Victoria leans over the balustrade and Daniel touches her arm, to pull her back. Dad nurses his bad hand and Ash says something. They're my family – I will never question their love again.

The judge enters, looking for all the world as if he's waiting for a doctor, or a bus. He's weary, his life won't be altered by whatever the jury has decided, it's just another day at work for him. The black-cloaked usher collects a slip of paper from the foreman, hands it up to him. He reads it with a resignation that suggests the bus has been delayed and he's not surprised. The foreman stands. He's one of the few people in the courtroom who looks at me; he wants to be acknowledged. Whatever the piece of paper says, he had no doubts.

'Members of the jury, have you reached your verdict?'

'We have, Your Honour.'

'And how do you find the defendant?'

The usher pauses, enjoying his moment of importance. Then, 'Not guilty.'

I really am innocent after all. The person most responsible for your death, Mum, was you.

48

Holly

The drive towards Kenley looked the same as it had last November, though just before the turning for Innocence Lane, there was a new addition: a sign, six feet high, navy blue, with silver writing that announced SAMPHIRE HEALTH SPA. Holly took the turning, and felt the change. For a start, the stench of pigs was gone, and the hedges had been trimmed along the lane.

The entrance had been levelled and white gravel crunched beneath the car wheels. Parking spaces were indicated by the positioning of olive trees in terracotta pots, and Holly pulled her Fiat 500 to a stop. The other cars in the car park were a BMW and an Audi. The entrance was sentinelled by lit candles in hurricane lamps and the door was a blue to match the signage. Each of the windows was gleaming, and the whole atmosphere was luxurious and tranquil. Holly left her car, and walked towards the entrance. She noticed, in the corner of the porch, a CCTV camera.

The brass handle was huge, and she pushed the door open, stepping forward onto a carpet so deep it was like stepping into sand. The mahogany reception table had been restored to its former shining glory.

On it stood an old-fashioned brass bell with a sign, PLEASE RING TO NOTIFY STAFF OF YOUR ARRIVAL. Holly ignored the instruction and walked along the hallway. To the left was the front room, where she'd sat with Cassandra, just hours after the shooting. Two women and a man in navy towelling robes sat on velvet sofas, sipping water and leafing through thick magazines. One woman looked up; Holly smiled and moved away.

Daniel was walking towards her. 'Holly, so good to see you – welcome to Samphire!' Presumably the camera had informed him of her arrival as she hadn't pressed the buzzer. 'Looks a bit different from when you were last here, doesn't it?'

'Yes,' agreed Holly, 'much plusher.' She hadn't been here since the trial had concluded, even though Cass had sent her an invite for the opening weekend. 'You've really transformed the place.'

'Book a spa day, then you can experience it first-hand,' he said pleasantly. 'I'll give you a Swedish massage, all on the house. We're very grateful to you, Holly – some Samphire Master Magic is the least you deserve.'

Holly felt distinctly uncomfortable; she hoped it didn't show. 'How's Cass?'

'She's grand: happy that we can move on with our lives. We'll go and find her – she's upstairs in the office.'

'I'd like to see Hector too, if he's around?'

'Of course he is. The old boy never really leaves the grounds since losing Maya. Come on, we can go and see him first.'

She followed Daniel down the hallway, and through to what had once been the farmhouse kitchen but was now a conservatory with low beds, each with a throw folded on the end. 'This is our sleep room,' he whispered, gesturing to one bed, where a curled shape was covered by a white blanket, bar the top of a blonde head. Candles had been lit in lanterns around the room, and sage incense was burning. Quietly, Holly followed Daniel through what was once the back door, but was now a bifold window that led to an herb garden, with benches placed strategically for clients to sit and take in the ambience. They crossed the garden and Holly realised where they were heading.

'The barn?'

'It's been converted, it's where Hector lives now. Cass, Tori and I live in the main house.'

The chickens were gone, the barn was no longer a place of straw and bird shit. It was now a single-storey home, Dutch-barn style and clad in black timber. Daniel didn't knock, just walked directly through the door into the front room. Where the barn wall had once been was a picture window looking out onto the copse at the back. The room was spartan and plain, and Holly thought it rather soulless.

There was a sharp bark and a black spaniel rushed forward to greet her. 'Hi, Jet, do you remember me?' He pushed his nose into her leg, wagging his tail. Yes, he clearly did.

Seated on the far end of the sofa, facing the copse but not seeming to see it, was Hector. He was still wearing his dressing gown, though it was almost noon, and his grey hair was unbrushed. Holly was shocked at how grief had aged him.

'Guess who's come to visit?' Daniel paused, but when Hector didn't reply, he asked her, 'So, do you like what we've done?'

'It's quite something,' she said. 'I'd never have known this was once a barn.'

'*My* barn,' sighed Hector, looking wistfully out of the window. 'No more workin' the land for me. Those days are gone.'

He touched his bad hand and Holly felt the touch, the mirror sensation of offered comfort, but felt its weakness too. Hector had been king here, and now he was exiled to life in the barn.

Holly went and sat next to him, Jet sat at her feet begging to be petted. She stroked his ears, and said, 'It's good to see you, Hector.'

'Shall I leave you both to catch up? You can find Cass in her study when you're ready,' said Daniel, looking at his watch. 'I've got to administer a deep-tissue massage now, so if it's okay I won't come with you.'

'It's fine. I remember the way.'

When he'd gone, she joined Hector in gazing out of the window, to land that was once farmed but was now being levelled. A huge machine was spreading seed over the area.

'That's the next stage of their big plans,' he said. 'It's being grassed.'

His comment made her look at him more closely, and she saw his eyes were cold.

'Where are Janet and Ash?' she asked.

'Oh, they got to keep their cottage. Janet comes over every day. She cooks all the funny food they serve here, salads mostly. And once those fields out there are flatter and covered in grass, it's gonna be a golf course. Ash'll be the groundsman.'

She said nothing: she could hear how much this hurt Hector. After the loyalty Ash and Janet had shown Cass, this was hardly the reward they deserved. And Ash was far more than just a worker to Hector, though it seemed this would never be acknowledged.

Holly climbed the stairs to the first floor and to the room that was once Maya's study. Very little had changed here: there was still a desk and filing cabinet, and lots of paperwork pinned on a cork board. But the woman in charge was different: the daughter had inherited and the mother was gone.

Cassandra looked better than Holly had ever seen her. She was wearing a fitted red dress with low heels, her blonde hair gleamed and her face glowed.

'Holly, so good to see you, please take a seat.' Beside Cassandra's desk was a small armchair. 'Sorry I wasn't downstairs to greet you, I was on a call with *Lifestyle Magazine*. They're featuring us in next month's edition.'

'That's wonderful.'

What a change this was. The woman before her was, seemingly for the first time, in command of her fate. Her dream was now a reality.

'Things seem to be going well for you, Cass.'

'Oh, they are. I can't tell you!' Just then light footsteps approached, and a young woman entered the study. 'Tori, do you remember Holly?'

The teenager looked at Holly, recognised her, and gave a beaming smile. 'Of course I do – you saved my mum.'

'Well, I wouldn't quite put it like that . . .'

'It's true, Holly,' Cass said, lightly rebuking her. 'Rupert Jackson said it was you who convinced the jury I was innocent.'

After Victoria had ambled away, Cass said, 'She's at the Academy in Felixstowe, and doing really well. Of course she's still adjusting. She misses Oakfield, but she'll get over that before too long.'

'Does she still see Dawn?'

'Oh yes,' said Cassandra, 'at weekends and holidays. They're still best friends and we help Monica with the school fees.' Her eyes passed over Holly and fixed on her hand, where the engagement ring glittered. 'Oh, congratulations!'

'Thank you,' said Holly.

'If you'd like to organise your hen weekend here, I'll give you a very special package. Mate's rate.'

Holly felt herself cool inside. 'Oh, I don't think I'll be bothering with that.'

Cassandra's smile dropped, and Holly saw that she was disappointed, not because Holly had rejected the offer, but because she was rejecting the possibility of friendship. As if to underline the point, Holly asked, 'Do you still see Clive?'

'I'm involved with Team Talk each Friday, but we run it here now, in one of the therapy rooms. Clive hires the space from me.'

'And the sleepwalking?'

'Under control. No repeat incidents,' Cassandra said simply, still dejected.

Holly found that she was unsurprised by this. 'Your dad seems . . . sad.'

'He's grieving for Mum. But look at how fortunate he is, living in a barn conversion with his family all around him. And look how close he still is with Ash. What more could he ask for?'

Despite herself, Holly shivered. 'I think Hector probably believes that Ash deserves more.'

Cass narrowed her eyes. 'He can only blame himself for what Ash got. If he felt so strongly about it, he should have acknowledged him, while Mum was alive.'

'Cass, that's so . . . ?' Holly searched for the right word.

'Cruel? What's cruel is Dad having a child with Janet, and betraying my mum. I've treated Ash fairly, but he's not my brother.'

'But he is,' Holly said simply. It had been obvious to her from the start, and now it was clear that this was an unspoken fact that everyone knew. 'You just don't want to give up your inheritance.'

Cassandra finished the tour herself, showing Holly the grounds where a spa bath was situated and a steam capsule amid the herb garden. 'All of our treatments are organic,' she told Holly. 'As well as the cancer treatments, we specialise in sleep disorders. We got quite a lot of publicity after the court case, and that always helps with bookings.'

She was shown the rooms, where reiki and Bach flower treatments took place. This spa was meant to heal but Cassandra's own healing came from a darker source, Holly was certain. She was thriving because Maya was dead.

Finally, they were done and there was nothing more to see.

Cassandra opened her arms for a final farewell. 'Congratulations again!' she cried, as Holly stepped into the woman's embrace. She felt it then, like a jolt of electricity: she saw, in her mind's eye, Daniel firing a rifle.

Holly pulled away and the question came from her mouth before she could censor it. 'Why are you protecting him, Cass? He shot your mother.'

There was no one around, no one to hear.

The subject was her own mother's death, but Cassandra answered coolly, 'Mum had me locked up. She paid for my daughter to be kept away from me and she was about to expose Daniel as a fraud. She was going to destroy everything.'

Holly, her hands still on Cassandra's forearms, saw it all. The struggle for the gun, Daniel pulling the trigger, Maya falling.

'He murdered your mother.'

'The case is closed, Holly. I was found not guilty because I was asleep. It's been proven, thanks to you, beyond reasonable doubt.'

'But all those suspicions you had. How can you trust him?'

'Because I know his secret, and I took the blame.'

'I'm going to the police,' Holly said, backing away. 'The case will be reopened.'

'No, it won't, Holly, not unless I appeal. Which I won't. The case is solved, and nobody wants it reopened. Look at the life we have now. Look at how happy we all are.'

EPILOGUE

Holly

'Are you okay in there? Remember, Holly, try not to move your head or swallow too much. Press the panic button if you need to.'

Holly knew she wasn't a good patient, but Clive's voice helped her relax as she was slid into the MRI machine. His tweedy tones of orange and grey comfort swaddled her, making her feel safe even as the gurney mechanically repositioned her within the scanner. She wouldn't have done this if Leif hadn't come with her – he was waiting in the hospital café. He'd convinced her it was better to know as much as possible about her synaesthesia, that she was helping the researchers as well as herself.

Holly stiffened as the machine began its whirrs and clicks. Inside the white plastic oesophagus, she listened to the bangs and ticks of the machine. She'd known for most of her life that she was different from other people, but now she knew she needed to embrace it. Leif had helped, and he was waiting for her now.

Returning to Innocence Lane had been the true tipping point. If she'd only trusted her senses all along, it would have ended differently. She'd mistrusted Hector's confession from the start, had sensed that something was amiss, and she'd been focusing on Daniel. If only she hadn't felt so guilty about the past, so keen to make amends to Cass, then he'd be behind bars.

'Okay, Holly, you're going to be shown a series of images. Just look at the picture and we'll see which part of your brain lights up. Okay?'

Memories came to her, like scenes from a film, of children in dark woods and the screams of a ghost. All of the moments that had triggered her synaesthesia. She'd be stronger, she would no longer hide her trait: synaesthesia was a gift to a paramedic, it helped her make sense of things.

From now on, she wouldn't fight her gift. She wouldn't make the same error twice.

'The test is over, Holly. You can relax now.'

ACKNOWLEDGMENTS

This book was inspired by a family anecdote about my great-uncle, George Hair, who owned a farm in Lincolnshire. After a day throttling chickens, he fell into a deep sleep, but was woken by his wife's screams in the early hours of the morning. He had his hands around her neck, and was strangling her, dreaming that he was still with those chickens. She lived to tell the tale, which is how I got to hear of it. This same uncle jumped through a glass window when he dreamed he was jumping fences on his horse. This book is dedicated to him.

I'm grateful to the many people who helped turn that story into the book you now hold in your hands. The team at Thomas & Mercer have, once again, been a tour de force of talent and I'm very lucky to be published by them. Victoria Pepe, commissioning editor, came to my manuscript with fresh eyes and helped turn it into something different, along with Sophie Wilson – such a sensitive editor that I felt fully supported even when I was ripping a new heart into the story. Thank you both for your insight, and for giving me the time to catch up. Thanks to Monica Byles, copy editor, for your astounding precision and thoroughness.

Thanks again to my trusty writing group: Elizabeth Ferretti, Morag Liffen, Sophie Green and Jane Bailey. Now I'm living on the other side of the pond, we're back to meeting on Skype, and I'm even more grateful for my monthly dose of feedback and friendship.

I'm very fortunate to have the world's best agent, Lorella Belli, whose support is unstinting and who is always on the other end of an email or phone line when I need her.

I have been blessed to have had DS Darren Bruce from Suffolk Constabulary as my guide on all things 'police procedural'. Darren, thank you for all those hours at Milsoms. Your knowledge is awe-inspiring and your stories made my jaw drop. This book won't be what you (or I) envisioned at that point, but I hope you like it.

Thanks to Professor Jamie Ward from Sussex University for his email correspondence, and especially for forwarding his report on mirror-touch synaesthesia. All remaining inaccuracies and fictional liberties are mine.

The name Kaitlin Burgess appears courtesy of her parents, who bought the right to have her name in the book at a charity auction to raise funds for The Literacy Council of Benton County in Bentonville, Arkansas. Its purpose is to teach adults to read English and help them become more successful in society. Kaitlin, I hope you like your character, as I have a feeling we'll be meeting her in my next novel too!

Finally, thank you to the readers who have found my books and enjoy them. I never take a single one of you for granted.

Ruth Dugdall
Palo Alto, California
December 2017

If you are affected by any of the conditions referred to in this book, you may like to contact:
UK Synaesthesia Association
http://www.uksynaesthesia.com/
The Sleep Council
https://sleepcouncil.org.uk/

ABOUT THE AUTHOR

Photo © 2017 Jemma Watts

Ruth Dugdall is an award-winning British crime author.

In 2005, she won the CWA Debut Dagger for *The Woman Before Me*, which also won the Luke Bitmead Bursary in 2009. Since then, her novels have been published internationally.

Ruth's novels are inspired by her previous career as a probation officer and she continues to be involved with the criminal justice system in a voluntary capacity.

Previously a resident of Luxembourg, Ruth now divides her time between the UK and California.